WARDEN OF THE QUEEN'S MARCH

There was a surge forward of the waiting crowd, so that the lofty ones at the front were in danger of being pushed off into the water, to their outraged cries, these lost however in the general cheering, as Mary paused in mid-gangway to smile brilliantly and wave. She was dressed all in black, unlike the others, save for white at throat and cuffs and the white silk coif, for the French court was still in mourning for the young King Francis the Second, her husband; and it was not much more than a year since her own mother had died, the Regent Marie de Guise.

Standing there, however, radiant, lovely, lissome, graceful and so obviously vivacious and mettlesome, she certainly showed no other aspect of mourning or sadness, joyful expectancy rather, and eager anticipation. That smile was a delight.

Thomas, for one, was fascinated, quite smitten. Perhaps romantically inclined anyway, he decided there and then that here was the most delicious creature it had ever been his fortune to set eyes upon; and that she should be his Queen, his liege-lady and sovereign, made her all the more a wonder.

Warden of the Queen's March

Nigel Tranter

CORONET BOOKS
Hodder & Stoughton

First published in Great Britain in 1989 by Hodder and Stoughton
A division of Hodder Headline PLC
First published in paperback in 1991 by Hodder and Stoughton
A Coronet paperback
This Coronet paperback edition 1997

10 9 8 7 6 5 4 3 2

British Library Cataloguing in Publication Data

Tranter, Nigel, 1909–
    Warden of the Queen's march
    1. English fiction – 20th century – Scottish authors
    2. Scottish fiction – 20th century
    I. Title
    823.9'12[F]

ISBN 0 340 54597 6

Printed and bound in Great Britain by
Cox & Wyman Ltd, Reading, Berkshire

Hodder and Stoughton
A division of Hodder Headline PLC
338 Euston Road
London NW1 3BH

To Peter and Antonella Kerr of Ferniehirst,
Marquis and Marchioness of Lothian.

PRINCIPAL CHARACTERS

in order of appearance

Thomas Kerr of Smailholm: Son and heir of Sir John Kerr of Ferniehirst; *Sir John Kerr of Ferniehirst:* Warden of the Middle March; *Lord James Stewart:* Commendator-Prior of St Andrews. Eldest illegitimate son of James the Fifth; *Lord Robert Stewart:* Commendator-Abbot of Holyrood. Later Earl of Orkney. Illegitimate son of James the Fifth; *Sir William Kirkcaldy of Grange:* Renowned soldier and prominent Reformer. Keeper of Edinburgh Castle; *William Maitland of Lethington:* Secretary of State; *Mary, Queen of Scots:* Lately also Queen of France. Only legitimate child of James the Fifth; *Mary Fleming:* Sister of Lord Fleming, *Mary Seton:* Daughter of Lord Seton, *Mary Beaton:* Kinswoman of the late Cardinal, *Mary Livingstone:* Daughter of Lord Livingstone. The Queen's four Marys; *Lady Fleming:* Illegitimate daughter of James the Fifth. Mother of Mary Fleming; *James Hepburn, Earl of Bothwell:* Chief Warden of the Marches. Lord High Admiral of Scotland; *John Knox:* Minister of St Giles High Kirk, Edinburgh. Leader of the Reformed clergy; *Janet Kirkcaldy:* Daughter of Grange. Married to Thomas Kerr; *Lord Ruthven:* Prominent Reformed noble; *Sir Walter Ker of Cessford:* Head of other branch of the clan, spelling name differently. Uncle of Thomas; *David Rizzio:* Italian private secretary to the Queen; *George, Lord Gordon:* Eldest son of the Earl of Huntly; *George, Earl of Huntly:* Lieutenant of the North. Leader of Catholic nobility; *James, Earl of Morton:* Leading Douglas noble; *James, Duke of Châtelherault:* Head of the Hamiltons. Heir-presumptive to the throne; *Henry, Lord Darnley:* Eldest son of the Earl of Lennox; *Lord Seton:* Great Catholic noble. Father of Mary Seton; *James, Duke of Rothesay:* Infant son of Mary, Queen of Scots. Later James the Sixth; *John, Lord Borthwick:* Hereditary Master of the Ordnance; *Ogilvy of Boyne:* Northern laird. Member of the Queen's household; *George Douglas, Younger of Lochleven:* Brother of the Laird of Lochleven and half-brother of the Earl of Moray; *Will Douglas:* Kinsman of above; *Sir John Maxwell, Lord Herries:* Great Galloway Catholic noble; *Claud Hamilton, Lord Paisley:* Son of the Duke of Châtelherault.

1

For mid-August it was surprising weather, even for Scotland – fairly dense fog, and cold. Already those so inclined were muttering about it being no good augury, presaging murky and chilling times ahead. But at least it was not stormy, the easterly breeze only moderate. Edinburgh was used to east winds off the Norse Sea, producing the notorious haar or sea-mist, which could indeed chill to the bone; but not usually in summertime. And on this occasion that easterly breeze had rather upset the folk, notably the great ones more than the ordinary citizens of the capital, confounding calculations, disorganising arrangements and imposing an abnormally early rising and hurried breakfasting for those in the know. For, fog or none, word had come by fastest horse from the Earl of Angus's castle of Tantallon that the Queen's flotilla of French ships had been sighted, dangerously close to the shore, between the Bass Rock and the Lothian mainland at dawn, considerably before expected. That was only some twenty-five sea-miles from Leith, the port of Edinburgh, which, with an easterly wind, even despite the fog, would be covered in less than three hours. So it was all haste, to dress, snatch a bite, get mounted, and hurry down the two miles to Leith, to be there when Mary arrived, to greet the returning Queen after so long, all this in no orderly fashion.

Young Thomas Kerr of Smailholm was eager, impatient, even with his father who, as chief of a Border moss-trooping clan, and superbly mounted, could surely have ridden faster; but Sir John Kerr of Ferniehirst was a quiet, deliberate and dignified man, markedly unlike his eldest son, and was not to be hurried, even for so important an occasion. Thomas, newly come of age, perforce had to restrain himself and his mount. His mother, two younger brothers and sisters had been left behind in their town-house in the Canongate of Edinburgh.

Astonishingly, as well as numbers of important folk like themselves, lords, lairds, clerics, the Provost of the city, even the English and French ambassadors, there were lots of citizenry, the commonality of Edinburgh, also hastening down the long Leith Walk, as the roadway was called which linked the capital with its port. How they had got to know of this so inconvenient arrival so soon was no mystery, for bell-men had been sent riding down through the city streets, the Lawnmarket, the High Street and the Canongate, from the castle, shouting aloud the news, so that those concerned were speedily informed; and the lower orders would hear just as well as their betters; but how they had got so quickly thus far, on foot, was a surprise, to Thomas at least, many actually running, men, women, children and dogs, in shouting, barking excitement, all highly unsuitable. Why they should be so interested and attached to a queen they had not seen for thirteen years was hard to understand.

"If we are too late, sir, what will happen?" Thomas demanded, the nearest he could go to rebuking his father's deliberate riding. And to somewhat relieve his impatience, shouted, not for the first time, for the wretched impeding foot-folk to get out of their road. This was no progress for moss-trooping Kerrs.

"There will be time enough, Tom," Sir John told him easily. "Fret you not. This fog will slow the ships as they approach the port. Getting them in to the quayside in this will take time."

Down through the narrow twisting streets and wynds of Leith, their passage was further delayed, all choked with folk. And when they came, at last, out on to the wide quayside, backed by warehouses, where the Water of Leith entered the Firth of Forth, it was to find the available space already packed with people. They had to dismount and leave their horses with a servant, and push their way through the noisy throng to get anywhere near the waterside. This was not being at all well organised, Thomas declared. What would the Queen think?

There was, however, no sign of the French ships, although the fog seemed to be lifting a little. That did not mean a great deal, for, even so, visibility was not more than three hundred yards, not even to the harbour-mouth.

"What now? Do we just stand here? Wait? Do nothing . . .?"

"What do you suggest, son?" his father asked, smiling. "Swim?" And when he got no answer, pointed. "Yonder is the Lord James. And Argyll. They will know what is to do."

They insinuated their way through the press of dignitaries

lining the quay, to where a notably richly dressed group stood. Amongst these, one remained not so much apart as aloof, head held strangely high, unspeaking where the others were loud of voice. For him Sir John made.

"Greetings, Lord James," he said. "Here is a broil! Most difficult. We just wait here?"

James Stewart, Commendator-Prior of St Andrews, merely inclined his head. He was like that, a man of few words, tall, good-looking after a fashion, but stern of features, sombre of demeanour. So it was not he who answered Kerr but an older, sallow-featured, slightly built man, Archibald, Earl of Argyll, chief of Clan Campbell and member of the Regency Council.

"Ha – Ferniehirst! You are here. This damnable fog! We have word that the French ships are lying off the harbour-mouth. The harbour-master is rowed out in his barge, to bring the Queen's vessel in. He has with him the Lyon King of Arms and Maitland the Secretary, to greet Her Grace." The softly sibilant Highland lilt came but strangely from that dangerous man.

"Scarcely the most auspicious welcome for the Queen of Scots to her ancient kingdom," Sir John observed. "After all the years of absence. And, if I mind it aright, she was held up by storms off Dumbarton when she left her land for France. I fear that she will have but a poor notion of Scotland! We must seek to improve it."

"Why yes, my friend. We must seek to improve much where Her Grace is concerned." That was said with a certain significance.

Something between a sniff and a snort came from the Lord James Stewart.

Ferniehirst glanced from one to the other. These two were probably the most powerful and influential men in Scotland, together with Master Knox the churchman, and these together had been more or less ruling the realm for the year or so since Queen Marie of Guise, the Queen's mother and Regent, died. There was a Regency Council appointed, but it was more or less a formality, and being composed of both Protestant and Catholic lords and prelates, seldom achieved any unanimity. That their young monarch was coming to take over the rule now meant that these two were going to have to play very different parts. Sir John knew just a hint of apprehension, for he was very well aware of their quality, having had to

9

cross swords with both more than once, as a member of the Scottish parliament and as Warden of the Middle March of the Border.

Thomas, listening, touched his father's arm. "Will the Queen come ashore in this harbour-master's barge? Surely not . . .?"

"No, no. Our sister requires better than that! They will bring her ship in to this quay for us to greet her here." That was not the Lord James speaking but one who stood close by, another of his many half-brothers – and therefore the Queen's – the Lord Robert Stewart, Commendator-Abbot of Holyrood, an amiable character although notoriously profligate. Others of King James's bastards were there also, none clergy but all bearing clerical titles – with their attached revenues and seats in parliament – conveniently made available by the blessed Reformation of a few years before. The late monarch, of partially blessed memory, had been a potent prince in this respect at least, although Mary was his only recognised legitimate offspring.

The Lord James, the eldest of the brood and the ablest, if not the most genial and voluble, found words now, turning to his half-brother Robert. "Discover if Kirkcaldy of Grange is here yet. Fetch him to me." That was quite peremptory.

Nodding, the amiable Robert moved off.

Quite quickly he was back, with a stockily built, strong-featured man of middle years, Sir William Kirkcaldy, Keeper of Edinburgh Castle.

"Sir William, your cannon? To fire a royal salute. Are they here?"

"No, my lord James. How could they be? There has been no time. They are heavy, drawn by oxen. Slow. They cannot be here for an hour yet. More."

"If fired from the castle itself? Would they be heard here?"

"Normally, yes. But this fog! It will much deaden sound . . ."

"Then you must find other cannon here. On ships. There must be some. Have these fired."

"Cannon could be difficult to find. And there may not be powder available on board . . ."

"Find some. See to it." The Lord James turned away. There was no doubt who was in command here, despite the presence of others more highly placed – the Chancellor, the High Constable, the Earl Marischal and so on. But this

James Stewart had an inborn authority, allied to ability, and a temperament which few found convenient to contest. Had he been legitimately born, he, the eldest of the late monarch's offspring, would possibly have made a strong and effective King. In fact he asserted legitimacy, claiming that his mother, the Lady Margaret Erskine, had been secretly wed to his father, unlikely as this was, she having been previously married to Robert Douglas of Lochleven. His bastardy undoubtedly preyed on his mind, and he had applied for and received papal papers of legitimacy ten years earlier – but this could not give him any claim to his sister's throne. Illegitimacy did not seem to worry any of his other numerous half-brothers.

His brother-in-law Argyll – he was wed to another of the late monarch's bastards, the Lady Jean Stewart – looking round, remarked that he saw no sign of the good Master Knox. The Lord James made no reply to this, but the Lord Robert chucklingly commented that that saintly presbyter no doubt considered that he had better uses for his time of a morning than waiting on the arrival of the Catholic Whore of Babylon – a remark which raised the eyebrows of some within earshot.

Thomas Kerr glared at the speaker and wished that his father would suitably rebuke him. But Sir John seemingly elected not to hear. Instead, he pointed.

"Is that not a ship coming in now? I think . . . yes, it is. This will be the Queen's Grace."

Slowly the bulk of a large galley loomed out of the fog, being towed into the harbour by three many-oared barges, only one of its sails unfurled, this painted with the Lilies of France. A tentative cheer arose from the crowd at sight of it, Thomas adding his voice strongly – although few around him did.

It took quite a long time for those barges to manoeuvre the large ship in to the quayside where the most important folk were standing, all eyes on the brilliantly clad group amidships on the galley, with exclamations, and demands as to which of the half-dozen women seen there was the Queen – for only the Lord James, who had been to France as an envoy recently, had seen Mary since her childhood. *He* did not enlighten anybody.

Thomas gazed. He had heard so much about Mary Stewart, or Stuart as they said she was now spelling the name, the French way, with no "w" in their alphabet. She was tall, spirited and beautiful, they said, with reddish hair. The trouble was, all these women wore coifs over their hair, and two were tall. But one looked older than the other, without being of any great age. The other, then . . .?

At length, ropes thrown, the galley was moored securely to the pier, and a gangway pushed out. And the tall younger woman was the first to move forward to it, almost at a run indeed, as though eager to be ashore, so that sundry men had to run also, in order to assist her up on to the gangway, these including two over-dressed characters, presumably Frenchmen, and the soberly clad William Maitland of Lethington, the Secretary of State. So it must be the Queen.

There was a surge forward of the waiting crowd, so that the lofty ones at the front were in danger of being pushed off into the water, to their outraged cries, these lost however in the general cheering, as Mary paused in mid-gangway to smile brilliantly and wave. She was dressed all in black, unlike the others, save for white at throat and cuffs and the white silk coif, for the French court was still in mourning for the young King Francis the Second, her husband; and it was not much more than a year since her own mother had died, the Regent Marie de Guise.

Standing there, however, radiant, lovely, lissome, graceful and so obviously vivacious and mettlesome, she certainly showed no other aspect of mourning or sadness, joyful expectancy rather, and eager anticipation. That smile was a delight.

Thomas, for one, was fascinated, quite smitten. Perhaps romantically inclined anyway, he decided there and then that here was the most delicious creature it had ever been his fortune to set eyes upon; and that she should be his Queen, his liege-lady and sovereign, made her all the more a wonder. How many other impressionable young men were equally stirred, it would have been interesting to know.

The cheering and shouting continuing, the Queen of Scots started forward again, but now, remembering a suitable dignity, slowed her pace so that she stepped down on to the quayside in more regal style, although having to hitch up her skirts to do so with something almost of a flourish, revealing white silken and shapely ankles. This young Queen was all woman, most evidently, aware of it and not averse for others to be aware of it also.

Pausing for a moment to gaze around her, a hand raised

to acknowledge the acclaim, she inclined her head now in wholly queenly fashion, turning this way and that. And who could have more right to seem queenly, for as well as being Queen of Scots, Mary was also Queen of France, or had been until her husband had died those months before, something hitherto unprecedented.

Unprecedented too, was this moment, as Mary Stewart set foot again on her own land. For never before had Scotland had a Queen-Regnant, a ruling female monarch not just a Queen-Consort of a King. This Mary came to *govern*, and although her mother, Queen Marie de Guise, had acted governor, or Regent, for her daughter in France, her role had been qualified by the Privy Council and parliament. Now, at least in theory, this young woman could rule and overrule, as well as reign. Were the Scots, a notably unruly nation, prepared for a female monarch? And a young one such as this, aged only eighteen years?

Mary, turning to scan the faces of those closest at hand, saw presumably the only one she recognised, her half-brother the Lord James, and moved impulsively to him. He allowed her to do the moving, for he was not of an impulsive nature, the warmth of his greeting a deal less evident than was hers as she embraced and kissed him. He was no smiler either, but he did return her kiss, if stiffly.

"Welcome to your realm, Madam," he said formally.

She trilled a laugh. "Oh, I have been here before, James. I was five when I left, you remember. I was . . ."

The rest was lost in thunderous noise as from somewhere much too close at hand, cannon-fire crashed out, reverberating from the close-packed warehouses, sheds and buildings and sending seabirds screaming up from roofs and steeples. Kirkcaldy of Grange had found at least one gun and some powder.

Startled at first, the Queen blinked, then laughed as she realised what it was. She turned, and beckoned forward one of the men who had followed closest behind her.

"Here is my uncle, the Marquis d'Elboeuf. You have met, I think?"

René de Guise of Lorraine was the youngest of the late Marie's three brothers, a foppish-looking individual of early middle years, with painted cheeks and lips, and sporting rings in his ears. The Scots eyed him distinctly askance.

"My lord Marquis," the Lord James said briefly. He turned. "Here, Madam, is another uncle, by marriage – my lord Earl of Argyll, wed to the Lady Jean Stewart."

"Ah, my lord. I have heard . . ."

Whatever she had heard was not disclosed, for another cannon-blast bludgeoned all eardrums. Some of the Queen's ladies clapped hands to coifs, but Mary restrained herself. Whatever ship boasted the artillery was just too close for comfort. Mary smiled round at the company. Thomas asserted afterwards that she caught his eye as she did so.

How long the cannonade might go on was open to question and presentations to the Queen were hurried through, in the intervals, with more expedition than dignity: the half-brothers she had never met, officers of state, ambassadors, earls and high dignitaries, these including the Warden of the Middle March, Sir John Kerr. Thomas was not included, of course, but he got a glance – or assured himself that he did. He was not a bad-looking young man, in a rugged sort of way.

Impatient with all this, the Lord James ordered a servant to go find Sir William Kirkcaldy and tell him to stop all the damnable noise. Then he commanded various of his half-brothers to clear a way through the crowd, and took the Queen's elbow, to urge her to walk on up the quay. They would go meantime to the house of one Andrew Lamb, a merchant, he said briefly, for refreshment, until all was ready for her at the Abbey of Holyrood.

So a move was made, Mary, flanked by the Lord James and Argyll and followed by her entourage and a long train of Scots notables, smiling and waving right and left and even pausing now and again to say a word or two to quite ordinary folk, a delay and gesture of which her half-brother obviously disapproved. Thomas got separated from his father in this long narrow column, and found himself walking with one of Mary's young women, a plumply pretty dimpling creature on whom he tried out his halting French, to be answered in a good Scots tongue and to be informed that this was in fact Mary Fleming, daughter of the late Lord Fleming. The Queen always kept a group of four high-born Marys as her closest companions, replacing them if they married, not the first to support this royal custom, this one's present colleagues, she told him, being the daughters of the Lords Seton, Livingstone and Beaton. Thomas found himself getting on well with Mary

Fleming, a cheerful and friendly character, on this very slow progress. She informed him that although they had applied for a safe-conduct for the French ships from Queen Elizabeth of England, that strange woman had refused to grant it to her fellow-monarch. However, although they *had* been intercepted by English warships, these had not actually attacked them, content apparently to show that they were in command of the seas; and they had made a swifter voyage northwards than had been feared – which, with the favourable wind, accounted for their early arrival.

Although it was not far from the quayside, through the pressing, noisy throng, it took some time to reach a very substantial and tall-gabled and stair-turreted house, set only a little way back from the river-bank; this Andrew Lamb must be a very prosperous merchant indeed to own such an establishment, better than most of the nobles' Edinburgh town-houses, although Thomas had never heard of him. Guards now stood at the door, and Thomas had little doubt that he would not have been let in had he not been with this Mary Fleming, who took his arm and ushered him past the scrutinising sentinels, who were forbidding most people entrance.

Even so, it was crowded within, and Thomas would not have dared to go upstairs when he saw his father held in the vaulted basement hallway, had his companion not drawn him up after her with entire confidence, declaring that she must always be at the Queen's side.

In the large room on the first floor, crowded also, refreshments – cold meats, fish, oatcakes, honeyed scones, with wines and spirits – were being dispensed in liberal fashion. The Queen was holding court up beside a well-doing log fire, for the fog had been chilly; and Mary Fleming, seeing her brother near her, pressed forward to his side, Thomas a little hesitantly following. He was introduced to the Lord Fleming of Cumbernauld, who nodded civilly.

There was a great chatter in that great room, but at least the booming of the cannon had ceased, and as Mary Fleming talked to her brother, Thomas was near enough to the Queen to hear at least snatches of her talk. She spoke in Scots, not unnaturally with a somewhat French accent, which he for one considered the more delightful – no doubt her four Scots Marys had kept her in practice.

He learned from the conversation that they were awaiting

15

word, to the Lord Robert, Commendator-Abbot of Holyrood, that the Abbey premises were ready for Her Grace, before proceeding up the two miles thereto. In theory, Edinburgh Castle was the royal residence in the capital, but in fact monarchs usually resided at the Abbey, where the abbatical quarters were much more comfortable and spacious than in the fortress on its rock. All should be ready very shortly — they had not expected the Queen for another day, at least.

Thomas missed what was being said thereafter by the Earl Marischal, and the next he heard was the Queen remarking to Archbishop Hamilton of St Andrews, a brother of the Hamilton chief, the Duke of Châtelherault, and her distant kin, that he must present to her the renowned Master John Knox, of whom she had heard so much.

There was a distinct pause at that, at least amongst those close at hand, and some embarrassment on the part of the archbishop. For one thing, Knox was most certainly not present; and anyway, presbyter and Primate were not on speaking terms. The so-called Reformation was far from complete in Scotland as yet, and although the Protestants had the upper hand and controlled parliament and most functions of state, the Catholics were still a power to be reckoned with, and the prelates still held their titles and privileges if not all their former lands and wealth; indeed the majority of the common people probably still upheld the old religion, as did the Kerrs of Ferniehirst.

The irrepressible Lord Robert Stewart answered for Hamilton, *his* religious affiliations being doubtful, if he had any, despite being Commendator-Abbot. "Master Knox is probably at his devotions, Madam, at this hour, since it is too early for him to be teaching folk the error of their ways! He is a very godly man, and not to be distracted by . . . frivolities!"

That caused at least one of his half-brothers to cough disapprovingly, the Lord James. "Master Knox will no doubt greet you at Holyrood, Madam," he said, in a voice that made it clear that this subject was closed.

This unfortunate incident was countered by the arrival of a further group of Frenchmen, loud in their demands to join the Queen. These proved to include two more de Guise uncles, brothers of d'Elboeuf, the Duke of Aumale and Francis, Grand Prior of France, who had voyaged north in another of the French galleys. This had now also been brought into the harbour. They were vehement in their complaints as to their reception, or the lack of it, at the quayside, their difficulty in finding their way here, and especially the fact that the Duke had lost his Duchess in the crowd, the good God alone knowing where she was now.

As some concern was expressed about this, the Queen declaring that her aunt must be rescued and brought to her, Thomas Kerr saw his opportunity. Raising his voice, he called out that *he* would go find the lady, who certainly could not be far away. No one else volunteering, he began to make his way out of the crowded room, when, near the door, he found Mary Fleming at his side.

"She is large and fat," the girl informed. "And she will speak no Scots. Perhaps I should come with you."

"No, no. I will find her, lady," he asserted, and hurried off downstairs. That young woman evidently did not think much of his French.

Out on the street, although it was thronged with folk still, and noisy, he had in fact little difficulty in locating his quarry. A big, red-faced and very voluble female was creating quite a furore not far away, waving her arms about and berating all in sight, in French, to a certain amount of unkind hilarity. Thomas pushed his way through the press, and clutched at one of those urgent arms.

"*Madame la Duchesse*," he shouted. "*Venez vous avec moi.*"

The lady eyed him suspiciously, treated him to a torrent of complaints in her own tongue, but came with him as he tugged at her.

Getting that Duchess through the throng was not easy, but at least her authoritative volubility got them past the sentinels at the door and up the stairs of the house, where she was reunited with her spouse, whom she lambasted for deserting her in this barbarous, uncouth land, and then fell on the Queen in a flood of Gallic eloquence. Mary sought to soothe her, and then looked over at Thomas, who was modestly now standing back.

"Who is this gallant young man?" she asked. And added, "With the bright eyes!"

When no one volunteered the information, Thomas, much affected by those last words, spoke up. "Kerr, Your Grace. Thomas Kerr of Smailholm." He was rather proud of that designation, which had not been his for long, having only received it on his twenty-first birthday from his father, a subsidiary property of the Kerrs. "Son to Ferniehirst."

"Then thank you, Thomas Kerr. Of, of . . . Smellum, did you say?" That delightful tinkle of laughter. "I am sure a goodly place, whatever its name, to have produced you! My thanks for finding the good Duchess for me."

Quite overcome, he bowed and backed away.

"Is it really Smellum?" That was Mary Fleming, at his side again, with a giggle. "I think that you should change that, Tom Kerr!"

"Not so — *Smailholm!* A notable strength, in the East March." He shook his head. "Is she not wonderful? Divine! She thanked me. Did you hear?"

"Ha! Another one! All the young men dote on her. Not that I blame you. She is an angel of heaven — but an angel with a temper, mind! But it is hard on the rest of us!"

Thomas found some refreshment for this frank young woman, and for himself, and was introduced to two more of the Queen's Marys; Seton, a fair, calm girl whose father, the Lord Seton, had also come with the royal party from France; and Beaton, a slim, lively creature, kin to the late assassinated Cardinal David Beaton. Also to the older, taller woman who had stood beside the Queen as the galley docked, and who proved to be this Mary's mother, the Lady Fleming, the former royal governess, and herself another bastard of the prolific King James. Thomas had lost count of these, but liked this one, although her reputation was not of the highest, she having been a mistress of King Henry the Second of France.

At length, with the refreshments demolished and many of the company becoming restive, the Lord Robert Stewart made announcement that he had word that Holyrood Abbey and palace was now ready for Her Grace, and a move thereto should be made by those concerned — a declaration which left not a few present uncertain as to who might be included in this invitation, Thomas Kerr amongst them. At any rate, the move away applied to all.

But down in the crowded street there was further delay, the difficulty being to get the horses of the great ones, and those provided for the new arrivals, through the great press of people. Fortunately, despite the heavy-handed tactics of the guards and lords' servants, the common folk remained good-tempered and cheerful, acclaiming the Queen if not many of her associates. In the end, the royal party had to make their way to the horses, rather than the other way round; and since these were scattered in such few open spaces as the port boasted, the business took some time. Thomas felt bound to escort the four Marys and Lady Fleming to find their transport, and since these were not to be separated from the Queen, he lost touch with his father and became more or less attached to the royal party.

When Maitland of Lethington, the Secretary of State, who appeared to have the task of organising the move – however disorganised it all seemed – got them to a drying-green for fishermen's nets and household washing, where a collection of horses was waiting, there was something of an outcry from the French visitors as to the quality of the animals provided, the Abbot of Brantôme in especial, a magnificently attired courtier of no more than Thomas's own age with no ecclesiastical aspect to him, declaring that these sorry beasts were not fit to carry more than the fish-baskets lying around, much less the Queen of France – and, by implication, himself. Admittedly, Thomas's own horse, nowhere near here, was an infinitely superior mount; presumably these were hired animals from Edinburgh. Mary Fleming confided that the Queen had shipped her own fine horseflesh for transport in two Dutch ships from Calais; but unfortunately, when the English warships had intercepted their flotilla, they had detained these while letting the royal galleys go on.

The young monarch, however, made no complaint about the steeds provided, and mounted one of them agilely and unaided. Unlike many of her attendants, she had obviously come prepared to make allowances and make the best of conditions. Thomas helped his ladies up on to the poorly saddled and caparisoned beasts, and, loth to leave this company, mounted another himself. His father could look after their own horses.

Maitland led them through a network of narrow lanes and wynds to the graveyard of St Mary's Church. Here they found the main assembly of the important ones, and Thomas for one felt distinctly ashamed at the sight of all those excellently mounted and heraldically caparisoned horsemen, nobles and clerics and even servants, compared with the Queen's sorry cavalcade. He saw his father amongst them and his own riderless black stallion, but decided that he could nowise switch mounts now.

19

So the procession formed up, the Lord James now taking charge, to ride up the two-mile Leith Walk to Edinburgh. The fog was almost gone, and, presumably spied from afar by the watchers on the city's fortress when halfway up the Walk, the gunners there thundered out their belated salute.

As the large company neared the outskirts of the capital, the roadway forked, both branches starting to climb, that to the right to mount Moutrie's Hill, in the direction of the castle; the left, which the procession took, to go on over a shoulder of the quite steep and high green Calton Hill. Here waiting crowds had assembled, in holiday mood, and to cheers and shouting they progressed upwards and over.

At the summit of quite a ridge, there were gasps from the visitors, even the most critical and unenthusiastic, impressed by what they saw. Ahead of them the land sank quite abruptly to a fairly deep valley. But beyond soared a mighty hill, almost a mountain, shaped like a crouching lion rearing its massive head skywards in majesty, an extraordinary feature, dwarfing all around it, especially the city housing which seemed to creep towards its foot. And directly below their present position, and near the hill-skirts, lay the Abbey of the Holy Rood, with its palatial extension built by Mary's father.

Waiting for them here was a large choir of singing boys, with accompanying fiddlers and flute-players, who led the way down with spirited music, to the Queen's evident delight, this apparently the cheerful Lord Robert's arranging. From now on, as Abbot of Holyrood, *he* would be in charge rather than his elder brother. Nevertheless the Lord James found cause for frowns, in that the cannonade continued to resound from Edinburgh Castle, which could be seen now about a mile to the west, rearing its proud head above the hilly city, its battlements presently wreathed in smoke from the busy artillery – a shocking waste of powder. Had Kirkcaldy not told them when to stop?

Down at the gates of the abbey the crowds were dense, and the music faltered as singers sought to force a way through, the Lord Robert sending guards ahead to clear a passage with the flats of their swords. It all made a lively and noisy homecoming for Mary Stewart, at least.

Thomas, much as he appreciated his becoming unexpectedly involved in all this, to some degree, could think of no excuse to attach himself further to the royal party. He told

Mary Fleming and the others, therefore, that he hoped that they would find their quarters here, and all else, satisfactory, and that it might be his privilege to attend on her, and on them all, on another occasion.

There appeared to be surprise that he was leaving them, the assumption being evidently that he was part of the Lord Robert's Holyrood entourage.

"Where do you go, then?" he was asked. "To your Smellum? Where is Smellum?" She seemed to find amusement in this version of the name.

"Not there, no. Smailholm is down in the Merse, the East March of the Border, fifty miles. No, I go now to my father's town-house, in the Canongate here."

"Ah, that is close at hand, then. So we shall see more of you?"

"That I do not know, lady – but I would hope so."

"Indeed yes. You have been most kind. Come and see us."

"I can scarce do that, uninvited," he said. "The Lord Robert cannot know me – although he knows my father . . ."

"Then we shall inform him. Shall we not?" And Mary Fleming looked at her friends.

They all agreed, heartily.

He coughed, almost hesitant. "These wretched nags we ride. We, the Kerrs, Borderers, use better beasts. We have a few with us here, in Edinburgh. Not many, of course. But if you would wish to ride abroad, to hunt or hawk or see the land here, I could see you better mounted. And, and accompany you if so you wished. Until the Queen gets her own horses."

"How good you are! We shall not forget. Where do we find you?"

"At the Ferniehirst lodging, beside the head of Bakehouse Close. That is near to the Canongate Cross and the Tolbooth. No distance from here."

"Good. I have that." And as he saluted them, and reined his horse round, "Thank you, Tom Smellum!"

He was not greatly enamoured of that designation, but was much too pleased with his day's involvements to let that worry him. He rode back through the crowd, thoroughly pleased with himself, to the Kerrs' house at the Bakehouse Close, no more than four hundred yards in fact. The Canongate opened on to the abbey precincts, as its name implied – the canons' gait or road to their Holyrood, the area a separate and distinct burgh from its large neighbour so close, Edinburgh.

His father not yet having returned, Thomas was able to give his mother, younger brothers and sisters a colourful and lively account of the day's proceedings, of the Queen's beauty and grace – she had actually spoken to him personally – the French oddities with her, and the excellence of her Scots ladies, in especial Mary Fleming. He did not, however, mention Tom Smellum.

Next morning, the excitement had worn off somewhat; none of the Kerrs had had much sleep, for all night long the noise from the abbey precincts had kept them awake, with half the population of the capital seemingly gathered there, singing, dancing, playing the bagpipes, shouting, even some urgent Reformers chanting psalms, all in honour of their Queen's return after thirteen years. Thomas's exalted mood was less in evidence therefore – that is, until, after a brisk ride round the royal park which encircled that great hill-mass called Arthur's Seat, after the semi-legendary Strathclyde King Arthur of the sixth century, to clear his head, he returned to learn that a messenger had come from the abbey, one of the Lord Robert's men. Come for *him*, not his father, to invite him to attend a celebratory banquet and ball that very evening, in the palace wing. Elation was renewed, for this call could have originated only with Mary Fleming. The Lord Robert did not know him, and the invitation was only for himself, none of his family included. So he must have made some impression . . .

That evening, then, dressed in his modest best, he walked down to the abbey gate. Noisy crowds had been there all day, and still were, making merry, with pedlars of meats and drink doing a literally roaring trade, troupes of gypsy dancers performing, pipers playing, even a bear-leader, and psalm-singing striving to compete. The common folk of Scotland had a greater regard for their ancient monarchy, and its present lovely representative, than had the aristocracy, it seemed.

The abbey gates were well guarded, in consequence, and Thomas had to wait whilst a minion went to ascertain his right to enter. But eventually he got inside. He did not have to be conducted to the scene of celebration, for music and laughter, again in competition with the noise outside, emanated from the palace wing to the south of the abbey proper with its great church. This was the handsome twin-towered building in the French castellated style erected by James the Fifth, Mary's father, that strange monarch, lover of women and things of beauty and art – he had built an even finer great hall at Stirling Castle – of sports and wild games, yet comparatively uninterested in the rule of his realm, which he had left largely to others, in especial to Mary Beaton's kinsman, the Cardinal, who had to all intents governed both Church and state. This palace was linked to the monastic premises by the abbatical wing, now the quarters of the Lord Robert and his odd establishment of mistresses, children of various ages, and hangers-on, where the Queen and her party were presently lodged, for the palace wing had not been used since her father died, her mother preferring Linlithgow and Stirling to the capital. But evidently the great ballroom was being used tonight.

Thomas entered this splendid apartment, its neglected finery and decoration temporarily hidden behind greenery and flowers, to find the first dancing already in progress down one half of the hall even though servants were still setting tables and bringing in foodstuffs in the other, a group of fiddlers playing lustily. The available space was fairly crowded, but he could see no sign of the Queen or her ladies, none that he knew at least. The Marquis d'Elboeuf he saw, capering with what he considered was an underclad female, his brother the Grand Prior of France only slightly more dignified in his comportment. Of the rest, he recognised some of the offspring of the Lord Robert – who had a large family by various ladies, all living together in approximate amity – cavorting with enthusiasm and laughter. The only other whom he identified was a strong-featured, burly, youngish man with notably hot eyes, dancing with one of their host's daughters, James Hepburn, Earl of Bothwell; him he knew only too well, for the Earl was Chief Warden of the Marches, and he and Thomas's father did not get on.

Thomas enjoyed dancing well enough, but judged that the present cantrips could hardly be called that, more suited to a fair-ground or barnyard, he thought. He was not priggish, but felt that in these stately premises some dignity should be observed. Besides, there was nobody present whom he would want to dance with, although more than one young woman eyed him assessingly.

He had a little while to wait before a servant appeared, in a motley gown, to mount the dais at the top end of the hall and clash together a pair of cymbals, which effectively silenced the musicians and halted the dancers. Then a rear door was opened and the Lord Robert ushered in his royal half-sister, on his arm, her ladies and a train of courtiers, French and Scots, behind. The fiddlers struck up again, changing their tune to a more formal measure, to which the Queen's party paced in, bowing and waving to all.

The Queen had discarded her mourning black for this occasion, and looked highly attractive in a gown of crimson and gold silk, which did full justice to her tall, lissome and excellent figure. Although Thomas's eyes quickly sought out Mary Fleming amongst her train, they were irresistibly drawn back to her royal mistress, who excelled all in looks and bearing. Only in the by-going, as it were, did he note that amongst the males of the party were few indeed of those who had been prominent at the royal reception at Leith the day before: the Lord John Stewart, Abbot of Melrose, was there, but not the Lord James nor most of the other dignitaries. Was there some reason for this he wondered?

Dancing did not resume meantime, and the Queen and her half-brothers, the Lady Fleming, her de Guise uncles and the Abbot of Brantôme, took their seats at the table up on the dais, while all others jostled for places at the tables which stretched the length of the great room, in competition for seats nearest the dais. Thomas, whilst a fairly modest young man, was a Border Kerr and certainly not apt for the lowest places, and was making for mid-table when he found his arm taken by Mary Fleming, and steered by her further up. She was all in white satin tonight, and fair indeed. A group of places had apparently been reserved for the Queen's ladies just below the dais itself, and to this the almost embarrassed Thomas was conducted, and there seated between Fleming and Beaton, opposite Seton and Livingstone, who had between them the young and handsome John Sempill, son to the westland lord of that name, who eyed Thomas critically.

"You see, we seek to pay our debts, Tom Smellum!" Mary Fleming said.

"No debt, Mistress Mary. It was my privilege. And, and pleasure. It was good of you to have me invited here tonight."

"Our pleasure. And, since we are all called Mary, you

24

had better name me Flam, as the others do. Or, when they disapprove of me, Flim-Flam!"

"I swear that can be but seldom!" he returned, heavily gallant.

She went on, "Beaton, here, we call Beth – for Beaton, the name, comes from Béthune, in Flanders. And Seton, who is vowed to eternal chastity – unlike the rest of us! – we name Ebba, from our Scots Saint Ebba, who cut off her breasts to keep men away from her . . .!"

"Hush you, Flim-Flam!" the ethereally beautiful Mary Seton said, but with a smile. "Your tongue will be the ruin of you!"

"I know St Ebba's Head, on our Merse coast," Thomas put in hastily. "And the story of her nuns . . ."

"Of course you will. Is Smellum near there? As for Livingstone . . ."

She got no further, for the Lord Robert clapped his hands for waiting servitors to march in, in procession, bearing aloft great silver trays on which steamed a flotilla of roasted swans, cleverly reinvested with their white feathering, a notable sight and delicacy. These were followed by a sounder of suckling piglets, most lifelike, with haunches of venison behind, great bowls of soup bringing up the rear. The abbatical kitchens had been busy indeed.

"We hunted the deer in this royal park, four days ago," Sempill confided, with some authority. "And the swans come from Duddingston Loch, at the far side of Arthur's Seat." He glanced across the table, less than flatteringly. "The pigs, perhaps, come from the Borders!"

Thomas was saved from having to counter that suitably by the Lord Robert announcing that before they commenced to eat his poor provision, they would drink a toast to his royal sister, so long absent from their shores but not their hearts, now joyfully returned to her ancient realm, God be praised.

That was about as far in the way of religious observance as the Commendator-Abbot of Holyrood was apt to go. But not the said royal sister. When they had all, standing, drunk the toast, followed by cheers, and the Lord Robert, grinning, sat to his steaming platter of swan's breast, the Queen held up her hand, thanked all, and smiling, called on the Grand Prior of France to say grace-before-meat.

That exquisite rose, crossed himself elaborately, and

launched into a lengthy gabble, in French, which ended with a further demonstrative signing of the cross over the entire company.

Somebody, well down the table, cried out, and there was a murmur from others. Thomas glanced sidelong at Mary Fleming, who presumably was a good Catholic, and coughed. This was Reformed Scotland, and such manifestations of popish behaviour expressly forbidden by the Confession of Faith passed by parliament. The Lord Robert, fortunately, was concerned to cut short any discomfort by signing for the musicians to strike up soft background melodies.

The banquet proceeded thereafter, with the incident forgotten in the lavishness of the provision and the excellence of the wines, Mary Fleming confiding that the French present would be getting a better and different impression of Scotland from the barbarous and backward place it was generally held to be. But Thomas recognised that that gesture of the Grand Prior, and the reaction to it, might be an ominous presaging of problems to come.

The meal over, there was a masque presented, on the swan theme again, swans being royal birds by tradition, and the three lochs of Arthur's Seat's royal park noted for their prevalence. A boat contrived in the form of a great swan, white-painted and with an arch-necked and beaked figurehead, two sails painted to represent upraised wings, was drawn into the hall by a team of scantily clad young women, with head-dresses of white feathers and diaphanous wings. Within the boat, on a sort of throne, sat a voluptuous female, a golden crown on her head but wearing nothing else at all, to the gasps and then cheers of most of the company. The Swan Queen was drawn round the hall, bowing, smiling and gesturing to all. The circuit completed, she stood, and melodiously sang a few verses of the "Ballad of Fionnuala", who was transformed into a swan and haunted the lochs and rivers until, wounded by a fowler's arrow, she died, singing most beautifully her swan-song. The lady's cygnets joined in the chorus, before all departed, to enthusiastic applause.

Thomas wondered whether the monarch and her ladies would find all this to their taste, but perceived no signs of disapproval. Of course, he had heard that the French court was the most indecorous and profligate in all Christendom, so such a display would be unlikely to shock.

Now, with the servants clearing the long tables away, the general dancing was resumed, but in more decorous fashion, the Queen first taking the floor with the Lord Robert. She danced, as she did all else, with grace and verve, and Thomas was admiring when he perceived that Mary Fleming was eyeing him expectantly. So he, informing her that he could make only a clumsy effort at the stately sort of dancing, such as this, being used to the more active Scots variety, led her on to the floor – and did none so badly, under her guidance.

He danced with the other Marys thereafter, but kept coming back to Fleming, even though she chided him that his attentions should be a deal more intent on his partner and not tending to stray off to watch the Queen, however fascinating the royal performance. He could scarcely explain that he was disapproving of the way her present partner was holding her when the dance called for any close proximity – for this was the Earl of Bothwell – and his attitude over-familiar in a Kerr's opinion. Although, indeed, when partnering Beth Beaton, that lively one, he himself experienced some closer embracing than he was used to. These French dances . . .

It was his turn, presently, when they progressed to typical Scots dances, and he was able to demonstrate and guide. The Marys had some idea as to these, of course, but were far from expert. He soon had them skipping and twirling in fine style and enthusiasm, even though some more intricate steps were bungled.

Some of these native dances involved considerable circling and exchange of partners, and it was in one of these that Thomas found himself face to face with the Queen, who, flushed, bright-eyed and even panting a little, took his arm in entirely natural fashion.

"Ah, Thomas . . . of Smellum! I . . . saw you . . . playing squire to . . . my Marys." That came out breathlessly, for this was an energetic exercise. Thomas was much aware of the royal bosom heaving so evidently and delectably so close to hand.

"They are very kind to me, Your Grace," he said.

"I . . . wonder why?" she asked, and tapped his shoulder, having to use the hand which had been hitching up her skirt to do so, for these dances called for a certain freedom of the legs.

He did not answer that, being all but overcome by the fact

that he was actually holding his sovereign-lady, this quite adorable creature – he, Thomas Kerr.

All too soon, he had to pass her on to another, the Lord John in fact – he was glad that it was not to the Earl of Bothwell – but even so she squeezed his arm and murmured something which he did not catch.

It was quite some moments afterwards before he realised that his new temporary partner was Mary Seton, and that she was speaking to him, less vigorous of action and therefore less breathless than had been her mistress.

". . . loves to dance," she was saying. "And has been denied it for some time, the French court being in mourning."

"Ah, yes. To be sure." He forced himself to concentrate on *this* young woman.

"You approve of Her Grace, I see! She is going to require approval here in Scotland, I fear." That was not said lightly.

This had a sobering effect on him. "You think so, lady?"

"Oh, yes. This land requires much governing. And she has not had to govern, as yet, only reign. The nobles here are out of hand, my father says. The Protestant ones in especial. I fear . . ."

"Yes. They can be bigoted. And unruly." That last, coming from a moss-trooping Kerr, might have raised some eyebrows. It was altogether an unusual conversation to be holding in the midst of a fairly vehement Scots dance, but this young woman was herself unusual, different from the others, quietly serious without being stiff, prim or restrained-seeming. He decided that he liked Mary Seton, chastely inclined or not.

Back with Mary Fleming, later, they noted that, as the evening wore on, the company in that hall was becoming progressively more boisterous, the behaviour indecorous and provocative, wines and spirits having their effect.

"I think that we shall be leaving you soon," the girl said. "The Queen prefers to retire if the night grows thus . . . noisy."

"That I can understand. Some here should know better!" And he looked in particular at the Earl of Bothwell, who was not so much dancing with as embracing and exploring the person of a young woman whose clothing was already sufficiently disarranged. "The Chief Warden of the Marches!"

"That is the Lord Bothwell, is it not? A lusty lord, I think! And also appreciative of Her Grace."

Thomas frowned.

Mary Fleming had guessed aright, for shortly afterwards Mary Seton, clearly the senior of the four, came to indicate the Queen's retiral, Flam looking a little regretful.

"It is goodnight, then," she said to Thomas. "Might we go riding tomorrow, perhaps?"

"To be sure. You? Or . . . others?"

She smiled at him. "I think that I would be safer with the others, no?"

He coughed. "No, no. Not so. I . . . you would be entirely safe with me, I assure you."

She pouted provocatively. "One could be *too* safe, I suppose?" Then she gestured towards Bothwell. "You March-riding Borderers! Sleep well, Tom Smellum! Until the morrow."

He left that celebration immediately after the Queen and her Marys departed.

2

Next forenoon Thomas arrived at the abbey gates with five horses besides his own. There had been words about this with his father, for these were all the animals the Kerrs had brought with them to Edinburgh, apart from the servants' nags, and Thomas had only got away with it by declaring that this was for the Queen's service. Actually it was a far-out hope that the fifth beast would be for the Queen herself; this was almost too much to hope for, even for that young man, for surely she would be provided with mounts, and good ones, by the Lord Robert should she wish to go riding. In fact, only Flam and Beth Beaton came out from the abbatical quarters to join him, so they had to return three animals to the Canongate lodging stables. He rather wished, now, that he could have been returning four.

However, both girls were in good spirits and soon he was enjoying their company without any such qualifications. When they congratulated him on the quality of his horses, he had to remind them that they were talking to the son of a chief of the Border Kerrs, and other than the very finest horseflesh was inconceivable therefrom.

They rode into the royal park – which, in the circumstances, was a strange term for that spectacular terrain out of which soared the tremendous Arthur's Seat and its foothill slopes, wooded on the levelish ground to the east and north, and still sheltering a few deer, he told them, despite the depredations of the Edinburgh poachers. In that direction, passing presently St Margaret's Loch, where clouds of wildfowl rose, he went on to inform his companions as to how the Blessed Queen Margaret's youngest son, David the First, whilst hunting hereabouts, had been saved from the charge of a wounded stag, as he believed, by a piece of Christ's true cross carried with him, his late mother's treasure, and in gratitude swore to build a great abbey on the site, which he named the Abbey of the Holy Rood, or cross, their present lodging. Neither of the young women knew of this story.

Thereafter they began to climb, quite steeply, up over a high shoulder of the hill and into a sort of pass swinging round southwards below the main summit. Here they skirted another, smaller, loch, called Dunsappie, also fowl-haunted, and a notable venue for hawking, Thomas said. Soon afterwards the pass opened out and a vast panorama of country was spread out before them, to the girls' delight. Thomas pointed down immediately below them, hundreds of feet, to where lay still another and larger loch, amongst woodlands, fringed by great reed-beds.

"That is where the swans come from – Duddingston Loch. But I doubt if you will find Fionnuala the Swan-Queen here today!"

"She was one of the Lord Robert's mistresses," Mary Beaton announced factually. "Well-shaped, did you not think? For her age."

Thomas forbore comment.

Flam was looking up, not down. "I would like to climb this mountain," she declared. "Is it possible?"

"Possible, yes. I have been up it many times. But not on horseback. Riding up the Hunter's Bog corrie, you could get halfway, mounted. But the rest, for women . . .?" He looked at her doubtfully.

"You think us weaklings?" she demanded. "Like so many men do. Poor feckless creatures, incapable of climbing a hill, good only for play and bed! To be ogled at and toyed with but not – "

"No, no! I assure you, no!" That was urgent. "I will take you up Arthur's Seat one day, if you wish."

"Yes. We will hold you to that, Tom Smellum! The Queen might like to climb it also."

"Lord . . .!"

Circling the great hill so that they were now trending northwards they began to come in sight of an extraordinary feature, a face of tremendous perpendicular, reddish cliffs, in columnar formation, thrusting out westwards from the main massif, seeming to frown over the city.

"Sarumsburgh Craigs." He pointed. "Sometimes called Sampson's Ribs. There are many stories about those."

"I have never seen the like," Flam admitted. "Does not

Edinburgh cower beneath it all? That fierce castle on its rock on the one side, this on the other – how strange a place to build a city."

"I suppose that I saw this as a child," Beth said. "But we were only five years when we left."

Instead of heading straight back to the abbey-palace, once they had dipped down to the lower ground again, Thomas took them round south-abouts so that they could see Duddingston Loch and the many white swans which sailed thereon. Flam wanted to know why swans were considered to be the property of royalty, but Thomas confessed his ignorance. It was so in other countries too, he had been told.

When returning through the eastern woodlands, they hoped to catch sight of deer, but were denied this, Thomas explaining that they were apt to lie up in the dense thickets during the day. At the abbey gates, the girls were cheerfully grateful for his kindness and escort, both kissing him frankly, there in front of the guards, Flam declaring that she would not forget to hold him to a climbing of the mountain. He had to warn her then, distinctly apologetically, that he would not be in Edinburgh for long, unfortunately. He was, although newly come of age and allotted his mother's dowery-house of Smailholm, still not entirely his own master, in that his father was very much the laird, chief of the Kerrs and Warden of the Middle March into the bargain. And Sir John had said that they would be returning to Ferniehirst, near to Jedburgh, on Monday. And this was Friday.

So their climb must await another occasion, he feared.

But Thomas's delaying tactics did not prevail, for that very evening a message came from the palace to say that, weather permitting, they would go climbing next day, Saturday. And he was to bring all five horses, for the Queen had decided to accompany them.

Wondering what he had let himself in for, Thomas at least had no problem this time over the horses, for this could be construed as something in the nature of a royal command, which Sir John could not question.

In the morning, when he presented himself at the abbey with his mounts, he found the forecourt thronged with horses and riders. Somewhat alarmed, he hoped that this was nothing to do with him, but feared the worst when he perceived Mary Livingstone's friend, Sempill, amongst the waiting company.

Presently Flam appeared, in something like glee, to come to him and declare that this was indeed going to be a notable day. For when the Queen announced that she was going to climb Arthur's Seat, practically the entire court said that they were going to accompany her, shamed into it by their liege-lady. There would undoubtedly be a great slaughter amongst them, she believed, many there apt to cock a snook and think themselves grand, who would never make it, she judged – and hoped. Some of these men . . .!

Thomas was less enheartened.

At length the Queen emerged, surrounded by a flock of brilliantly dressed and noisy folk, most of them strangely clad indeed for hill-climbing. The monarch herself was more suitably clad in serviceable riding-clothes, fairly short of skirt and with knee-length boots. She came straight across to where Thomas and Flam waited, the other Marys, as ever, close behind.

"A good morning to you, Thomas of Smellum," she greeted him. "Today you take us up yonder mountain? It is long since I climbed a hill. I hope that I do not fail you!"

"Your Grace, it was not my notion." He glanced almost guiltily at Flam. "I would not wish that you should be put to any trouble, any discomfort . . ."

"No, it will be good for me, I think. A challenge. We must face challenges, no? We now ride with you?"

"Your Grace honours me . . ." He brought a horse to her, and aided her into the saddle.

The Lord Robert, at her back, hooted a laugh. "God knows what we are at, this day!" he said. "I have never been up that hill, in all my life. What have you put upon us, young Kerr?"

"None need go to the top, my lord. It is but an outing, meant to be a pleasuring . . ."

The Marquis d'Elboeuf, nearby, made some comment in French.

Laughing, the Queen rallied him. "Come, Uncle – you are in Scotland now! You wished to discover it all, did you not?"

While Thomas assisted the other girls up, the men went back to select other horses from the many assembled there, and there was a great mounting amidst much calling and to-do.

At the Queen's side, with considerable lack of confidence, Thomas led a sizeable cavalcade out into the royal park.

33

They rode, as they had done the day before, eastwards, but not quite so far as to St Margaret's Loch, to turn off right-handed near a stone-canopied well and under a strangely placed chapel perched on a rock-top, which Thomas explained was dedicated to St Anthony. Almost immediately they began to climb into a wide, scoop-like green hollow which led up and up towards the main towering summit of the hill. This made fairly easy riding, and the company behind chattered cheerfully. But a fair height up, that cleuch or corrie levelled off into a sort of great basin, and this, lacking drainage, had a soggy, reedy floor into which the horses' hooves tended to sink. This was the Hunter's Bog, a noted hazard, and its wet going produced some alarm and complaint amongst the riders. But Thomas sought to steer them round the rim of it, on somewhat firmer ground; and here they glimpsed their first deer, three hinds some distance off, sufficient to arouse spirited shouts and halloos from the company.

However, not a few spirits were dampened thereafter when it was perceived that there was no way out of this basin ahead save by suddenly rising slopes too steep for horses. Thomas pointed to a sort of little plateau about one hundred feet higher, to which he thought they ought to be able to get their beasts; but after that, he said, they would have to go on foot. He set his mount zigzagging its way up, picking his difficult route, his Border horse quite used to hilly ground. There was outcry and all but consternation behind – although not from the Queen and her ladies – as animals slithered and stumbled, pecked and sidled.

At the grassy shelf, dismounting, he noted that perhaps half the party had already turned back, misliking this terrain, to Flam's scurrilous comments.

With still steeper climbing obviously ahead, some proportion of those who had got thus far decided that their place now was with the horses, which it seemed must not be left untended in such dangerous territory, these including the Lord Robert. The Marquis d'Elboeuf seemed in two minds on the matter, but the Earl of Bothwell rallied him and he allowed himself to be persuaded. His brothers, the Duke and the Grand Prior, chose the wiser course.

In some doubts about leading his sovereign up that rough and slippery ascent – it was more than any mere slope – Thomas wondered whether offering a hand to help would be in order. But he found the Queen tackling the task without hesitation, hitching up her skirts with one hand, the other out to aid her progress by grasping at tussocks and rocks – the incline was sufficiently steep for that. With this example before them, her Marys could do no less. Another six, including unfortunately the Earl of Bothwell and John Sempill, both agile young men, were concerned to demonstrate their ability, and this pair quickly forged ahead. Challenged thus, Thomas would have liked to prove his own mettle, but felt that his place was with the young women. D'Elboeuf and the others were less ambitious.

Soon all were panting, some more deeply than others, with the female form apt to show to pleasing effect. The dozen of them lost all coherence and became spread out, Thomas however keeping close to the Queen – who indeed was the foremost of the ladies, scrambling up with vigour. Ebba Seton, oddly enough, was the next most effective, with poor Flam, who had instigated it all, bringing up the rear – no doubt her plump and well-rounded figure being less advantageous here than on some occasions.

Arthur's Seat rose to nearly nine hundred feet, and they had got the horses up almost two-thirds of that, so they had some three hundred feet to climb to the summit, not a great height but the ultimate crest steep, with much bare rock, although Thomas sought to pick a somewhat circuitous route up, to avoid the most difficult features. Frequently he urged the Queen to pause, to rest, but she shook her head, breathlessly but smilingly determined. Perhaps Bothwell and Sempill, away ahead, spurred her on. She did accept, however, Thomas's tentatively outstretched hand more than once – to his major satisfaction. Although now he felt a little guilty when he glanced back and saw Flam toiling unaided well behind.

There were respites of a sort, of course, where the hill's steepness eased off temporarily a little; but these had the effect of creating false crests ahead, and the summit seemed to keep receding. But at last the final crown presented its demand on them, and laboriously they surmounted it and reached their goal, the Queen's hand now firmly clutching Thomas's elbow. It may be that it was the sight of this which roused Bothwell, sitting now on a summit rock in nonchalant style, into belated gallantry. He rose, to come forward and take the royal arm in almost proprietorial fashion – to Thomas's scowl. Equally belatedly, he himself turned back to assist the pink and gulping Flam up over the last score or so of feet.

It took some time for the ladies, at least, to fully recover themselves, and so appreciate the magnificence of the reward for all their efforts. The prospects from that hilltop must be the most exciting and dramatic in all southern Scotland, so all-embracing and far-reaching their scope. On every side the seemingly limitless vistas spread, infinity itself.

Soon all were exclaiming, however, or most – for it was beneath the dignity of some of the men so to do – the Queen in especial spellbound, her regard rising from the dwarfed city crouching below under its pall of chimneys' smoke, northwards to the blue, sparkling, isle-dotted Forth estuary, the green hills of Fife beyond, backed by the distant purple mountains of the Highland Line; eastwards over fertile Haddingtonshire, out of which soared the leviathan-like Traprain and North Berwick Laws, to the Norse Sea from which thrust the mighty Craig of Bass and the gleaming white cliffs of the Isle of May; southwards across Lothian to the Lammermuir, Morthwaite and Pentland Hills, range upon range; and westwards, far beyond the towering Edinburgh Castle on its rock, to fair demesnes, spreading woodlands and rising moors, to further mountains far off.

"It is said that you can see sixty miles and more in all directions from here," Thomas declared.

"My kingdom!" the Queen breathed. "So fair, so very fair."

"And so ill-disposed, Madam!" Bothwell, at her other side, jerked. "A land of rogues and scoundrels – and, yonder, barbarous Hielandmen!" And he gestured northwards.

"Surely not, my lord!" she protested. "You are too harsh, too critical."

"Your Grace will learn!"

"I think that you cannot have slept well last night!"

"For thinking of you!" That was quick, and he touched her shoulder.

"La – your loyalty overwhelms me, my lord!" she said, but lightly. He was, after all, Lord High Admiral of Scotland as well as Lieutenant or Chief Warden of the Borders and Sheriff of Edinburgh and all Lothian. She turned to Thomas. "Name me the places I see, the towns, villages, lands, mountains. So many, I am bewildered . . ."

He did his best, interrupted and amplified by Bothwell,

Sempill and Maitland, the Secretary of State, who had arrived with the exhausted d'Elboeuf.

Flam drew Thomas aside a little. "There are more of us here than just the Queen!" she reproved.

"I am sorry. Yes. You did well."

"I could have done better – with a little help!"

"Flam is jealous!" Beth Beaton announced, laughing. "*She* discovered you, Tom. You had better be careful!"

He looked from one to the other.

"Heed them not, friend." That was Mary Seton. "They will both grow up, one day!"

When all made their way downhill, considerable assistance was now forthcoming from the men, now that prowess had been displayed, the steep slope being even more slippery in descent. Thomas discreetly left the Queen to Bothwell's attentive handling, and whilst concentrating on Flam, gave a certain amount of aid to Beth Beaton also. Livingstone was being looked after by Sempill, and Seton seemed to be very competent on her own. But presently Secretary Maitland came to take Flam's other arm, and appeared to be more appreciated. So Thomas transferred his services to Beth, who hung on to him, giggling. It was all very high-spirited, after their achievement.

Back at the horses, they discovered that some of the party had already departed. The remainder were treated to a catalogue of what they had missed by their feebleness, with general scorn, even d'Elboeuf twitting his de Guise brothers.

They returned to the palace.

In the forecourt, dismounting, the Queen came to Thomas, to thank him. "It was a notable venture, friend Thomas. I much enjoyed it. I shall not forget this day, nor you. We are in your debt. Tomorrow, after morning church, will you come and eat with us? It would pleasure me."

"Your Grace is kind . . ."

Flam had already disappeared indoors, with Maitland, but Beth gave him a generous kissing, and Seton a warm smile.

He went off with the horses, not a little pleased with himself.

The next morning Thomas was not alone in repairing to the abbey for worship, for the Chapel Royal there in fact also served as the parish church of the burgh of the Canongate, and thither the faithful congregated of a Sunday morning.

Probably the Queen had not realised this. So all the Kerr family, with servants, accompanied him, amidst large numbers of other denisons of the Canongate and elsewhere, more than usual indeed, because of the royal presence.

The church therefore was fairly full before the Queen's party arrived, but a space at the front had been reserved. At the chancel steps the parish minister, the Reverend John Craig, a sober, elderly divine, waited to receive her. The Lord James Stewart was in evidence, keeping a watchful eye on all.

The royal entry was a little late, led in by a choir of singing boys. The Queen and her ladies were all in mourning black again, although most of her entourage were anything but, the Grand Prior and the Abbé Brantôme being in full, colourful canonicals, which drew frowns from most of the congregation. As did the Queen's genuflection before what had been the altar up until a year or so before and was now the communion-table, in the chancel. But she smiled kindly to the Reverend Craig and after a moment of hesitation, went to take her seat in the middle of the front row of pews, no throne-like chair being provided. In the Reformed Church monarchs were equally God's vassals with everyone else. Her party had to jostle for seats as best they could. The only person who did not have to do this was the Lord Robert, who as Commendator-Abbot of Holyrood had a stall provided for him near the pulpit. He did not look particularly abbatical even so, dressed as was his usual.

Once all were seated – save for the majority of the congregation behind, who had to stand for lack of pews – the minister led off with a lengthy prayer, at which the Queen and her people knelt, although nobody else did. John Craig had a resonant voice, and addressed his Maker with confidence – after all, he had been a priest of the Romish Church for many years, until recently, and had had plenty of practice.

This was followed by a psalm, everyone standing, the congregation, led by the choirboys, singing heartily, even though the visitors from France clearly knew neither words nor tune. The Apostles' Creed was then recited, the monarch and her party crossing themselves at each mention of the Trinity, which caused some faltering elsewhere. The minister then read from the Old Testament, sternly, declaring woe unto the pastors who destroy and scatter the sheep, from Jeremiah twenty-three; and thereafter came a second long

38

prayer and another psalm. Then mounting the pulpit, John Craig read briefly from all four Gospels, in their mention of Bartholemew, this being St Bartholemew's Day; and although the Reformers were not too happy about saints, Bartholemew was fairly harmless.

The sermon that followed was shorter and less dogmatic than usual, even though the royal company, unused to such, stirred in their seats as it proceeded. However, for others, it was more interesting than often, for the preacher explained that although Bartholemew was referred to as a called apostle in all four Gospels, as they had heard, nothing more was heard of him. The fact was that he was probably Nathanael, whom Jesus specifically called, with Philip, named the Israelite in whom was no guile. The name Bartholemew merely meant son of Tolmai, so the apostle's true name would be Nathanael, thus resolving a mystery for those who knew their Scriptures. This was delivered with distinct satisfaction, however much above the heads of most present.

There was another prayer and psalm and then the final benediction, with more crossing from the front seats.

The minister, closing the great Bible, was about to descend from the pulpit, service over, when a tinkling sound of a bell came from the west end of the church, and turned all heads – or most of them. As well as this, there was noise from outside, for not all who had come this morning had been able to get into the crowded building, and the west door had been left open for their benefit. Shouting now arose, and in came a little procession, scurrying somewhat but attempting to retain some dignity. Two young robed acolytes led, bearing tall lighted candles, ushering in a priest in full vestments – as distinct from Craig's sober black with white bands – bearing a silver tray on which lay a platter of eucharistic bread and a flagon and chalice of wine. Two more candle-bearers brought up the rear.

As this group paced up towards the front of the church, it dawned on most of the congregation that this was preliminary to a Mass being celebrated, Romish Mass, forbidden in Scotland, not only by the Reformed Church but by parliament and the law. Outcry, protests, shouting arose and maintained. The little procession quickened pace but pressed on.

Everywhere, except in those front seats, there was commotion, turmoil. Thomas found himself elbowed aside as people pushed past to get out, to leave that suddenly bedevilled place. Some excited young men rushed forward and managed to knock over two of the candles, amidst cheers. Nearby, a man whom Thomas knew, Patrick Lindsay, son and heir of Lord Lindsay of the Byres, yelled out that the idolatrous priest should die the death, and this was enthusiastically taken up. Still on the pulpit stairs, John Craig raised hands, palms out, as though to banish the newcomers. Chaos reigned.

The Lord James, who had been standing near the back, not with the royal party, sought now to take charge; for whatever else he might be he was an able and determined man, a leader. He strode forward, to pull Lindsay round, and pointed peremptorily to the door. Glaring all around, he gestured for others to leave also. There was a concerted rush to get out.

Up at the chancel, the priest was seeking to elevate the Host, to the imminent danger of its collapse, for his arms were shaking visibly. The Grand Prior and Brantôme went to support him.

Uproar continued, but the church was emptying.

The Lord James was at his most coldly authoritative, directing the exodus – ignoring his half-sister's party. The Kerrs, like many others of the aristocracy, were still inclined towards the old religion, but had to be discreet about it, doing their Catholic worship in private, since it was illegal in public, and offices of state could not be held by its practitioners.

In the circumstances, Sir John was taking the prudent course, and ushering his family out. Thomas would have preferred to stay, since the Queen had invited him to be there, but his father was commanding.

They were amongst the last to leave, and the Lord James came out behind them, slamming the door shut and then standing with his back to it, to prevent an entrance.

Surrounded by the angry crowd, Sir John herded his family to push their way through. "There will be trouble here," he said, somewhat unnecessarily. "That was folly! Come, it is home for us."

Thomas felt differently. "I stay. I am to eat with the Queen."

His father shrugged. "It may be none so happy a feast, boy. You would be better at home this day, I think."

"Yes, Tom – come with us," his mother said.

40

He shook his head. "She asked me, herself."

Thomas went with his family sufficiently far as to see them through the noisy throng, then turned back. The Lord James still stood at the Chapel Royal door, barring it. Presently he sent for aid, for soon a group of armed servitors appeared from the abbey premises, to form up, under his instructions, at the doorway. Leaving these in position, he opened the door and went within again, closing it quickly behind him.

Thomas bethought him of the vestry door, at the other end of the building, the clergy's normal entrance. He edged out of the crowd and slipped round to the east end – and discovered the Lord James now standing there, on guard again, and eyeing him levelly. No one else, thus far.

"You are young Kerr, are you not? Go you to the corner there, and keep watch," he ordered briefly. "If any such come round here, sign to me. I will get the Queen out this way."

Thomas nodded and went to where he could see the south side of the building, to wait.

It was not long before the Lord James, presumably hearing what went on inside, turned to go in through the vestry doorway. Evidently the Mass service had been shortened, and wisely. He reappeared quite quickly with the Queen, her Marys close behind and the rest of the party following on hurriedly. Last came his two half-brothers, the Lords Robert and John, with the priest between them. At a gesture and pointing from James, these hastened with the frightened celebrant across to the abbey stables nearby, and inside. The Stewart family were closing ranks, for once.

The royal party moved off, not into the stables but round a back way to the abbatical quarters, keeping out of sight of the crowd. It was scarcely a dignified proceeding for the monarch, but Mary did not hurry, her head high, however closely she was pressed on by some behind. Thomas came along at the end, and as the group strung out, moved up beside the Marys. They were all looking tense, but seemed glad to see him.

"That was . . . unfortunate!" he said.

"It was wicked, shameful!" Flam exclaimed. "How could they dare? In the Queen's presence!"

"And God's!" That was Mary Seton.

He shook his head. This was no time nor place for explanations.

They got into the residential quarters without further difficulty – and the first person they saw waiting for them there was the Earl of Bothwell. So he had not been to church, perhaps foreseeing trouble. Thomas was prepared to believe the worst of that one.

The Marys conducted him along to their rooms at the end of a long corridor, Flam taking him into one she shared with Beth. She seemed to have forgotten her pique of the day before, and went on at some length about the disgraceful scenes in the chapel. He did not seek to defend the perpetrators but pointed out that the service of the Mass was now forbidden in Scotland, in public, against the law, and that perhaps this morning's celebration had been inadvisable.

"Is the Queen of Scots subject to your new laws?" Flam demanded. "Does she not rule here?"

He forbore to answer that.

Such grievous matters were rather moved to the back of his mind thereafter, for it was distinctly pleasurable for a man to be permitted to remain in a young women's chamber as they prepared themselves for a meal in the Queen's company, a new experience for Thomas Kerr. He was fully appreciative.

Presently Mary Seton came to say that the Queen was almost ready to proceed to the abbot's dining-hall. The girls trooped back along the corridor, Thomas, somewhat doubtfully, behind, unsure as to where he fitted in. But at the royal apartments they found the Queen waiting, with Lady Fleming, and her greeting reassured him. If she was upset by the morning's events she did not show it, and clearly assumed that he would follow her, with the Marys. He thought it best not to mention the Chapel Royal trouble.

The Lord Robert appeared, to lead the group to the dining-hall. Thomas still felt self-conscious at being the only male in a party of six females, and he was aware of odd glances being thrown at him when they entered the room. Not that there were a great many people waiting there, only the Queen's de Guise uncles, the Lords James and John, Bothwell and Secretary Maitland. Now he felt still more the odd man out in such lofty company. At least John Sempill was not present.

As the Marys distributed themselves amongst the waiting men, Flam took his arm and steered him to a seat beside her. Lady Fleming was at his other side, which was a comfort, for in the next chair was the Marquis d'Elboeuf, Thomas's French

42

being halting to say the least. Flam's mother was easy to get on with, royal blood or none.

Preoccupied with the situation as he was, Thomas could not but be aware also of the noise outside. This dining-hall faced westwards, towards the city, and so was not screened from sounds in that direction. And although it was placed well back from the forecourt and area in front of the Chapel Royal, outcry was evidently still going on there, the crowd by no means wholly dispersed.

"Much fuss!" Lady Fleming said lightly. "Who would have thought that the citizens would take their religion so seriously? Extraordinary!"

"Not all will," he suggested. "These will be the more extreme Protestants, I think, not the ordinary folk."

"There seems to be plenty of them," Flam said. "In France this would never be permitted, for a moment."

"Hush, my dear – or that brother of mine might hear you!" Her mother, smiling, glanced across the table to where the Lord James sat silent, expressionless, beside the Grand Prior, to whom he seemed to have nothing to say.

"Is even *he* one of Tom Smellum's extreme Protestants?"

"How extreme I do not know. But it seems to serve his purposes to appear so! And James has the wits of our odd family!"

"I do not like him," her daughter said frankly, if with lowered voice.

"Then you would be wise not to let him see it, *chérie!*"

Despite the noise from outside, the talk around the table, as the meal progressed, was far from gloomy or apprehensive, with the Queen evidently determined to be cheerful, laughing frequently, and on two occasions throwing a word down as far as Thomas, referring to aching muscles and the like after yesterday's exploits on Arthur's Seat, concerned clearly to put him at ease in that company.

The repast was nearly over and the wine-flagons circulating when there was a distinct increase in the volume of noise coming from the west, and the diners exchanged glances. Presently a servitor of senior aspect came in, to bow to the Queen and then moved to speak in the Lord Robert's ear.

"Knox!" Thomas heard that man exclaim, and he looked down at his brother James. He leant over to speak to the

Queen. She eyed him interestedly, and then nodded. The servitor backed out.

There was no question as to the impact of that name, Knox, on the diners: concern, alarm, apprehension. Even the Lord James looked troubled.

After a moment or two that man strode into the room, to halt just within, and to stare. He did not bow towards the monarch, as was customary, nor even concentrate his regard on her, but stood, gazing round on them all. And, strangely, one by one all in that chamber rose to their feet, even the Queen, such was the effect of the man. She soon sat again, but the significance of it was not to be denied.

John Knox was not particularly impressive physically, of medium build, somewhat gaunt of feature, with a long beard, dressed all in black save for white at throat and wrists, a man in his late forties, a farmer's son from near Haddington. Yet there was no escaping the sheer and extraordinary personal power and presence of him, the strange authority and vehemence which emanated from him, projected to all, in his stance and bearing, and above all in the shock of those hooded but burning eyes. Here was perhaps not the most powerful man in Reformed Scotland but the one whose word carried most weight, swayed thousands. Behind him came two others, earls both: Arran, heir to the Duke of Châtelherault, chief of the Hamiltons, and next in line for the throne, and Glencairn, the Cunningham chief and a foremost Protestant lord; but these were scarcely noticed in the humbly born Knox's presence.

There was silence for moments, until the Queen found words. "Master Knox?" she said, a little uncertainly for her.

"Madam," he replied, and that was not uncertain. And still he did not bow.

A further pause, uncomfortable for most there. Then, clearing her throat, Mary gestured. "Come, join us, Master Knox. Sit in."

"That I will not, Madam." Here was a throwing down of the gauntlet, with a vengeance. There were gasps from around the table.

"Then why have you come, sir?" the Queen asked, her young voice of such different modulation to the man's. Somehow, Queen or none, she was only an eighteen-year-old girl in the face of this dominant, middle-aged man.

"I come because I must, Madam. To pronounce this day's

outrage as wickedness, a grievous offence against Almighty God! I have heard that Mass was performed in your presence in the Chapel Royal."

"Yes, Master Knox – in the Chapel Royal. *My* royal chapel! On my royal authority." Spirit was returning to Mary Stewart.

"But contrary to God's authority and command. And against the law of this land."

"Not *my* God! *Your* strange God perhaps, Master Knox – not mine."

"The Mass is idolatry!" the other thundered. "Evil! We have purged God's Church of all such popish sin. One Mass is more fearful to me than ten thousand enemies landed in Scotland on purpose to suppress our whole and purged religion. The Mass is an abomination before God!"

"Only to you and your like, sir. The rest of Christendom declares you in error, wicked error. As do I."

"Then you, Madam, and the rest of Christendom, are in grievous sin. Your worship is false, and you will not bring the plague of it back here!"

"My worship is between me and my Maker, sir! My own!" It seemed as almost with difficulty she withdrew her gaze from those piercing, accusing eyes, to look down the table to the Lord James. "My brother, here, came to France and assured me that, returning to Scotland, I could worship as I chose . . ."

"In private, Madam – that is *your* concern, God pity you! But not in public. Never in a public place."

"Is my Chapel Royal a public place?"

"It is the kirk of the Canongate."

"I attended your Protestant worship therein first, Master Knox. Was I not entitled to hold mine, thereafter?"

"No, you were not. Not in a congregation of the faithful. It must not, will not, be!"

"In my realm, Master Knox, I will not be told by you, or other, what will or will not be. I am your Queen."

He raised a hand to point an accusatory finger. "I heard that you were contumacious, Madam, a headstrong but light young woman, shallow and pleasure-loving. I see that it is true. But this is Scotland, not France. And here *God's* will prevails over those of earthly rulers."

Mary actually conjured up a smile, however brief. "Ah yes, Master Knox – I too have heard tales! Of *your* mislike of my sex. Of your prejudice against women. A sad burden for you to bear! I think that perhaps you are to be pitied in this?"

Knox frowned. "Against women I have no quarrel, Madam. It is against the *rule* of women over men that I condemn, as contrary to God's word. It is unnatural."

"Yes, you call it the 'monstrous regimen of women' do you not, in your writing? What made you so to inveigh against me, those two years ago, sir? A girl of only sixteen years, as I was then. Whom you did not know, had never met."

"Not so much you, Madam, as that Jezebel of England, Mary Tudor, now no doubt paying for her sins, elsewhere! And the woman Catherine of France. Both murderesses of God's elect."

"You speak of the royal mother of my late husband!" Mary exclaimed. "I urge you to watch your words, sir."

"God will judge my words, Madam – not you! Religion does not derive from princes, so subjects are not bound to frame their religion according to the appetites of their sovereigns. But kings should be the nursing fathers of the Church, queens its nursing mothers . . ."

"Perhaps. But *you* are not the Church which I will nourish. I will defend the Church of Rome, for I say that it is the true Church of God!" That was almost defiant, a declaration of war.

Knox stared at her for long moments. Then nodding his head grimly, rather than bowing, he turned about and, pushing his way past the two earls, strode out as he had come in. After a somewhat sheepish pause, Arran and Glencairn bowed, and followed him.

Something like a sigh of relief rose from the company, relief which changed to some concern as the Queen's attractive features crumpled and, with tears starting, she buried her face in her hands, abruptly overcome.

The Lady Fleming went to comfort her former charge, followed by all the Marys.

Out of the incoherent discussion and outcry which now arose, the Queen got up, and mustering a brave smile to all, moved to leave the room, her ladies in her train. The remainder of the company were left somewhat at a loss, except for the Lord James who quickly departed, set-faced. His attachment to the Protestant cause had been one of Knox's achievements, allegedly.

Thomas, much perturbed, indignant and unhappy, was uncertain what to do. His urge was to go and express his feelings and sympathy, if not to the Queen herself then to her Marys. But he imagined that Flam and the others would be fully occupied with their mistress meantime, and any hanging about on his part of no help.

Quietly, somewhat dissatisfied with himself and all else, he took his leave, to head for the Canongate. His first royal repast had scarcely been a success.

3

Next morning the Kerrs were off early, for it was a long way south to Jedburgh and Ferniehirst, a very full day's ride, with the women and the servants. Thomas would have liked to have at least called at the abbey-palace, and if he could not see Flam and the others, leave a message; but his father declared it much too early for anything such. Besides, in the present situation, it was better for his son to be less involved with the royal household, he asserted; he had not been too happy about this sudden attachment to these young women anyway. Altogether, Edinburgh would be a good place to get out of for the time being. The Kerrs knew where they were in the Borderland. So it was a start soon after sunrise, with nearly fifty miles to cover. They had good horses admittedly, but it was a rough as well as a long road.

Thomas went reluctantly, especially when they passed the west end of Duddingston Loch on their way to Dalkeith, and he recounted to his family that day with the two Marys, and went on to extol the Queen's prowess in climbing Arthur's Seat. He could, he supposed, perhaps have refused to leave Edinburgh with the others, for he was now of age, even though only newly so; but his father was very much head of the family, as well as of the clan, in his quiet way an autocrat, as befitted a Warden of the Marches, and Thomas had hitherto never thought to run counter to his expressed wishes. And Sir John was strangely adamant for a quick return home.

After Dalkeith, in the Lothian Esk valley, they started the long climb towards the Soutra pass through the Lammermuir Hills, gateway to the Borderland. It was, of course, good to be riding free after the constrictions of the city, even though now he would have liked to have ridden faster. His mother, herself a Ker of Cessford – the rival line of the clan spelt the name with only one "r" – and his young brothers and sisters were good riders, but they were not so urgent on a horse as he was. And of course they had the servants and baggage-animals to consider.

High on Soutra Hill, at the monkish hospice and travel-lers'-rest – still being maintained by the Lord John Stewart, as Commendator-Abbot of Melrose, but now making a charge for shelter and provision where the monks had given it free – they drew rein, and whilst Sir John went inside, gazed around. From here the vista was magnificent, although not quite rivalling that of Arthur's Seat, for here the hills themselves blocked off distant views to east and west, but were tremendous nevertheless to north and south, over Lothian and Edinburgh and the Forth, and ahead down Lauderdale, to the green, lovely but bloodstained Borders, where the three summits of the Eildons, the Trimontium of the Romans, stood guard over the Tweed valley, and far beyond stretched the great range of the Cheviots which divided England from Scotland.

They were halfway down to Lauder, with the empty sheep-strewn hills yielding to upland farmeries and lairds' tower-houses, when Sir John rode ahead a little, waving Thomas on with him.

"I want a word with you, lad," he said. "It is time. You are a man now, and must begin to play the man's part, in sundry matters. You have your grandmother's Smailholm, and so can set up your own house. But, more than that, you may be Laird of Ferniehirst before very long, and I would have you . . . prepared."

Thomas stared at his father. "Ferniehirst? *You* laird it there. How could I . . .?"

"I am not the man I was, son. Have you not noticed? For some time I have been . . . less than myself. My inward parts have been troubling me. Bleedings. An old wound I won in a fray over the Border, reminding me that I am mortal, perhaps! The physicians can do little. I am not dying . . . yet, I think. But it may get the better of me at any time. So – I am concerned that my eldest son and heir is readied to succeed me."

"But, Father – this is scarcely to be believed! Dire. I had no notion . . ."

"No. You have had other matters on your mind, son!"

"Does my mother know?"

"To be sure she does. But I told her to say nothing. To the others either. But now – this word with you."

"I cannot credit it. You, you seem the same as ever."

"Hardly that. You saw that I visited that hospice back yonder, for a space. As I shall have to do at Melrose and

49

Ancrum, belike. This bleeding. I am as bad as any woman in her monthly flow! Long riding is not the best for me any more – and me the Warden! So, you must marry, Tom."

He gulped and gazed at his father. "Marry! Me . . .?"

"Yes, marry. Wed. I would see you wed. And before . . . long. A settled man, to be chief of the Kerrs, and to follow me."

"But . . ."

"No buts, lad. You have your responsibilities, as had and have I. You were born to this. As your son will be, God willing. Marriage is fell necessary, your duty. The Kerrs must have their chiefly line."

"I, I will think on it, Father."

"You will do more than that, son – you will wed! And quickly. I must see you married before I . . . move on."

"But – who?" Thomas wagged his head. "I cannot just wed *any* woman! I know of none . . . Flam Fleming . . .?"

"Not any woman, no. But *I* know of one suitable. Janet Kirkcaldy. Daughter to Sir William Kirkcaldy of Grange."

"Lord!" He stared.

"She will be an excellent match. An heiress. She is Kirkcaldy's only child. And comely, I am told."

"But . . . I do not *know* her! I cannot wed someone I have never even met!"

"It has been done before! And her father assures me that she is fair, of equable temper and of a kindly disposition. You could do a deal worse, son."

"You have spoken to him of it? Already!"

"To be sure. It is all arranged. For the best."

"But – have I no say in this? My own marriage! If I favour another . . .?"

"*Do* you? Have you considered marriage, then?"

"No-o-o. But, when I wed I would wish it to be with someone *I* favour and admire."

"And there is someone?"

"Well, I had not thought so far ahead. But I much favour Mary Fleming, one of the Queen's ladies . . ."

"I feared this. You should not have let yourself get entangled there, Tom. That was a folly. Those young women are far beyond you, especially Fleming. She is not only a lord's daughter but she is of royal blood, a granddaughter of King James."

"There are not a few of them!"

"Perhaps. But they are not for such as you. When she weds, it will be to much higher than a Border laird."

They rode on, silent.

"See you, boy, use your wits. I have spoken to Kirkcaldy of Grange, and he is willing. His wife is dead, and he would see his daughter wed. He has only a brother, Sir James, who is not wed either. He would have heirs to his lands. It is all most suitable."

"He is a Protestant and a leading one. A friend of the Lord James. And of Knox."

"Precisely. That is another advantage. See you, lad, you may well be glad to have friends in the Protestant camp ere long. You saw what happened in the Chapel Royal yesterday. There is going to be trouble in this realm. *We* favour the Queen and her religion, of course – but this is now a Reformed kingdom, as they say. If Her Grace insists on celebrating and conducting the old religion, there will be dire clash, all but war, I fear. And those who hold to that old religion, like ourselves, will be endangered, our peace, our lands, even our lives! I tell you, that is so. And we will require friends on the Protestant side. For they will win, believe me."

"There are many powerful Catholic lords."

"In the north, yes. And many who will bide their time, further south, to see who wins. But far more who will support the Reformers. You know how it is. Holy Church possessed half the best land in Scotland. All that was taken from her, and shared out amongst the reforming lords and lairds – which was why many of them supported it. These, whatever their religion, or none, are not going to give up those wide lands if they can help it. So they do not want the old Church restored to power here, and the lands taken back by it. Think of all the commendators, abbots, priors, even bishops, with the seats they have won in parliament formerly held by churchmen. Think you they will allow all that to be lost to them?"

Thomas did not answer.

"So, lad, Sir William Kirkcaldy could be an excellent good-father for Kerr of Ferniehirst! He is a brave soldier and a fine man, Protestant but not against the Queen, moderate and honourable . . ."

"Was he not one of those who murdered Cardinal Beaton at St Andrews?"

"He was young then and led astray by his friend the Master of Rothes. And the Cardinal was the main obstacle to their Reformation, and a hard fighter. Kirkcaldy paid for that, in his French prison, afterwards. But that was long ago. Now he helps to rule the land, and could serve *you* well."

"I do not desire his services."

"You may well *need* them! But – enough of this. My mind is made up, and all is in train. We will go over to Fife and see the young woman shortly – and you will go willingly and kindly. Reaching man's estate carries its burdens and responsibilities as well as its privileges, for such as us. Remember it."

Sir John reined up, to let the others catch up with them.

For the remainder of their ride southwards, Thomas was notably quiet.

It was early evening when they came to Jedburgh, the Kerr "capital", nestling amongst the Border hills near where Jed Water joined greater Teviot, the town dominated by the splendid abbey, one of the finest in the land, or had been, for now it was in ruins, burned by English raiders, the borderline being only some ten miles to the south. The Kerrs rode through the streets that August evening to greetings, salutations and bows – nothing servile, for the Borderers were not that way inclined, but respectful, almost affectionate. Sir John was well liked, and, as had been his father before him, hereditary Provost of the burgh, bailie of the abbey, as well as laird. Even in his present state of mind, Thomas felt it good to be home amongst his own folk.

Ferniehirst Castle stood on high ground about two miles up Jed Water southwards, a fine L-shaped tower-house only recently rebuilt – for like the abbey it had been burned by the English, and not once only. It was larger than most of the Border peel-towers, and rose within a high-walled courtyard lined with lean-to building housing stabling, men-at-arms' quarters and brewhouse. A pleasance, orchard and garden-ground stretched to the east on slightly rising terrain; in the other directions the ground fell away sharply towards the river-valley, forming a defensive site.

After two weeks of absence Sir John returned to much and pressing work, for being Warden of the Middle March was no empty title but a major task and responsibility. The Borderers were always a vigorous and unruly people, and seeking to govern them and adjudicate in their frequent quarrels and disputes no sinecure, the theft of cattle and sheep being of almost daily occurrence and that of women not far behind. Then being Provost and chief magistrate of Jedburgh brought further judicial and other duties, the townsfolk being little more peace-loving than the countrymen. Even being bailie of the abbey carried responsibilities and problems of an administrative kind, for there were lands attached. In all this Sir John now increasingly sought the help of his eldest son, and Thomas was kept busy for the next week or two, being sent especially to deal with cases in distant dales and valleys deep in the Cheviots, demanding of much riding, and inadvisable for his father now. In all this he had to make fullest use of his wits and judgment, as well as his sense of fair play, interpreting the Border laws more liberally and practically than exactly, especially the nearer he got to the borderline with England, where different standards tended to apply. It was, no doubt, excellent training and discipline for a young man, whatever it proved to be for the subjects of his decisions. And it helped, in some measure, to keep his mind from dwelling too much on the matter of dictated marriage.

But this was not to be postponed for long, for Sir John was urgent and determined. In mid-September he announced that they must now take the road again, northwards, while still he could face the long journey, to go see the bride-elect in Fife. They would ride by Smailholm, to see to matters there and give orders for the place to be made ready to receive its new mistress. Thomas did not enthuse.

Smailholm Tower and parish lay about fifteen miles due north of Jedburgh. But because there were two great rivers to cross, Teviot and Tweed, and fords on these infrequent, detours were necessary and the journey much lengthened. Moreover it was almost like entering a different land, for Smailholm lay on the west edge of the Merse, that great fertile spread, almost level land compared with the hills and valleys to south and west, and out of which rose sundry isolated humps and ridges. There was a difference in jurisdiction also, for this was the East March, the Wardenship all but hereditary in the Home family; indeed the Merse was all but wholly Home territory, their lairdships so numerous as to tax the memory. Which made Thomas's holding of Smailholm unusual, indeed somewhat precarious, since it was generally resented by the Homes.

Thomas's great-grandfather had been laird of Smailholm, and, having married the only child of his kinsman and chief, another Sir Thomas Kerr of Ferniehirst, had found it expedient when he succeeded to the chiefship to exchange Smailholm with the Homes for the more typically Kerr properties of Crailing and Hounam. But his son, Sir Andrew, the famous Dand Kerr, had himself married a Home, Thomas's grandmother, who had, strangely, received Smailholm as her dowry. So it had come back to the Kerrs and she, fond of her grandson, had left it to Thomas for when he came of age. Hence this detached holding in the Berwickshire Merse, which, it seemed, was now to have a resident mistress for the first time for long.

Smailholm in fact was no more to be overlooked physically than it was proprietorially, for it crowned one of the major crests which rose out of the Merse plain, its tall tower a landmark for miles around. About a long mile from its village, which huddled on the lower ground, it thrust up on a steep, rocky bluff above a small loch, in dramatic fashion, challenging all, a reddish stone keep of four storeys, rising to a parapeted wall-walk on north and south sides, these flanking a gabled stone-flagged roof, all surrounded by a small, irregularly shaped walled courtyard with gatehouse, all clinging to the outline of the rock-top, limpet-like. Within the courtyard were outbuildings, stable, bakehouse and store, with the well. With only one apartment on each floor of the keep, it was a modest establishment compared with Ferniehirst, however spectacular its appearance, but it was strong, and had defied the English raiders time and again – as well as more local assailants – where greater places like Ferniehirst had fallen.

Thomas was proud of it, of course, in a way; but climbing to it now, their horses having to pick a precarious, zigzag way up over the naked rock, he asked his father whether the gently born heiress of a powerful national figure like Kirkcaldy of Grange would wish to come to dwell in such an eagle's nest of a place, remote from her own kind, especially in the midst of Home territory – for the Homes were a wild lot, and unlikely to prove friendly. Not so very long before, they had ambushed and stabbed to death the Sieur de la Bastie, a French nobleman and commander whom Albany, Regent for the present Queen's father, had appointed Warden of the East March, to help pacify the area and keep out the English. The Homes looked on this position as theirs by tradition. So they cut off the Warden's head and rode to hang it on the market-cross of Duns, their "capital". One of the most senior lairds, Home of Wedderburn, had led in that, supported by Home of Cowdenknowes and others. Cowdenknowes was only five miles from Smailholm, Wedderburn itself none so far away.

Sir John said that Kirkcaldy's daughter would be no shrinking violet; besides, it probably would not be so very long before she would be the mistress of Ferniehirst rather than of this Smailholm.

Rob Cranstoun and his wife looked after the tower meantime, and Thomas left it to his father to tell them that this particular service would no longer be required of them, although they would be welcome to remain on in one of the nearby farmery cottages, and to help in domestic matters. While they were being so informed, he climbed the narrow turnpike stair, up to the topmost floor, from which there was access to the two parapet-walks. These, in fact, were his favourite features of Smailholm, viewpoints for perhaps the most tremendous vistas in all the eastern Border. In every direction the land was spread out far and wide, to the coast of the Norse Sea, into England, to all the Cheviots and the distant West March uplands; only due north was the prospect limited by the Lammermuir Hills, twenty miles distant. Gazing now, it occurred to him that he would rejoice to show all this to those appreciative young women whom he had taken up Arthur's Seat, rather than to this Janet Kirkcaldy for whom it seemed to be destined. Perhaps that might be arranged, even so?

Thomas checked above his head, on the roof-top, reached by the crow-steps of the gable, where the iron cage was affixed, to see that Rob Cranstoun was keeping it well filled with highly inflammable pitch-pine. For that was a responsibility of the laird of Smailholm, to maintain a beacon there. In the event of an English incursion over the borderline, a chain of high-placed towers and castles, by lighting such balefires, could send a warning right across the Borderland in a matter of mere minutes, so that precautions could be taken and men mustered for defence, the custodians having ever to be on the watch, fire by night, smoke by day. He looked eastwards by north, six miles, to Home Castle on a similar ridge, westwards to the Black Hill of Earlston, above Cowdenknowes, where there was another beacon, and to other warning-points, north and south, all Home-owned. The Merse had need of those beacons – even though the Homes themselves were often the menace.

Thereafter the Kerrs spent the rest of the day, with the Cranstouns, arranging for the accommodation to be made suitable and comfortable for occupation by the lairdly couple; for hitherto Thomas had never lived at Smailholm, only roosted there for an odd night or two. Some furniture and plenishings would have to be brought from Ferniehirst to improve the amenities, some extra coffers, wall-hangings, tapestries, sheepskin rugs and the like, with the Cranstouns' daughter, from the farm, brought in as extra maid. Thomas wondered what Janet Kirkcaldy would think of Smailholm – although that was by no means his most major concern in the matter.

In the morning they rode on north by west to Lauderdale, to reach the Soutra hospice by midday, where Sir John rested for an hour. Then downhill into the Lothian plain, for Edinburgh.

As governor of the great rock-crowning fortress there, Kirkcaldy had excellent quarters in the castle itself, and here the Kerrs sought him out, having to undergo considerable questioning and inspection before they were admitted at the gatehouse, security being tight here.

Sir William himself, however, was welcoming and friendly, even though Thomas was aware of being fairly thoroughly scrutinised and summed up thereafter, as a prospective son-in-law. At the evening meal, they were surprised to be joined by the Lord James Stewart who, it seemed, also had quarters in the castle, indeed adjoining the governor's house. He largely ignored Thomas but questioned Sir John on conditions in the Borders, especially the Middle March and its wardenship; it seemed fairly obvious that he knew of the present incumbent's ill-health and was concerned, not so much for that, apparently, as for who would take his place. There was a tradition that the office should be held in turn by the chiefs of Ferniehirst and Cessford; so Sir Walter Ker of Cessford would expect to be the next Warden. The Lord James, who had a fairly firm hand on the helm of the realm, knew little of him and seemed to wonder whether he would be strong enough a man for the task. Without actually saying so, he implied that a notably strong character was needed, not so much to cope with the Borderers in general but with the Earl of Bothwell,

Chief Warden of the Marches as he was. The Lord James undoubtedly did not like nor trust Bothwell.

Not much was said, therefore, about the proposed marriage terms.

Sir John, weary, retired early, and Thomas, at a loose end and feeling himself to be distinctly misplaced in the two older men's company, excused himself, saying that he had business down in the town. No hindrance was put as to his departure, and he sallied forth thankfully. He did not take his horse, and informed the guards at the gatehouse that he would be back in due course.

The castle on its precipitous rock rose at the west end of a mile-long slantwise escarpment, a whaleback which sank to the base of Arthur's Seat and Holyrood, the walled city stretching down this spine and its flanks in towering tenements and lands, as they were called, honeycombed with alleys and wynds and closes, teeming with folk all living one atop the other, the merchants' booths and premises, with many taverns, on the ground floors and basements, the gentry on the first and second floors, their servants immediately above, and the commonality filling up the three or four top storeys and attics. This pattern prevailed all the way down the Lawnmarket and High Street to the Netherbow Port, and thereafter into the Canongate. The streets were thronged, noisy and smelly — fortunately the winds which blew all but continuously from off the Firth of Forth helped to disperse the stink — and a walker had to be careful where he placed his feet, for not only dogs, cats and poultry wandered about, but donkeys and ponies, even pigs. City life did not appeal to Thomas Kerr.

He picked his way down past the Mercat Cross and the High Kirk of St Giles, John Knox's headquarters. Here, above the booths and stalls were the town-houses of many of the highest and noblest of the kingdom, owners of vast lands yet living cooped up here like coneys in a burrow. Not that the Kerrs' house in the Canongate was very different.

Passing through the handsome Netherbow Port, he entered that separate burgh. He was making for Holyrood, of course, hopefully.

Reaching the abbey-palace precincts, Thomas was not long in recognising that festivities were afoot again — not that this was in any way unusual for the Lord Robert's unconventional and unruly establishment. It was strange that the Queen, newly returned to her realm, should be put up in these conditions. There were splendid enough palaces scattered around the realm – Stirling, Linlithgow, Falkland, Dumbarton, Kincardine and the rest – but while she remained at the capital, Holyrood was the royal seat; and the palace wing was still not ready for her apparently.

Thomas found no guards on the doors here, and looked in at the hall from which the noise was emanating – not the palace great hall of the previous festivity and masque but a lesser one in the abbot's wing. However, although he saw the Lord Robert himself and the Marquis d'Elboeuf disporting themselves amongst a motley crowd of men and women, there was no sign of the Queen or her ladies.

Knowing where the royal quarters were, he made his way thereto, none hindering. At that door, however, he *was* challenged, but the servitor recognised him and admitted him without fuss. Indeed the man conducted Thomas along the corridors to where he said the Queen and her attendants were passing the evening with music.

It was very different music and scene which met him, when he was ushered into a moderately sized panelled apartment where a small fire burned on the hearth, now that autumn was here, and six women sat stitching at various embroideries and tapestries while Mary Seton plucked at lute-strings and sang in a melodious, soft voice, in French, slow and sweet. It made a pleasant and domestic picture.

"Tom Smellum!" the impulsive Flam Fleming cried out – and then glanced apologetically towards her royal mistress, who should of course have been permitted to make the first acknowledgment.

"Ah – our friend from the Border Marches!" the Queen said, smiling. "We have missed you, to escort us around. My Marys have taken me to see the lochs you showed them. But I am sure that there are other places you could take us to?"

Thomas bowed. "Yes, Your Grace, that would be my honour and pleasure. But . . . I am not here for long. Indeed only tonight. I . . ." He hesitated, as it occurred to him that the monarch could *command* that he stay, to attend on her – which might get him out of this marriage difficulty. But he could hardly suggest that, and against his ailing father's wishes. ". . . I am off to Fife tomorrow."

"How sad! But, another time. Come, sit, friend Thomas. You will take a cup of wine?"

"I thank you, Ma'am." He turned to Mary Seton. "My regrets for interrupting your music, lady." He was uncertain where to sit, but Flam edged along on the settle where she sat and patted a place beside her.

"I do not know Fife," the Queen went on. "Indeed I know all too little of my realm, to my sorrow. But I shall correct that. I suppose that I would be taken to Falkland Palace when a child – that is in Fife, is it not? But I remember nothing of it."

"Falkland is in Fife, yes, Your Grace. Or in Fothrif, rather."

"Fothrif? What is that? I have never heard of Fothrif."

"It is the western part of Fife, Ma'am. Not part of the ancient earldom. The area formerly under the spiritual jurisdiction of the abbots of Dunfermline, I understand – as against that of the Archbishop's St Andrews. At least, it *was*." He coughed. "Until the, the Reformation."

"Ah! Changes, while I have been away! So this Fothrif no longer exists?"

"That I do not know . . ."

"Is it a large area? As I say, I have never heard the name. A strange word. What does it mean?"

"I am not sure, Your Grace. But I would think that it once would be Forth Reeve. That is, the shire-reeve or sheriffdom of the upper Forth districts, on the north side of Forth. And it is large, yes. It stretches, I think, from the Cleish Hills on the west to the Lomond Hills on the east. I know that Collessie is on the eastern boundary and that is well east of the Lomonds. That area, south to salt water at the Forth."

"That is a great deal of land," Lady Fleming put in. "I know some of it. But I too have never heard of Fothrif. There must be many miles of it?"

"Yes. Perhaps a score of miles each way, at least, lady. But I am very ignorant about it all."

"But you go there. But to Fife, you said – not this Fothrif?" That was Flam.

Again he hesitated. "I am not sure whether it is Fothrif or Fife. I go to Hallyards Castle. In the parish of Auchtertool I am told. I am not sure just where that lies . . ."

"I have heard of Hallyards," her mother said. "Does it not belong to the Kirkcaldy family? Kirkcaldy of Grange? The noted Reformer!"

Thomas swallowed. "Yes. That is so. I . . . we go there. With Sir William, tomorrow. My father has arranged it. Not . . . myself."

That faltering half-explanation was worse than none at all. All there looked at him interestedly, obviously stimulated to hear more.

Flam, of course, could not let it lie thus. "Not *you*, Tom. But you go? To this castle you do not know. What to do there?"

He sighed, almost audibly. It had to come out, sooner or later. As well now, probably, however reluctant he was to tell.

"My father has arranged a marriage, I fear. Between myself and Janet Kirkcaldy. And we go to, to see her."

Whatever reaction he had expected, it was not what followed. There were exclamations, questions, congratulations, laughter even, clapping of hands. It was as though he had announced excellent tidings. Even Flam sounded intrigued rather than concerned – to his disappointment. Women were a mystery.

"Marriage, Tom! You are to wed? How happy a lady this, this Janet, did you say?"

"Aye, Janet, I believe." That was less than enthusiastic.

"You believe . . .?"

"I have never met the lady."

All the women exchanged glances.

"How exciting a meeting, then," the Queen exclaimed. "For you both. She will be wondering, I think, also; this Janet Kirkcaldy, as to her fate! I judge her fortunate!"

Thomas had not considered that, the fact that the young woman could be equally, if not more, concerned and in doubt than was he. It was quite a thought. He rubbed his chin.

"You will be eager to see her, I swear!" Flam said. "How old is she?"

"I do not know. It is all . . . difficult."

"You do not sound very pleased." That was Mary Livingstone. "No way to go meet your bride!"

"She might be ugly! An ogress!" the provocative Beth Beaton suggested. "Then, what?"

"Hush, stupid!" The Queen laughed. "You will further afright poor Thomas. Who, I think, is already less than assured! But I prophesy that all will be well. When you return, my friend, you must come and tell us all."

Thomas looked unsuitably doubtful at this flattering royal interest.

Fortunately the Queen, recognising his discomfort, changed the subject, to say that she had heard that they had many colourful and interesting ballads in the Borderland. Did Thomas know any which they might not have heard of? Could he tell them some? Or better, sing them?

This was more to his taste, and although he was a little hesitant to raise his voice in song in this company, it would be better than talking about Janet Kirkcaldy. He admitted that he knew many ballads and Border songs, but declared that he was no singer – which was not quite true, for he had a fair voice. Did Her Grace know "Jock o' Hazeldean"? Or "Fair Helen"? Or "The Battle of Otterburne"?

All shook their heads except Lady Fleming, who said that she remembered "Jock o' Hazeldean" a little, and "Fair Helen" too, from her youth. Did not "Jock" go like this? And she hummed a lilting melody tunefully.

Thus encouraged, Thomas said that if she would accompany him like that, he would dare to raise his voice, however like a corbie-crow's it was. And so he launched out into the sad but romantic and haunting tale.

Why weep ye by the tide, ladye, why weep ye by the tide?
I'll bed ye to my youngest son and ye shall be his bride.

Flam's mother joined in here and there, and quite quickly Mary Seton picked up the rhythm of the music and plucked a further and pleasing accompaniment on her lute.

The applause which greeted this effort emboldened Thomas to offer others, and soon he had the young women, the Queen included, joining in the refrains with increasing enthusiasm.

When he had exhausted his repertoire, and was glad to sup his wine, Ebba Seton reverted to her French minstrelsy. It all made a most pleasant evening, however awkwardly for Thomas Kerr it had started.

When he eventually made his way back up to the castle, he had not actually forgotten Flam Fleming's reception of his dire news, but he was prepared to forgive her. He even hummed the tune of the eerie "Young Tamlane" as he walked. Such was the effect of challenging female company.

*

Thomas had rather hoped that Sir William would find his pressing responsibilities on the realm's business preventing him from making the journey to Fife, or Fothrif, the next day, so that he himself could have another day at least in preferred company; but in this he was disappointed. They duly set off next morning, with a small escort, westwards from the city, making for Queen Margaret's Ferry over Forth, ten miles.

As they went, the two knights were soon in deep and concerned discussion on the political and religious situation. It seemed that there had been developments whilst the Kerrs had been in the Borders, quite dramatic ones involving the Queen, however little of that she had evidenced the night before. Apparently she had summoned John Knox to her presence, for a conference and debate, no less, with only the Lord James present, and there had been an extraordinary clash between the unlikely pair of protagonists, the eighteen-year-old girl and the stern divine, on the subjects of worship, the role of women and the rights of monarchs, neither greatly restraining themselves apparently. On the Sunday before, Knox had preached vehemently and authoritatively against the idolatory of Rome from the pulpit of St Giles Kirk, asserting the rights of the subjects to rise up against any unworthy ruler who opposed God's word, especially one of the frail, weak and feeble sex. Even the Lord James had been shaken by his friend's fierce attack then, and now, and surprised at his half-sister's spirited rejoinders and refutations. No sort of accord seemed to have been reached, and the next day Mary had issued a royal proclamation declaring that she intended to summon the Estates of Parliament to take order in the matter and to pacify the religious disharmony in the kingdom, allowing all to worship God according to their own consciences and beliefs. None were to assail or intimidate others, meanwhile, in matters of faith, as in all else, under dire penalties; and in particular none were to molest or interfere with her own servants and those who had come with her from France.

So it was all but a declaration of war between monarch and subject, for Knox would never climb down, that was certain.

Thomas listened, and had to restrain himself from indignant vocal support of the Queen, and anathema against Knox and his like.

At that so valuable facility, the Queen's Ferry, instituted by the sainted Margaret five centuries before to enable pilgrims to Dunfermline Abbey and others to cross the Forth estuary, here a mile wide, and so save a seventy-mile detour round by Stirling and the only bridge, they embarked themselves and their horses on the flat-bottomed scows which plied across the narrows. There were no pilgrims now, but no lack of passengers, and in half an hour they saved a long day's journey, blessing the long-ago Queen of Malcolm Canmore. On the north shore, they did not make for Dunfermline as did most of their fellow-passengers, but set off parallel with the coast eastwards, to the town of Inverkeithing and on to Aberdour, passing the castle there of another of the royal Stewart brood, the Lord Doune. Here they turned inland, through pleasant rolling wooded country now, commencing to climb through the modest Cullaloe Hills, by the baronies of Dunearn and Knockdavie and Balmuto, to more level and fertile land, loch-dotted, apparently Kirkcaldy's own territory in the main. His family's principal seat was the Grange of Kinghorn, near to the town of Kirkcaldy itself, but this had been ravaged and burnt in the troubles of some time before and was still in a bad state.

They rode through the village of Auchtertool, where the folk greeted their laird respectfully, and on by the pleasant Camilla Loch to where Hallyards Castle rose on a strong site above a sharp bend of a well-doing burn, a fine fortalice somewhat smaller than Ferniehirst but larger than Smailholm, an L-planned keep within a high-walled courtyard which was lined with lean-to outbuildings.

They had ridden, thanks to that ferry, little over twenty miles, but Sir John was much fatigued nevertheless, actually near to collapse. Sir William went calling for his daughter, but servants came to explain that Mistress Janet was outby, down in the den picking brambles for the jelly. So while Kirkcaldy superintended rest and refreshment for the older Kerr, he suggested that Thomas might like to go down into the steep little valley of the burn, downstream of the castle, where brambles grew in profusion, and introduce himself to his wife-to-be, an unexpected development as to which that young man was more than doubtful. But as well this way as otherwise, he supposed – although well was not the way to describe any of it, he felt.

A track led down below the castle walls into the wooded dean and its chuckling burn. Along the path he went, scarcely hurrying, listening to the gurgle and tinkle of the water, wondering what he was going to see and how he was to introduce himself to this female. Suppose she was as Beth Beaton had suggested, ugly, a horror? Must he, in fact, go through with this, whatever the older men had decided? Could he not claim to be his own master now, not just something to be disposed of conveniently?

Presently he was aware of another sound than the noises of the burn and the bird-song, a different sort of singing, soft and murmurous but melodious. He did not recognise the tune, but knew a tuneful voice when he heard one, as lilting as any raised the previous evening.

He saw her there, round a bend in the stream, standing beside a patch of rioting bramble bushes, pulling berries to drop into a bag on the crook of her arm. He halted to gaze, uncertain indeed. And he did not want to frighten her.

Forty yards away he could not distinguish her features fully but he could see that she was a well-built young woman, dark-haired and simply dressed in a sort of sleeveless waistcoat over a white bodice, and a short knee-length skirt. There was a distinct impression of suppleness about her as she bent and stooped and twisted to gather her fruit.

Thomas coughed, but, singing and intent on her reaching and plucking, she did not hear him. Undoubtedly, if he suddenly appeared at her side, even if he shouted, she would be startled. It occurred to him that if he sang approximately the same melody, in time, she might be the less alarmed. Why had her father sent him thus to confront her?

The tune was a simple one and he had no difficulty in accompanying it in a fair tenor. Almost at once she looked up, to stare.

He was bareheaded, so he could not doff a bonnet. But he waved a hand, and bowed briefly. "Mistress Janet Kirkcaldy?" he called.

She did not answer right away but continued to eye him as he approached. But she did not appear scared or apprehensive, merely questioning, interested. She was the laird's daughter, of course, and on her own ground.

He perceived that she was far from ugly, indeed quite worth looking at, not beautiful or even very pretty, but attractive, with lively dark eyes to match her hair, finely moulded features, nose a little tip-tilted, and with a creamy complexion.

64

If this was indeed Janet Kirkcaldy, some at least of his fears might be dismissed.

"You *are* Mistress Janet?" he repeated. "Sir William's daughter? I am Thomas Kerr of Smailholm."

She nodded and bit her lip. Then mustered a tentative smile. "A, a good day to you, sir. I . . . you . . . yes, I am Janet. I did not know . . ." She spread purple-stained hands eloquently. "I am sorry. I did not know."

He cleared his throat. "But you did know? Of me? I mean – you know what is . . . intended?"

"Oh, yes, sir. My father has told me."

"Yes. Then . . ." He did not know what to say next, himself.

Nor did she, evidently. They stared at each other for moments on end. Then she raised a little laugh, tremulous but unforced and amused. "So, we meet! Thus!"

He shook his head. "It is strange. For us both. Our fathers – they think to know best. And we, we have little say."

"No. And you wish it . . . otherwise?"

He could hardly say that he did. "I would prefer to have made my own choice. As, no doubt, would you?"

"Perhaps. But we women frequently are given little choice. Especially if . . . heiresses!"

"Ah, yes." Thomas looked at her sidelong. "That is another matter. No concern of mine. This of your heiring lands. I have my own. I would not wed for that."

"No? Many men do. What would you wed for, Thomas Kerr? For love?"

"If I might, to be sure. But . . ."

"And you have someone whom you love? And would prefer to wed?"

"I did not say that. Not . . . yet. But . . ."

"But you might have hoped? And now – you are saddled with Janet Kirkcaldy! I am sorry."

"It is no fault of yours. And you, too, may have looked elsewhere?"

"I could scarcely have looked towards you, sir! For I did not know that you existed until a few days past."

"No. Nor I you. So we have that in common!"

"A sufficient start for a marriage?"

Warily he considered her. This young woman, he realised, had a mind of her own, no shrinking female to humbly walk where she was pointed. "I do not know. But perhaps we have more than that?" He paused. Was this him *encouraging* this creature now? He would have to be careful. "How old are you, Janet?" That was asked in more suitably authoritative tone.

"Twenty years, in the past June. And you?" She was picking the berries again.

"A year older. But not yet my own master, it seems! Although I have my own house. Smailholm Tower. And I will heir Ferniehirst." Did he have to recommend himself thus? He found himself picking the fruit also, to add to her bag.

"I have never visited the Borderland," she told him. "Is it as wild as they say? Reiving and raiding and feud? Do I hazard my life and, and my person, at your Smailholm?" That held just a hint of amusement.

He managed an answering smile. "I think that you will be safe. My father is Warden of the Middle March. As I may be one day. And the Kerrs are a large and powerful clan. The English, of course, we have to watch!"

"So! My principal hazard will be my . . . husband?"

Thomas blinked. "As to that . . ." He did not finish, eating a berry instead.

"I am warned, then?" she commented. "I shall have to come prepared!"

After a brief silence, he nodded in a sort of acknowledgment. "You face your, your destiny stoutly," he said. "You make no complaint?"

"Would there be any profit in complaint? It is to be, it seems. So I should make the best of it. And . . ." she looked away ". . . since seeing you, I think that it might have been worse!"

"M'mm." He did not say it, but the same thought had occurred to him.

"That is a sufficiency of the berries," she declared then. "Shall we return to the house? Or they will wonder what has become of you. And me!"

She led the way back along the narrow path, and from behind he did not fail to note that her hips swung not exactly challengingly but in quite promising fashion. She walked well. Not as well as Flam Fleming, of course. Or the Queen. But . . .

At the castle, they found Sir John much recovered, and interested to size up his good-daughter-to-be. For her part,

Janet took charge of provision and hospitality, making it clear that she was used to managing a household, competent at it, the servants doing her bidding deftly, Sir John approving of what he saw obviously.

Over an excellent meal, Sir William announced that they had decided that the wedding should be quite soon, the "they" referred to clearly meaning Sir John and himself. It would take place, not here at the parish church of Auchtertool, which was a poor place for such, but in St Margaret's Chapel within his Edinburgh Castle. This would be of great convenience to all concerned, for it would avoid Sir John and his family having to come all this way again, guests likewise, and not too greatly distract him, Kirkcaldy, from his duties. The chapel was a tiny building, which would mean that few guests could be actually at the ceremony; but ample celebrations afterwards could be held in the governor's lodging. Two weeks from yesterday would be a suitable date.

Thomas forbore to ask for whom it would be suitable, with himself and Janet apparently not to be consulted; presumably his father wanted it all settled quickly and before the winter set in. He caught a glance and a raised eyebrow from the young woman, who however made no comment.

Later, when she conducted him to his bedchamber on the topmost attic floor of the castle, Janet referred to these marriage arrangements. "Our good sires have it all resolved most carefully, have they not? Except that they do not confer with us! Even foolish females may have their preferences and concerns. The time of their month, for instance, could be of some consequence in this matter! Would you not think so?"

"Oh. Ah . . . yes. To be sure." Embarrassed he looked away.

"Women can be awkward creatures, I fear. Let us hope for the best in this as in all else. So, goodnight, Thomas Kerr. Do not let your sorry fate spoil your sleep!"

Despite her admonition, he went to bed with quite a lot on his mind, and did not sleep for some time.

They were to be off again in the morning, back to Edinburgh, Sir William with them.

4

As he waited, Thomas wondered who last had been wed in
this little, ancient chapel, probably, he thought, the oldest
surviving building in Edinburgh, erected on the very crown
of the castle-rock by Queen Margaret some years before she
died in 1093, and so well before her youngest son, the pious
King David the First, had established any of his many abbeys,
Holyrood, Jedburgh, Kelso and the rest. He imagined that few
indeed, if any, would have thought of it as suitable for a celebration of marriage, for it was tiny, the Ferniehirst dovecote
larger. But it was certainly pleasing in its stark simplicity, bare
whitewashed walls, slit windows, a plain stone altar – no, he
must now call it a communion-table – the living rock of the
fortress for flooring. That Sir William had so chosen for his
daughter's nuptials said something about the man perhaps; he
was, of course, the first of the new Reformers to govern here,
and he would be against pomp, display and ritual in religious
matters – but even so, this was a strange choice, however
convenient for dining in the governor's lodging afterwards.
Thomas doubted whether they could get a score of people
into the chapel; he did not turn round to count them as he
stood waiting alone, only a yard or so from the altar-table.
He could understand his father, in his present state of health,
agreeing to this so limited wedding venue for his son and heir,
since it would greatly simplify and shorten the proceedings.
For himself, he cared not, this marriage being no great concern
of his – although no doubt that was a wrongful way to consider
so important a step in his life. The trouble was, he just could
not feel that it *was* important; and this cramped little white
cave of a place therefore suitable enough. Perhaps, however,
he ought to be deeming himself privileged to be married in
this royal oratory, which the sainted Margaret had built for
her own private devotions? What Janet might think of it he
had no notion.

It was warm, almost breathlessly so, as he stood there, what with the pack of folk behind him and the place being lit with innumerable flickering candles – these necessary, since little light got in through the few and narrow window-slits. He sought to loosen the fine crimped and pleated ruff round his neck.

His cogitations were interrupted by an unexpected sound, the ponderous, sonorous tones of a man's deep voice declaiming something solemn, all but funereal, the murmuring of the small congregation dying away. Thomas could not prevent himself from taking a quick glance back, as through the open door of the place paced in the Reverend John Craig, minister of the Canongate – the same who had conducted that fateful service in the Chapel Royal at Holyrood – clad in his sober black Geneva gown and white bands, intoning the words of what seemed to be a psalm. Behind came Janet Kirkcaldy on her father's arm. That was all.

There had been some discussion about this day's celebrant – not with Thomas who was little consulted – but between the fathers. The castle was not in the Canongate parish, even though the Kerrs' town-house was, but in that of St Giles High Kirk. But even Sir John would have jibbed at having John Knox officiate, and his son would have rebelled quite – even if the great man would have consented to act. The parish minister for Auchtertool could have been brought over, but Kirkcaldy did not seem to think much of him, a reluctant Reformer; and the private chaplains of sundry lords were hardly suitable. And of course no priest would be acceptable. So here paced John Craig, at his most sober.

The man had to brush against the bridegroom to get past and up to the table, where he turned to face them all. Thomas found Janet at his side. They exchanged glances, hers with a flicker of a smile, his all but wary.

The minister now announced sternly that they were here to bind together in the holy estate of matrimony this man Thomas and this woman Janet, in the sight of Almighty God and the presence of all there as witnesses, and in accordance with the purged faith of Christ Jesus His Son. This was a solemn and exacting occasion, not to be celebrated nor undertaken lightly, enduring for the earthly span of their lives, their vows to be broken only at their eternal peril. He all but glared around, not only at the happy couple but at all present, presumably having his doubts about some of them. They would now pray.

69

There followed a lengthy address to their Maker, not so much a petition as an injunction and exhortation as to what was expected of Him, with side-thrusts at the earthly hearers as to the sins and dangers of levity, looseness, carnality, lechery, lasciviousness and the like, all of which apparently their Creator and the Reformed Kirk frowned upon – the implication being that the old and discredited popish religion was less concerned. Thomas found himself being eyed directly; Master Craig would know that the Kerrs were still Catholic. He wondered whether in fact they would have been just as well with Knox, after all.

When this homiletic invocation was at length over, it was announced that they would say a psalm of David, of the number sixty-five, which they all would, or should, know, that commencing:

> *Praise waiteth for thee, O God, in Sion, and unto thee all the vow be performed.*
> *O thou that hearest prayer, unto thee shall all flesh come.*

Craig launched into this with vigour and volume – which was just as well, perhaps, for nobody else greatly contributed, the bridegroom not at all, not knowing a word of it. A glance at Janet saw her equally silent. At least the amens were loud and heartfelt when it was finished.

The Lord's Prayer followed, and most there knew that, even though some were used to saying it in the Latin. Then Craig stepped one pace nearer the bridal pair – any further and he would have been on top of them – and adopted a quite challenging attitude. Who gave this woman, he demanded?

Sir William raised a hand.

The celebrant demanded if any there knew of any reason or impediment why this Janet and this Thomas be not joined together? If so, their souls were imperilled if they did not declare it, so help them God! This was most deliberately said, with a long stare around, as though in suspicion that there well might be something being held back.

Thomas wondered what would happen if he announced now that he had never wanted this marriage, had had some slight knowledge of certain young women in the Ferniehirst vicinity, and could scarcely in honesty vow that he would love this Janet, however much he might try to honour and cherish her? Needless to say, he forbore.

After all that, Master Craig seemed to feel that it was now a matter of getting it all over as speedily as possible, and Thomas discovered himself repeating flatly the form of words presented to him, and taking the ring from his young brother Dand, who was pushed forward to give it, there being no room for him alongside. Janet for her part murmured all but inaudibly.

Suddenly it was all over, the pair were pronounced man and wife, and John Craig, declaring an authoritative benediction on all, pushed past to lead the way out, starting to intone one more psalm.

Janet took her husband's arm, and even gave it a little squeeze. Was that relief, satisfaction or sympathy?

Congratulations thereafter were formal rather than enthusiastic.

The wedding-feast which followed at least was conventional and generous, Sir William making a good host, and a number of guests appearing who had not been in the chapel, including, Thomas was surprised to see, the Lord James Stewart, the Earl of Glencairn and the Lord Ruthven. In due course it fell to him briefly and less than eloquently to acknowledge speeches of goodwill and admonition, while in fact only wishing to be elsewhere. Could he get away? Or *they*, it should be now, he supposed. From now on he would have to think frequently in the plural.

He had had no opportunity for private discussion with Janet. He wondered what her feelings might be as to their immediate course and doings hereafter? She might wish to remain meantime with her father, or spend this first evening and night at the Kerr house in town? But for himself, he had a great urge to be away, away from here, from Edinburgh, from all these people, back to his own Borderland. It was still only early afternoon. What sort of a horsewoman was she? *He* could be at Smailholm in just over four hours, before dark. Could he suggest that?

It occurred to him, then, that he was now this female's husband, master of her destiny in some measure – however little he felt the part. He could *command* this. No, he would not, could not, do that; he was not cut out for that sort of attitude. But he could urge it . . .

Low-voiced, he spoke to her at his side. "How good are you on a horse?" he asked. "Do you ride well?"

Brows raised, she eyed him. "Sufficiently well, I think. I have been riding horses all my days. Why ask? Now?"

"Smailholm, my, our house, is nearly fifty miles. Could you ride that now? Or, after a little time. This day? Four hours, or five."

She considered him questioningly. "You are so . . . eager?"

"No, no. Or, at least . . . eager to be away from here, from all this. And these. Is that so strange?"

"Perhaps not." She shrugged. "I am at your disposal, husband!"

"No. Not that. If you do not wish it . . ."

"I do not *not* wish it. And I like to ride. Yes, do that if you would have it so. But – I will need time to change clothing. And to pack my gear . . ."

"My people will bring on your gear, later. I have good horses."

"Very well. So soon as we may, I will tell my father and go to my room, to change."

"Yes. I will hasten down to our house here, change also, and collect another horse for you. Then come back here. If folk think it strange, let them think!" All this whispering was already attracting looks.

She smiled. "What have I married, I wonder?" She did not sound really perturbed.

So soon as he decently could, he excused himself to his host, gestured towards his parents and made his escape, stares notwithstanding.

He all but ran down the Lawnmarket, High Street and Canongate, an odd bridegroom.

It did not take him long to don more suitable clothing, while a servant readied the horses. Then up to the castle again, eager to be off.

Nor did Janet keep him waiting. She was there, in travelling clothes and with a satchel packed. He sought out his father, announced that they were for Smailholm that night, and waited for no protests or comments. He had been a subservient son for sufficiently long. Sir William gave his blessing to his daughter, eyed his new son-in-law levelly, all but warningly. Then they were off.

As soon as they were beyond the city walls, Thomas perceived that his acquired comrade on life's journey, whatever else she might be, was no mean horsewoman, at ease in the saddle, lissome in the motions of trot and canter, well in control of a mettlesome steed. Encouraged, he set no careful pace.

This sort of progress offered little opportunity for conversation as they covered the miles southwards, Janet observant and interested in a countryside she did not know. But at the long climb up through the Lammermuir foothills to Soutra, they let their sweating beasts take it slowly, and could talk.

"This Smailholm," she asked, "is it near to the border with England?"

"Not very near. Fifteen miles, as the corbie flies. You can see where the line lies, on the Cheviot Hills, from my tower. And we have a beacon to light, to warn of raiders, a balefire." He looked at her. "You are not fearful of this?"

"No, not fearful. But it will add a challenge to living. Does it not?"

He nodded. "I suppose it does. All my days I have lived with it, and so scarcely think of that." This clearly was a young woman of some spirit in more than horse-riding.

"You have never been attacked by the English?"

"Oh, yes. Not at Smailholm, in my time, but at Ferniehirst twice. Once when I was but an infant, and the castle was burned. But I remember naught of that. And again, when I was six years, and Hertford attacked it on his way north, the time he was besieged in Haddington. We, my father and family, had to flee to our house of Ancrum for some months, while Ferniehirst was repaired."

"So I am going to live dangerously!" She did not sound unduly distressed at the prospect.

Soon they were riding fast again, across the high levels of Soutra Muir and then down into Lauderdale. It was many miles before, climbing again out of the dale into the hills beyond Ersildoune, they slackened pace and were able to talk again.

"You ride well enough to be a Borderer!" he conceded.

"Do I thank you for that? Are Borderers such notable horsemen?"

"We have to be, yes."

"Is that on account of your cattle-reiving, raiding into England, or chasing and being chased?"

"I think that you have been listening to bairns' tales! We are not so ill a folk as some would have us."

73

"I wonder! I have been well warned as to the lawless land I was bound for!"

"Tales and blethers! I should know, son of a Warden."

"Is that so sure ground? When your own Borders Chief Warden, the Earl of Bothwell, behaves as he does?"

"Bothwell . . .?"

"Yes, the Earl. Have you not heard? He and the Frenchie, the Marquis uncle of the Queen, have been misbehaving, in Edinburgh. Grievously. They broke into the house of an Edinburgh merchant, one Craik, to take his daughter Alison and abuse her. This because she was said to be the mistress of the Earl of Arran, and Bothwell hates the Hamiltons. Or it may have been that she attracted them on her own account. They did it a second night, with the Lord John, Abbot of Coldingham, at Cuthbert Ramsay's house, where this Alison had taken refuge. The Hamiltons trapped them there, and there was great fighting in the streets. The Queen had to use her influence to prevent them being locked up in the Tolbooth. That, from the Lieutenant of the Borders, Chief Warden and Lord High Admiral!"

Thomas shook his head. "I mislike the man. But Bothwell is no true Borderer. The Hepburns are a Lothian clan, from Haddingtonshire. He should never have been made Chief Warden, my father said. Do not judge the rest of us by him."

"And the Homes? Are *they* not true Borderers? Did they not slay and cut off the head of that other Frenchman, the Sieur de la Bastie, another Warden?"

Thomas decided that their horses were sufficiently rested and time to be spurring on.

They approached Smailholm as the sun was setting, and having to come to the tower from the east, Janet saw it for the first time silhouetted black against the gold and crimson afterglow, high on its crag, stark, strong, dominant, its little loch before it reflecting the colours and blackness both, and but seeming to emphasise the thrust and challenge of it all. She reined up, to stare.

"Is that . . . it? Your Smailholm?"

"Aye. It is not so large as your Hallyards. But a strong place. It has never been captured, they say."

She made no comment on that, but continued to gaze.

"We climb up round the far side. There is a track amongst the rocks. Come."

It was scarcely a welcoming arrival for a bride, even an involuntary one, as their mounts picked their difficult way up the steep slope amongst the outcrops, hooves striking sparks from the naked rock. But halfway up the west face they did see a gleam of yellow light shining palely from a narrow window on the first floor, and Thomas claimed that he saw smoke rising from a chimney. Janet had become noticeably silent.

At the massive, iron-studded gatehouse door into the small courtyard, Thomas clanged the great bell loud and long, rousing quacking mallards from the loch below. He had to ring again, after an interval, before a voice sounded from within.

"Whae's there, at this 'oor o' nicht? Chappin' at Smailholm's yett?"

"It's myself, Rob. Thomas Kerr." He changed that, for Janet's benefit. "Your laird, man."

There was a muttering beyond, and then the clanking of bolts and chains, and, creaking, the heavy double doors opened.

"Och, I wasna lookin' for you the nicht," the custodian declared, in part apology, part protest. "The morn, maybe, or the next day. Sakes, and the leddy, tae! You should hae tellt us, sent us word . . ."

"Never mind that, Rob. We're here, now. This is your new mistress, the Lady Janet . . ."

In the very constricted and uneven courtyard they dismounted and Rob took the horses while Thomas led the way to the single door on the south front of the keep, where Meg Cranstoun stood peering out in some alarm. Clucking like a motherly hen, when introduced, she preceded them up the winding turnpike stairway from the vaulted basement chamber, both newcomers climbing somewhat stiffly after their long riding.

The hall on the first floor was bright, with a well-doing birch-log fire and lamps lit; and here Janet was fussed over while Rob was sent upstairs to light fires in the upper rooms.

A meal of cold meats, porridge, cream and scones with honey was provided for them in the private withdrawing-room directly above, and they were informed cheerfully that bedpans would be duly warming the couch in the chamber still higher, an announcement upon which the newly-weds made no comment. They were left to themselves.

Thomas, for conversation's sake, spoke of the Queen and her arrival and impact, and of her ladies, dwelling particularly on the climbing of Arthur's Seat and the rides around the lochs, becoming quite enthusiastic in the process.

"You admire Queen Mary, I see," Janet commented. "I have never seen her, of course, but she sounds lively and of spirit. And good-looking."

"She is indeed. And although so young, but eighteen years, no weak and simple creature. She stood up to Master Knox, your father's friend, with great ability and courage. He ought to have known better than to have spoken to his sovereign-lady as he did, to be sure."

"But then, she ought not to have had the Mass performed in that church, should she?"

"She let Master Craig, as parish minister, have *his* service first. Why not hers, later?"

"It is against the law, is it not?"

"She is the Queen. Is she bound by laws passed in her absence?"

"That I do not know." She shrugged. "Nor do I think that we ought to argue on such matters, do you? We have different views on it all, the way our fathers reared us. You are Catholic and I am Protestant. Let us just accept that."

"Aye, no doubt you are right. But I wonder that your father *let* you marry a Catholic. Or mine a Protestant."

"Perhaps it was for our mutual safety, partly. And their own?"

"How mean you . . .?"

"Well, who knows how matters may go in this kingdom? Now that we have a strong Catholic monarch reigning in person. Many of her lords are still Catholic, in heart at least. Many more, Father says, will be prepared to change sides again if it is to their advantage. So, there could be benefit for both of us, the Kerrs and the Kirkcaldys, in having friends on either side. Shelter, whichever way the wind blows!"

"M'mm. That could be, yes."

She changed the subject, advisedly. "You admire not only the Queen, I think, but her ladies? Do you not? Particularly the one, Fleming. From your account."

"I . . . well – yes, I like Flam Fleming. And the other Marys. I found them very friendly. Flam is kind, good company, attractive . . ."

"In fact, you would much prefer to have been marrying Mary Fleming than this Janet Kirkcaldy, no?"

Thomas gulped some ale. "I, I do not say that. Not for me, I am assured, to wed such as her. Of royal blood, her mother a daughter of the late King James, her father a great lord, dead now, but her brother . . ."

"So – you have to be content with lesser things, Thomas Kerr! I . . . sympathise!"

Warily he considered her. This one was going to take careful handling.

They spoke on safer topics, before that fire, for a little, Thomas for one very much aware of that bedchamber awaiting them above, and doubtful, to say the least, as to procedure.

It was the young woman who, in the end, took the initiative. She yawned a little, tapping her lips. "It has been a long day, and a long ride, husband," she said. "Do you not think that it is time to . . . retire?"

"Ah – yes. To be sure. You will be weary. I, I should not have kept you talking."

"Your Meg Cranstoun said that the bedchamber is above. I shall go up now, I think."

"Yes. I will show you where."

When Thomas opened the creaking door for her, a voice came up from below. Meg must have been listening for them.

"Bide just a wee, sir and leddy," she called up. "There's warm watter in the tub for you. But Rob'll fetch up some mair hot, for it. Just a wee."

Thomas rubbed his chin, but Janet called down a thank-you.

He led her up the twisting stair to the topmost floor, and opened the door to usher her into a pleasant chamber, slightly larger than below, for the walls thinned somewhat as they rose. It had larger windows too, for at this high level there was no risk of ingress by invaders. There were two other doors, apart from that at the stairhead, to north and south, opening on to the two parapet-walks, but these were covered by heavy hangings to keep out draughts. Another fire blazed welcomingly at the gable-end, and there were two lamps lit. A great four-poster canopied bed occupied the centre of the room, sheepskin rugs dotted the floor, there were three chests for linen and the like and wall-cupboards for hanging clothes.

And before the fire, steam rose from a boat-shaped wooden tub, lined with beaten silver.

"How good . . . comforting!" Janet said. "All kindly thought on."

He went over to put another log on the fire. He patted the bed, dipped a finger in the water, opened the lids of two chests, seeking to seem busy.

"You will be sufficiently warm, I hope?"

"Warmer than I would be at home, I think!"

"Yes. Well, I will leave you. For, for a little. I will . . ." He went to the stairhead door. A knock sounded as he reached it.

This was Rob Cranstoun with a great jug of hot water to add to that in the bath. His laird was escaping when Janet called.

"Thomas, I have left my satchel downstairs in the hall, I think. Will you get it for me?"

He hurried down.

Meg had the satchel, and also a posset of warm wine and milk, which she declared knowingly to be a great comfort for ladies in a strange bed. There were oatcakes too, in case they wakened hungry in the night. One never knew on such occasions.

Rob reappeared with the empty jug, and announced that he had a droppie of French brandy, if the laird felt in need. Too much would be no' wise, but . . .

Thomas cut short this kind care and advice, declined the brandy, and taking the satchel and the posset, climbed back upstairs. He presumed that there might be some sort of nightdress in the bag.

The door was ajar and he entered, to halt abruptly. Janet had not waited for him and the satchel. She was, in fact, already in the tub, sitting up, splashing water over her upper parts.

He stared, blinking.

"Ah, there you are," she called. "I shall not be long in this. So it will still be warm enough for you."

Thomas stood there for moments, confronted by a situation new to him; never had he seen a grown woman taking a bath – his sisters, yes, as children. So, if he continued to gaze, could he be blamed? Especially as she was so exceedingly good to look at, and making no pretence at hiding anything. Gleaming white in the firelight, her physique was estimable indeed, neck longish and graceful, shoulders as though sculpted, breasts shapely, prominent with just a hint of upturning about their tips, torso slender by comparison but well-rounded. Further down he could not see, for the tub and the water, but what was visible had no small effect on him.

She turned to look at him almost questioningly, perhaps not quite so bold as she might seem.

Thomas cleared his throat once more, but found no words.

"Perhaps . . . you will bring me that towel?" she suggested. "I have left it on the bed."

"Yes. To be sure. The towel . . ." He moved over to the bed, deposited the satchel and picked up one of two towels. When he turned back to her, Janet was standing up in the water, to his further education and edification, rounded hips and bottom, dark triangle at groin, firmly smooth thighs and long legs. He handed her the towel, unspeaking.

She draped it over her shoulders, eyeing him in the flickering light. "I . . . I thought that this . . . might be the best way of, of . . . what has to be," she got out, a little thickly for that young woman. "A help, perhaps?"

"You are lovely!" he exclaimed then. It burst out of him.

Her face cleared. "I am glad. That, that you find me so. Very glad." Relief was in her voice.

"Yes. So, so lovely." He had seen women in various stages of undress, of course, but apt to be in huddling, part-covered embracing or in coy hiding and semi-darkness, never thus frankly offered for his inspection. "I, I thank you!"

She had begun to dry herself, stepping out of the tub on to a sheepskin. He still stood watching, lips parted, fascinated by the way she lithely twisted her body to her towelling.

"I have never done this before," she told him, small-voiced now.

It came to him that she had indeed made a major effort and gesture in this matter, something that must have taken a deal of resolution. "I thank you," he said again, inadequately. And then, "See you, give me that towel. Your back – I will dry your back for you."

She handed it over without demur and turned to face the fire.

He made quite a project of it. Seldom had a back been so thoroughly and carefully dried. He even tended to edge a little way round at the sides, especially where they swelled to her bosom – which after all needed the drying also. And in furtherance perhaps of her declared intentions, she turned to face him again, but left the towel with him.

Thomas did not require instructions now. He commenced a meticulous patting, wiping and rubbing process, paying especial heed to those splendid breasts which seemed to become more pointed indeed for his attentions as the nipples hardened. He proceeded downwards, finding it necessary to hold on to sundry parts and sections of those soft, smooth surfaces, to keep them firm with one hand whilst he towelled with the other. This was all going effectively, nothing to be left wet, when unfortunately there occurred an interruption. A knock sounded at the stairhead door and Rob Cranstoun's voice penetrated.

"Mair hot watter!"

Thomas did not actually curse, however like it he felt. He thrust the towel back at Janet and hurried to the doorway. It was essential that the wretched man should not open and see what went on. So he all but ran.

However, when he reached the door and ordered Rob to wait, there was no answer. Half-opening the door cautiously, he found the steaming jug left on the landing, its bearer discreetly gone. Relieved, he picked the thing up and turned back.

But the situation had changed in the interim. Janet was no longer by the fire but getting into bed, with a flash of white limbs, a tinkling if rather nervous laugh accompanying the process.

"Your turn now," she called. "If you do not disdain the water I used!"

Actually he could well have done without the bathing, but could hardly say so. Pouring in the new water, he began to strip off his clothing hurriedly, casting it on the floor – and having a certain problem with his breeches on account of aroused masculinity, which of course became very evident when he stood naked and stepped into the tub. Perhaps she was not looking?

It is to be feared that he made a very sketchy and token bathing, priorities now otherwise. Nor did he dry himself nearly so thoroughly as he had done his partner – and for her part she quite failed to offer a reciprocal service. Parts of him undoubtedly were still damp as he discarded that towel and hastened to the bed.

Even then there were delays, for Janet declared that the bedpans were burning her toes and would he kindly remove them. This entailed throwing back the covers to get at the things, and thereby revealing a most challenging sight in the firelight, that delectable body lying there in warm invitation – at least, from his point of view.

Having got rid of the bedpans, and burning his fingers, he was further advised to put more wood on the fire – why, he did not pause to ask. Tossing two logs on, he hastened back to the couch before she could think of any more delaying tactics, to fling back the covers again. He climbed in, to take her in his eager arms, without pause and, it is to be feared, distinctly roughly.

And a rewarding armful she made, all rounded, ripe and kissable delight, warm in most places, strangely cool in others, just a little stiff as to inner tension at first, perhaps, although that faded – whereas his brand of stiffness certainly did not. Soon he realised that her arms were now round him and a distinct undulating motion about her person. He responded quickly, too quickly perhaps, male urgency all too evident in his fumbling.

Thereafter activity was vigorous, compelling and pronounced – but so, unfortunately, was brevity. In much too short a time for his own satisfaction, apart altogether from hers, or any woman's, his manhood erupted in vehement and most positive fashion, whereafter his person more or less collapsed on top of hers in a groaning strange admixture of fulfilment and the reverse.

For a little, then, they lay quiet. Presently he found his tongue. "I am sorry, lass – sorry! I . . . I could not wait. Keep it back. Too . . . much. Too soon. Too hasty – for you. And for me! I am sorry . . ."

"Hush you," she whispered. "Hush you – never heed. It is . . . but natural." She stroked him in almost motherly, comforting fashion. "Perhaps . . . later."

"Yes. Oh, yes, later. I, I . . ."

"Just let be, now. Lie, holding me. I am . . . well enough. Fret not."

"You are good, kind . . ."

As he lay after that, in her arms, sundry thoughts came to

him. One, that although he did not love this woman, he had made love to her with no least hesitation or trouble. Perhaps love might come later, for he was beginning to admire her, undoubtedly. Another, that almost certainly she had not been a virgin – but then, neither was he, so why should she be? Also, that she had a very desirable person, and had been most thoughtful and considerate in all this matter, must have considered it all well beforehand. Were women all like that? And he thought he now knew why she had suggested more wood on the fire. That the night was young, yet.

These thoughts came in desultory fashion, not out of any deliberate cogitation, for he was in no state for that, in fact half-asleep as, heavy-eyed now, he watched the flickering light and shadow on the walling.

Presently he did sleep, for a while.

He wakened with Janet stirring at his side, seeking to extract her arm from under his weight.

"I am sorry," she murmured. "My arm has gone to sleep. Like you!"

He was all self-condemnation now, and as he turned to her enticing, velvet-smooth body, criticising himself even for allowing all this attractive pulchritude to go unappreciated beside him as he dozed. He ran his hands over her, and quite speedily realised that perhaps his dozing had not been entirely wasted after all, for rest seemed to have revived his male faculties, and desires too. He did not keep this recognition to himself.

Her kindness persisted.

This time, all went well. He was able to offer his vigour without overdrawing on his withholding abilities, and so to bring her the satisfaction denied previously. And that satisfaction it was, she made perhaps involuntarily but abundantly clear – to his own masculine satisfaction; after which he added some further attentions for good measure, before himself letting nature take its course again.

Thereafter they lay in peace in each other's arms, in as near contentment as humans are apt to know, even though of only an immediate and temporary sort, sleep near. The fire was allowed to sink in on itself also.

At some half-waking stage it crossed Thomas's mind that perhaps his father might not have done so badly by him in arranging this wedding; also that he himself had not in fact mentally substituted Flam Fleming's image and person under him on either occasion on this bed, as he had rather anticipated that he would do, however deplorable a reaction that would have been. Vaguely he wondered about that.

5

In the days that followed, Thomas Kerr found no reason to change that first sleepy assessment of this wife of his – nor in the nights. Janet proved to make a kindly, interesting and interested companion, suitably concerned to be a good wife, but not to the extent of negating her own quite pronounced personality. Whatever her inmost feelings were, or had been, she was clearly determined, as far as she was able, to make this marriage as successful as was possible – which attitude of course did not fail to rub off on Thomas also. Appreciation of her forethought and quite noteworthy gesture of the bridal night came back to him not infrequently, especially of an evening, for although she was obviously of a quite lusty and spirited temperament, that performance must have demanded no little resolution on her part, in the circumstances.

Not that the man's thoughts and urges did not frequently turn towards Flam, the Marys and the Queen. This was inevitable, with the impact made on him those weeks ago, not only the effect of those attractive young women of romantic and exciting background, but the royal presence involved – for he had been reared to esteem the monarchy highly, hold it in some awe. Undoubtedly Flam's hold on his emotions was partly that of the Queen herself, and so not to be dismissed readily. He could not explain this to Janet, of course – even if he fully realised it himself.

So his awareness and appreciation was in more than in bed, Thomas finding himself to be quite eager to show Janet something of his Border country. So they rode often, eastwards into the Merse, as far as Swinton and the Blackadder and Whiteadder Waters, not actually avoiding Home properties – since that would have been practically impossible – but not calling on them either; westwards to Tweed, and Melrose with its great devastated abbey, where the Bruce's heart was interred, and on over the three challenging summits of the Eildons, Thomas Learmonth's, the famed Rhymer's, territory and the Trimontium of the Romans; southwards to Kelso, the Teviot and the Cheviot foothills and dales, wilder country but picturesque as it was ballad-haunted. Janet was fully appreciative.

They visited Ferniehirst, of course, and possibly somewhat surprised Thomas's parents with the assiduity with which he showed this young woman all to be seen there, introduced her to the town of Jedburgh and took her to see their kinsfolk at Ancrum and Cessford. They were not quite sure whether he was showing it all off to her, with some pride, or showing *her* to all.

For Thomas's part, in these introductions, seeing his own heritage with new eyes, perceiving more consciously and thoroughly much that he had taken for granted all his life, recognising the importance, scope and responsibility of it all, he was sobered considerably, the more so in that he saw how grievously and swiftly his father's health was failing, how marked was the change in him, and therefore how near might be the day when he himself would be called to take over Ferniehirst and so much else. Apart altogether from affection and concern for his sire, he found himself scarcely looking forward to this burden and responsibility.

They were not long back at Smailholm when a messenger arrived from Sir John to announce an unexpected development. The Lord James Stewart had arrived at Jedburgh, and was in fact lodging at Ferniehirst Castle. He had come, it seemed, to hold a Justice Court, in the Queen's name, but clearly on the authority of the Privy Council and of parliament rather than Mary's. It appeared that the Queen had in fact summoned a meeting of the Estates, as she had said she would, to endorse by statute her royal command that all private worship was sacred to the individual, and none should be interfered with, Catholic or Protestant; nor were the practitioners of either faith to be harassed by others, under penalty. This had been grudgingly accepted by the Estates, where the Gordon chief, the Earl of Huntly, had led the Catholic supporters in what almost amounted to a riot, hardly aiding the Queen's cause but at least indicating that the Catholics were still a force to be reckoned with. And this parliament had, amongst other and unrelated decisions, concerned itself with the state of lawlessness in the Borderland, and the failures of the Wardens there to keep order, more particularly on the East and West Marches, the Middle one being less troublesome at the moment, despite Sir John Kerr's ailing state. The overall blame for this was firmly laid on the shoulders of James Hepburn, Earl of Bothwell, as Chief Warden and Lieutenant, who was not only failing to take the necessary action but himself all but encouraging trouble by his own misbehaviour; indeed he was accused of consistently neglecting his Border duties and hanging about the Queen's court. So this Justice Court was ordered, at Jedburgh and elsewhere, and the Lord James Stewart commanded to conduct it in place of Bothwell, whose duty it should have been. And now Sir John wanted his son and heir to come and deputise for himself where necessary.

So it was back to Ferniehirst again. This was not an occasion for women, but Janet sought to go with Thomas rather than remain alone at Smailholm, and he found no fault with that.

Something of the Lord James's abilities and methods as judge and lawgiver were evident for all to see, at Jedburgh where, up at the small royal castle above the abbey, much loud hammering and sawing was going on, as no fewer than a round dozen gallows were being constructed and erected, to be eyed askance by the citizenry. Thomas himself did not like the look of that, even though they might be intended only as a warning.

The Lord James, never the most genial of individuals, showed scant welcome for Thomas's arrival on the scene, but was rather more forthcoming, without being actually amiable, to his friend Kirkcaldy's daughter. Thomas was very much a minor figure in it all, at this stage, with the Lords Home and Maxwell, East and West March Wardens, present, as well as Sir John Kerr, and their deputies. Also Sir Walter Ker of Cessford, Thomas's mother's brother, who would become next Middle March Warden presumably. He wondered, indeed, why he had been summoned.

The Lord James, it seemed, was going to hold two days of trials here at Jedburgh, to deal with the most serious offenders, before proceeding east to Greenlaw and then west to Dumfries, to hold similar courts in those jurisdictions.

As Provost of Jedburgh, it fell to Sir John to conduct the judicial party to the town and castle. But he, in no state for such ongoings on a chill and damp November day, nominated Thomas for the task. So he had to lead the illustrious procession thereto, his first official duty. Most of the folk of Jedburgh, on this occasion, contented themselves with peering out from windows and doorways, distinctly warily, at the passing show, however apt normally to appreciate public displays.

Up at the castle high above the town, they rode past the new thicket of gibbets into the courtyard. Dismounting, they proceeded into the hall, where quite a pack of roped-up prisoners were already awaiting them, under strong guard. Here Thomas changed his role, from Deputy Provost to deputy governor of the castle, to lead the Lord James and the two Wardens to their places on the dais, at a table, with their supporting officers seated behind where, thereafter, he joined them, his introductions brevity itself.

James Stewart took over without delay or any preamble. He called upon the clerk of court to read out the names of offenders and the charges against them, in the Queen's royal name.

The first charge was very much a multiple one and notably simple and uncomplicated, and the names involved as easily comprehended in that they were all Armstrongs, from the West March – reiving and stealing cattle, burning decent folks' houses and buildings and assaulting their women, these last mainly Maxwells apparently, which was no doubt why the perpetrators had been apprehended in the first place. The list of Jock o' the Dean, Pate o' Parkheid, Little Will o' Doonbyres, Dod o' Langsyke, Rab this and Dand that, was rattled through, all Armstrongs. Then silence, as the Lord James stared at them.

"Who speaks to this?" he demanded, levelly.

"I do," the Lord Maxwell declared. "They are all notour rogues and arrant thieves, caught red-handed. Armstrongs!"

That was all that was needed to be said.

"Who seeks to deny the charges?"

There was silence again. After all, what could any of them say? It was a way of life. They had been caught, that was all. Whereas the Maxwells had not.

The Lord James nodded, expressionlessly. "Guilty, then," he said. "All to hang forthwith. Next."

There was some disturbance as this group of eight were led and pushed out, not exactly protesting but expressing defiance. Thomas and some of his neighbours eyed each other questioningly at this so summary justice, but had no opportunity to do more before a new group was brought forward: only three this time, Johnstones it seemed – also enemies of the Maxwells.

The charge was that these three, all brothers apparently, sons of Johnstone of Gillenbie, had abducted the daughter of one Matt Maxwell in Kirkblain, had all taken her carnally at the side of the Queen's highway in Lower Nithsdale, and then abandoned her, naked. They had not, however, abandoned the horse on which she had been riding, which was a sturdy nag and worth good siller. The beast had not been seen since, although searched for. It was thought to have been sold into England.

Clearly this of the horse was considered to be a serious matter.

"Who speaks to this?"

"I do." Lord Maxwell nodded. "There is no getting a beast back from the English."

"Does any deny this charge?"

One of the young men spoke up. "She is a noted wanton, near a whore! Many have had her. I laid her myself, one time, in Annan."

"So you admit it! And what of the horse?"

Silence.

"Very well. Guilty. All three to hang. Next."

The youngest of the Johnstones began to shout, but was quickly hustled out.

The Lord James tapped fingernails on the table, expressionless.

The clerk glanced at the Lord Home uneasily. He happened to be a Home himself. He coughed. "This charge is against John Purves of that Ilk. Of trading and conspiring with the English, not once but many times. Treason!" He paused. "The said John Purves has not compeared to answer the charges, my lords."

There was no least murmur in that hall, as all looked at the Lord Home. Purves was a property in the East March. And it was seldom indeed that lairds of ancient name were summoned thus.

Even the Lord James raised an eyebrow. "Who speaks to it?"

Alexander, fifth Lord Home, spare and now elderly, raised voice. "Purves was ordered to compear. By myself, as Warden. He has not done so. That in itself is a punishable offence. But his guilt is established and indeed well known. He maintains constant and shameful relations with the English, and frequently is seen in Berwick town. Also across Tweed at Cornhill and Wark. He droves herds of beasts there. He has lands near to Eyemouth and owns three fishing-craft there, which fish he sends to sell at Berwick market." He held up a hand. "And, my lord, in the last two invasions his properties were spared by the English. Treason, I say!"

The Lord James nodded. "Does any substantiate this most serious charge?"

"Aye! Aye!" Thomas's neighbours, supporting Home lairds, backed their chief. He himself frowned unhappily. The Lord Home was some distant kin to himself, not only through his grandmother but in that an aunt of his, Sir Walter Ker of Cessford's sister, was the man's wife. The great Border families were apt to be like that. And this charge made him wonder indeed. It was common knowledge on the East and Middle Marches that the Homes themselves had frequent cross-Border relations and often visited and traded with the Northumbrian English; also were apt to expect their properties to escape attention of the English raiders. So this present summons was odd, coming from them. There must be some reason for it.

The reason was forthcoming. "Purves is known to have dined in Berwick Castle with the English governor there," Home went on. "Could there be more clear evidence of treasonable conduct? And the penalty for treason is death. With the forfeiture of lands."

So that was it – forfeiture of lands. Purves lay in the Merse between Polwarth, Home itself and Eccles. Sir John, the chief's son, was Home of Eccles, and Home of Polwarth was kin. If the estate was forfeited, there was little doubt as to whom it would go.

The Lord James was no fool and undoubtedly would see the connection. But Home was the Warden of the East March, and part of Stewart's task as Justiciar was to strengthen and uphold the authority of the Wardens. And this Purves had not appeared to answer charges. He smoothed his chin.

"Warrant to be made out for the apprehension of Purves of

that Ilk," he announced levelly. "When taken, to be brought to Edinburgh for trial before the Privy Council, on charge of treason. Next summons?"

The Homes looked less than pleased but could not argue with the Queen's Justiciar.

The clerk read out another group charge. Six men, all indwellers in the burgh of Coldstream, also in the East March, accused of taking salmon-fish, with nets, from the waters of Tweed belonging to the Hirsel barony, for sale at Berwick Mart. This wicked trade known for long and of much prevalence. Now these six had been caught in the act. The Hirsel, near to Coldstream, was likewise Home property.

"Do the accused deny the taking and selling of the salmon-fish?"

The netters, two of whose names, read out, were Home also, but of the lower sort, said nothing.

This then was simple, and none need be disappointed. No need to seek confirmation.

"Repeated theft and forbidden traffic with the English found proven. All to hang. Next."

Thereafter a succession of fairly uncomplicated and easily disposed-of cases followed, from all three Marches, mainly concerned with the abstracting of cattle, sheep, horses and women from various localities, usually by night, none of which presented the Justiciar with any problems, although wearisome. The only one demanding questioning being where, Grahams involved, the cattle were from the English side of the line, which was of course legitimate; but two women had been picked up on the way home to Eskdale on the Scots side. These women, being Armstrongs, the thing had been doubly foolish, and had provoked almost clan warfare, with many of the cattle, in consequence, lost. So a modified penalty was called for here, right ears to be cut off, as warning for the future, all others just to hang.

That was ample justice for one day, and should send a clear message round the Borderland. It was back to Ferniehirst, duty done. As the official party filed out, for their horses, they found the dozen gibbets already full, some of the corpses still twitching. Thomas, for one, had difficulty in keeping his stomach under control.

He absented himself from the company that evening, with Janet, preferring the servants' quarters for their meal. He doubted now whether he was cut out to be a Warden, if the office came to him one day.

The next day's programme was very similar, with the gallows emptied and ready. However, the Lord James perhaps felt that his warning notes for the Borders were becoming clear to the deafest ears, for he condemned a mere three to hang that day. Instead, he consigned no less than forty offenders to be sent to Edinburgh for the Privy Council to deal with, most no doubt usefully destined to become galley-slaves in the Lord High Admiral's ships – which fate being worse being a matter of opinion. So the gibbets were comparatively empty as the Justiciar left Jedburgh Castle.

Thereafter Thomas learned that his services were required for the next day, to conduct the forty prisoners to Edinburgh, whilst the judicial party went on to Greenlaw and then to Dumfries, on further duties.

This of escorting was scarcely an enjoyable task, for of course it was nobody's concern to provide horses for the miserable miscreants, which meant that they had to walk, and at the pace of the slowest; and it was forty-eight miles from Jedburgh to Edinburgh – at least three full days of trailing along for Thomas and the guard, probably more, with very careful watch to be kept at night to counter almost inevitable attempts to escape.

Janet went back to Smailholm on her own, after all.

Thomas eventually and thankfully delivered his charges into Privy Council care – actually to Sir William Kirkcaldy at Edinburgh Castle, where there was ample cell accommodation – four days later. Feeling a free man again, he was not long in making his way down to Holyrood Abbey and palace. His father-in-law had told him that, although the Queen had been making a progress round parts of her kingdom – Linlithgow, Stirling, Perth, Dundee and St Andrews – she was now back again and in residence for the winter at Holyrood, in the palace wing itself now, repairs and renewals being completed at last.

It was not the abbot's quarters which Thomas approached, therefore, that evening; but he found more difficulty gaining entry past armed guards than at the Lord Robert's unconventional and happy-go-lucky establishment. But once inside and seeking the ladies, he went unchallenged, and was in fact joyfully received by the Marys – that is, save for

Livingstone, whose romance with Sempill apparently was reaching culminating stages. Flam Fleming was especially glad to see him, and demonstrative about it – which by no means displeased him.

She, and the others also, were of course full of questions as to his marriage, how he got on with his new wife, how he esteemed connubial bliss, whether she was all to be looked for in a woman, and so on, some of the queries, in particular those from Beth Beaton, frank to say the least, even verging on ·the embarrassing, to Ebba Seton's gentle remonstrances. He responded as best he could, not unaware of a certain need for loyalty towards Janet, and skirting intimate details, even though pressed somewhat – but not displeased that they were so concerned with his fate. On his part, he learned of the recent progress through the country, how the Queen had visited her birthplace in Linlithgow Palace by its loch; admired her father's magnificent buildings atop Stirling Castle rock, allegedly the finest in the land; travelled on to Perth and the edge of the Highland Line, which all had wanted to see, the further mountains already snow-capped and exciting; seen Scone where the Queen's ancestors had been crowned and where the Stone of Destiny should have been; on eastwards by the Carse of Gowrie to Dundee, where she had had a most notable reception, which greatly lifted her spirits, for she had been somewhat ill at Perth, a situation not helped by the canopy of her bed catching fire while she was in it; then across Tay to St Andrews, where there had been some trouble about Mass, and a priest actually slain by over-zealous Protestants. They had returned by Falkland Palace, in Fife, or Fothrif, where the Queen's father had died a week after her birth. All in all, it seemed, they had enjoyed the tour, and felt that they all knew Scotland a little better now – Thomas, of course, asserting that until they had seen the Borderland they were abysmally ignorant.

He asked after the Queen, needless to say, concerned that she had been unwell, and was told that she was fully recovered – her illness was a recurring one, and not serious. She was at this present moment holding an audience for Randolph, the English ambassador, and Throckmorton, a special envoy, about a projected visit the Secretary of State, Maitland, was to pay to Queen Elizabeth Tudor in London on the subject of the succession to the English throne, to which Mary was the obvious and closest heir, as a granddaughter of Margaret Tudor, Henry the Eighth's sister, and Elizabeth's full cousin therefore – however much the Tudor disliked any talk on this important subject. It would be a highly dramatic situation if the Queen of Scots and former Queen of France became also the Queen of England – and clearly the so-called Virgin Queen was not going to produce any offspring now. Thomas did not know that he personally would welcome any such development and the extraordinary change in circumstances that would result.

Flam said that the Queen would surely wish to see Tom Smellum, when she was free. She would go and inform Davie Rizzio, the Italian personal secretary, that he was here.

In the event, Flam was soon back with Queen Mary herself, the conference over. She was looking very beautiful and vivacious, and Thomas's heart turned over, especially as he was greeted with flattering warmth.

"*Pardieu* – the bridegroom himself!" she exclaimed. "How good to see Thomas of Smellum! We have much missed you. Yes. You should have been with us on my progress. Did I not say so, at the time?" She glanced round her Marys. "The next one you must come on – that is my royal command!"

He bowed low. "That would be my great honour and pleasure, Highness." He took his chance. "I would humbly suggest that this next one should be round your Borderland – which I swear would much interest you. You would be warmly received. It is long since a monarch visited my country. Your royal father, when he was a young man . . ."

"Ah, yes – when he hanged all the Armstrongs!"

"H'mm. Yes. Although he came later, more than once." He hesitated. "Your Grace's brother, the Lord James, has been hanging more Armstrongs, I fear, a few days back."

"Is that so? Are they such an ill breed, these Armstrongs? My lord of Bothwell seems to get on with them reasonably well."

Recognising that he had let himself get on to dangerous ground here, Thomas shifted his stance a little. "The Borderers have their own customs and even laws. A little different from some prevailing here, perhaps! But, then, life is different also . . ."

"So wild and unruly, Thomas? Only fifty miles away, I am told?"

"Not so, Madam – at least, not unduly so. But the English threat is ever present, and . . ."

"To be sure. But we have just been seeking to do something about that. I send an envoy to Queen Elizabeth. Let us hope for much improvement there. But – you say that my brother James has been hanging more Armstrongs? I am sorry to hear that. Parliament and the Council were much concerned about the Borders, to bring order there. But not by . . . hanging!"

"No. So say I. It was done in warning, I think. But . . ."

"Has my lord of Bothwell been too weak, too easy with them, think you? He is not a weakly man, is James Hepburn!"

Thomas shook his head. This was difficult. "Not weak, no, I would say. Uncaring perhaps. For the, the violence. There is too much raiding and reiving, yes. But then, men have to be ready to take to arms all the time against the English raiders. Not just great invasions but constant sallies across the Border by Northumbrian and Cumbrian parties. It, it *breeds* violence! Perhaps the Earl of Bothwell seemed uncaring, Your Grace. But all this hanging . . .!"

"And in *my* name, no doubt! I would not have it so."

"Then, Your Grace may perhaps be pleased to say a word for the prisoners I have just brought to Edinburgh, from Jedburgh? At the Lord James's command. Forty of them, remitted for sentence by the Privy Council. It would be grievous if they too were to be punished over-hardly. They are up at the castle now."

"Is that so? I will see to it, Thomas."

"Yet despite all this wildness, Tom would have you make a progress to his Borders, Ma'am," Flam put in impishly. "He declares them worth seeing, dangers from wild men and all!"

"There would be no danger, I assure you!" he declared, looking at the girl reproachfully. "And I would conduct you all around, my own self."

"Then we will do that, Thomas, one day. And before long," the Queen said. "The Council is planning another progress for me to the north, to Aberdeen and the Highlands. But not until the springtime. Perhaps we could come to your Borders a day or two before that? It is none so far."

"That would be excellent, Highness."

"My lord of Bothwell urges it also."

Thomas's face fell somewhat.

"We have been to your Fothrif," the Queen went on. "To the palace of Falkland. And to Dunfermline Abbey and the old palace there. Few knew the name Fothrif, we found, even there. But the abbot did and one or two others. I was able to surprise them, thanks to you!" She waved him to a chair. "Now – I would hear of your marriage . . ."

Why these young women were all so interested in this, he did not know. But after he had disposed of that, as briefly as he might, they settled down to a most pleasant evening of talk, music and song, Border ballads in demand again, whilst needlework and embroidery proceeded. Thomas asked for no better.

The only flaw in it all was when Beth Beaton, commenting on one of the ballads, which was said to have taken place on the Hermitage Water in Liddesdale, observed that perhaps they would see Hermitage and its great castle when they came to the Borders. It was Lord Bothwell's seat, as Lieutenant, was it not? Who knew – they might even see the renowned but elusive Anna Throndsen, who was said to dwell therein, with her bairn.

Thomas expressed ignorance of the lady.

With just a flicker of a glance at her royal mistress, the mischievous Beth explained. The dashing Earl had been in Denmark and had brought back a Norse mistress, this Anna, the High Admiral of Norway's daughter, no less, by whom he had a child. She was said to be an interesting creature, and notably beautiful. Again the glance at the Queen. Few had seen her, however.

There was a little pause after that, slightly uncomfortable. Mistresses and illegitimate children were sufficiently prevalent at court as in the land generally, especially in the royal family; but with the Queen obviously favouring Bothwell . . .

When Thomas reluctantly took his leave he was given royal good wishes for the coming Yuletide, which would not be long now, in case he had no cause to be in Edinburgh before that. And they would hope to come to the Borders for a brief visit in the early spring. He could not say it, but he hoped that this would be minus the Earl of Bothwell.

He was conducted to the main palace entrance by Flam and

Beth, one on each arm. At the doorway he was presented with a smacking kiss on the lips by both of them. Apparently his married status did not preclude this.

On his way up the Canongate thereafter, he assessed, appreciatively, that Flam's had been the more lingering.

6

That Yuletide proved to be less happy than the royal wishes had hoped for Thomas, for his father took a serious turn for the worse on Christmas Eve and died three days later. The death came as no great surprise, of course, but its suddenness was a shock, and the sense of loss no less grievous for all concerned. He had been a good husband, father and chief.

For Thomas, after the interment in the family crypt at Jedburgh Abbey, it meant a great upheaval in more than emotions. His life had to change drastically. He was now abruptly head of the family and clan, with major responsibilities. He had to move back from Smailholm to Ferniehirst. Although he was not Warden of the Middle March, which office now went to his mother's brother, Sir Walter Ker of Cessford, he was hereditary Provost of Jedburgh, bailie of the abbey and Keeper of its royal castle. At twenty-one years, it was all more than he would have sought. Janet accepted the changes without demur, and was in fact very helpful in the transition.

An early and obvious problem, of course, was that of his mother and the family. Ferniehirst was their home, and he had no least wish to dispossess them. He would have been well content to remain living at Smailholm Tower, but that would not have been acceptable to the Kerr tribe; he was now Laird of Ferniehirst and must live there. Any mere exchange of residences would not serve, for Smailholm on its rocky hilltop was no place for Lady Catherine and the young people, too small and too remote. Yet it was unsuitable to impose on either his mother or Janet that they should share house and housekeeping. Indeed Lady Catherine would not have it so. The estate had other houses, to be sure, but all were presently occupied. Crailing, only four miles away and a fine property, was the obvious choice, and the uncle and his wife, who presently occupied it, had no family and could surely move to Smailholm, or Prymsideloch, another smaller place. Meantime, Lady Catherine solved the problem by declaring that she and the young people would move temporarily to quarters in Jedburgh Castle. It was a royal property admittedly but its hereditary Keeper was entitled to lodgings therein – never used because of its near proximity to Ferniehirst, but available. Thomas was doubtful, for in his opinion the accommodation there was less than admirable or comfortable. But his mother, who was still a woman of only forty-two years, declared that she could make it adequate as a temporary home until Crailing should be available. And it was conveniently near at hand, so the family could see each other and their friends frequently.

So, for the remainder of that winter and early spring, there was no lack of activity in the Jed Water valley, and much coming and going with Cessford Castle over the transference of the wardenship and its duties and records.

Thomas was pleased to receive a letter in the Queen's own handwriting expressing her sympathy over the loss of his father, and adding in a postscript that perhaps in the circumstances her visit to the Borders should be put off meantime?

He wrote back, to the contrary.

In the event, the visit – it was to be no royal progress, this – took place even earlier than anticipated. It transpired that the projected northern progress and tour, important apparently for political reasons, had been postponed until August, and that meantime there was to be a fairly prolonged visit to St Andrews to settle sundry matters of religious divergence with the clerical authorities there; this the Privy Council had arranged as from 10th March. So any Border tour, however brief, would have to be before that. As it happened, the Queen had arranged to pay an important visit to the castles of Crichton and Borthwick on the third day of March, reasons unspecified; and since she reckoned these to be on the way to the Borderland, she purposed coming on thereafter. It could be only for a day or two, of course.

So Thomas had a sufficiency to occupy his mind, for any newly married man. Janet made no reproaches.

On the fifth day of March, then, with an escort of a score of Kerr moss-troopers, to look suitably chieflike, he rode northwards to meet the royal party. Coming from Crichton and Borthwick, in the southern section of Lothian, they would presumably travel down Wedale, the valley of the Gala Water, by Stow and Torwoodlee to Galashiels, to reach Tweed soon thereafter and follow that great river eastwards to Melrose and St Boswells, forty miles. The Queen and her ladies were good horsewomen all, so he ought to meet them perhaps halfway, twenty miles or so, which he reckoned would bring him, and them, to Bowland in long Wedale, or thereabouts.

That proved to be a fair calculation, for he was at the great bend of Bowshank amongst the close-pressing, rounded green hills when he perceived a long column of riders coming down the winding road towards him, which could be nothing else but the royal party.

The meeting was cheerfully exclamatory on the women's part, less so on the men's, the Queen in excellent spirits. She declared that she was already loving Thomas's Border hills, with their fair green valleys. Why was this one called Wedale, when the river flowing down it was the Gala Water? None of her company could tell her. Thomas declared that he was not entirely sure, but he had heard that it was because this valley, in especial the place of Stow in it, was anciently a sanctuary or girth, to which offenders could go to the protection of Holy Church whilst their cases were fairly considered. Stow church was famous for having a portion of Christ's true cross, the reason for the sanctuary. The name should be Wad-dale, wad being the old Scots word for a pledge of security, as in wadset. He did not swear that this was correct, but it was what his father had told him.

The very Catholic Queen delighted in this account, even though her half-brother sniffed.

The Marys were all there, and Lady Fleming too, Flam calling to him to come and ride beside her. He had thought to ride with the Queen, to point out and explain what was to be seen. But the Lord James did not move from one side, and the Abbé Brantôme was as close on the other – so perhaps protocol operated. At least there was no sign of Bothwell in the party, indeed few of the lordly ones. David Rizzio, the Italian secretary, was there, and the poet Chastelard. Thankful that the company was not greater – for of course he would have to provide hospitality for all – he reined in between Flam and her mother, immediately behind the Queen. The roadway was only wide enough for riding three abreast.

When, quite soon, they reached the wide Tweed valley area

99

and the land opened out notably before them, the Queen, at sight of the three shapely and outstanding peaks of the Eildons ahead to the east, turned in her saddle to enquire. So Thomas was able to give some information that these were the Trimontium of the Romans, where they had had a great camp; and the famed territory of Thomas the Rhymer, Learmonth of Ersildoune, who had allegedly met the Queen of the Fairies and gone off with her to Elfland for seven years – as the ballad recounted.

The Lord James looked disapproving at such pagan fairy tales and nonsense.

Down Tweeddale they could ride in more open order, and Flam largely got Thomas to herself for much of the time. She was as full of news as an egg of meat. She revealed that what they had been doing at Crichton and Borthwick was connected with alleged misdemeanours on the part of the Earl of Bothwell – why he was not present now. Apparently it had been discovered that he and the young Earl of Arran, heir to the Duke of Châtelherault, the one-time Regent and Hamilton chief, were in a plot to kill the Lord James and Secretary Maitland and to abduct the Queen herself and take her to Dumbarton Castle, from which, in her name, Bothwell and Arran would rule the kingdom; Arran was in line for the throne anyway through his princess-grandmother. The Lord Borthwick had been part-source of this extraordinary information, and Borthwick Castle was quite close to Bothwell's Castle of Crichton. But the Earl had been warned and had got away in time. The Queen did not take it all very seriously, but the Privy Council and the Lord James certainly did, and had instigated a confrontation, with a large armed force ready in the background. The Queen's ladies had been encouraged to come along, to give the impression of a mere social visit. Disappointed in dramatics, the armed force had returned, with most of the lords, to Edinburgh, whilst they had come on southwards. Incidentally, the Lord James had now been created Earl of Mar – which, oddly, was not pleasing him. For he had wanted the earldom of Moray, much larger and more wealthy, and which it seemed he had been promised at some time. But the Earl of Huntly, the Gordon, had gained this from the Queen's mother, when Regent, and was not going to give it up. So Mar had been produced instead – itself causing trouble, for the Lord Erskine was also claiming it. Much fluttering in doocots.

Thomas, ready to believe almost anything of Bothwell, wondered why the Queen seemed to be so partial to the man. Should he not be deprived of the lieutenantship of the Borders and the office of Lord High Admiral? Flam thought that the Queen, all her life surrounded by dandified and courtier-like men, found his rough maleness and dashing behaviour attractive. Women could so think, he must realise! That was accompanied by a significant glance.

Down past the village of Darnick, with its little Heiton tower and bastle-house for the population to flee into in the event of raiding, they came to the splendid red-stone abbey of Melrose immediately below the Eildon Hills, still part ruinous after the last English invasions. The Queen was distressed to see this, and said that it must be repaired, although the new Earl of Mar, suitably Protestant, declared that it was, after all, only a monument to the discredited popery, and the new house being built alongside – with some of its fallen stonework – for their brother, another of the late King's bastards and now Commendator-Abbot of Melrose, was of much more interest. They did examine the desecrated high altar, before which the heart of Robert the Bruce was buried; and the Queen was delighted when Thomas pointed out the stone carving, higgh on the south front, of a pig playing the bagpipes.

It was a mere seven miles from Melrose to Smailholm, and although Thomas much wanted to show this off, he preferred not to with this large party. Besides, the shortish March daylight required them to get to Ferniehirst before dark. So they pressed on down Tweed, and then over the rolling ridges between its dale and that of Teviot, the glorious vistas drawing exclamations from the womenfolk.

They crossed Teviot by a ford at Monteviot, and climbed the final ridge over into the Jed Water valley, reaching Jedburgh and Ferniehirst just as the sun set.

Janet received the large company with quiet dignity and no fuss, however much of an ordeal it must have been, her first major hostess-function a royal one. The Queen and her ladies, although obviously highly interested to meet Tom Smellum's wife, were friendly and helpful towards her, and all went well, Thomas considerably relieved. A fine repast was provided for them in the castle's great hall, a notable effort on Janet's part. This was done full justice to, by all.

For his part, Thomas had arranged for fiddlers from

Jedburgh to be present, and after the meal they had music and dancing, even some ballad-singing, on demand.

With insufficient bedchamber accommodation available for all the royal party, some had to go down to Jedburgh's hospice and inns for the night.

In their own room, after all had retired, Thomas told Janet that he was proud of her, for all that she had done, and her expert handling of the situation. In return she complimented him on *his* expertise, especially in the dancing, which he had managed to keep secret from her up till now – but not, she gathered, from Mary Fleming particularly and even the Queen! She had noticed how effectively they co-operated.

He had to do some fast talking over that.

In the morning Thomas was well pleased when the Earl James announced that he was going to see the new Warden, Sir Walter Ker, at Cessford. So they could go off to Smailholm, which clearly was being anticipated as the highlight of the trip by all the young women, with less critical company. In the event some of the others elected to go with the Earl to see the major castle of Cessford rather than some small, remote Border tower which they had never heard of, and only David Rizzio and one or two others came with the Queen's group – which was all to the good. Thomas quite liked Rizzio, a darkly good-looking, sardonic character with a pronounced sense of humour.

He took the little party down Teviot to the river's junction with Tweed, at Kelso, so that they could see that attractive small town, really just the abbey-town of Roxburgh. It was strange to have another great abbey so close to that of Jedburgh, a mere ten miles apart; indeed, with Melrose not much further to the north, and Dryburgh a mere five miles from the latter, they formed a curious constellation of magnificent monuments to the piety and wisdom of King David the First, who had set them up, all thus near to his favourite seat of Roxburgh Castle, so that he might keep an eye on them, not only as places of worship but as training-centres for a vast increase in the numbers of priests, for he it was who had instituted the parish system in Scotland for the betterment of his people in moral, spiritual and governmental well-being, and as a check on the excesses of the nobility. On all this Thomas held forth to the Queen – he rode at her side today unquestioned – to her evident interest, admitting that she had not known of it. But then, there was so much that she did not know of her kingdom, having been so largely reared in France.

They called at this abbey, which also showed signs of English assault, and where a kinsman of Thomas's was Commendator-Abbot – but he was from home. Thereafter they crossed another ford of Teviot, westwards again but on the north bank, a bare mile, to the site of Roxburgh Castle on the narrow peninsula between the two rivers, King David's palace, now ruinous but impressive still. To the west of it again had been the once large and busy town of Roxburgh, one-time capital of Scotland, and now largely derelict, only a few broken-down houses still occupied, Kelso, more accessible, having superseded it.

Thomas, explaining all this, began to fear that he might well be becoming something of a bore to these young women, and warned himself to restrain his flood of information – not that his hearers exhibited signs of a surfeit, save perhaps for Rizzio, whom he noticed eyeing him amusedly.

Back across both rivers, he led them west by north through the fertile and fairly level Merse, Home country, by Stodrig and Luntonlaw. And soon he was able to point out, miles ahead on its hilltop, the tower of Smailholm upthrusting on the skyline. The closer they got to that challenging fortalice, the more appreciatively vociferous grew his visitors; and by the time that they had climbed some way up its hill and rounded a little spur to find the lochan before them and the tower soaring high above it, dominant, all were loud in admiration and almost wonderment. None had ever seen the like. Wildfowl obligingly flew up for them from the water's edge.

Leading the string of riders up the steep and circuitous track to the tower was something of an adventure.

The Cranstouns were much flustered at the arrival of this very vocal company, and quite overwhelmed when they were presented to the Queen herself. They hid themselves thereafter.

The keep's interior held little to impress the visitors, of course, but once up on the parapet-walks, the exclamations resounded again, at the prospects in every direction. Thomas was kept busy identifying this feature and that, near and far, ranges of hill, forested areas, castles, villages. The Queen declared that Smellum was a place she would never forget.

Before they went downstairs, she asked whether they could see Hermitage Castle from here, which she had heard much of. He had to point out that it was a good fifty miles away, and anyway hidden far behind that furthest range of high hills to the south-west, where Teviot, Esk, Liddel and other rivers were born, the lofty watershed of the Borderland. Flam nudged Thomas with her elbow as he informed, in case he missed the significance of the enquiry.

Below, the Cranstouns had not been inactive, hastily seeking to conjure up refreshments, however inadequate for royalty: not much wine but plenty of ale, some home-brewed cordials, that made with honey especially popular with the ladies, scones, oatcakes and cheese. Chastelard, the poet, made up an impromptu rhyme to celebrate the occasion, and as they ate and drank before a newly lit log fire, Thomas was urged to give them the ballad of "Young Tamlane", which seemed to have become a favourite with the young women. This over, and Rizzio complaining that it was too sorrowful and unearthly for words, in his esteem, being pressed to provide an antidote, obligingly rendered them a spirited Italianate song, all flings and skirls. When the girls picked up the lilt and joined in, he rose and grabbed Beth Beaton, and went skipping about the floor with her in antic style, to the cheers of all. And when Meg Cranstoun arrived with additional warmed scones, Beth was discarded and Meg whisked off instead, to her gasping protests – which, however, soon died away as she began to kick up her heels in astonishingly lively fashion, to applause. It was as well that the Earl James was not present.

When, at length, they left Smailholm Tower, the Queen presented the Cranstouns with a brooch of silver wire, which she wore to keep her headscarf in place, in the shape of a heart, to their speechless delight.

For their return journey, Thomas took them to the abbey of Dryburgh, only a few miles to the west, set deep and tucked away in a sharp bend of the Tweed valley, almost at the riverside, a quietly lovely place which, because of its hidden position, had partly escaped the despoilers, even though no monks resided there now, only the caretakers of the Commendator-Abbot, one more James Stewart. As it happened, all the party this day were of the old religion, and so the Queen herself led a brief prayer-session before the high altar, a touching little gesture in the circumstances, Thomas mentioning to her that St Modan, an Irish Celtic missionary, was the founder.

Thereafter it was back to Ferniehirst by the village of St Boswells, named after another early Celtic saint, Boisil, and where the somewhat later St Cuthbert was said to have come to worship, the Queen remarking that the Borderland seemed to be a great place for saints and sanctity, despite its reputation for wild men.

That evening, at Ferniehirst, she told Thomas that she wished him to take her to Hermitage on the morrow.

Thomas did not personally hear the discussion, next morning, but Flam told him that the Earl James had strongly advised his sister against making this visit to Hermitage. It was highly injudicious, he had said, and could be dangerous. Almost certainly Bothwell would be there, after fleeing from Crichton, and in such wild and remote surroundings he could display his unruly spirit unchecked, in menace to them all. Indeed, if he and Arran had planned to abduct the Queen before, she would be positively presenting him with the opportunity to do so now; and they had an insufficiency of armed men to protect her, whereas he would have a host of Border ruffians, Armstrongs, Johnstones, Elliots and the like, at his beck and call. But the Queen had been adamant, declaring that James Hepburn would not hurt her, and she wanted to hear his own side of the story. Flam asserted that what she really wanted was to see the Norse mistress, Anna Throndsen.

Thomas himself thought that this visit was injudicious, but could not say so. He did what he could to improve the situation by calling up as many of his Kerr moss-troopers as he could rake in at short notice, to accompany the party. For once, he assessed, the Earl James approved.

It was, Thomas reckoned, fully thirty-five miles from Ferniehirst to Hermitage, and over some of the roughest terrain in southern Scotland. They had to follow Teviot right up, past Lanton and Denholm-on-the-Green and Hawick, nearly all the way to Teviothead itself, amongst the ever-heightening hills, near mountains now, almost to Caerlanrig, where the Queen's father, aged fifteen, had hanged all the Armstrongs. Just before this, they swung away south by east and started to climb still more steeply into a very jumble of summits by a difficult drove-road, reaching at length a lofty plateau area where there were the remains of Pictish settlements, stone circles and earthworks, which much interested the Queen. Thereafter, making for the actual watershed area, deep in the wilderness of heathery heights, to follow up what Thomas declared was the Priesthope Burn, a few dramatic miles brought them to the highest point of their journey between two soaring summits. It would be mainly downhill from now on.

The panorama southwards from here was breathtaking, over the widespread Debateable Land, so called, he explained, because so much of it was doubtful as to its actual allegiance nationally, the borderline being less than clear and apt to local alteration – and in fact of no very great interest to most of the inhabitants – in the Liddesdale, Eskdale, Ewesdale, Keilder, Lynedale, Sark and Kirtle valleys. On the edge of all that, another five miles or so on, would be Hermitage Castle.

The Earl James commented that anyone who chose such a place to hide away in *must* have a guilty conscience.

When at length they reached the Hermitage Water, and the castle rose on a shelf above it in stark, frowning dominance, all fell silent, such was the impact of it. This was a fortress rather than just a castle, massive, stern, much larger than any other in the Borderland, its five great towers squared and linked by high curtain walls, its parapets, bartisans and machicolations sheerly threatening. Even the Queen looked askance at it.

"Why . . .?" she asked, of no one in particular.

"Well may you ask!" her brother said.

"It had need to be strong, in this country," Thomas declared, but with no great conviction.

"I think that evil could be done here!" Mary Seton said.

"Evil has, yes. More than once, I think. But here it was that the noble Sir Alexander Ramsay of Dalwolsey was starved to death by his own friend and fellow-leader, Sir William Douglas of Liddesdale, the Flower of Chivalry. After the Bruce's death."

"I have heard of that," the Lady Fleming said. "I never could quite believe it."

"It is true. One of the most shameful deeds told of the Borderland."

While they were still almost half a mile off, they saw a large party of horsemen coming from the castle area towards them. No doubt their approach had been under view from those towers for some time. As they drew near, these riders looked a wild and menacing lot, armed to the teeth. The visitors could be glad of the Kerr moss-trooping escort. The leader of this party, a villainous-looking character with a red beard, superbly mounted, hailed them from four score yards off, bull-bellowing.

"Who comes to Hermitage, unasked and unannounced!" he demanded.

Thomas was about to answer when the Earl James outvoiced him. "Better folk than you, sirrah! The Queen's Grace herself, and the Earl of Mar. Is the Earl of Bothwell here?"

The other did not answer at first, clearly put out. Then he nodded, curtly. "He is, yes." No more than that.

"Then bring us to him, man. And who are you that speaks so bold?"

"I am Armstrong of Mangerton. And I do not know of any Earl of Mar!"

Thomas all but smiled at that. But at James Stewart's scowl, he found opportunity to assert himself. "You will have heard of your sovereign-lady the Queen, no? Even of my poor self, Kerr of Ferniehirst, Mangerton?"

The Armstrong – and Mangerton was the chief of the name – nodded again, and, reining round his fine horse, gestured his people back to the castle, without further parley, the royal company following on.

The Armstrong spurred ahead.

By the time they got to the ditches which separated them from the castle shelf and the main moat before the walls, they saw a single man standing awaiting them on the lowered drawbridge – James Hepburn himself.

"Welcome, Madam – welcome!" he called cheerfully. "Here's a pleasure!" And he flourished an almost mocking bow, before coming forward to aid the Queen down from her saddle. He ignored everyone else.

There was a great dismounting, and they all trailed after Bothwell and the Queen over the drawbridge and under the great gatehouse arch into the first of three inner court-yards; that is except for the Kerr riders, who followed the Armstrongs to nearby stabling on the west, itself strongly fortified. Bothwell held the Queen's arm familiarly, the Earl James, still ignored, looking daggers at their backs.

That castle within seemed little more friendly and hospitable than without, its notably small and high windows letting in scanty light, its bare stone walls largely devoid of hangings and tapestries. But at least there was no lack of food and drink, acceptable indeed to the visitors after their long riding. They ate in the great hall, on the first floor of the largest tower, a vast barn of a place but with a wide fireplace at either end.

Bothwell seemed in excellent spirits, certainly giving no impression of guilt, attentive to the Queen, and to some of her ladies, in his over-familiar way. There was no sign of a mistress.

Presently the new Earl of Mar grew tired of being ignored, an unusual state of affairs for him. "My lord of Bothwell, we looked to find you at Crichton," he announced, levelly. "Her Grace, and the Privy Council, required information as to certain charges laid against you. And against the Earl of Arran."

"Had Her Grace advised me of her coming, I would have awaited her." That was easily said.

"Would you? I wonder! And Arran?"

"James Hamilton is no concern of mine. The man is crazed, anyway!"

"He is not here, with you?"

"No. Why should he be?"

"You were said to be in a plot together. A dire and treasonable plot. Against Her Grace."

"Against Her Grace?" Bothwell turned to the Queen, grinning. "I wonder if there is more than Arran crazy! Think you, Madam, I would ever plot against *you*? Save perhaps to seek win some little kindness or token of affection!" That was boldly suggestive.

Mary shook her head, unspeaking.

"You deny, then, that you and Arran were plotting to take the Queen by force, to Dumbarton Castle, and hold her there? Aye, and contrive the deaths of sundry of Her Grace's Council, including myself!"

"Lord! What bairn's tale is this? Have you indeed lost your wits, my lord? Like Arran?"

"You will learn otherwise, Bothwell, I promise you! We have means of discovering secret iniquities!"

The other hooted. "I am no saint! But *my* iniquities are none so secret!" he exclaimed. "*Yours*, now, my lord, may be otherwise? Sundry young men might inform us?"

The Queen raised a hand, this having gone far enough. "My lords – sufficient!" she said, half-commanding, half-pleading. "This is unseemly. I come to Hermitage on a kindly visit, not . . ."

Almost as though signalled to introduce at least one reason for this kindly visit, movement at an inner doorway caught the Queen's eye, and in came a small fair-haired boy, part-dragged by a tall deerhound, the collar of which he clutched. Dog and boy headed straight for Bothwell.

There was silence in that hall for moments on end.

The child came to take the Earl's hand, saying something in a foreign tongue.

Bothwell ran his other hand over his face, but did not reject the boy. He looked over at the Queen. "This is Sven. From Norway."

"Ah, yes," Mary said. "A pretty child. And . . . the mother? I would meet her."

"As Your Grace wishes. You have been informed, I see!" Bothwell strode to the doorway. "Anna – come!" he commanded, loudly.

After a moment or two a tall, well-built, exceedingly good-looking young woman, in a rather gaunt way, appeared, smoothing back her long blonde hair. She looked about her at the crowd in the room nervously.

"The Queen's Grace desires speech with you, Anna," he said. He turned. "The Lady Anna Throndsen, daughter to the Admiral of Norway."

Mary stepped forward, a hand out to the newcomer, who dipped a deep curtsy. Neither spoke as they eyed each other almost assessingly.

Then the Queen smiled. "You are a beautiful woman," she said. "My lord is to be . . . congratulated!"

The other dipped another incipient curtsy. "The Highness is kind," she said, in a heavily accented, husky voice.

"I have known Anna long," Bothwell added, as though in explanation.

"To be sure. I know little of Norway, nor of Denmark. The Lady Anna and I must talk." She turned, to eye the little boy thoughtfully. Talk was resumed generally.

The Queen went to consult with the Earl James. Then she came to Thomas.

"I had thought to return to your Ferniehirst this night,"

she said. "But it is further than I had foreseen. And scarcely easy riding. We could not be back before darkening, I think?"

"No, Highness." It was mid-afternoon and it had taken them over four hours to come. And the horses were no longer fresh. "We would be fortunate to reach even Teviot."

"Then I fear that we must pass the night here. But I must return to Edinburgh tomorrow. Is it possible to ride from here to Edinburgh in one day?"

"It would be a long ride, Madam. Over seventy miles, I would say. By Teviothead and Ashkirk, then Galashiels and Wedale." He hesitated. "I think that *I* could do it. But . . ."

"If you can, I can, my friend! Even though some others may not. If we leave early. I shall be sorry not to say farewell to your wife. But, another time . . ."

She went to inform Bothwell.

What that man thought of having all the royal company and their escort imposed on him for the night, without warning, was not disclosed. At least there was plenty of accommodation, and meat was no problem in the circumstances.

The evening was a strange one. The underlying tension was very evident, although Bothwell and the Queen themselves showed little sign of it. Apart from the eating and drinking, there was little in the way of entertainment. The enmity between the two earls, however, was very apparent; indeed few of the royal party looked in favour on their host. Anna Throndsen kept herself very much in the background. Thomas, on demand, sang a few ballads, and got some help from the Marys. But nothing could make it a joyful occasion. Nothing more was said about the alleged plot, however much was thought. By common consent, retiral was early, with an early start required next day.

Thomas found himself sharing a lofty tower chamber with the poet Chastelard, who went on at considerable length, in a mixture of quick French and slow English, on the beauty, charm, merits and accomplishments of the Queen, the glories of her court in France, the uncouth conditions in Scotland, her patience with it all, and his own readiness to die for her. Also his detestation of the man Bothwell. At length, Thomas had to feign sleep in order to bring the recital to a close.

In the morning, they were off in good time, the weather threatening rain. Bothwell escorted the Queen up as far as the watershed, bluffly assured to the last.

110

Thereafter, Thomas said that he would conduct the party through the hills as far as Ashkirk, near to the town of Selkirk in the Ettrick Forest, whence it would be straightforward all the way north to Edinburgh, forty more miles. As well that they had all excellent horses.

They rode by Teviothead, by a drove-road across the heights of Dryden Fell to the valley of the Borthwick Water. From there, past Hoscote, by Borthwickshiels, by high passes through the empty hills to the source of the Ale Water and so to Ashkirk. Selkirk on the Ettrick, and the Tweed were only a few miles ahead. Thomas and his moss-troopers drew rein, his own Ferniehirst still a score of miles away.

He was surprised when the Queen dismounted – and so must all others.

She smiled at him. "Thomas, you have been goodness itself, my true friend. I am much beholden, in your debt. We all are. I am grateful."

"It has been only my loyal duty, Your Grace. And, and much esteem."

"Not all are so loyal. Nor so . . . esteeming, I fear! But . . ." She turned. "James – come. And your sword, if you please."

The Earl James came forward but doubtfully, hand on his sword-hilt.

"Out with it, brother. I wish to knight our friend Thomas here. You shall bestow the accolade for me." She turned back. "Kneel, Thomas of Smellum."

Astonished, quite overwhelmed, he stared, scarcely able to believe his ears. It took her pointing at the ground in sham peremptory fashion to gain his obedience to the royal command.

"James!" she said. That also was a command.

Less than eagerly, as Thomas knelt on the grass, head bent, the Earl tapped him first on one shoulder and then on the other with the flat of the sword-blade, although it was the Queen who spoke the words.

"Thomas, I hereby dub thee knight, as is my right, in the sight of God and of these present. Be thou faithful and a good and true knight until thy life's end. Arise, Sir Thomas Kerr!"

Mind in a whirl, he got to his feet, seeking to swallow his emotions. From all around came cries of approval and delight, especially from the Marys – but noticeably not from the Earl James.

When he tried to thank her, the Queen cut short his halting words. "No, no, my friend – it is little enough for your deserts. We part now – no? But I will see you again shortly. For you come with us on our North Country progress, you remember? I shall send you word when we are to go. Meanwhile, my thanks and salutations to Lady Kerr at Ferniehirst. *Au revoir*, Sir Thomas." And she held out her hand, which he stooped to kiss, as in a dream.

That was not all the kissing done, for as the Queen moved back to her horse, Flam and Beth Beaton came running to embrace him enthusiastically, followed by Ebba Seton and Mary Livingstone, Lady Fleming bringing up the rear. David Rizzio and Chastelard, with others, came to shake his hand.

As the two parties separated, to go north and south-east, Thomas Kerr, knight, rode wondering. His moss-troopers, however, seemed quite unimpressed.

7

Thomas had considerably longer to wait for his summons to accompany the Queen on her northern progress than anticipated: four months, indeed. This, oddly enough, was caused by Queen Elizabeth of England, who was using delaying tactics to bring pressure to bear on her sister-monarch over an accord between the two realms which would end the English raiding into Scotland – and, to a much lesser extent, vice versa. Secretary of State Maitland had returned from London empty-handed; and then Elizabeth's special envoy, Sir Philip Mewtas, arrived in Edinburgh with counter-proposals. The English demands were that all French troops in Scotland should be sent home – there were still considerable numbers remaining from Marie of Guise's regency, with their advanced artillery, which expressly worried the English; also that the ancient mutual-protection Auld Alliance of France and Scotland be abrogated. The Scots Council and parliament were against this. Elizabeth was offering little in return for these major concessions save, of all things, offering to find a suitable husband for Mary, a strange preoccupation for the Virgin Queen, linking this with the suggestion that until Mary produced an heir, she herself could not sensibly accept her as heir-presumptive to the English throne, a peculiar argument. She was nominating her favourite, the Earl of Leicester, as most suitable; and as alternative, Henry Stewart, Lord Darnley, son to the exiled Earl of Lennox, and, more importantly, to Margaret his wife, who was a daughter of Queen Margaret Tudor, James the Fourth's widow, by her marriage to the Earl of Angus, Queen Elizabeth's aunt. This last, of course, had some point to it, since this Darnley could claim links with both royal houses.

All this, of ambassadorial meetings and discussions with the Privy Council, meant that Mary had to be available and accessible, reasonably near to Edinburgh that spring and summer. Actually she did not greatly like that city, or Holyrood, complaining that Edinburgh's smelly, narrow streets, closes and middens, with the prevailing westerly winds, contaminated the air of the palace, especially in warm weather; she preferred Linlithgow, Stirling and St Andrews, with considerable time spent at Falkland in Fife, the hunting palace, excellent for her favourite outdoor sports of archery, falconry and deer-driving. She sent messages to Thomas that he was most welcome to join her there. But meantime the north, Aberdeen, Inverness and the Highlands, were out of the question.

For his own part, Thomas, although missing seeing all the attractive females of the court, found more than enough to keep him occupied in his own Borderland. Being Baron of Ferniehirst and other properties, and chief of the Kerrs, even though not a Warden of the Marches, entailed much more work and heavier responsibilities than he had realised, the provostship of Jedburgh also making inroads on his time; as chief magistrate he found the Jeddart folk particularly unruly. And he had come up with an especial project – partly at Janet's suggestion. In gratitude for his knighthood he decided to build a house for Queen Mary in Jedburgh itself. The small royal castle on the hill above the abbey was more suitable for a gaol than a palace; and there was just insufficient accommodation at Ferniehirst for the size of party which always accompanied the Queen. He had been ashamed of having to send many of her company, that time, down to the hospice and inns of the town – and he hoped that she would come back to Jedburgh frequently. So he began the erection of a fine house for her down at the east end of the town, with gardens down to the Jed Water bank, quite an ambitious design for a young man of twenty-two years.

He and Janet did not see much of Smailholm in those months.

Certain items of news reached them, on occasion, from outwith their Borders. The poet Chastelard had been discovered hiding under the Queen's bed, presumably with romantic intent, and although Mary had been annoyed, she pardoned him despite the demands of some, including the Earl James, that he should be executed for the crime of *lèse majesté*. The monarch had been again publicly criticised by John Knox, from the pulpit, for playing backgammon, chess, cards and dice, especially on the anniversary of her late husband's death.

And the Earl James had to some extent got his own back on Bothwell by having the Privy Council order him into ward whilst they investigated the alleged plot – this also to apply to Arran. But since the Council was nowise in any position to take Bothwell out of Hermitage Castle, he was ordered to ward himself therein, which would not unduly worry him; and Arran was put in ward of his father, the Duke of Châtelherault.

All this left Thomas wondering about affairs of state.

Then in early August the call came. Some sort of temporary agreement had been reached with Elizabeth Tudor, and Queen Mary felt able to leave for the north now, especially as there was trouble brewing with the Gordons, which ought to be dealt with before it became serious. The Earl of Huntly, chief of that great clan and the senior Catholic nobleman, was still in theory Chancellor of the realm, but with Council and parliament predominantly Protestant, attended few meetings. Called on to resign, he would not; and since he hung on to the Great Seal of Scotland, sign of the Chancellor's authority, up in his northern fastness of Strathbogie, replacement was difficult. And now a son of his, Sir John Gordon, a roystering character, already in trouble for almost killing the Lord Ogilvy in a duel and refusing to yield himself up, was actually proposing himself as a suitable husband for the Queen. Something would have to be done about the Gordons. The Queen would be leaving Linlithgow on 11th August, making for Stirling, Perth and the north. Thomas should join them at his convenience.

On the 12th, then, he said goodbye to Janet and set off. Considering that there might well be trouble with those Gordons, he decided that it would be sensible, and consonant with his knightly dignity, to take a score of his Kerr riders with him. He reckoned that the Queen's party would be at Stirling before he caught up with them.

He went, therefore, by the westerly route, right up Tweed, passing near to Selkirk again, all the way on through that great dale, by Elibank, Innerleithen, Traquair and Peebles, to Broughton, where the river turned southwards to its source on high Tweedsmuir and he turned north, not far from the headwaters of the great rival stream, the Clyde. Sixty miles of rough riding, and they halted for the night in a haugh of the River Medwyn near Dolphinton.

Next day they headed as consistently north by west as the terrain allowed, mainly by high and bleak moorlands flanking the western side of the Pentland Hills, country little known to Thomas, and little esteemed by Borderers, being largely Hamilton territory. Skirting the Calders and Torphichen, eventually they came in sight of the wide strath of Forth above Falkirk, with the Highland hills blue far beyond, and reached Stirling at sundown, after well over one hundred miles of riding, horses weary, riders stiff and sore.

Thomas found Stirling town in a stir indeed, for it seemed that the Queen had brought a host with her on this progress, not only her court but almost the entire Privy Council, the corps of ambassadors and nearly all her lords, with their trains. The royal castle up on its majestic rock, so like that of Edinburgh, the true home of the Scots monarchy, could hold only a small proportion of all there, and the town which mounted its narrow streets up towards the citadel was packed to overflowing.

Latecomers, the Kerrs found no accommodation available, and had to go on a further couple of miles to Cambuskenneth Abbey, amongst the extraordinary meanderings of the now quite narrow Forth, for the night.

In the morning, Thomas made his way back to the town and up to the castle, alone. He had no difficulty in gaining admittance, at least, for the gates were wide in the succession of ramparts, with folk coming and going freely. Even up at the fine royal palace, built anew by the Queen's father, he met with no challenge, so crowded were all the premises, so busy everybody. It seemed that a Privy Council meeting was in progress, a continuation of one held the day before, presumably with major matters to be discussed, the Queen presiding.

He ran the Marys to earth in a handsome chamber looking out west and north over the wide Flanders Moss and the vales of Forth and Teith, to the noble escarpment of the Highland Line, a prospect to draw the eye indeed. He was welcomed with enthusiasm, even hilarity, Flam and Beth taking his arms to waltz about with him, to the astonishment of their new recruit, Mary Carmichael, a quietly shy girl, but seemingly amiable.

Thomas learned, then, that great things were afoot, problems, excitements. Something far more serious than the alleged Bothwell–Arran plot was now preoccupying the Council and the Protestant lords. It was the Gordons, this time,

Huntly, his sons – all nine of them – his clan, and all the other northern and Highland clans allied to them, these mainly Catholic. Huntly was, in fact, proposing a Catholic rising of all the north against the Protestant-dominated south, civil war. And this was no idle threat, with the enormous manpower of the clans, some of the fiercest fighting men in the land. It was, of course, all a grievous headache for the Catholic Queen. In one way her sympathies were with her co-religionists, of course – but Huntly was scarcely going about his plans wisely or with care for the royal interests. Apart from actually supporting his son John's insolent offer of himself as husband for the Queen – Huntly's mother had been an illegitimate daughter of James the Fourth, so he was claiming cousinship – he was giving shelter to the said son, who had been imprisoned over the Lord Ogilvy wounding and had broken out of custody at Edinburgh and was now in the Huntly town-house in Aberdeen, openly challenging the Privy Council to do its worst. Huntly had garrisoned the royal castles of Inverness and Inverlochy, as well as his own strongholds of Strathbogie, Aboyne, Gight, Drummin, Lochindorb and Ruthven-in-Badenoch, and instructed other Highland chiefs to do the like. And he had ordered the entire great earldom of Moray to arms, possibly the most flagrant challenge of all, since it was of course a royal earldom and always claimed by the Earl James. Some were saying indeed that this entire progress to the north was James Stewart's devising, in order to grasp the important and wealthy Moray thus, and that the Privy Council, which he so largely dominated, was primarily concerned with this. It so happened that the Lord Erskine, hereditary Keeper of this Stirling Castle, who claimed the earldom of Mar which had meantime been granted to James, was heartily co-operating, over Moray, so as to get Mar for himself. The Earl James's mother had been Erskine's sister, as it happened.

The poor Queen, in all this, was torn this way and that, grievous pressure on a young woman of nineteen years.

However, when at midday the Council meeting broke up, and she arrived back in the royal quarters, she quickly recovered her gaiety and cast aside her cares for the moment, delighted to see Thomas, and telling him that he was just in time to accompany them on a visit she had been looking forward to making – to the Loch of Menteith and the island in it where she, and indeed three of her Marys, had been sent for safety when she was almost five years old, to escape Henry of England's attempts to abduct her and marry her to his six-year-old son, in what was still referred to as the Rough Wooing. She had happy memories of her months on this tiny island, before her removal to France, and longed to see it again. Tomorrow they were all leaving Stirling, so they would go this afternoon. It was only some fifteen miles away.

It made a very pleasant and carefree excursion for a party of no more than a score – for the lords and nobles were all busy now sending out instructions to their various lordships and baronies to mobilise men to form something like an army to accompany the Queen northwards, a Council decision. They rode westwards a mile or two along the southern skirts of the vast Flanders Moss, an area of lochans and pools and bogs and mire, the flood-plain of the River Forth, twenty miles long by five wide, which stretched all the way to the high mountains and formed the great natural barrier between Highlands and Lowlands, impassable by armies – which was what made Stirling the most strategic place in the land, the only crossing of Forth, where invasions innumerable had been halted. They crossed that river at the Ford of Drip, to proceed northwards now, to avoid the quagmires of the Drip Moss, part of the greater swamp, to get to the slightly higher ground between Forth and Teith. Thomas had never understood why the great estuary eastwards was called the Firth of Forth and not the Firth of Teith, for the Teith was the greater of the two rivers; none could tell him. Keeping necessarily to this higher ground, no ridge, but named the Mounth of Teith – hence the name Monteith or Menteith, they skirted the mosses of Blair Drummond and Coldoch, by Thornhill and Ruskie till, with the great mountains now drawing ever closer, they saw ahead of them the fair, island-dotted spread of the Loch of Menteith.

As they went, the young women spoke of their sojourn in the loch, so long ago, a happy time as they recollected it, despite the grim reasons for their stay there, the games they had played, the boat-trips, the garden they had created, their attempts at fishing, and the like. Lady Fleming, who had looked after them, shook her head over *their* versions of some events.

At the ambitiously named group of cottages and little pier, Port of Menteith, they hired a couple of boats to take them out to Inchmahome, the largest of the islets, whereon was a quite famous priory, which had been the royal refuge, abandoned since the Reformation but not yet ruinous.

It was over fourteen so very eventful years since the young women had been here, and they all but reverted to childhood in their excitement and pleasure, Thomas being dragged hither and thither to see this and explore that. The Queen was particularly delighted with her little enclosed garden, weed-grown now but still showing flowers; and the two recumbent effigies of Walter Stewart, Earl of Menteith, and his Countess, lying together over their tombs, arms around each other. They must have loved each other greatly in their life, and she was sure did so still in a better one now. She wondered aloud whether she would one day find an equally loving and beloved husband to lie beside?

Thomas, a fairly honest young man, could not say that he thought it likely, in the circumstances, so said nothing.

After exhausting the delights of Inchmahome, they rowed across to the two other islets, Castle and Dog Islands, where the earls had had their hunting seat and kept their hounds. There was no Earl of Menteith at present, the earldom having reverted to the Crown.

It had been a carefree afternoon, but as they rode back eastwards, with the towering battlements of Stirling Castle far ahead beckoning them on, the Queen grew silent and preoccupied, as well she might, problems and responsibilities reasserting themselves. She was now scarcely looking forward to her northern progress, however much she had done so originally.

Thomas fell back to ride beside Flam, who told him, low-voiced, that the Queen was greatly worried that war and battle could be looming ahead, and racked by the thought that this would probably seem to be between the Protestant and Catholic interests, with herself, Catholic, all but tied to the ruling Protestant side. It was crazy, maddening, and so unnecessary. But Huntly and his Gordons were so arrogantly unreasonable, there seemed to be little chance of avoiding a clash. Why, oh why, must men be so thrawn and unyielding, when a little compromise could let all live in peace?

There was no dancing and music at Stirling Castle that night.

Next day most of the great company went on to Perth, which

had been set as an assembly-place for the large numbers of lords' retainers summoned; but the Queen herself made a detour to Coupar Angus Abbey, which she had promised to visit. It made another welcome break from affairs of state.

Two days at Perth, and all the hoped-for muster of men not yet complete by any means, the Queen decided to ride on ahead, through Angus and Strathmore, to call at sundry great lords' houses, Finavon, Glamis, Airlie, Melgund, Edzell and others, leaving the mass of armed strength to come on – so long as they caught up before reaching the Gordon country of Aberdeenshire.

This proved all satisfactory, reasonably pleasurable and undemanding. It was a pity that the shadow of trouble ahead of them loomed ever darker as they came near to Aberdeen, where the word was that Sir John Gordon, and possibly his father, awaited them. Flam told Thomas some further details of the younger Gordon's indiscretions, a complicated story. It seemed that the ageing Ogilvie of Findlater's young wife, who was in fact a mistress of Gordon, had persuaded her husband to withdraw the lands and property of his son, James Ogilvie of Cardell – who was the Queen's Master of the Household, with them here – and give it to Gordon, the reason for the Gordon–Ogilvy brawl, in which the Lord Ogilvy had been seriously wounded; the Ogilvy family spelt their names in two ways, the southern with a "y", the northern with "ie". Thomas wondered why it was the Borderers who got the name of being the wild ones.

The royal company, although numerous and illustrious as to composition, still lacked its main armed manpower as at length they approached the Aberdeen area, where none knew quite what their reception might be at that city. The Queen was advised to wait meantime at the Earl Marischal's strong castle of Dunottar, on its detached headland above the sea some fifteen miles to the south, whilst investigation went forward to ascertain the position. So there was a welcome interlude of two days in this dramatic spot, in the golden late-August sunshine, with the Queen's personal group exploring the exciting seaboard of cliffs and coves, caves and hidden beaches.

The news, when it came from Aberdeen, was not good. Huntly, who had been ordered by the Council to ride abroad with no more than three hundred men, had arrived at the city with fifteen hundred, clearly intent on a confrontation. With their own host still not available, this was clearly to be avoided. What to do, then? They could wait here for their reinforcements – but Huntly, no doubt well-informed in his own country, could also summon greater strength from all around. The Queen thought to move on to the city, in peace, to reason with Huntly, as his monarch and co-religionist; but her councillors would not consider that. She would be as good as asking for herself to be taken, abducted and held as a pawn in the Gordons' ambitions. It was the Earl James's suggestion that they should move on, but bypass Aberdeen well to the west, and leave it behind meantime, heading northwards to the great royal earldom of Moray, which should be made aware of its duties and where its allegiance lay, while they awaited the arrival of their armed strength. This ought to confuse the Gordons. Most there saw it as another step to gaining the earldom for James Stewart; but it was agreed that it would put Huntly in a quandary, and moreover would indeed interpose themselves between him at Aberdeen and his main base area of Strathbogie, good strategy.

So a move was made, the Earl Marischal remaining at Dunottar to await and marshal the royal host when it arrived, as was his hereditary duty.

They rode westwards, avoiding the Marischal's burgh of Stonehaven, to reach what was known as the Slug Road, a corruption of the Gaelic *slochd* or throat, a route through the hills to the valley of the Dee, many miles west of Aberdeen, to ford the great river at Banchory. They were verging on Forbes country hereafter, and that clan could probably be looked on as allies of Huntly, so they did not look for any welcome or amicable gestures in this territory.

But they had miscalculated. For awaiting them at the Banchory ford of Dee was quite a large and splendid party, not warlike-seeming and by no means disputing the crossing. Surprised, they were more so when they saw that it was a woman who rode, alone, forward to meet them.

The Earl James, at Mary's side, exclaimed, "It is Huntly's wife! Elizabeth Keith, the Marischal's sister."

The lady was of middle years, plump, richly dressed and assured. "Loyal greetings, Your Grace. And welcome to Aberdeen!" she called. "You come the long way round! I am the Lady Huntly."

The Queen glanced at her brother, unsure how to react. She got no help from him. "I, I thank you for coming to greet me, Countess. I had not expected it. Here."

"We could not allow Your Grace to cross Dee unwelcomed. Wherever you chose to cross!" She reined her horse closer. "The city awaits you eagerly. As do my husband and sons."

Presented with something of a poser, the Queen's companions eyed each other. Was this a trap, to lure them into the city, when they were so evidently avoiding it? Sending the Countess to allay suspicions? Obviously the Gordons were kept very well informed. On the other hand, if this was the Earl Marischal's sister, would she be apt to lend herself to such a device?

The lady presumably recognised this indecision. "The Earl, my husband, awaits Your Highness in leal duty, a few miles outside Aberdeen," she added. "So that the Provost and magistrates may greet Your Grace to the city, suitably. And he has commanded our third son, Sir John, to humbly yield himself into your royal mercy and custody, after his foolish flight from ward at Edinburgh."

"Indeed! Then . . . I am glad to know it . . ."

The Earl James interrupted, less appreciatively. "Lord Huntly, told to bring no more than three hundred men to the Queen's presence, has, we are assured, brought five times that number, lady. Is this in leal duty?"

"Why yes, sir. The House of Gordon does not measure its loyalty in petty numbers! My husband's clansmen flock to show *their* duty. But he keeps them well outside the city. To which I am come to escort you, Highness."

"M'mmm."

The Queen allowed her natural trust to prevail. "Very well, Countess. You are my good Earl Marischal's sister, I understand, as well as my lord of Huntly's wife. We will visit our city of Aberdeen, assured of your goodwill and loyalty."

"That is well, Highness. And I personally will deliver my foolish son John into Your Grace's keeping."

With mixed feelings the royal party turned eastwards instead of continuing towards the north.

It was seventeen miles along the north bank of Dee, by Drum and Peterculter, to Aberdeen, and it was evening before they reached the city, the Countess describing all they passed, a confident and attentive guide, displaying no signs of unease, whatever some of the visitors might feel. The Queen got on well with her, although the Earl James remained stiffly hostile. At Peterculter, riders were sent spurring ahead to inform the city fathers of their approach.

So the Provost and magistrates were awaiting them, at the western gates, with a great concourse of the citizenry, with cheering and every sign of warm welcome, not at all what had been anticipated. The Queen was presented with the keys of the city, with laudatory speeches, and thereafter the Countess conducted them through crowded streets to the palatial Huntly town-house near the great harbour at the mouth of the Dee. Here a banquet was awaiting the royal entourage, whilst her escort was provided for nearby in Church properties of Greyfriars and Blackfriars. There was no sign of Huntly himself, although the Lord Gordon, his eldest son, a quiet and reserved youngish man, aided his mother as host.

The meal was half-over when a newcomer made an entry into the fine chamber – and an entry it was, the door at the dais end being thrown open and bowing servitors ushering in a notably handsome, brilliantly clad, supremely confident young man, who strolled forward smiling, two tall deerhounds at heel. He flourished an elaborate bow in the general direction of the Queen and waved to all around.

"My son John," the Countess murmured.

They all gazed. Nothing more unlike an escaped felon yielding himself up to justice was to be imagined.

He came up to the Queen's chair, and with an exaggerated genuflection, sank on one knee, to reach for and take the royal hand and kiss it, not once but many times. "Most beautiful princess and gracious lady," he declared, "your most humble, worshipping servant and admirer!" He had a voice to match his appearance. He still held the Queen's hand.

Mary was, of course, put in a very difficult position. She was sitting beside this young man's mother and brother, partaking of Gordon hospitality in a Gordon-dominated city, his father, in name, still Chancellor of her realm. And he was very good-looking. She did manage to withdraw her hand.

"Sir John," she said, "I have heard much of you. Too much, perhaps! This is not how I thought to see you!"

"No, lady? Then I must hope that you are not disappointed?"

123

"As to that, I must consider. But, rise up, Sir John." And she turned back to the table.

Not in the least abashed, he stood, grinning, and went to kiss his mother ostentatiously. She did not exactly frown at him but made a toning-down gesture, and waved him towards the far end of the dais-table.

But that was no place for Sir John Gordon. He went there, but only to pick up an empty chair and bring it to place just behind his mother and the Queen, and there sat, at ease.

Mary tried to ignore him, but found it difficult. Nearby, the Earl James glared. Further away, Thomas, between Flam and Beth, wondered what he could do to help in this peculiar situation.

William Maitland of Lethington, the Secretary of State, did more than wonder. He rose and went to the Gordon. "Sir John," he said crisply, "I would remind you that you are still under arrest, at the order of the Privy Council, of which I am secretary. You should not be sitting here. You are required to go deliver yourself to officers of the royal guard. And tomorrow to go, under escort, to ward in Stirling Castle – from which you will not abscond so easily as you did from Edinburgh's Tolbooth!"

"Of course, of course, sir – just as you say! That was my intention, I assure you. But you would not have me depart from Aberdeen without coming to pay my loyal respects and duty to our sovereign-lady? My Queen as well as yours, I'd remind you!"

"That you have done, then. Go, now." That was peremptory.

"*Now?* Who says that I must go now?" And Gordon looked at the Queen.

"I do!" That was the Countess.

"Ah, cruel, cruel mother!" But he rose, smiling, and bowed low, to her and to the Queen. "Are not women supposed to be kind?"

Lady Huntly waved him off, and the Queen did not turn. Still smiling, he strolled away to the door and out, the deer-hounds following dutifully.

"That is a dangerous man," Beth Beaton confided to Thomas. "But . . . very attractive!"

Soon thereafter the meal was over, and the Queen rather

124

promptly announced that she would seek her couch, a signal for all to break up.

On the way to his bedchamber, actually with Thomas Randolph, the English ambassador, with whom he was to share it, Thomas noted that Secretary Maitland was assiduously escorting Flam Fleming to hers, followed by Beth Beaton making faces.

The arrival of Huntly himself next forenoon was suitably dramatic. He appeared in front of his own town-house, with as many of his Gordon horsemen as he could crowd into the limited space, and there, under the faintly stirring Gordon boars'-heads banner, sat his mount, waiting. The Queen was quickly informed of his presence, and went to a window to look out.

He was a great bear of a man, massive, portly and red-faced, with greying hair and beard. He made no move, just sat there expressionless in front of his ranked supporters.

After a while, with Huntly looking as though he was prepared to wait there indefinitely, the Queen sent for the Countess. What was he doing, she wondered? What was *she* to do, in the circumstances?

Lady Huntly said that she thought that probably her husband was waiting for royal recognition, for Her Grace's invitation to come to her. After all, he had been more or less warned off, had he not?

Mary would not have that. She went out, to confront the uncrowned king of the north.

When Huntly saw her, he heaved himself heavily, awkwardly, out of the saddle, his corpulence very evident, and jerked his head. He was not so good at bowing as his son John.

"Salutations, Cousin!" he declared, thick-voiced. "Welcome to this my land."

Mary blinked at that. "Yours – or *mine*, my lord?"

"Both," he all but growled. "Yours, in name. Mine, in fact."

At least, here was plain speaking.

"You hold it *of* me, my lord – never forget it. And the Crown can forfeit. But . . . here is no way to greet each other. And I have been favoured with the hospitality of your house here."

"I come to take you to my house of Strathbogie. There you will taste of true hospitality. It is, I swear, the finest house in this kingdom."

125

"M'mm." Her councillors had been adamant: Strathbogie was to be avoided at all costs, palace though it was. "That may not be convenient, my lord."

"For whom the inconvenience? That forsword by-blow of your father's, who calls himself Prior of St Andrews? Or Earl of Mar as I now hear it? Who wants my Moray."

"*My* Moray, my lord. It is a royal earldom."

"Granted by your mother to me."

The Queen shook her head in some exasperation, so aware of the glowering ranks of mounted Gordons, listening. "We appear to be at odds always, my lord. I am sorry for it. But this kingdom has to be ruled, and by me. I have to consider all interests. To weigh and judge."

"And come down in favour of the accursed Protestants! You, of the true faith. Who wed the Most Christian King of France. And are niece of a cardinal!"

"I have to rule a mainly Protestant realm, sir."

"I can make it a Catholic realm again, for you, tomorrow!"

"By force of arms? That I will not have."

"Your mother was made of sterner stuff!"

"Perhaps. But this realm and people were not hers by birth, as they are mine. I must seek the good of the majority."

"Even when it is against God's word?"

Quite a group had gathered at the Queen's back, by now, including the Earl James, Argyll and Maitland, Thomas with them. An angry growl arose from the Protestant lords. Mary turned round in some agitation.

Her half-brother spoke up. "Enough of this talk! Your Grace is not here to listen to such. It is shameful and little less than treason, I say!"

There were cries of agreement. Somebody called out that Huntly should be arrested here and now – impracticable advice with the crowd of grim-faced Gordons there watching.

Lady Huntly came forward to the Queen's side, and eyed her husband levelly. "My lord, this is not the time, I think," she said. "I assured Her Grace that you would remain, with your men, outside the city. Would it not be best to return there, meantime?"

George Gordon put a hand up to cover his mouth, almost as though he was seeking to control his lips, as he stared at her heavily. For long moments there was silence, while their gazes locked. Then he inclined his head.

126

"Perhaps you are right, woman," he got out. And without another word or glance, turned back to his horse and laboriously hoisted himself up into the saddle. Reining round, he kicked his mount into movement, and his cohort sidled this way and that to give him passage. But, before they closed in behind him, he looked back.

"I shall look for you at Strathbogie!" he barked. That was all.

He left an astonished and exclamatory party there on his town-house doorstep.

Thereafter, of course, there was much discussion and conjecture as to the reason for the fierce and proud Gordon's sudden departure at his wife's behest, so out of character as it seemed. Flam later told Thomas that Maitland – who seemed much in her company these days – had said that the Earl Marischal had informed him that his sister had always claimed to have the second-sight, and was believed to consult with witches on occasion. Possibly her husband was superstitiously afraid of this, and deferred to his wife in consequence.

What to do now? The Queen and her advisers were in some disagreement as to procedure. Nearly all were still against any visit to Strathbogie, although Argyll and, strangely enough, Randolph the Englishman advocated it, as it would have the effect of gaining them time while they awaited their reinforcements. Also, a collection of royal cannon were there, lent by Marie of Guise to Huntly years before when she appointed him Lieutenant of the North; and these should now be recovered. But the Earl James was vehemently against it, as highly dangerous. They should press on at once to Moray, as had been earlier decided. And they should persuade Lady Huntly to come with them, since she seemed to have a restraining influence on her husband. Most agreed with that.

Mary herself, however, felt that she could scarcely hurry away from Aberdeen so quickly, after the kindly and loyal reception they had had from the citizens. The Provost had urged her to pay a visit to the ancient university, second in importance only to that of St Andrews. She claimed that this was the least that she could do. They would move on northwards tomorrow.

So the rest of the day was spent in a royal tour of the city's main features, not only the university but the Cathedral Church of St Machar, the almost equally renowned church of

St Nicholas, the Grammar School, William Wallace's House, the Brig o' Balgownie, which Robert Bruce had had built over Don, and other landmarks – the Earl James fretting the while.

Next morning, with still no word of their armed host – which of course would be largely unhorsed and therefore able to travel only slowly – they set off. It was now 6th September. Lady Huntly agreed to accompany them for some of the way – although she also urged that they visit Strathbogie.

They rode up the wide and picturesque valley of the Don for many a mile – and saw no sign of Huntly himself or his fifteen hundred, although no doubt he was not far away and keeping an eye on them. The country being fertile and attractive, green rolling hills of no great height save for the dominant and shapely peaks of Bennachie, new territory to most there, the fear of being intercepted by the Gordons gradually died away and appreciation could develop. The Countess was an able and informative guide. They left Don at Inverurie, to follow the River Urie northwards, passing many fine castles, properties, ancient churches and a great wealth of stone circles and Pictish remains, reaching Rothiemay by evening, a long but rewarding ride of some forty-five miles.

Gordon of Rothiemay was distinctly surprised and less than enthusiastic about putting up the Queen and her close associates in his house – the rest, including Thomas, had to camp where they could – which was scarcely to be wondered at which the palace of Strathbogie only four miles away. In view of the lack of accommodation, Lady Huntly, who was not going to accompany them further, did persuade three or four of the party to go with her to Strathbogie, and Argyll and Randolph did so. They came back next forenoon, Randolph at least loud in his praise of the hospitality and magnificence, and Huntly's conduct.

Mary was very much confused in her mind over the entire question of George Gordon.

They made a short day of it after a late start, going only as far as the Grange of Strathisla, where there was ample accommodation in the priory farm and monastic purlieus formerly belonging to the Abbey of Kinloss.

They were in Banffshire here but shortly left it for Moray, the Earl James now eager to get to Darnaway, the main seat of the earldom. So, although this was supposed to be a royal progress, the Queen showing herself to her subjects rather than just a lengthy journey, they did not delay long in the walled city of Elgin, the principal town of Moray, promising to come back on their return southwards.

They had crossed innumerable rivers, some of them large, in their valleys, flowing eastwards from the Highland mountains, including the Ythan, the Deveron, the Isla, the great Spey, the Lossie and the rest, passable fords a recurrent problem. They now crossed the swift-running, peat-stained Findhorn near Forres, with Darnaway amongst its forests at last before them.

This important castle had once been mighty but was now, they found, sadly declined and neglected, indeed part ruinous. James Stewart was furious. Was this not a royal earldom, and the upkeep of its main seat an elementary duty? Huntly must be made to pay for this!

They camped in and around that sorry establishment for a couple of days, the Queen going to visit the towns of Forres and Kinloss and Nairn. Also the famed castle of Cawdor, whose Thane, Mary was surprised to learn, was now a Campbell, kin to Argyll; how that came about was recited to her gleefully – but not by Argyll or in his hearing.

The second day, there was news at last of their armed host – but scarcely the tidings they had anticipated. It had, in fact, been attacked, soon after crossing Dee, and by none other than Sir John Gordon, who, instead of going to immure himself in Stirling, had eluded his escort and hurried home, to round up a large band of Gordons from his own properties, over one thousand it was said. They had been beaten off, apparently, but there were quite heavy casualties on both sides, and considerable delay.

The anger of the royal company was scarcely to be wondered at. A Privy Council meeting was convened there and then, at which the Gordon was declared guilty of treason, outlawed, and his properties forfeit to the Crown, every effort to be made to apprehend him. At the same time, taking his opportunity, the Earl James declared the failure of the Earl of Huntly in the matter of this Darnaway, plus his other misdeeds, and pronounced him unfit to hold the royal earldom of Moray, and sought formal transfer of that earldom to himself, James Stewart, as promised. None there contested it, and the Queen, so advised, agreed to sign the papers, at the same time transferring the earldom of Mar to the Lord Erskine, James's uncle.

There was some question whether to turn back now, to link up with their oncoming host and thereafter seek to deal with Sir John Gordon; or to proceed on to Inverness as intended. The Queen expressed herself strongly as in favour of the latter course, and her brother, having got what he wanted, backed her. So a move was made, westwards now, with messengers sent back to the royal army with orders to move to take over the castles of Findlater and Auchindoune, held by Sir John Gordon, as now forfeited. It was 13th September.

The approach to Inverness, accepted capital of the Highlands as seat of the ancient Pictish High Kings of Alba, excited the Queen. At the head of its extension of the great Moray Firth, and where the River Ness reached salt water, the mountains guarding it on three sides, its setting delighted. But delight was changed quite quickly to wrath and indignation when, arriving at the royal castle on its steep escarpment above the town, they found the gates shut against them and admission refused. Angry shouts that this was the Queen's Grace herself only produced from the captain of the fortress that he opened to no one save on the direct orders of the Earl of Huntly, Lieutenant of the North, or of his son the Lord Gordon, governor of this place. Fury had no bounds amongst the lords, and Mary was much upset. Since Huntly was still presumably at Strathbogie and the Lord Gordon, his eldest son, known to be down at his father-in-law's house of Châtelherault in Lanarkshire, there seemed to be no answer to the situation.

They retired down to the town, where the Provost and magistrates, with different ideas as to loyalty, were greatly concerned, and found quarters for the royal party, the Provost himself going up thereafter to the castle to plead with the captain, but to no avail.

It was Thomas who, that evening, taking a walk with Flam and Beth round the town, was struck by what he saw as a weakness in the fortress's defence. The place was set high on its rocky spine above the river, in a strong position, yes, and the approaches from all other sides effectively guarded by high curtain walls, flanking towers and bastions. But at the northern, river, side, there was a stretch of less high walling and no parapet-walk apparently, no doubt because of the steep rocky climb here and the impossibility of bringing cannon-fire to bear on it at that angle. Thomas, with some experience, as

a Borderer, of assailing castles and towers without artillery
– he had been at the taking of the English castles of Wark
and Norham three years before – believed that he could get
himself and his Kerrs into this one.

Back at the royal quarters, he put the matter to the Queen,
who, at first doubtful, presently, with the approval of the Earl
James and Maitland, agreed to the attempt being made –
if Thomas was careful, careful. Promising extreme caution,
he declared that all he needed was ropes and hooks: thick
ropes and strong hooks. They would make the attempt that
very night, in the small hours. According to the Provost, the
captain there had no more than a score of men to keep the
place.

There were plenty of stout ropes to be found down at the
harbour, some already attached to anchors, which would serve
as hooks, although only the smaller crafts' and fishing-boats'
anchors would be light enough. Knots were tied in the ropes
at eighteen-inch intervals and the hooks firmly secured. As
word of the attempt got round, Thomas found that his Kerrs
were to be added to by many enthusiastic volunteers; but
too large a party would be to risk discovery, and he was
prejudiced in favour of his moss-troopers and their ability to
scale those rocky heights skilfully and quietly. Forty men, no
more, would serve.

In the event, the Queen and her Marys waited up to see
the assault-party off, with a variety of encouragements, good
wishes and pleadings not to do anything risky, not entirely
practical advice. Thomas drew the line at having a group of
them coming to watch at the rock-foot.

At two hours after midnight they set off quietly through the
deserted streets, with their ropes and tackle; also, of course,
their swords and dirks. It was a dark, moonless night, and
no lights showed up at the castle.

Eyes quickly becoming accustomed to the gloom, they
found their way to the foot of the rock slope, steep but
not actually precipitous. There Thomas held a whispered ·
conference. There was, he reckoned, about one hundred feet
in length of the lower walling, up there, no more than twenty
feet in height. They must scale this slope as silently as they
could, keeping the anchors from clanking on stone, then
spread out along the wall-foot. When all were in position,
he would whistle a signal, like a night-bird's call. Then, as

nearly together as possible, their hooks were to be thrown up, ropes attached. This would be the difficult part, both to toss the things high enough to get over the wall, and then to grip beyond. Some undoubtedly would have to be pulled back and thrown again. And this could not be done without noise, iron on stone. So speed was of the essence. Just as soon as a hook, tugged on its rope, held, men were to climb up, the knots serving as ladder-rungs. Behind that wall-head how deep a drop there might be he could not tell them. They might have to use their ropes in reverse, jerk loose the hooks, haul them up and anchor them again on the wall-top. Then wait at the bottom until all were assembled. All to be done as swiftly and silently as possible. Was it understood?

Impatient to be off, men asked no questions. The climb began.

It was not difficult, although the thick ropes and heavy iron were no help. Thomas did not have to wait long to give his whistle, up at the wall-foot.

Thereafter it seemed to him as though his instructions as to silence were ignored quite, such a clattering and clanking and muffled cursing followed, as ropes fell short and iron landed on rock, even a yelp resounding, no doubt as one of the hooks hit an unsuccessful thrower. Thomas's own rope, for that matter, did not grip at first try and made its quota of noise. The second attempt did hold, however, and after a reassuring tug, up he went, hand-over-hand, others doing the same around him.

Panting, on the wall-head, he found satisfaction in that the drop on the other side was no more than eight feet or so, thanks to a buttressing platform. Some of his men were already down on it. Getting to his knees, he turned and lowered himself carefully, clinging to the wall's edge, and dropped.

There proved to be another helpful circumstance. It could be seen now that there was quite a wide open space within the walling before the loom of any buildings, caused, they discovered, by the very uneven and bare rocky surface of the hilltop, this discouraging mason-work — which meant that the garrison would be the less likely to hear any noise from here. No lights showed, there were no signs of stirring.

His party in tight grip, Thomas led the way towards the buildings. Any guards on duty would be apt to be at the gatehouse towers. He detached ten of his men to go and seek

132

to deal with these. Where would be the barracks? Chimneys? At this hour, fires would not be burning, but there could be the smell of wood-smoke from smouldering embers.

They found the barrack block otherwise – by snoring coming from an open doorway. Moving quietly in, it was almost too easy. None of the occupants was awake. Thomas whispered for no unnecessary killing, and signed his people forward, dirks drawn. He waited only long enough to assure himself that the dozen sleepers, rudely roused with cold steel at their throats, made no trouble or outcry, left a score of his men to tie them up, and with his remaining ten went in search of the captain and any officers.

The smell of smoke did help this time, leading them to a nearby angle-tower. Here the door was shut, but it opened without difficulty or noise, and they tiptoed up the turnpike stair after ensuring that the vaulted basement was empty. The first-floor chamber proved to be empty also, living quarters, where the remains of a fire still glowed. They went higher.

On the second floor, the door creaked slightly as they opened it, and, as Thomas entered first, it was to see a large bed and movement thereon – and it was not so dark as to hide the fact that it was a woman who sat up, naked. He was about to mutter some sort of apology when the lady emitted a cry, and at her side a man grunted and half-rose, to peer, blinking. Gleefully the Kerrs pushed past and in, to take charge of these two. Thomas himself, however, hurried on alone further up the stairs to the remaining storey of the tower – but found only another empty room.

It turned out that the man below was indeed the castle's captain, one Alexander Gordon; whether the lady was his wife or otherwise they did not enquire. It seemed moreover that the fortress was now theirs, however simply gained, for the gate-house party came back with two prisoners, one slightly wounded, the only casualty, save in feelings, of the entire operation, no other premises producing any occupants. Seldom can a fortress have been stormed so bloodlessly and so quickly.

Leaving most of his party to keep the place and guard the prisoners – and ordering them to respect the woman – Thomas took the captain, wrists bound, emerged through the great gateway, the portcullis specially raised and the drawbridge lowered for them, and proceeded in modest triumph down into the town.

He was received with rousing acclaim, the Queen declaring that he deserved a second knighthood, the Marys kissing him and even the Earl James commending him briefly. It was all somewhat embarrassing.

Thomas could have had a compliant bedfellow that night, had he been so inclined.

The Queen went to visit the Priory of Beauly, ten miles along the north shore of the firth, one of the most renowned in the Highlands, and there met the young Lord Lovat, chief of a branch of the Frasers, hitherto allied to the Gordons. He was clearly impressed, and it was to be hoped would thereafter transfer his support to his attractive monarch.

On their return to Inverness, they discovered that the Earl James and the other lords had been otherwise engaged. The body of the captain, Alexander Gordon, now hung from a gallows erected before his castle gate. The Queen was much distressed, as indeed was Thomas, whose bloodless victory was now spoiled.

The day following, the royal party left Inverness, to retrace its steps to Elgin, where they would lodge in the sumptuous palace of the Bishop of Moray, Patrick Hepburn, uncle of Bothwell, and alleged to be the most dissolute prelate in the land, the Earl James wondering righteously how he might unseat him.

8

Back in Aberdeen, decision fell to be taken by the Queen and her Council, important and challenging decision. The Gordon situation was anything but resolved. The royal armed host had at last reached them, and indeed just in time for, returning southwards when they arrived at Spey near Fochabers, they had found a Gordon force of fully one thousand waiting for them at the far side of the ford. Placing themselves there, and that number, the assumption was that they had intended to contest the crossing, and possibly capture the Queen, presumably unaware that her party had been so notably strengthened to no less than three thousand. Perceiving this, they had drawn off and disappeared into the hills, and the fording of the great river had been accomplished. Presumably also, this had been Sir John Gordon's men, the same who had attacked at Dee; but it could have been Huntly himself, as the Earl James proclaimed – although Thomas for one would have expected the Earl to have been better informed about large numbers in his territories. Auchindoune Castle, Sir John's main seat, was only some fifteen miles away, so a move was made thither, amongst the low hills. But they had found no force there, only a small garrison, so they were able largely to destroy the place, a square massive keep in a square courtyard, before resuming their journey southwards.

So, at Aberdeen, decision. The Queen was for moving on, back to Stirling or Edinburgh, avoiding further trouble. But her Council was all but unanimously against this. It would be as good as surrendering all the north to Huntly, it was claimed; more than that, perhaps encouraging counter-revolution in the entire kingdom against the Protestant regime. The Highlands were insufficiently trustworthy as it was; this could be to invite civil war. The Gordons must be shown who ruled in Scotland. And this was best done, at this stage, by passing sentence of outlawry on the father as they had already done on the son. And to remain at Aberdeen meantime.

Reluctant as the young monarch was to agree to this, she felt that she could not go against the advice of almost her entire Privy Council.

So letters of horning, as the outlawry proceedings were called, were drawn up and signed, a copy being sent to Strathbogie.

They did not have long to wait for a reaction. First of all, Lady Huntly arrived alone at Aberdeen, but was turned back by the lords, recognising the danger of that persuasive lady being able to influence the Queen unduly. She was sent away. Then, only a few days later, scouts informed that Huntly and his son had set out southwards from Strathbogie at the head of a large armed force, thousands strong. So he had been gathering his strength whilst his wife made her effort.

It was to be confrontation, which the Queen had dreaded all along.

Commands were sent out for all loyal men to rally to the royal banner. The Earl Marischal was sent for, from Dunottar, to perform his duties in the field.

There were conflicting views as to procedure: to go to meet the Gordons head-on, or to await them in the Aberdeen vicinity, allowing them to make the first hostile moves. The Queen was for the latter; after all, she pointed out, there was no certainty that Huntly intended actual warfare; he might only be showing his strength. The Earl James, however, was in favour of taking the initiative, going to attack. And he was strongly supported by two important nobles who had come with the reinforcements – the Earls of Morton and Atholl, the former a tough and aggressive character indeed.

Not mary of the Aberdeenshire clansmen appeared to be anxious to demonstrate their loyalty; indeed the word was that such of them as were on the move, Forbes, Leslies, Grants, Frasers and the like, were more likely to attach themselves to Huntly, the Cock o' the North as he was known locally, than to the Queen's force, although some might well hang back to see which side looked likely to win.

This waiting period ended on 27th October when, in the evening, scouts came to inform that Huntly's array, mixed cavalry and foot, had crossed from Donside to Deeside, well west of Aberdeen, and had taken up a strong position on the Hill of Fare, north of Banchory, some fifteen miles west of the city. Whether they were just camping there for the night, or to make it their strongpoint, was not to be known.

In the royal camp, all was mustering and marshalling.

The morning brought word that the Gordons were still at Hill of Fare. Moreover, quite a large force of the local clans had materialised out of the hilly country between the great rivers and was now also converging on this Fare area, and almost certainly not to *attack* Huntly.

The Earl James and Morton now had their way. They would advance westwards with all their strength, and if possible seek to come between Huntly and his probable allies. The Queen was advised to remain in Aberdeen, but she refused to do this. When her powerful subjects were to be locked in any kind of struggle, she desired to be present, to seek to be an influence for restraint and the right.

So almost all the court followed on behind the armed host, Thomas and his Kerrs acting as a sort of bodyguard.

They marched up Dee to Peterculter and then, under local guidance, turned up the Gormack Burn, north by west, the heights of the Hill of Fare soon in sight ahead, perhaps six miles off.

This Fare, it seemed, was not so much a hill as an isolated range, of no great height but a commanding feature. There proved to be at least eight distinguishable summits, the highest to the north and west, all but enclosing a wide, kidney-shaped amphitheatre or central hollow, in which was a mire, a swamp, out of which ran southwards the Burn of Corrichie, the whole covering perhaps four miles by three. Just where Huntly was based in it all was unclear, but there could be many strong positions therein.

As they drew near, scouts came back to inform them. There were two distinct bodies of men in the hill area, both large, one high in the upper reaches of the great corrie or hollow, the other down in the low ground where the Corrichie Burn spilled out of the said corrie's mire, these last mainly foot, whereas there was much cavalry higher. So the former would probably be Huntly's main force, waiting on the high ground, and the latter his allies of Leslies, Forbes, Fraser and the rest.

A leadership group of earls and lords rode forward to a lofty viewpoint to survey the ground, as far as possible, Morton, a Douglas and a trained soldier, insistent on tactics. The others waited.

When the leaders came back they were agreed as to procedure, as much as the situation would allow, although conditions could change. So much would depend on Huntly's strategy. If he remained up there near the hilltop, there was not much that they could do to assail him, with any hope of success. But the fact that his secondary force of allies was down there below in the corrie-mouth, a good mile away, was surely significant. Almost certainly the wily Gordon would be using them as a sort of bait for a trap. For nothing was surer than that *they* would not successfully attack any royal army further up, especially with the wet miry ground in the foot of the corrie intervening. So Huntly's plan would likely be that this, the vulnerable grouping, should draw the assault of the Queen's force first, and while that was preoccupying them the Gordon cavalry would charge downhill upon them and overwhelm by sheer impetus. It seemed a reasonable hypothesis, and none could think of other.

So their course surely, now, was to seem to be enticed by this, and to bring Huntly down. But in fact to spring their own trap. Send some part of their strength, mainly foot and the least effective troops, five or six hundred of them perhaps, to go and put in an attack on the Forbes, Leslies and the like, while their main mounted host turned and rode due northwards, uphill, this side of a spine which ran down from the most easterly prominent hill, called, they were told, the Meikle Tap. This spine or shoulder ought to hide them from Huntly's force in the top of the corrie, at least until they were at a similar level. Then, if and when the Gordons charged down, they would be in a position to cross over and to do the same, at an angle, and so take the enemy at major disadvantage, in mid-descent, when it would be all but impossible for them to halt, turn and seek to meet this flank attack. This clearly was Morton's device, and commended itself to practically all – save for those who were destined to go and do the fighting down below the corrie.

The Earl Marischal, therefore, had to do considerable marshalling, dividing the sheep, as it were, from the goats, holding back a rearguard in case of need to change tactics, and arranging for the Queen to be safe, whatever happened, and able, if possible, to view the scene of operations.

Thomas himself had a marshalling of his own to consider. His impulse was to go with the horsed host uphill for the charge; but a part of his mind said that perhaps he ought to go with the downhill group, who undoubtedly were being allotted the most dangerous and least dramatic part of the action; while a third course was to remain with the Queen, for her protection, even though this might seem to be shrinking from the battle, lack of spirit. But, after all, he was only here on this entire expedition on the royal invitation and because of his loyal affection for her – and, to be sure, her Marys. For most of the others there it would not have troubled him not to see again. So be it, then – he and his moss-troopers would guard the monarch. This turned out to be the royal command anyway, so his debate with himself had not been necessary.

Local guides they had picked up at Banchory said that there was a flat-topped hillock called Tornadearc, the Berry Hill, overlooking the mouth of the corrie where the Corrichie Burn ran out, well above where Huntly's allies' force was said to be assembled. If anything went wrong, Her Grace would there be in a position to retire swiftly back and downhill to Banchory and safety.

The dispersal began.

At first the Queen's small party went with the Earls of Atholl and Argyll, who led the low-ground force, south by west now. But after a mile or so their guides turned them off, right-handed, to climb a modest hill with the promised flat summit, this Tornadearc; on that, admittedly, they would be in full view of Huntly's host at the head of the corrie; but so, quite soon, would be those they were leaving – indeed this was part of the strategy. With mixed feelings, they wished the others good fortune, and parted.

At the summit of the hill it was seen that this was certainly an excellent viewpoint, with the entire amphitheatre area spread before them. They could see both of the enemy forces – if enemy they were to be called – on the low and high ground. Also the force they had just left, approaching the defile and valley of the Corrichie Burn, where the mixed clans were. They could not, however, see their own main cavalry array, climbing behind that shoulder of the Meikle Tap.

The Queen and her party dismounted, to wait, excited, apprehensive. It seemed as though they might be going to watch a battle, although the ladies hoped that this still might be avoided. Thomas was less sanguine. It was a strange situation to be in, inactive spectators of major drama.

They had not long to wait for the first signs of action. High up there above the corrie they saw quite a large body of horsemen suddenly detach themselves from the main mass of Huntly's force and spur off eastwards, not downhill but approximately at the same level, banner at head. Thomas pointed.

"I fear that means our cavalry has been seen, reported. Behind the ridge. These will be going to head them off. And that banner – it must be one of the leaders. Not Huntly himself, for his main host remains. Sir John Gordon, possibly . . ."

"Will this make ruin of the Lord Morton's plan?" That was David Rizzio, the secretary.

"It could spoil it, yes. But surely they will have considered this possibility? Have some other plan . . ."

"Perhaps it will only be to parley?" the Queen said hopefully.

The men said nothing.

Unfortunately, because of the contours of the hill, they could not see what went on once the Gordon group crossed that shoulder. And soon their attentions were elsewhere anyway, for their low-ground force had reached the burn valley, and there delayed nothing in assault. It was prompt and furious fighting, there in the confines of the Corrichie glen, a constricted battlefield indeed. Argyll and Atholl were not going to be outdone by Moray and Morton and the rest. So all hopes of a peaceful solution were banished.

From their hilltop, all seemed to be chaos down there, a wild and close-packed mêlée; impossible to tell how the struggle went, even to distinguish friend from foe. Faintly the noise of it all came up to them, savage, however distant and indistinct.

The Queen wrung her hands and Flam gripped Thomas's arm. Never had the women seen anything like this, their viewing of martial struggles hitherto confined to tournaments.

But even so there was distraction for the onlookers. The poet Chastelard yelled and gestured, right-handed. Up there at the corrie-head, Huntly's main mounted array was on the move, and in spectacular fashion, banners flying. Straight downhill the Gordon host thundered in headlong career, a dire but eye-rivetting sight.

That charge had the best part of a mile to cover, in fairly steep gradient, to reach the lower battle; but once it did, the impact would be appalling, overwhelming, its momentum able to sweep through and aside friend and foe alike, irresistible. Fascinated, in a sort of dread, the watchers stared.

There was, however, that green, treacherous bog and mire in the corrie-floor. The Gordons would know well about this, but it still had to be got around or avoided to reach the battleground. Thomas, after the first few moments, switched his gaze between that and the shoulder of the Meikle Tap. Where was the Earl James and the rest? Had the Gordon diversion succeeded in spoiling their strategy?

"What will they do? Those in the battle? In the valley?" Flam cried. "Our people – Atholl's and Argyll's men? When that, when that . . ."

"Oh, the good God help them!" the Queen prayed.

Thomas, his glance back to the valley, shook his head. "They knew the plan. They will be hoping for interception first. If not, they will have to try to withdraw, I think, to extract themselves from the fighting, pull back . . ."

"See – they divide! *Ma foi* – they divide!" That was Rizzio, not referring to the low-ground battlers but to the downward-charging Gordon horse.

All eyes thither now, they saw Huntly's hurtling host splitting into two, clearly to circle either side of the green swamp. It was a reasonable expedient. Moreover, if they did not attempt to rejoin thereafter, they would descend on the battle on two fronts, left and right. Which could well be the more effective.

It was Beth Beaton who changed the direction of their gazing. "Look! Look! They come!" she cried. "At last!"

All eyes turned north-eastwards. There, over the shoulder of the hill, lower down than the watchers had anticipated, horsemen appeared, many horsemen, in compact troops – and assuredly these were not Gordons. On and on more and more came, riding hard.

In agitation and concern the onlookers exclaimed. What had happened? Were they too late? What would they do? What had happened over there?

What they did was to slant across the slope of that hollow at an angle, to bear down on the left-hand Gordon charge. For whatever reason, the newcomers had left it almost too late, indeed. Had it not been that the level floor of the corrie widened, and even beyond the actual mire was less than firm ground, so slowing the enemy descent just a little, the Gordon horsemen would have been past it and hurtling, on either side of the burn, down into the glen. But that so slight lessening of pace, and the spreading-out on the softer terrain, had two effects. It gave the royal riders that little more time; but more important, it allowed Huntly's people to perceive the threat coming in on their flank, and this was in fact not to their advantage. For many of them saw it as the major menace, as to some extent it was, to be met and repelled, and so sought to rein round to face and meet the attack head-on, not in flank. But not all, some driving on, leadership less than evident. So there was a further splitting of force and some confusion, all at the speed of racing, pounding horseflesh. And, of course, half of Huntly's force was already four hundred yards away, at the other side of the corrie.

The royalist charge therefore was more successful than it deserved to be, with so much suddenly in its favour. Down on only perhaps one-quarter of the Gordon host it swept, and these somewhat scattered and in no effective formation, were crashed through, bowled over, unhorsed or otherwise rendered inadequate, in a matter of mere moments. And some of those who had plunged on, perceiving what was happening at their backs, sought to turn round; others elected to try to rejoin their fellows at the other side of the mire; and some charged on downhill. It was sheer chaos now.

Significantly, the Earl of Huntly himself was on this eastern side, and found himself all but isolated, save for his banner-bearer, who clung close, a general abruptly deprived of his command.

The Earl, when he managed to rein up, sat his horse as though stunned, bewildered. Then, as his standard-bearer saw their enemies coming directly for him, and his lord sitting there inactive, pulled over, grabbed the Earl's reins, and jerking his mount round, kicked both beasts into urgent motion, away. And he headed, not on down, nor back, but over towards their partners across the corrie. That is, into the skirts of the mire.

Only a few yards into the green treachery, the Earl's horse sank hock-deep, stumbled, and out of the saddle pitched the heavy, corpulent person of George Gordon, to crash to the soggy ground and lie still.

All this the watchers could see from their viewpoint. What they could not see was that the Cock o' the North was in fact dead, his heart given out on him.

After that, although it was difficult to make out any detailed sequence of events, the general development of the battle was fairly obvious. The Gordons on the west side of the mire, seeing their opposite numbers in dire trouble, instead of plunging on down into the lower conflict, swung round to cross the stream below the corrie and come to the aid of their fellows. This put them lower down than the royalist horsemen, and so in a less advantageous position. Their own fleeing colleagues bearing down upon them there did not help; and they were of course outnumbered now. When Moray's and Morton's men came charging down, they were swept aside, and although most fought bravely enough, they could not prevail. In almost less time than it takes to tell, these also were no longer a fighting force, only dead, injured and fleeing individuals.

Now the Queen's cavalry host re-formed in some fashion, to hurl themselves downhill to the aid of their friends in the ongoing battle in the glen below.

The effect of their massive and headlong intervention, of course, was predictable, a swift ending of the struggle, the Gordon allies left in no doubt that the day was lost and that they should be elsewhere. From Tornadearc, the watchers saw enough to recognise that all was over, save for a sort of mopping up. Great was the relief and thankfulness.

A move was made down towards the battlefield, little as the Queen and her ladies wished to view the scene of carnage at close quarters. However, they met the Earl James coming up to inform them. All was well, that unemotional man announced without any visible signs of triumph. Huntly was dead, seemingly of heart failure, too fat a man for battle. They had captured Sir John Gordon and his brother Adam, who had led a flank attack over yonder ridge of hill, which they had countered and broken up. The Gordon menace and possible revolt in the north, therefore, could now be esteemed as over. He advised his sister briefly that she should return to Aberdeen while the light lasted.

In a mood of gratitude mixed with some doubts and a kind of sorrow also, the royal party left that fatal area and headed eastwards for the city.

*

It was two days later that Queen Mary's feelings of doubt and sorrow over the Gordon debacle were honed into something more intense and searing. The Privy Council had met, and decided that Sir John Gordon and his brother Adam must be executed. She had been against this, vehemently, but they had been insistent – and of course Sir John had very much earned that fate, in the laws of the land, in attacking in arms the Queen's forces, breaking out of royal custody, announcing that he intended to marry Her Grace, even boasting here in Aberdeen that she would be well advised to wed him, not behead him. She had managed to persuade them to reprieve Adam, on account of his youth and inexperience – he was only seventeen years – but about his brother they were adamant.

That was not all the Council's decisions, to be sure. Aberdeen and all the north was to be made aware of the cost of treasonable revolt. Many of the dead were brought from Corrichie and their corpses set up on prominent positions in the town. Huntly himself was publicly disembowelled outside the Tolbooth. Prisoners and wounded were marched through the streets and herded in the burying-ground of St Nicholas's Church. And the victorious forces thereafter made their own impact on the city.

So that forenoon, all was astir in Aberdeen. John Gordon was to pay the price, before all, in the public place of Broadgate, suitably right in front of the Provost's House, where the Queen was presently lodging – some declared to his everlasting damnation, others merely to face his Maker. The streets around had been thronged for hours, even the house roofs being utilised as viewpoints. Such as this had never before been seen in all the north.

Only the Lady Fleming did duty with the Queen, in that first-floor chamber of the Provost's House that morning, for there was insufficient room for many, and certain lords must be there. Thomas and the Marys found a stance on steps outside. The crowd was noisy enough to drown even the screaming of the gulls which always haunted the nearby fish-market.

But the gulls prevailed presently, when the window of that first-floor room was flung open and two men in black appeared therein, one the Earl James, who always dressed soberly, the other in the Geneva gown and white bands of the Kirk, the minister of St Nicholas's Church. James Stewart raised a commanding hand, and gradually all but the birds fell silent.

This quiet let all hear the clatter of hooves on cobbles, none so far off.

"Let us worship Almighty God," coldly level but penetrating, Moray's voice proclaimed. "Let us glorify His name and thank Him for His grace towards us, His elect. We seek His blessing on what is done this day, for the furtherance of His rule and worship of this *His* kingdom of Scotland!"

Silence.

The minister took over. In a very different voice, sonorous, powerful, carrying, but as stern as the other, he launched forth, whether addressing his Creator or merely his fellow-men was not quite clear. He thundered on about the just and inevitable downfall on earth and everlasting and excruciating punishment elsewhere of all idolators, recusants, papists and defiers and defilers of the Word, this at some length. The crowd began to stir and murmur, until, behind the two men at the open window, the Queen moved into view.

She was dressed today all in white, and looking sadly beautiful. In her hand she held a black crucifix.

Then, the hoofbeats growing loud, the minister drew to a close. Into the Broadgate, forcing a way through the crowd with the flats of swords, rode a dozen armed men, amongst them, very much unarmed, John Gordon of Findlater and Auchindoune.

The scene was extraordinary in more than it being the first time a prominent Gordon had come thus through the streets of Aberdeen, bound with ropes and set on a mean garron of a horse. It was the man himself who held all eyes, head held high, proudly, splendid fair hair falling to wide shoulders, looking straight ahead of him with a sort of humorous disdain, his bearing as though he was bound for a triumph. And handsome, brilliantly handsome. From all around there was exclamation, and acclaim in the main rather than cursing and menace.

The escort rode up with the prisoner to the timber scaffold and its block, set so directly before that window of the Provost's House. Without waiting for aid in dismounting, Gordon threw a leg over the bare back of his garron and leapt lightly, agilely, despite bound arms, from beast to platform. He strolled over to inspect that ominous block, shook his head over it, and then turned to bow towards the Queen's window.

A newcomer appeared, to mount the platform, a hulking

figure with a large axe over his shoulder, unease in every line of him. Sir John greeted him, casually.

There was movement at the window. The minister stepped back, Moray turned, and the Earl of Morton, all but pushing the Queen in front of him, moved forward. The crowd fell silent again.

For long moments monarch and captive stared at each other. It was the woman whose glance fell – to the cross in her hand. Gordon was about to speak out.

The Earl James made a swift cutting motion of his hand, to stop him. It was Morton whose voice rose, loudly. "John Gordon," he bellowed, "ye are condemned to die a traitor's death. Ye have taken up arms against your Queen and her Council. Ye have broken ward, slain the Queen's servants and been put to the horn. Ye now meet your just doom – to the rejoice of all true men!"

Gordon did not so much as raise an eyebrow.

"Have ye nothing to say?" Morton cried.

"Not to such as you!" the other returned, clear-voiced. And then, in a changed tone, "Madam, your true lover stands here before you now, at last. And to say his farewell." He spoke it quietly but distinctly so that none failed to hear him. "I have loved you well, and could have loved you still better. But . . . methinks you make but a cruel mistress!"

Something like a growl rose from many in the crowd. Moray and Morton exchanged glances. The Queen answered no word, although she bit her lip.

"You are the loveliest amongst women, Madam – but your heart, I think, is of stone! I embrace death now, as the warmer lover!"

Mary, bosom heaving, clutched that crucifix and shut her eyes.

"I have cared nothing for throne and honours, Your Grace – empty words! It is for men – and women – that I care. But . . . perhaps you are only a Queen and no woman?"

The noise in the street grew greater. Fists were shaken – and towards that window rather than at the scaffold. A seething began amongst the densely packed mass. John Gordon smiled.

The Earl James frowned. This was going too far obviously – there could be danger in it. "Enough!" he jerked. And to the executioner. "To your duty, man!"

"I salute you, Highness, and bid you adieu," the Gordon

146

said, apparently unperturbed. "Who knows, perhaps we may meet again elsewhere . . . without benefit of Reformers!"

The headsman tapped him on the shoulder.

Sir John bowed again to the window, as deeply as he could with hands tied behind his back. Turning, he knelt, and after a brief pause, laid his head on the block, without fuss.

Something like a corporate sigh arose from all around.

The executioner ran a thumb along the edge of his axe, grinning his embarrassment. He raised his weapon.

"Tut, man – the other way round," Moray called into the hush. "Have him facing here."

Almost a shudder ran through the crowd.

Blinking, the headsman lowered his axe and jogged Gordon's shoulder with his knee.

That man rose awkwardly to his feet, he whose movements were so seldom awkward, and turned to face that window, features set now. He stared for a moment, then knelt once again.

The Queen could be seen to be sobbing, soundlessly.

Raising his head from the block, Sir John saw that her arm was now outstretched. She held the crucifix out towards him, urgently.

A sudden smile came to soften that set handsome countenance. He sank his head, and the axe fell.

A whimper swelled from the street, swelled to a wail, rose and sank again.

But it was a bungled beheading. The axe was sharp enough, but the executioner was either inexpert or nervous, and his first stroke inaccurate. The second was little better. At the third the crowd was yelling, and the Earl James was having to hold up his sister who appeared to have half-fainted away to semi-consciousness.

Thomas Kerr hoped that John Gordon had reached *fullest* unconsciousness at that first bungled stroke, and declared it so to the Marys, whatever it looked like. None of them was looking, anyway.

The crowd was now in a strange and unpredictable mood, and Thomas was quick to escort his charges away, waving to his moss-troopers to come and guard them. The girls, however upset, wanted to get back to their mistress as soon as possible, for she would be needing them. They blamed the Earl James loudly for making her go through this dreadful ordeal. She had not wanted to, they said, had pleaded not, but he had declared that it was her royal duty as monarch, treason to be seen by all to attract the Crown's direst displeasure. Thomas rather wondered about treason, and who decided what was so.

After that day's doings, few desired to remain longer in Aberdeen, certainly not Mary Stewart. Two days later the royal train set off for the south.

9

Thomas returned home, after an absence of over three months, to sundry developments, mostly satisfactory. He found himself delighted to see Janet again, her welcome warm and sincere – and her personal news joyful: she was pregnant, and was sure that she was going to present him with a son in due course. His mother and the rest of the family were getting on with the improvements to Jedburgh Castle; and the house that he was building for the Queen, in the town, was progressing well, what he had planned on paper beginning to look as he had visual-ised. A great deal of work, and the making of many decisions, had accumulated for him as Provost of Jedburgh and Baron of Ferniehirst, Oxnam, Crailing, Hounam and Smailholm, and more as chief of the Kerrs. And there had been another raid by the Northumbrians over the Border and Sir Walter Ker of Cessford, the new Warden, was requiring his help in making representations, and threats of counter-measures, to the English Warden.

Amidst all this, Thomas much enjoyed Janet's company and attentions. Considering that he had never been actually in love with this young woman, he realised that he had grown very fond of her, appreciating more and more her many excellent qualities. She was warm, understanding, but by no means over-humble or submissive, with her own views and opinions which she could maintain but which she never thrust upon him. She was utterly reliable, and had a quiet sense of humour which she found to his taste. Compared with Flam Fleming and Beth Beaton, for instance, she was perhaps less effervescent and exciting, and less beautiful than the Queen; but she made a good, loyal, rewarding and attractive companion, and he more and more was coming to trust her judgment. His late father had probably served him better, in this matter of finding him a wife, than he had realised.

This of the looked-for child was, of course, a joy, and brought them the closer together. Janet reckoned that he would be born in April – she was assured that it would be a boy; indeed they chose the name Andrew – or Dand, by Border usage – although Thomas kept an alternative Mary up his sleeve, as it were, in a different aspect of loyalty.

So the winter passed, with no lack of preoccupations for Thomas Kerr, however often his thoughts turned to the Queen and her Marys. He had no direct communications from the court, but heard, in roundabout fashion, of goings-on thereat, the most sensational being that of the French poet Chastelard. That rash and romantic individual was, like so many another, in love with the so-attractive monarch, and made no secret of the fact – indeed penned and recited to her passionate verses to that effect. Mary, it was said by some, was much too patient with him, allowing him liberties; but then that was being said about David Rizzio the secretary also, and sundry others, Knox and the other strait-laced Protestant divines being particularly and persistently critical. The young Queen herself wrote poetry and was of a romantic and outgoing nature, and so had sympathies. At any rate, after being found hiding under her bed on the one occasion, and being forgiven, Chastelard, in Burntisland Castle in Fife, went altogether too far, bursting at night into the Queen's bedchamber, to her alarm. He would not leave, and she had had to cry out for help. This had brought her Marys and then the Earl James, who took stern charge, arresting the poet there and then and charging him with the crime of *lèse majesté*, before the guard took him away. And two days later he had been executed, at St Andrews, as the law prescribed for this offence, once again the Queen being forced to witness the beheading, to her horror and eventual collapse – but not before she had heard his last words, said to be "Adieu, most beautiful and most cruel princess in the world!" All something of a repetition of what had happened at Sir John Gordon's death. If execution did indeed seem an over-drastic punishment, the word circulating was that the Privy Council had evidence that Chastelard had in fact done what he did on the orders of certain persons in high positions in France, deliberately to compromise the Queen's virtue and blacken her reputation, for political reasons.

Various versions of this sorry tale swept round the land, to the mixed outrage and fascination of the lieges.

However, Thomas's news of royal matters came usually from a more reliable source than common hearsay – oddly, indeed, through Janet. For her father, fond indeed of his only child, proved to be a conscientious correspondent, and sent her frequent letters. And one of these, a little later, was illuminating indeed as to the Queen's situation. Whether or not as a consequence of these romantic overtures of Gordon and Chastelard, international pressures, or merely the need to ensure the succession to the throne, the Council decided that the Queen must marry, and soon. Apparently there was a host of suitors, possible, suitable, or less so. The madcap Hamilton Earl of Arran was still proclaiming that he was the obvious choice, since his father, the Duke of Châtelherault, was present heir-presumptive to the said throne. Because his sanity was in doubt, few took his claims seriously. But he was a Protestant, which had its importance. Dynastic pressure was also forthcoming on the Protestant side, from London, where Queen Elizabeth was putting forward quite strongly the name of her favourite, Robert Dudley, Earl of Leicester, whose wife, Amy Robsart, had died in mysterious circumstances; and as an alternative, Henry Stewart, Lord Darnley, son and heir of the Earl of Lennox, whose mother was a daughter of Margaret Tudor, Henry the Eighth's sister, and who therefore might one day make claim to the *English* throne. On the Catholic side there were further proposals. Pope Pius, much concerned over the death of Huntly, the Catholic leader in Scotland, was urging Mary's marriage to a powerful Catholic prince, and suggesting either Don Carlos, son and heir to the King of Spain, or the Archduke Charles of Austria, son of the Emperor. This did not suit the Queen's French mother-in-law, Queen Catherine de Medici, who was ruling France, more or less, for her younger son; and she, desiring to maintain and strengthen the French influence in Scotland, proposed the Duc d'Aumale, son of the Constable of France, or else the Duc de Nemours, of the royal house. The former had a wife already, but this could be got over, apparently.

So there was no lack of suitors. At least the Bothwell problem seemed to have solved itself, for that strange and unpredictable character announced, of all things, that he intended to wed the Lady Jean Gordon, the late Huntly's daughter; just why was not clear.

Of the Queen's own reaction to all this, Sir William did not say.

Kirkcaldy's next letter did refer to the royal state of mind. He wrote that she was sad and depressed – not so much over the marriage proposals and arguments apparently, but over the untimely deaths of her de Guise uncles, within weeks of each other, the Duc de Guise himself, and the Grand Prior of France. Brought up largely by her de Guise relatives, she was very fond of them, and most unhappy over this loss.

Thomas wondered whether there was anything that he could do to help.

His own affairs, however, tended to put such loyal consideration to the back of his mind, for in mid-April Janet was brought to bed, and after a somewhat prolonged labour produced the looked-for son and heir, amidst great rejoicings at Ferniehirst and Jedburgh. Andrew he was duly christened, and Dand he was called, a fine, healthy, gurgling infant. Janet recovered quickly. With the first swallows appearing and the cuckoos calling from the Border hillsides, the spring sun shone for the Kerrs.

It was in this state of euphoria that Thomas remembered the Queen's depression, and thought of something that he might do to help. She had enjoyed her previous visit to Ferniehirst, and in this excellent spring weather, with the Borderland looking at its loveliest, a return here would be just the thing, perhaps, to take her mind off the cares of state, and cheer her up. If she would come – and if possible without all those oppressive Protestant lords and the clamorous court, but with her Marys of course. It occurred to him that he might suggest that he required her presence in order to decorate and furnish suitably the interior of the house he was erecting for her in Jedburgh, now roofed and nearing completion. That might be a sufficient excuse? Janet agreed.

So he wrote a letter to Holyroodhouse, as the palace wing of the abbey was now being called, and hoped that he was not being presumptuous.

The reply he received, quite promptly, gave no such impression. The Queen would be delighted to visit the Borders again and see the house he was so generously building for her by the Jed Water. She had missed seeing her Thomas Smellum this past sad winter, and would look forward to repairing that neglect. She would come, God willing, at the end of May, for first she had to go to Glasgow and the west. She rejoiced to hear that he now had a son, and would look forward to seeing them both, and the Lady Kerr, soon. She was lodging meantime at Craigmillar Castle, a mile or two from the city, for there was a visitation of the plague in Edinburgh; she prayed that the good Lord would be merciful and remove it speedily, even though it might be for their sins, as Master Knox declared.

The royal party arrived at Ferniehirst on St Brendan's Day, and Thomas was pleased to see that it was only a small one, with few of the court, but Lady Fleming, the Marys, and, strangely, the English ambassador, Thomas Randolph, also David Rizzio. He was especially thankful that the Earl of Moray was not present, who Thomas was apt to consider represented trouble and a dampening of spirits.

The Queen looked somewhat wan, he thought, but was cheerful and obviously glad to see him, as were her ladies, a lively crew, full of reports, stories and gossip, none clearly sickening of the plague. A great fuss was made of the baby, of course, with presents brought and assertions that he was going to be like his father, but better-looking. Janet was congratulated on her production, and details sought as to delivery, feeding and the like, only Lady Fleming there being experienced in such matters.

They had only three days for their visit, it transpired, affairs of state demanding an early return – some of the Council apparently having expressed disapproval of even this brief expedition. Clearly being a young queen in Reformed Scotland was no joyous progression.

That evening, round the fire in Ferniehirst's great hall, notably long and narrow, the talk was wide-ranging and not all light-hearted – and somewhat inhibited by the presence of Thomas Randolph who, although good enough company, inevitably, as Queen Elizabeth's representative, had the effect of restricting subjects of interesting debate, that of the royal marriage in particular, which was of course so prominent in all their minds. Not entirely restricting, however, for Beth Beaton did rather turn the tables on him, by naughtily quizzing him on the matter of the Lord Robert Dudley, newly made Earl of Leicester – to Randolph's slight embarrassment. Was not he the English Queen's favourite, some even naming him her paramour?

The diplomat tried to be diplomatic. Queen Elizabeth was fond of Dudley, yes, but entirely properly – or she would not be proposing him as husband for Her Grace here. He was a notable and personable man, and the Queen sympathised with him in his difficult position. For he was, of course, a son of the late Duke of Northumberland, who had been executed for treason over the Lady Jane Grey affair by the late Queen Mary Tudor, and the title put under attainder. But the son was innocent of all offence, and would make an excellent husband.

Had he been an excellent husband to Amy Robsart, Beth persisted – although the Queen shot warning glances at her.

Randolph shook his head. The Lady Robert's death was most unfortunate, he asserted; but nothing to do with Dudley. The Queen was most distressed about it, and about the ill stories unscrupulous persons put about on the subject. Malicious tongues were ever ready to plague royal persons – as Her Grace here had learned well over the affair of the Frenchman Chastelard.

That silenced Beth Beaton for the moment. Flam Fleming sought to cover any discomfort by asking if the ambassador was acquainted with the other Elizabethan nominee, Henry Stewart, Master of Lennox; she used the Scottish title rather than the English Viscount Darnley.

Randolph was obviously more at ease on this subject. The Lord Darnley was a fine, tall, pretty fellow, he declared, much seen about the English court and well liked by the Queen. He was younger than the Lord Robert, and of course, had royal blood both on his father's and his mother's sides. Her Grace would find him much to her taste, he was sure.

The Queen did not comment on that, and carefully changed the subject, suggesting that they should have some music. Signor Davie would give them some of his Italian melodies, and Mary Seton contribute her French songs. But first they must have Sir Thomas's Border ballads, commencing with her favourite, "Young Tamlane".

So the evening passed pleasantly thereafter, with no more discomforts.

Escorting the ladies to their chambers later, Thomas, ending up with Flam, asked why the Queen had brought the English ambassador with her on this visit. Laughing, Flam said that he had pleaded to come because of Beth Beaton, with whom he had become enamoured, following her about everywhere, despite being old enough to be her father. When Thomas, surprised, said that Beth did not give the impression of returning his devotion, he was told that she thought it all only a great joke, and rather delighted in twitting and bantering the poor man.

Next day they went down to inspect the new house in Jedburgh, the Queen expressing herself as delighted with it. She was full of ideas for its plenishing and decoration, and said that she and her Marys would make tapestries and embroideries for the walls and furniture. Then they went up to the little royal castle on the hill, to meet Thomas's mother and family and to see the improvements in hand there; ending up at the abbey, splendid still in its ruins, where Thomas told them of his namesake, Thomas the Rhymer, and his remarkable vision here, of the Queen's remote predecessor, Alexander the Third, he who fell to his death at Kinghorn soon after and left Scotland with an empty throne, the cause of the Wars of Independence, Wallace, Bruce and the rest, and the ghostly scene which had predicted this. His hearers were enthralled; he promised to give them the ballad of Thomas of Ersildoune and the Queen of Elfland, that evening.

For the second day's entertainment he took them eastwards eight miles into the Cheviot foothill country, to introduce his uncle at Cessford Castle to the Queen, privately not a little pleased with himself to be thus able to demonstrate his close association with the monarch to the new Warden of the Middle March, of whom he had used to be somewhat in awe. Cessford was an older and more massive fortalice than was Ferniehirst; but then, it had not had to be rebuilt so often consequent on English demolition, being more remotely situated and not on the main invasion route into Scotland. They rode on from there to the ancient church of Linton, near to Morebattle in the Kale Water valley, to see the sculpture and hear the story of the celebrated Linton Worm – no worm or serpent but in fact a great dragon-like creature which was reputed to have terrorised this district, centuries before, until it was slain by the gallant efforts of one Somervail, from whom the present family of the Lords Somerville were descended. The creature was thought to have been the denison of Linton Loch, from which it sallied to seek its prey. Thomas found these Border stories of his much appreciated.

The day following was Sunday, and wet, so after Mass in the castle chapel they occupied themselves with more stories, games and dancing – which would have greatly offended

Master John Knox – the last to the music of David Rizzio, who proved to be a very talented musician; indeed it transpired that this was how the Queen had come to know him, he being one of a group of Italian entertainers at the French court.

It was not all entertainment, however, for when little Dand was being bathed and prepared for his cradle, the Queen and her ladies looking on – not the men, needless to say – Thomas found himself sent for. There, in the ante-room of his and Janet's bedchamber, beside the steaming tub, he was greeted with encomiums as to the pink infant's enchantments, and then, to his mystification, sent off to fetch his sword. Returning with this, he was informed by the Queen that he might recollect that one day she had told him that he deserved a second knighthood – but that was impracticable. However, she had heard that her sister-monarch Elizabeth had recently knighted an infant-in-arms, for some reason – and what one Queen could do, so could another. So draw the sword, Sir Thomas.

Astonished, even wondering whether he was being cozened, he did as commanded, Janet squeezing his arm.

"Now, my friend, you yourself must bestow the accolade," Mary said. "Any knight, I am assured, has the authority to create a knight, given the command. And only a knight may perform the knighting – as I, a woman and therefore no knight, may not. But I can command it, and speak the words." And in a different voice, "Now, be you careful with that sword, of a mercy!"

So, careful indeed, and head ashake, Thomas, holding the sword not by its hilt but far down the blade, tapped his little son on each tiny plump shoulder, while the Queen intoned: "Andrew Kerr, Younger of Ferniehirst, I hereby name and dub thee knight. Be thou a good and worthy knight until thy life's end. I salute you, Sir Andrew!"

To the cries and clappings of the women, and to the father's incoherent manifestations of mixed gratitude and doubts, the new knight was laid in his cot, burbling.

Here was something to make a ballad about, indeed.

In the morning, the royal party left Ferniehirst, with many expressions of appreciation for a most happy interlude. Thomas escorted them all the way north to Soutra Aisle, Edinburgh in sight. He was urged to come to court, and soon.

10

Thomas repaired to Edinburgh rather sooner than he, at least, expected thereafter, summoned to court -yes, but to the High Court of Parliament rather than to Holyroodhouse. Strangely, no parliament had been held in Scotland since the Queen's return, or indeed for a considerable time before that, although there had been conventions, called by the Privy Council, less authoritative assemblies – all this an indication of the ruling power of the Council itself, since the Reformation. However there were certain measures which only a duly called parliament could enact, and more than one of these were now required. In Scotland, unlike England, the monarch sat in parliament with her subjects' representatives, lords, barons and burgh nominees, all together – indeed, without the monarch or regent no parliament was possible, hence only conventions.

So infrequent had these occasions become during the years of Mary's minority and absence abroad, that many had almost forgotten the existence and need therefor. Thomas certainly had, nor considered the fact that both as holder of baronies and as Provost of Jedburgh, he was entitled and required to attend. So the summons came as something of a surprise.

He rode north with his Uncle Walter of Cessford, also summoned, as Warden as well as baron, with whom he now had to have frequent dealings. They discussed, of course, the whys and wherefores of this parliament, whether it was merely a ceremonial occasion or called for a specific purpose. The Queen had not mentioned it during her visit, so it looked as though it was a decision taken elsewhere, presumably by the Council; the summons had come in the name of Secretary of State Maitland, Flam's admirer, who acted as secretary of the Council also. They hazarded a guess that it would have to do with the Queen's marriage negotiations.

Since Sir Walter, who had no Edinburgh town-house, was to stay in the Kerr lodging in the Canongate, Thomas could scarcely leave him, on arrival, to hurry down to Holyroodhouse, as was his inclination. But later in the evening he did make his escape, and took his way thither – and was not surprised to discover great activity at the palace and abbey, servants and retainers everywhere, with the many notables, from distant parts evidently, descended upon the Queen's hospitality, including, it seemed, a host of Hamiltons, under the chief thereof, the elderly Duke of Châtelherault, heir-presumptive – though not, it was to be hoped, his peculiar son, Arran.

As a consequence, Thomas did not manage to attain the royal presence that night, so thronged was the Queen with high-born luminaries; but he did see Flam Fleming, briefly, who was full of excitement about it all, declaring that there was going to be a notable battle of wills on the morrow, in spite of all the ceremonial, the Queen determined not to be over-ridden at her first parliament, not to be a mere figurehead – the clash seeming likely to be mainly with her brother, the Earl James, and the so-called Lords of the Congregation, the militant Protestant faction. Bothwell's position came into it, apparently, the marriage situation, and the ever-controversial issue of religion. So it was not to be an occasion for mere display and formalities. Flam suggested that Thomas should join the Queen's train, and proceed up to Parliament House with them, as it were in state, but he said that he would have to be in his place in the assembly before the royal arrival. He hoped that he might see them all afterwards.

Parliament House stood nearer the castle than the palace, in the High Street, quite close to Knox's High Kirk of St Giles, scarcely an auspicious location in present circumstances. Next morning, then, Thomas and his uncle had to fight their way up the packed Canongate and through the Netherbow Port into the city proper, and then up the equally crowded High Street, to reach the venue, much of Scotland, as well as the citizenry of Edinburgh, seeming crammed into the wynds and closes and streets, such as were not hanging out of the windows of the tall tenements, to watch. The Queen would require quite a regiment of her guards to clear a way for her presently.

The hall itself was already well filled, large as it was, and a great noise arising. Thomas could have joined the burgh representatives, provosts and magistrates representing the towns; but he thought it best to sit beside his uncle on the barons' benches, being well aware that he was only a *hereditary* Provost, not truly a nominee of Jedburgh's townsfolk, and others would likewise recognise this. He saw that the visitors' gallery at one end of the hall was also crowded, save for a space left at the front, no doubt for the Queen's party. The only other space vacant was the earls' stalls, these magnates no doubt finding it below their dignity to come in and wait amongst the rest. Thomas was rather amused to see the former clerical benches now occupied by the commendator-bishops, abbots and priors, none clerics – why, of course, they had retained the clerical titles, on gaining the Church lands, to give them seats in parliament. Amongst these were some kin of his own, including a brother of Sir Walter, Mark, Commendator-Abbot of Newbattle, now a Protestant.

They had quite a wait, inevitably; indeed Uncle Walter fell asleep. Then, with the sound of cheering coming from outside, the earls began to file in two by two behind the Earl Marischal: Morton and Mar, Bothwell and Atholl, Glencairn and Cassillis, Home and Rothes, and the rest. And almost simultaneously there was something of a stir up in the visitors' gallery as three black-gowned clerics came in and pushed their way down to the front, the stern, bearded figure of John Knox foremost. Since the Reformation the clergy no longer sat in the Scots parliament, in which they had been so prominent and influential before, now having their own General Assembly; but Master Knox, it seemed, was not going to miss this one.

He was barely seated when all must stand, as trumpeters marched into the hall, to blow a stirring fanfare. Then, behind the Lord Lyon King of Arms and his heralds, came in procession the elderly Duke of Châtelherault carrying the crown on a purple cushion, followed by the Earl of Argyll with the sceptre, then the Earl of Moray bearing the great sword of state, held high. There was a slight gap and the Queen appeared, dressed magnificently in her robes of state, walking with great dignity and looking straight in front of her.

While the trumpeters changed their blowing to a slow march, Lyon led them up to the dais, where he seated Mary on the throne, taking up his own position behind her, the three symbol-bearers placing the crown, sceptre and sword on the table in front of her, before bowing and moving down, two to their stalls amongst the earls, Argyll to a table nearby, where Secretary Maitland stood. When all were in place and the music ceased, Lyon raised his staff of office for silence – glancing up to the gallery where Lady Fleming and the four Marys were the only moving figures as they insinuated themselves into their places at the front, and so next to those three clerics. He spoke loudly.

"Hear ye all. The high and mighty princess, Mary, Queen of Scots, has called this parliament of her realm for the due and proper governance of the kingdom and the welfare of its people, as is her right, only hers. Let all heed the Queen's Grace." He bowed towards the throne and then gestured for all to sit, although he and his heralds remained standing at the Queen's back.

When the stir ended, Mary, whose head had been sunk as though in prayer, sat up and eyed the great waiting assembly, only hands clasped tightly together revealing something of the ordeal this must be for a young woman, however regally raised. For moments she paused, as though hesitant, and then spoke slowly, carefully but clearly, in the melodious slightly French-accented voice.

"I, Mary, greet you all, my friends, my officers of state, my lords, barons and representatives of my beloved people, and welcome you all to this the first parliament of my own attending. I rejoice to be with you, and will hear and attend on your deliberations . . ." She paused, and amended that: ". . . *our* deliberations, with the greatest interest and concern, for there is much to be discussed and decided, much of great import to the weal of this kingdom."

She looked around her, even up at the gallery. "First, there is my own state and position. For the well-being of the realm it is required that I, who have no offspring by my late and beloved husband, King Francis of France, should remarry, and, if God is willing, produce a child to heir this ancient throne, perhaps the most ancient in Christendom, to ensure the succession." She gave a slight smile in the direction of Châtelherault. "And thus relieve my lord Duke, here, of the problems of being heir-presumptive!"

Everyone there recognised those problems, at least, for if the Hamilton chief died, the half-crazed Arran was *his* heir, and heaven save Scotland from a mad king.

"A number of illustrious names have been put forward for our consideration," Mary went on, solemnly. "It is not, I think, the duty of this parliament to decide on who should be chosen for *my* husband." A pause. "But guidance is perhaps necessary in this situation. Whose say in the matter should carry most weight – my own, or my councillors'? Never before has there been a Queen-Regnant in Scotland. Therefore, whoever weds that Queen-Regnant will, it is to be presumed, wear the Crown Matrimonial, and be called King. This, of introducing a new King in Scotland, although not King of Scots, is, to be sure, a most vital matter for the subjects of this realm. Should they, therefore, have the greater say in the choice? Or, on the other hand, I, Queen of Scots, must take to my person and bed the said choice, the father of any child I may bear. Which, shall we say, makes *my* concern of importance! So here is a great matter, on which there are differing views. I shall be glad of the guidance of this parliament. Other grave matters fall to be discussed. But this, I think, we may deal with first, my lord Chancellor?" And she turned and gestured to the Earl of Argyll, who had succeeded the errant and late Huntly as Chancellor of the Realm, amongst whose duties was acting as chairman at parliaments, as well as of the Privy Council – one reason why no parliaments had been held before this.

"Yes, Your Grace, so be it. The royal marriage," the Campbell said, in the soft, sibilant Highland voice which was so little indicative of his nature. "Who speaks to this?"

There was no hesitancy now. The Earl James was on his feet. "My lord Chancellor, when a King or Queen of Scots is crowned, he or she swears ever to place the good and interests of the people before all else. Therefore, I say, there should be no question here. That the identity of the Queen's husband is of no little importance to her subjects, could indeed be momentous. Amongst names being put forward are those of certain foreign princes, most of them Papists. This realm has eschewed papacy, God be praised! To have a Catholic brought in to wear the Crown Matrimonial would, I say, be contrary to the needs and interests, yes indeed the law, of this land. Therefore, in this aspect at least, choice *must* be governed by the wishes of the people, which this parliament represents, the ruled rather than the ruler." He glanced up at that visitors' gallery as he sat down – and it was not at the Queen's ladies that he looked, that was certain.

"I agree." That was Morton, brief but positive.

There was exclamation and murmur, for and against, throughout the hall.

Bothwell rose, as positive as Morton. "This parliament may

advise the Queen," he declared. "It cannot *tell* her who she may wed or who she may not! Her Grace must choose her husband. Would any other here permit the like, save perhaps by a father or guardian? And the monarch is the guardian of the people. I say advise only, not choose."

"So say I." That was Erskine, the new Earl of Mar.

There was a snort from the gallery.

The Chancellor tapped on his table to still the swell of comment. "There appears to be a conflict of direction here. Two issues raised. One, the question of whose final choice. The other, conditions which must limit the choice. Take the latter first. In a Protestant realm, with the Reformed faith by law established, can a Catholic prince be considered to wear the Crown Matrimonial? Especially one who may bear rule in another and Catholic land . . ."

"We have a Catholic monarch now!" Bothwell cried, without rising. "None can gainsay that!"

Argyll banged his gavel. "I am not finished, my lord," he said sternly. "If this parliament's duty is to advise the monarch, then I judge that it would advise against a Catholic marriage."

There was some applause at that, on which the Chancellor did not frown.

"I so advise, and make motion of it," the Earl James said.

"I second," Morton added.

"I say otherwise. Reject." That was Bothwell again.

"I also," the Catholic Earl of Menteith said.

As the Chancellor was about to speak, the Kennedy, Earl of Cassillis, a fervid Protestant, stood. "Ere we go further, there is another side to this," he asserted. "The *English* succession. Queen Elizabeth of England is unwed. There is no closer heir to her throne than Her Grace here, granddaughter of Elizabeth's father's sister, Queen Margaret Tudor. There are other possible heirs, less close. Yet Her Grace of England delays any declaration as to her intentions in the matter. She is a good Protestant monarch of a Protestant realm. It would, I say, aid her in her decision if *our* Queen's choice should be for a Protestant suitor put forward by herself. And thus bring Scotland and England together hereafter, an end to ancient hostility and warfare." He sat.

There was silence as all digested that.

"Do you make a motion of this?" Argyll asked. "If so, what is your motion?"

"No, my lord Chancellor. It is but an observation."

"I agree with the Lord Cassillis. And my motion stands," the Earl James said.

"As does mine!" Bothwell cried.

The Queen looked unhappy. Thus early, the parliament was going to be divided into a Protestant versus Catholic confrontation.

"The amendment first," the Chancellor directed. "Those in favour of the amendment of my lord of Bothwell, show."

Comparatively few hands went up, Thomas's included.

"In favour of the motion?"

Many more were raised – but a surprisingly large number of those present did not vote at all.

"Motion carried."

A buzz of comment and talk went round the assembly, but little in the way of cheering.

Moray rose up at once. "So this parliament chooses to advise Her Grace. In what terms? I move that she choose a Protestant husband."

"Seconded." That was the Earl of Glencairn, the Cunninghame chief.

Thomas was thinking that it was high time that others than these earls spoke up, for they had no more right than anyone else to hold the floor here, when someone appeared to hold the same opinion – the Queen herself.

"My lord Chancellor," she said quietly but quite firmly. "I have heard what has been said and decided. I am advised by parliament. And I will take heed of that advice. But I must declare that the decision will and must be made by myself, mine the choice of *my* husband. I say that there is no need for my lord of Moray's second motion, since I have heard and will heed. *I* move that we proceed to the next business."

There was a distinct hush at that as men eyed each other. And then, despite Knox's furious leaning forward and glaring from the gallery, somebody raised a cheer, which Thomas at once took up, and which then swept round the assembly, and maintained, a spontaneous and surprising development.

Argyll had to hammer with his gavel for silence eventually. But he bowed to what most clearly was the will of the majority.

163

"As Your Grace wishes," he said. "We move on to the next matter."

The Earl James was not a good loser, nor easy to put down. He rose again. "Apart from the Queen's marriage, there is a grave concern of religion and equity to be decided," he asserted. "That is the shameful injustice still being imposed on many good and valiant supporters of the true Reformed faith who were adjudged guilty of offences during the period of the Reformation struggle and who still suffer sentences imposed on them then, some fines, some forfeiture, some still imprisoned or otherwise punished. These by prejudiced judges, sheriffs and magistrates and barony courts. All should have been absolved and released long since. I now move that an Act of Oblivion be passed, freeing all from any remaining reproach or untimely punishment. An Act of Oblivion, I say." Again he glanced up at the gallery.

Half a dozen seconders rose to support that, to Master Knox's grave nods of approval.

Lord Seton, Ebba's father, spoke. "My lord Chancellor, some perhaps of such folk should be acquitted. If any indeed there be remaining under punishment, honest protesters for their religious beliefs. But most of those so receiving punishment were rogues and thieves, notour disturbers of the peace, destroyers of property, attackers of their fellow-citizens, even murderers, who used the protesting cause to cover their own evil works. Surely it is not right that such disturbers of the Queen's peace should be released and restored?"

Thomas Kerr, much aware of some scoundrelly Jedburgh law-breakers, jumped up to second that, but was told coldly, by Argyll, that no counter-motion had been proposed, merely a question asked. Somewhat crestfallen, he sat.

The Earl James was on his feet again. "To decide who were the few such felons amongst the many honest protesters would demand retrial for all," he contended. "That is beyond all consideration, and taking much time, profitless. I say the Act must cover all – it is not pardon, since pardon implies offence in the first place. Wiping out, oblivion, is what is required. So I move an Act of Oblivion."

"Is there any counter-motion to this fair and honest proposal?"

Lord Livingstone rose, a Catholic to be sure. "Are there not other injustices stemming from that protesting period still being perpetrated, my lord Chancellor? I refer to the persecution of good and loyal citizens who hold true to the old faith, especially in the west of this kingdom." And he looked directly at some of the occupants of the earls' stalls. "I say that if this Act of Oblivion is to be passed, it must ensure the end of persecutions and attacks on subjects of *all* religious faiths, not just Protestants."

There was some agreement expressed, some otherwise.

Argyll nodded. "If my lord of Moray will agree to include a clause to that effect, will this parliament accept his motion for an Act of Oblivion?" And at the Earl James's curt nod, "Mr Secretary, will you so word a writing for our later approval?" Without waiting for any further comment, he went on. "Next business."

The Earl of Cassillis, perhaps smarting a little from that allegation of persecution of Catholics in the west, jumped up. "There are many manses and glebes of the former churchmen standing denied to the lawful Reformed parish ministers," he complained. "And many churches standing empty and falling to ruin. Owned by Catholic sympathisers. I say that all such should be repaired and made available for the new incumbents. I so move."

He was strongly backed, and the motion passed by a considerable margin.

So the ding-dong warfare went on, attitudes hardening rather than modifying for the good and peace of the realm, with of course the Protestant majority there tending to win. A law against Catholic lords permitting assemblies of the lieges was promulgated – to hoots of laughter from the Earl of Bothwell – with the odd rider, 'without the Queen's consent'. The Catholic earldoms of Huntly and Sutherland were forfeited. The attending of Mass, publicly, except in the Chapel Royal, was to be punishable by loss of goods, lands, and on repetition, even of life.

As this all became a positive battle, with tempers rising, the Queen herself took an extraordinary step. In the midst of unseemly clamour, she rose to her feet from the throne.

As angry men perceived it, they fell silent. All recollected that when the monarch stood, all must stand. So all rose, slowly, amidst notable hush, the first for some considerable time.

She spoke, her voice quivering a little, but not hesitant.

"My lords and commissioners to parliament, I must speak. I must remind you that this *is* a parliament, meeting here at my express command, for the weal, comfort and better government of *all* my people. It is not a gathering for religious dispute and debate and enmity, but for peace and the rule of law in my kingdom. For myself, I have sought, and will seek, ever to put peace and goodwill first and foremost. I belong to the old faith, but I keep my faith, as it were, private, as all have a right to do, and support and proclaim tolerance for the faithful beliefs of all, and amity in religious matters. In this I have agreed to many measures which some of my Catholic subjects may well frown upon – that I recognise. Others should note it. Nevertheless I am the anointed Queen and monarch of this realm, and declare to you, as is my concern and duty, that all Scots must learn to live with each other in such amity, and allow the worship of God to the conscience of all." She waved a hand. "You may sit."

Mary sat also, but she was not finished. "My lord Chancellor, my royal wish is that this parliament moves on to discuss its remaining business, avoiding matters of religious discrimination."

Thomas Kerr, for one, could not restrain himself. He stood up. "God bless the Queen's Grace!" he cried.

All around him men rose, lords, barons and representatives of the people, not all there but a clear majority, especially of the last, and took up the cry. "God bless the Queen's Grace! God bless the Queen's Grace!" On and on it went.

Argyll raised his gavel, but wisely did not bring it down to bang for silence. He eyed the Earl James, eyebrows raised questioningly.

That man sat inscrutable. That is, until there was a commotion up in the visitors' gallery, as Master Knox stood up, to stalk out in obvious fury, followed by his two companions. Then the Queen's half-brother half-shrugged and briefly nodded.

"Next business," Argyll said levelly.

The Earl James was not going to suffer reverse lightly. He stood up immediately. "It is the concern of this parliament, I say, that the position of the Earl of Bothwell be considered." He did not glance along the stalls to where the Hepburn chief sat. "He still fills the offices of Lord High Admiral and Lieutenant of the Borders. Yet he has refused to answer charges that he was engaged, with the Earl of Arran not here present, to abduct the Queen's Grace, imprison her treasonably in Dumbarton Castle, and seek mastery of this kingdom thereafter by bringing pressure on the captive monarch. If he cannot deny this, is it right and proper that he should remain at liberty, and indeed sit in this parliament, as well as hold these high offices?"

"I do deny it." Bothwell did not even trouble to rise.

"And if witnesses are brought to swear to it?"

"This is not a court of law."

"It is the High Court of Parliament! There is none higher."

The Duke of Châtelherault stood, no doubt to defend his absent son's name, but Bothwell forestalled him, looking around him.

"I see no witnesses here!" he observed, grinning widely. "But perhaps they are outside? In the street. I have many good men there awaiting me. Perhaps *they* may be able to find your witnesses, my lord!"

The hush at that most obvious threat was tense. The Hepburn men-at-arms were notorious for their savagery as well as their numbers. Bothwell had clearly come prepared.

The Chancellor looked around him, recognising the danger. A riot outside could be so easily sparked off between the followings of rival lords, Catholic and Protestant, as well as clan against clan, and that would help nothing.

"You are not making any motion, my lord of Moray?" he asked, significantly emphasising the word not.

The Earl James saw the point. He shrugged. "I but ask for the matter to be considered." He sat down, the realities of the situation all too evident.

Bothwell gave a single bark of laughter.

"Any other business?" Argyll demanded hurriedly.

"New appointments to the Court of Session," the Lord President thereof requested, also hurriedly.

"Ah, yes . . ."

That comparatively non-controversial matter took some time to complete, and had the notable effect of lessening tension and cooling tempers. When it was finished, the Chancellor, after another glance at Moray and Morton, turned to the Queen.

"A sufficiency for this day, I think, Highness? With Your Grace's royal permission, I will adjourn this session?"

Almost visibly thankful, Mary nodded.

"My Lord Lyon . . ."

The King of Arms signed to his trumpeters to blow their fanfare. Thereafter, stepping forward, he waved to the symbol-bearers to collect the crown, sceptre and sword from the table, and bowed to the Queen. Mary rose, as did all, and the royal procession began to move out.

Mary's first parliament had been not uneventful, and significant as to a number of truths relative to Reformed Scotland.

That evening Thomas found his way to Holyroodhouse again, and had no difficulty in gaining the royal presence this time, for the Queen, claiming a headache after the stresses of the day, had early withdrawn from a banquet for the illustrious and excited guests, and closeted herself with her ladies for a quiet evening.

Clearly Thomas was not considered to spoil the evening's quietness. He, in fact, was all but submerged under a flood of chatter and questioning, relative mainly, of course, to the parliament ongoings. Did he hear this, what did he think of that, was not it all quite extraordinary, telling, shameful, splendid? When he could get a word in, he declared his great admiration for the way that the Queen had conducted all, in especial her upstanding intervention which had brought the assembly to much-needed order and duty. He recognised how difficult this must have been for her, in the circumstances, and rejoiced that it had had such good effect. Also that it had shown how, despite all the arrogant and power-seeking lords, most there loved and supported her. For her part, the Queen acknowledged and thanked him for *his* so evident loyal and unfailing support, which she had noted, and admitted her nervousness at having to take the stand she had done.

Flam it was who put into words the recognition of them all. "The man who would have controlled that parliament, had Your Grace not acted as you did, was not part of it at all, but sitting in the gallery beside us," she declared. "The former and renegade priest Knox. The Earl James and the other Protestant lords were, I swear, dancing to *his* tune. They kept looking up to him – we could see it – seeking his yea or nay. And he was exclaiming and muttering all the time. He is the puppet-master, pulling the strings! That man would rule this kingdom if Your Grace was to permit it."

"When you took charge, in the end, and he stormed out, he was beside himself with rage," Beth Beaton said. "He was spluttering about the infamous wickedness of women in power. He hates our sex, does Master Knox!"

"He is a hard man, yes, but strong," the Queen agreed. "Why he is so hard against me, and womankind, I do not understand. It is not all a matter of religion, I think."

"I do not know that he hates womankind," Thomas observed. "My uncle, Sir Walter, was telling me as we rode north that he had word that Knox is about to marry again. His wife died not so long ago. And now he is going to wed a seventeen-year-old – and he a man of over fifty! The Lady Margaret Stewart, a daughter of the Lord Ochiltree."

"Save us!" the Queen exclaimed. "Seventeen! This is scarce believable. Perhaps it is not true? I know her – indeed, she is far-out kin of my own. Extraordinary!"

"It surely says something about John Knox, does it not?"

"If true, yes . . ."

"And she, poor young creature!" That was Lady Fleming. "Our Stewart family is having marriage problems, not only yourself, my dear. For I am told that my half-sister, and yours, Jean, Countess of Argyll, has left her husband."

"*Mon Dieu* – Jean! My good Jean? She has left Archibald Campbell? I did not know of this, either."

"So – beware then of Henry Stewart of Darnley, this possible husband!" the irrepressible Beth Beaton put in. "If it comes to anything."

The Queen looked away, thoughtful. "As to that, I have to consider well. He, the Master of Lennox, is Elizabeth's second choice, I am told. And I certainly will not wed her first, this Dudley, her plaything! Even as she created him Earl of Leicester she was nibbling and kissing at his neck! This Darnley is too young even for her – he also is but seventeen. His mother, the Countess of Lennox, came to see me in France, two years ago, soon after my Francis died, suggesting a marriage. For *her* mother was Henry the Eighth's sister Margaret, so next to myself he is closest to the Tudor throne. And he is a Protestant, of course, so that would please the lords. Also he is personable and good-looking, they say. Two years younger than myself. I might do a lot worse."

None there ventured comment, even Beth.

The Queen clearly wanted now to be done with such subjects and the affairs of state. She asked after Janet and her little Sir Andrew, and thereafter insisted on music and ballads and embroidery.

Thomas went back to the Canongate under female escort.

11

The next that the Kerrs saw of the royal entourage was when word reached Ferniehirst that the Queen would like to come to stay for a few days in her new house in Jedburgh, if it was ready for occupation. It seemed that Queen Elizabeth had finally become serious about the English succession situation – or her ministers had – and recognised that her sister-queen's marriage was important in the matter. She summoned Thomas Randolph her ambassador down to London, for guidance and instructions, and was sending him back, with the Earl of Bedford, to Berwick-upon-Tweed, for a conference with Scots representatives. The Earl James and William Maitland were to meet these. The place being only half a day's riding east of Jedburgh, the Queen would there be near enough to be consulted and informed.

So all was bustle in putting the finishing touches to the handsome building, part tower-house, part mansion, and completing its furnishing.

The party arrived rather sooner than was anticipated, but made no complaints. Secretary Maitland came with them, *en route* for Berwick; but the Earl James was apparently making his own way thither. It transpired that, since the parliament, he and his half-sister had not been on the best of terms – and James Stewart was not the man to hide his feelings. Maitland, as it happened, was not good at that either, and whatever his attitude to Catholicism and the monarch, was hopelessly enamoured of Flam Fleming and anxious to be with her as much as was possible. He would have taken her to Berwick with him if she had been willing.

After a due interval, when Thomas enquired about this conference and the royal marriage situation generally, he was told that the choice was in fact narrowing. The Archduke Charles of Austria had found an alternative bride; and the King of Spain's son, Don Carlos, was showing signs of insanity. So the two Frenchmen, the Dukes d'Aumale and de Nemours, both Catholic of course, remained, and the English nominees, Dudley and Darnley – and Mary, whatever ambassadors might urge, was not going to consider the other Queen's playthings. So unless new names were put forward . . .

Sir James Melville had been sent south to London to express Mary's concern over the succession issue, hence this conference. Otherwise, the only evident reaction of the Virgin Queen was to allow the Earl of Lennox, virtually her pensioner, to return to Scotland, from which he had been banished all those years before, Mary agreeing. Which seemed to point to Darnley. The Earl James had strongly advised against Darnley, oddly enough.

The second day after the Queen's coming, the Earl of Bothwell arrived unannounced, from Hermitage, news travelling swiftly in the Borderland. Thomas, who did not like the man, was glad at least that he did not have to entertain him at Ferniehirst, for there was ample room for him at the new house in the town. But he admittedly did feel a sort of jealousy, unsuitable as this was.

Smailholm was a particularly good place for the sport of hawking, with much passage of wildfowl between its lochans and the nearby Tweed, and it had been arranged for an expedition there, for Mary was fond of falconry. Bothwell had to come too – which rather spoiled things, at least for Thomas, although the Queen seemed to enjoy the Earl's challenging company.

Bothwell was the sort who was proficient at all sports, and not averse from demonstrating the fact. He did not think much of Thomas's hawks, and made that clear also. So the exercise was less successful than it might have been. David Rizzio was there also, and he seemed to share Thomas's antipathy towards Bothwell, who treated him as though he was little more than a servant.

Riding back to Ferniehirst, Rizzio it was who, perhaps seeking to repay the Earl's discourtesies, broached the subject of that man's fairly recent and unexpected marriage.

"Your lady wife, my lord, you have not brought her with you? She is in good health, I trust? And recovered somewhat from the sorrow of her father's and brother's deaths? So grievous for her." That was suavely said, but significantly near the bone.

The Earl looked at him coldly. "Sufficiently well, yes," he answered briefly.

"That is good. You must greatly have comforted her."

The Queen may have been looking for some such opening to touch on this subject, for she spoke up. "Your marriage somewhat surprised us, my lord. It must have required no little decision to wed the Lord Huntly's daughter . . . after what happened in the north. And the forfeiture of the Gordons."

"Jean Gordon I have known for long," Bothwell answered easily. "And when I perceived that there was no likelihood of marrying *you*, Madam, I so chose!" That was added with the flourish of a gloved hand.

Mary drew a quick breath, and found no words.

Thomas spoke for her. "And the good Mistress Throndsen, my lord? How goes it with her?"

If the other was put out by that, he did not show it. "Anna has returned to Denmark," he said. He turned shoulder on Thomas, and back to the Queen. "My marriage is of little import, save to myself. And Jean, to be sure. But Your Grace's now – that could shake thrones! How does it feel, as a woman and a desirable one, to be at the disposal of others, in this? Of those who seek their own advantage in policy and statecraft?"

"I am at no one's disposal, my lord. I shall make my own choice, in the end."

"But the choice for you is much limited, is it not?"

"Perhaps. But that is the lot of those born to sit on thrones! They must needs accept it. So we learn from the cradle."

"You have my sympathy. But – heigho, that is only marriage, after all! There are other pleasures to savour. Other than the marriage-bed! And sweet pleasures. As your royal father made proof!"

That blatant proposition was such that even the tolerant Queen could hardly swallow it. "Enough, my lord!" she said, and turned in her saddle. "Sir Thomas, you promised to take us to the Abbey of Dryburgh. Shall we go there tomorrow?"

"With pleasure, Your Grace. It is a fair place, hidden in a bend of Tweed. Not like Jedburgh and Kelso and Melrose, in the midst of towns. It was a White Friars' house. Burned by the English Hertford, a score of years ago . . ."

"Ah, yes – like the others. Tell me of Dryburgh, as we ride, Thomas my friend . . ."

Bothwell grinned and, reining back a little, transferred his attentions to Beth Beaton meantime.

On returning from their Dryburgh visit next day, to a modest banquet Janet had prepared for them at Ferniehirst, they found William Maitland awaiting them there. The conference at Berwick was already over, he informed – and to little real progress. Queen Elizabeth was proving dilatory and awkward still, refusing to commit herself as to the succession. Randolph, in private, had told him, Maitland, that she had an irrational fear that if she once named her successor on the throne, she might be signing her own death-warrant, that she might well be assassinated or poisoned, so that the named one should succeed. As to marriage, she was still preferring Dudley – or Leicester as he should now be styled – over Darnley, even though she had allowed Lennox to return to Scotland. And Lennox, he revealed, was already sending presents to those in a position to influence the decision; he himself had received an orloge set with diamonds. No doubt gifts would be coming to Her Grace also. But Leicester himself, Randolph reported, was less than eager to come to Scotland. It was thought that he still had hopes of gaining Elizabeth and the *English* Crown Matrimonial for himself. William Cecil, the English Secretary of State, was in favour of Darnley and so was Bedford, the other ambassador. But their own Earl James was not. He had something against Lennox, it seemed, and therefore against his son. So it was all very much a case of divided counsels, with "many obscure words and dark sentences" as Maitland put it, with little achieved.

The Queen herself was in two minds over it all. She personally was in no hurry to be wed again, content to remain meantime as she was. But her Council was strong on the issue of the succession, the Scots one; but they were keenly interested in the English one also, which could end the five centuries of war between the two realms, if they united. Again, if marry she must she would have preferred one or other of the two French dukes, both of whom she knew and liked, more especially d'Aumale, good Catholics both. But obviously her Council and the parliament would not be happy with these, and there would be much trouble. So, since her pride would not allow her to consider Leicester, this Darnley seemed to be the best possibility – especially as,

Maitland reported, Randolph said that although he supported the established Church of England, his mother was a fervid Catholic and the son was thought privately to lean that way also. At seventeen, of course, his religious views could be less than settled.

There and then the Queen asked her Secretary of State to compose a letter for her to send to Elizabeth asking that the Master of Lennox, the Lord Darnley, should be allowed to come to Scotland soon, to visit her còurt – so that she could at least see the young man, to aid in her decision.

That night, match-making and amours being very much in the air, William Maitland proposed marriage to Flam Fleming – and was told to wait awhile.

12

That was a hard winter, with heavy snow and frost, and for much of the time the Borderland was cut off from the rest of Scotland, roads and hill-routes choked. Not that Thomas Kerr would have been apt to be travelling far afield anyway, for Janet was pregnant again, and not doing so well with it as last time. He was concerned, wondering whether he was to be blamed for making her so too soon. Also, his Uncle Walter, who was in fact rather old and portly for very active Warden's duties, was seeking to use his nephew more and more as assistant; and since one day, presumably, Thomas would succeed in turn to the wardenship, it was good practice.

It was in fact early February before he heard anything from the Queen. Then a messenger came, not from Holyroodhouse but from Wemyss Castle in Fife, where she appeared to be staying. She requested her "friend and protector", as she put it, if it was not too much of an inconvenience to him, to go to Berwick-upon-Tweed, or at least just north of it, to welcome, in her name, to Scottish soil, Darnley, Master of Lennox, who was now travelling north as requested, and to bring him either to Holyrood or to this Wemyss Castle. She was uncertain as to the day of his arrival, weather conditions bound to have affected him; but he had left London at the end of January, so he might be expected, if a good horseman as reported, before the middle of February. Would her good Sir Thomas do this for her? She sent her fond good wishes and hoped to see him, therefore, shortly.

Distinctly surprised, but flattered too, at this mission, and assured by Janet that she was much improved and could be left with an easy mind, he set off the next day eastwards, by Kelso and Coldstream, following Tweed. He took four of his Kerr horsemen with him.

Like all Scots, particularly Borderers, Thomas resented the fact that he could not enter the town of Berwick without the express permission of its English governor, for of course it had been Scotland's principal port once, as well as capital of Berwickshire or The Merse. But by trickery in diplomacy, after having occupied it in arms, during the reign of the weak Robert the Third, the English retained possession, and now it was a jealously guarded part of England.

So Thomas and his men spent the night at the hospice for travellers at Lamberton, three miles north of the town and the Tweed, where now was the borderline, to await his charge.

They had to pass all next day there also, before in another snowstorm young Darnley arrived, with an escort of a dozen, come cursing the weather and taking a jaundiced view of Scotland, having spent the night in the Berwick governor's castle. His greeting of Thomas was less than cordial.

Darnley was, as had been reported, tall, over six feet, slender, fair-haired and good-looking, with an almost girlish complexion and no beard. Indeed it looked as though he did not yet shave. This impression of immaturity was added to by a certain weakness about the mouth – or so Thomas judged; but perhaps he was biased.

They rode northwards, in snow, scarcely companionably. Thomas did, dutifully, attempt to point out various features and landmarks, for this was the other's first visit to the land of his forebears, but weather conditions did not help and the visitor showed no great signs of interest.

However, when they halted for the night at Dunbar, at the former Trinitarian monastery, the great royal castle on its rock-stacks rising out of the sea looking singularly inhospitable, Darnley, warmed by wine and a good meal, shed something of what seemed like petulance and without being affable, became less difficult. He began to ask questions, as to conditions in this land, its powerful lords, the man Knox, the balance between Protestant and Catholic, and of course the Queen, her views and attitudes. Thomas was cautious about his replies. He recognised that this young man, whatever he might lack in geniality, was knowledgeable and evidently highly educated. What his impact on the Queen might be, he was unsure.

The snow stopped, and, succeeded by frost and brittle sunshine which painted brilliant scenery, next day they came to Edinburgh amongst its hills, with Darnley exclaiming that he had never seen the like. At Holyroodhouse, they discovered that the Queen was not there, still at either Wemyss or St

Andrews apparently. But the Lord Robert entertained them with his usual hearty if unconventional hospitality.

Uncertain whether to go on to Fife, or to wait in Edinburgh, they stayed a day to rest the horses and then resumed their journey, Darnley anxious to meet the Queen and possibly learn his fate. They rode nine miles westwards, to Queen Margaret's Ferry, over the sudden and temporary narrowing of the Firth of Forth, where large scows were available to transport men and horses across to the Fife shore, thus saving a sixty-five-mile detour round by Stirling and the only bridge. Turning east thereafter, they proceeded some twenty miles along an attractive coastline, Thomas indicating Burntisland Castle, where the Frenchman Chastelard had so recklessly invaded the Queen's privacy; Kinghorn where King Alexander the Third had fallen to his death, thus precipitating the Wars of Independence; and the ruined castle of Grange, belonging to his father-in-law.

They reached Wemyss Castle, past Kirkcaldy town and just east of the port of Dysart, as the sun was sinking, a large fortalice perched on the sea-cliffs which were honeycombed with caves, these giving the place its name – Wemyss being merely a corruption of the Gaelic *uamh*, cave. They found that, despite the late hour and the weather the Queen was still out hunting, or rather hawking along the cliffs where many wildfowl roosted; but Ebba Seton, who was less sportingly inclined than the other ladies, welcomed them kindly.

Presently and privately, Ebba asked Thomas what he thought of this Darnley. He had been with him for a few days now and must have gained some notion as to his worth and character? The Queen was greatly anticipating his visit, needless to say. Was she going to be well impressed, or otherwise?

He was cautious about answering that also. He said that the young man was able, talented, good-looking as she could see, and could be, he thought, fair company, if so inclined; whether he was reliable was not for him to say, but he seemed to be moody – although perhaps the circumstances warranted that. Her Grace must judge for herself.

When Her Grace arrived, presently, flushed with exercise, bright-eyed and lovely, Thomas went to greet her in the castle stableyard, and was affectionately received and even given a little royal hug. Then asked the selfsame questions. What was Darnley like? Had he found him agreeable? Was he as handsome as reported? Or was she going to be disappointed? She had deliberately not come to Holyrood to await him, or gone out of her way to welcome him here – until she had seen him. For she did not want to raise his hopes of any marriage in case he was not the man for her.

Thomas hesitated, as well he might. He did not really like Henry Stewart. But then, there were many around the Queen that he did not like – Bothwell, the Earl James, Morton, and of course Knox; he was prejudiced undoubtedly, and admitted to a kind of jealousy for Mary Stewart – so he was not the best one to ask.

"I fear that I cannot answer all Your Grace's questions," he said. "For *you*, no man could be worthy, as I see it! The Master of Lennox would have to be an angel out of heaven to be fit to wed Your Highness! And he is scarcely that! But he is of good appearance and sound wits, that I can assure you."

She looked at him a little doubtfully, as perhaps was not to be wondered at, but nodded, and introduced him to her host, Sir John Wemyss, and then yielded him to her Marys, and passed inside.

The meeting between the two Stewarts, significant as it had to be, was not dramatic in any way, of the Queen's intent. By arrangement, it took place at the evening meal in the castle's great hall; and for that, of course, all had to be in their places at table before the royal party's entry. Sir John, and Lady Wemyss, his mother, since the laird was as yet unmarried, had their due seats on either side of the Queen, and a place was set for Darnley next to their hostess, with Lady Fleming, another Stewart, on his left. Other lofty ones were also on the dais. Thomas sat with the Marys just below it.

When the duty herald appeared, to bang a gong and announce the Queen's entry, all arose, and Sir John led her in and to her place at table. So Darnley could only turn round and bow, at this stage, and receive, like others there, a kindly inclination of the royal head before the Queen sat and signed to the herald, who announced that the Wemyss parish minister would say grace-before-meat. This, at some length, over, and general conversation recommencing as servants appeared with the steaming viands, the Queen leaned forward and looked past her hostess to the visitor from England, and smiled again.

It was all skilfully done, not committing herself to anything

179

specific at this stage, yet treating Darnley as a special guest. At her smile, that young man rose, and came to stand behind the royal chair and bow again, deeply. He was notably clad now, in the height of London fashion, and indeed looked singularly attractive.

The Queen held out her hand for him to kiss. "So, my lord Henry, we meet," she said. "This is a pleasure. We are far-out kin, and I have heard much of you. I trust that your long journey to Scotland was not too sore a trial, in this weather?"

"No journey, however far, would be a trial, Madam, to meet Your Majesty," he asserted gallantly. "And now that I see the reality is even more brilliant, more lovely, than all reports proclaimed, I am overwhelmed!" And he dipped knee in another bow.

"La, sir, we have a flatterer here, I think! And from the English court, where feminine charms command all, I am assured!"

Only for a moment he hesitated, as Flam nudged Thomas with her elbow. "No beauty there could surpass yours, Majesty," he said. "As for charm, I made an unprofitable target, I fear!"

The Queen nodded, smiling, clearly approving. "Thank you, my lord. You are a diplomat, I see, as well as all else." And, in case that sounded over-appreciative, she added, "And here in Scotland we use the term Grace, rather than Majesty."

"Ah – I beg Your Grace's gracious pardon. I would, h'm, esteem grace before majesty, anywhere!"

She tapped his wrist in mock reproof. "We must not forget that you are an English citizen! Now I keep you from our host's good provision. We shall talk more later." And she waved him away, but graciously.

"He came well out of that," Flam whispered. "She set a trap for him there. For he is a subject of Queen Elizabeth and her cousin. Could hope to succeed her, one day. He must be careful indeed what he says of her and her court. All will be reported to Randolph, you may be sure, and so to London."

Thomas nodded. He had to admit that Darnley had performed well and seemed to be making a good impression. He appeared a very different young man to the one met in the snow at Lamberton.

After the meal the tables were cleared for dancing, and

musicians struck up. The Queen danced first with her host, and then with his brother, a young man also in his late teens, coltish rather than accomplished, while Darnley partnered first Lady Wemyss and then Lady Fleming, all noting that he danced most expertly and gracefully for a man. Thomas, with Flam and Ebba, and then Beth, found himself getting scant attention and reaction from two of them at least, so intent were they in watching the visitor from the south.

When Darnley danced with the Queen, at length, there was no question but that they made notable partners, a target for all eyes, suiting each other's movements and gestures in an excellent unison. Knowing the Queen's love of dancing and music, Thomas's heart sank, for he could not feel that this man was the man for her, yet most evidently he was impressing her.

When the evening's entertainment was over and Thomas escorted Flam and Beth to their high tower chamber above the cliff-girt shore, he was not encouraged by learning that they both thought well of Darnley, seeing him as romantic, attractive, even appealing, almost in need of cherishing. Obviously, superficially at least, his qualities and style commended themselves to young women. Somehow he did not think that many *men* present had eyed Darnley with any great approval.

"There is a weakness there," he insisted. "I am sure of it. Something to the mouth. A pettiness, also, I think. And vanity . . ."

"All men cannot be paladins of strength, like Tom Smellum!" Beth declared. "And he is young. I say Her Grace could do much worse."

"If he *is* a little weak in will — not in body, I warrant! — that might be no grievous failing," Flam suggested. "For he will always have to yield to her in great matters. She will take the decisions, as monarch, not him. A strong-willed man could find that difficult, trying."

Thomas had to admit that there was something in that. But still he held out. Their beloved sovereign-lady deserved better than this.

"*You* — you are half in love with her yourself!" Flam accused, even as she kissed him goodnight. "Like so many another. Even the man Knox looks at her devouringly even as he thunders at her! So your judgment in this is suspect, Tom Smellum!"

"As well that the Earl James is not here," Beth added.

"For he is strong against any Darnley match, for some reason. Would he and you join forces for once?"

Thomas went to his more humble room in the stable block thoughtful.

The day following, being damp, misty and chill, with an easterly haar off the Norse Sea, and so unsuitable for both hawking and hunting, or even archery, Sir John Wemyss took his guests to visit the caves in the cliffs. These were rather special, in more than just giving name to the parish and barony. They had evidently been occupied by their Celtic ancestors at some remote period, and the walls of some were decorated by typical Pictish carvings and symbols. Later occupants appeared to have been Christian missionaries, who also had left their marks and inscriptions. And in one, Sir John recounted, with tactful lack of detail, an episode therein between Mary's own father, James the Fifth, and a gypsy woman. In it all the Queen was clearly highly interested; but watching Darnley, perhaps less than kindly, Thomas saw him as bored, and little caring who noted it, save when *she* turned to him to point out or comment. Not that he was the only one there to become bored, Beth Beaton amongst them.

That evening there was more dancing and music, also song-singing and ballads. And Darnley revealed some talent for versifying, reading out a brief poem he had composed, somewhat floridly extolling the Queen's beauty, charm and grace, which was well received – if hardly by Thomas Kerr.

It was perhaps as well, in his present frame of mind, that that man felt that he had to leave next morning, to get back to Janet and his duties at Ferniehirst, even though the Queen and her ladies urged him to stay. He rode off westwards moodily – he who had accused Darnley of being moody. Perhaps his mood was not helped by what Flam had told him last night at her bedroom door: that she had decided to accept William Maitland's oft-repeated proposal of marriage, and they would be wed soon. It was ridiculous – the man was twice her age. Why . . .?

13

Janet presented Thomas with another son, in May, oddly
enough an easier birth than the previous one despite all the
earlier discomforts. They named him William, and were happy
indeed. Thomas found great satisfaction in his children, family
life much to his taste. Much as he enjoyed the recurrent visits
to court and the company there, in especial the ladies, he came
to recognise that he was a home-loving man.

Word of what went on, or some of it, in the Queen's
circle, reached him intermittently, in no great detail. Darnley,
inevitably, was apt to be the main focus, of reports and gossip
both. He was behaving himself well, by most accounts, doing
the things that the Queen liked doing, outdoors and in, in
sports and games and entertainments. But as well as that he
was clearly seeking to please, or at least not to offend, the
ruling magnates of the Council, the officers of state and the
religious authorities, even to the extent of attending St Giles
High Kirk on the first Sunday of the return to Edinburgh to
listen to the celebrated John Knox. The Queen, apparently,
was showing mounting appreciation.

But Darnley's efforts were not entirely successful, for the
royal approval angered the Earl James sufficiently for him to
insult the young man to his face and then to have a violent
row with his half-sister, resulting in that usually calmly cold
individual storming out of the royal presence and consequently
being banished from court to his hard-bought northern earldom of Moray. Since he had in effect been the principal ruler
of the land, and the Queen's most influential councillor, this
affected and excited the entire country. And to Thomas Kerr
at least it spoke loudly and sadly as to the royal inclination
towards Darnley.

All this left Thomas with mixed feelings, but he told himself
that these were really no dire concerns of his, happy husband
and father and growing luminary in the Borderland.

Then he heard that Darnley was ill, at Stirling Castle. At

first it was reported as only a chill developing into a fever; then it turned out to be, in fact, measles – a diagnosis which produced a hoot of unkind laughter from Thomas over what he esteemed to be a child's disease, coming to emphasise his own assessment of the other's immaturity. But his mirth soon changed to gloom as word came in that the Queen had established herself as Darnley's personal nurse, attending on him day and night, nothing too much for her to do for him. That very youthfulness and appeal to a woman's kindly protective instincts towards those in need of cherishing, was now bringing the pair close indeed.

Thomas now feared the worst, but prevented himself from praying for the patient's relapse.

As it happened, Thomas was not alone in his reaction to this development, much loftier folk than he becoming alarmed. Mary's de Guise uncle, the Cardinal of Lorraine, wrote to her warning against a false step and strongly urging a French match; as did the French Queen-Mother, Catherine de Medici. The Pope sent word that a Catholic marriage was essential, and declaring that his papal dispensation would be necessary before Mary could wed Darnley, as they were step-cousins. And Queen Elizabeth of England changed her tune once more and announced that she was not going to commit herself to declaring the English succession, with Leicester being spurned by Mary. Messengers, couriers, legates and ambassadors hastened to Scotland; and at Stirling, Mary Stewart received them politely – and continued to nurse Henry Stewart back to health.

Then all protests and advisings were shown to be ineffective. The Queen officially announced that she had created Henry Stewart, Duke of Albany, the royal dukedom second only to that of Rothesay which was reserved for the heir to the throne. And only a week later, Thomas received an invitation, indeed a royal command, to attend the Queen's marriage in Edinburgh on Sunday, 29th July.

On arrival at the capital, short notice as it was, Thomas found the city in a great stir. And not only on account of the royal wedding but because the Earl of Moray, of all men, was said to be raising the standard of rebellion – not in Edinburgh fortunately but at Loch Leven in Kinross-shire. His enmity to the Darnley match was known to all; but now he was carrying his objections to an extraordinary length; and scarcely believably was said to be receiving Queen Elizabeth's support and funding, on the grounds that the Protestant religion was being threatened in Scotland by this marriage – this despite the fact that Darnley was a Protestant, and had been more or less sponsored by Elizabeth herself in the first place. Moray had refused to attend a convention of the nobles, at Perth, summoned to agree that Darnley should be given the Crown Matrimonial, on the grounds that there was a plot by the Lennox faction to assassinate him there, a charge which few believed. Now Moray was calling on all good Protestants to rally to his cause, and was being backed up by Argyll and Châtelherault, the latter seeing his position as heir-presumptive endangered. So there was considerable unrest and excitement in the capital – with John Knox, oddly enough, remaining strangely silent.

Whether from fears of possible disturbances in the city or out of the Queen's personal choice, the wedding was to be held at the extraordinary hour of five o'clock in the morning, in the Chapel Royal at Holyrood, this occasioning much talk. Thomas, arriving only the day before, had to refrain from visiting the palace that evening, guessing that all would be in a great to-do there. He would have liked some first-hand information from the Marys.

He was in his place in the Chapel Royal next morning, and found it crowded, despite the hour. They were by no means all Catholics present, although the ceremony would be by the Catholic rite; he saw the Earls of Eglinton, Cassillis and Glencairn there, all strong Protestants. These had links with the Lennox family, of course, the Scots nobles' allegiances and alliances being not all of a religious persuasion.

Brides traditionally have the privilege of being late, and Queen Mary was no exception. But in the quite lengthy wait there was a development, the Lord Lyon King of Arms with his heralds coming in, and, after a fanfare of trumpets, announcing that by Her Grace's royal command, the Prince Henry Duke of Albany, was hereafter to be known as the King of her kingdom and addressed as such. There were not a few scowls at this declaration.

Then the Bishop of Brechin and the Dean of Restalrig, with acolytes and choristers, appeared, to conduct the service. The choir sang.

At length more trumpeting heralded, not the bridegroom to await his bride, but the Queen herself, a hand on the arms of the Earls of Lennox and Atholl. Unexpectedly also, she was clad wholly in black satin, gown, mantling and hood. Nevertheless she looked very lovely and serene. Behind came her Marys and personal attendants. The two earls led her up to before the high altar, then turned back to leave the chapel, the Queen standing alone.

A single trumpet-blast, and in came Darnley escorted by the same two earls, clad in great splendour, cloth-of-gold with the red Lion Rampant of Scotland blazoned on the short cloak slung over one shoulder, jewelled chains around his neck. Carrying himself proudly, he paced up to stand beside the dark Mary, his father and Atholl stationing themselves behind the notably contrasting pair. It was as though the widowed queen was deliberately seeking to invest the young man with the trappings of majesty which he lacked and of which she had no need. Yet the effect was, in fact, to emphasise their two years' difference in age, and the bridegroom's callow immaturity.

The two clerics came forward to commence the service.

By Romish standards it was a very simple ceremony, with a minimum of invocations, responses, genuflections and priestly gestures, clearly to appease the Protestants. The couple exchanged their vows, she more clearly than he. Then, with something of a flourish, Darnley placed three rings on her finger, the centre one with a great diamond which sparkled in the light of the altar candles.

Then they knelt down together to receive the benediction, the clerics intoning it in unison. And kneeling there, Mary turned to her husband and held out her arms, and they kissed before all.

Rising, they bowed towards the altar and then turned to face the congregation. The Queen, one hand on her bridegroom's arm, raised the other.

"I rejoice to present to you all Henry, King of our kingdom, sharer of my throne to be, wearer of the Crown Matrimonial. Hereafter he is King Henry; and all documents, charters and edicts will be *signed* jointly in the names of Marie and Henry. So be it."

There was silence. That is, until the new father-in-law, Lennox, raised his voice.

"God save His Grace! God save His Grace!" he cried.

None echoed that. The silence descended again.

The Queen bit her lip. Then, turning to her husband, she inclined her head, unspeaking.

He bowed jerkily and, set-faced, swung about to stalk out of the chapel. After a few moments, the other Protestants therein moved to do likewise. Nuptial Mass would now be celebrated, without the bridegroom.

Thomas Kerr was probably not the only one there who knew considerable misgivings.

Back in the palace thereafter a more cheerful atmosphere developed, fortunately. Undoubtedly this was much helped by a version of the traditional and much-demanded bedding ceremony. Since it was far from bedtime, and of course unsuitable that the Queen should have to undergo the full ordeal of public undressing by the men present – whatever the women might have desired regarding Darnley – a very modified procedure was adopted. While the new King Henry stood by, such men as could crowd into the great bedchamber with the large, canopied double bed, all watched and to some extent restrained by the grinning Lord Robert Stewart, began, one at a time, to undo the strategically placed pins which kept the Queen's dark outer clothing in place, hood first, then mantling and finally the gown itself, a deliberate superfluity of the said pins. At length, with a shake of her person, the gown fell to the floor and Mary stood there clad only in a brief white silken shift, shoulders and much of a fine bosom bare – and a delectable sight she made. For a moment or two she remained thus, and then, with a smile to them all, raised a finger and wagged it, signifying enough. There were exclamations from all around, admiration, approval and the reverse, disappointment that it did not go far enough, even a few crudities – which had Thomas for one frowning angrily – before the Lord Robert shooed all the males out of the room, save for Darnley himself, leaving the Marys to dress their mistress in suitably gorgeous clothing, a widow no longer. Her husband stood watching, left severely alone.

The wedding banquet which followed, at not yet even midday, was a splendid affair, quite the most ambitious Scotland had seen for a century, both as to provender and entertainment. Thomas was seated, as usual, just below the dais, between Flam and Beth Beaton – Secretary Maitland was away in London seeking to change Queen Elizabeth's present attitudes. But if at this level the company was little altered from normal, at the dais-table above there were notable variations. Apart from Darnley himself, at the Queen's right hand, and his father, mother and young brother nearby, there sat the bishop and the dean, with the Lord Robert, the Earl of Atholl and the Lord Seton, Ebba's father. Significantly missing were the Earl James of Moray, Argyll the Chancellor and the Duke of Châtelherault, with other leading Protestants. Also, the Earl of Bothwell. Thomas remarked on this last to Flam.

"He is gone to France," she told him. "Why, none knows. I fear that he does not approve of our new lord and master, King Henry. Like so many another, it seems! You yourself, I think? And he preferred not to witness the wedding. He is a law unto himself is James Hepburn."

Thomas nodded, unspeaking.

"You *do* mislike this match?" Flam persisted.

"I think it . . . mistaken."

"You all are jealous, I swear!" That was Beth.

"Scarcely that. Darnley is weak, I judge, weak. And the Queen needs a strong helper and support. He is very young. And vain, it seems . . ."

"He will grow older," Flam said.

"His will be a difficult part to play. A King in name only, the first to wear the Crown Matrimonial in all Scotland's long history – for we have never before had a Queen-Regnant. And with few of those in power favouring him. The Queen says that all will be done now in their joint names. But in fact that must be only a token. He will have no *power*. Always having to defer to his wife. Few men would enjoy that. For a vain young papingoe like him . . . !"

"You are hard on him, Tom Smellum!"

"Perhaps. But I fear for this marriage. And the Queen's happiness. She is surrounded by strong, hard men. She will have to carry her husband, not he her. And with the Earl James and Argyll already in rebellion . . ."

"What think you they will do? They cannot undo this marriage."

"The good Lord knows! But Moray is no fool. He will have his plans, you may be sure. And if he has Elizabeth of England's backing, and general Protestant support . . ."

"Save us – this is a wedding-feast, not a wake, a burial!" Beth Beaton exclaimed. "Spare us, of a mercy!"

Thomas apologised.

The banquet over, there was dancing, singing, entertainment by jugglers, acrobats, dwarfs, even a dancing bear. Also set masques, in which the Marys took part. They were joined, for the occasion, by a very pregnant Mary Livingstone.

Thomas had the privilege of having one dance as the Queen's partner. She was obviously happy and he was careful not to show any hint of his misgivings. She asked kindly after Janet, young Sir Dand and the new baby William, and declared that she would come down to Jedburgh as soon as she could.

There was thereafter a promenade outside and a distribution of largesse to the waiting crowds thronging the palace yard and the foot of the Canongate, the Queen, as ever, eager to show her affection for her people, too much so by Darnley's expression. Thereafter, although few were ready for it, there was another feasting, done but little justice to, this followed by the ceremonial send-off for the royal couple – which none, fortunately, tried to convert into the explicit bedding scene, a feature of so many weddings.

It had been a long day, and Thomas took his departure soon thereafter, escorted to the gates as usual by Flam and Beth, this time with Ebba Seton joining them. She it was who, as he was leaving, with embraces and kisses, echoed the man's fears.

"Pray God this day has a happy outcome," she said. "Our beloved mistress deserves joy and blessing."

"More gloom!" Beth exclaimed. "*You* now!"

On that note they parted.

Thomas headed back to his Borderland next morning.

14

In the circumstances, Thomas was surprised to receive a royal summons again less than three weeks thereafter – and this time to no courtly function. He was to report, with all speed, not to Edinburgh but to Glasgow, and with as many of his Border moss-troopers as he could muster, in armed strength. No explanations were vouchsafed.

Two days, and he was on his way north-westwards, with fifty horsed men, some of them Cessford Kers.

In the event he did not have to wait until he reached Glasgow for at least some of the explanation, for they met sundry other bands of armed men heading in the same direction, and the leader of one such, John Home of Blackadder, was a fairly near neighbour to Smailholm; and being kin to the Lord Home, much in favour at court these days, was knowledgeable as to events. Apparently Moray's rebellion had reached very serious proportions and become active; indeed there had been an attempt to kidnap the Queen and Darnley. Fortunately this had miscarried. The Earl James and the other extreme Protestant leaders had been ordered to yield themselves to the Queen's mercy, and when this was ignored, were put to the horn and outlawed. Thomas was alarmed to learn that his father-in-law, Kirkcaldy of Grange, was included amongst the uprising leadership, and, whilst not actually outlawed as yet, had been ordered to ward himself in Dumbarton Castle, with the Erskine Earl of Mar taking over the governorship of Edinburgh Castle. So now it was suddenly all but civil war, with the Queen determined to exert and maintain her authority. She was assembling a major army at Glasgow, to separate Châtelherault, the Hamiltons and their allies in the south-west, from Moray's and Argyll's forces in the north-east and north-west respectively, and was leading her host in person, all equipped for war – a new aspect of that young woman's character displaying itself.

Most of the way up Tweed and by its upland passes to the

infant Clyde, they came to Glasgow, where the latter river reached salt water. Thomas had never been here, and found it a smaller city than he had expected, the large port area being further down the Clyde estuary at Dumbarton. Glasgow, not really in any important position strategically, had remained essentially an ecclesiastical centre and seat of learning ever since St Mungo had founded it in the sixth century, second only to St Andrews, with its own archbishop and a university, something which Edinburgh could not boast.

Moderate in size the place might be, amongst its green meadows with the blue ramparts of the Highlands visible to the north, but at present it was teeming with folk, some ten thousand armed men already assembled there, its citizens, clerics and scholars scarcely enjoying the influx, even if the students found it all exciting.

Leaving their men at the great camp established on the extensive Glasgow Green, Thomas and Home made their way to the Provost's House, where the Queen and Darnley had taken up quarters. There Thomas was astonished to find all the Marys; he had hardly expected the Queen's ladies to be taking part in a great military exercise such as this; but since the monarch herself was so doing, they accompanied her. Good horsewomen all, they seemed to be enjoying the experience thus far. What would happen if fighting began was another matter.

Thomas was welcomed with acclaim. The Queen was not present when he arrived, being gone, with Darnley, to visit the royal castle of Dumbarton down-river, but she would be back that evening.

The military situation, he learned, was confused, to say the least. They had come to Glasgow on information that Moray was amassing his troops in the Campbell country of Argyll, with the Hamiltons doing the same much nearer at hand, in Lanarkshire and north Ayrshire. Then they had heard that the Earl James and Argyll had moved, in force, south-eastwards, to Castle Campbell, Argyll's Lowland seat in Kinross-shire. The royal forces had been preparing to march thitherwards when it was reported that the enemy leadership had moved once more, south-westwards now, not seemingly to assail the Glasgow position but, bypassing this city, to go and join the Hamilton force further south. Now Moray was alleged to be at Ayr. So it looked as though confrontation would be in that

191

direction. Estimates of the rebel strength varied from six to eight thousand.

Thomas enquired as to how the royal marriage was progressing. Answers seemed to him a little guarded for those forthright young women. Darnley apparently fancied himself as a military commander. He had acquired for himself a magnificent suit of gold-plated armour, and was talking ambitiously of tactics and strategy – such received but doubtfully by more experienced warriors. The Queen was a little perturbed, it seemed, in that her husband was now tending to associate with less than reputable characters to game and drink with – perhaps hardly to be blamed, in that few of the nobles and magnates would have anything to do with him. There was no rift between husband and wife, but hints of problems. Quite possibly this military adventure was no bad development, in that it brought and kept the pair close together and well away from some of Darnley's new and raffish friends.

When Thomas asked who, in fact, was the overall commander of the royal host, under the Queen, he was told that, in name, it was the Stewart Earl of Atholl; but in fact it was the Lord Home, who, on account of the unending Border warfare, was an experienced campaigner. This information made Thomas a little uneasy, for despite the fact that Home was married to one of his own aunts, a sister of Ker of Cessford, he was a strong Protestant and former associate of the Earl James. Scotland's family and religious alignments were apt to be like that, confusing. And nothing was more sure than that both Atholl and Home would much resent being told their military business by the new and youthful King Henry.

Thomas learned also that the Queen had sent to France for Bothwell to return to her aid; for whatever else he might be he was a fighter.

When the Queen returned that evening he was surprised to see with her and Darnley an unexpected companion – George, Lord Gordon. This young man was the eldest son and heir of the late Huntly. He had not been at the Battle of Corrichie, and despite Earl James's demands that he should be executed, like his brother Sir John Gordon, had been spared by the Queen and only warded in the royal castle of Dunbar. Now he had been released; and although not yet restored as the new Earl of Huntly, was, it seemed, to be sent north to rally the great clan of Gordon, if possible, to the Queen's cause, this as counter to Moray's influence up there. Mary was learning to play the complicated game of statecraft, using men and interests rather like chessmen on a board.

Wearing a leather jack, less spectacular if rather more effective than her husband's gleaming gilt armour, and with a pistol at her saddle, the Queen expressed herself as delighted to see Sir Tom Smellum. But she had distressing news for him. His goodsire, Sir William Kirkcaldy of Grange, had failed, along with the Lord Rothes, to ward himself in Dumbarton Castle as ordered, and consequently had to be proclaimed outlaw – which she had been loth to do, for Thomas's sake. But with all the other rebel leaders now put to the horn, he could not be excepted.

Next day, the army was prepared to march southwards to challenge the insurgents. They would leave Glasgow at first light on 2nd September.

But, although leave they did, it was not to march southwards. For overnight, a messenger arrived from the Earl of Mar, in Edinburgh Castle, to report the surprising news that Moray, Châtelherault, Glencairn, Rothes, Kirkcaldy and the rest, with twelve hundred horse, had made an unlooked-for and hurried dash eastwards to the capital and were now more or less in possession of the city. He, Mar, had turned the castle cannon against them, to the admitted danger of the citizenry; but he urged the Queen's arrival, in fullest force, at speed.

So it was eastwards that the royal host moved that wet and blustery early morning, to head the forty-five miles to Edinburgh. With haste of the essence, the slow-marching infantry were left behind, under the Lord Seton, and the horsed squadrons, to the number of some four thousand, including Thomas's moss-troopers, pounded ahead. Unfortunately the heavy rain delayed them considerably, thousands of hooves churning up the roadways into muddy quagmires. The Queen and her ladies, however, were by no means backward.

It took them nearly seven hours, despite flogging the horses, to reach Edinburgh – and they had to traverse Hamilton country, in West Lothian, on the way. This did not produce any active opposition, but it almost certainly meant that information, carried on fresh horses, would be despatched to the capital, warning of their approach in large numbers. And when, at length, they did enter the city, it was indeed to find the enemy gone, having suddenly departed an hour or so earlier, southward apparently.

Clearly Moray and his friends were not yet ready to face the Queen's strength.

Mary was for following the rebels there and then, but this was advised against as impracticable. Not all the horses were of the quality of the Queen's and her nobles', and the difficult forty-five-mile dash had taxed them. An army cannot move at the pace of a few keen riders. They must rest. So, although it was only early afternoon, still raining, the troops were settled on the city's Burgh Muir, to recover and prepare for another early-morning start, and the royal party repaired to Holyrood. But not Thomas. His moss-troopers and their mounts were a tough stock, and the Queen besought him to go on after the rebels, not to attack, of course, but to discover their route of retiral and establish their whereabouts.

No enjoyable task as this was in these conditions, Thomas had no real difficulty in carrying out his instructions. Twelve hundred horsemen leave a very evident trail, especially in wet weather; and people along the way were informative. By the Leper-town and Straiton and Penicuik they went and, turning due south there, by Leadburn, it was obvious that the enemy were heading down for the Tweed valley in the Peebles vicinity. Presumably they would turn west there, for the upper Clyde and Lanark or Ayr.

Thomas followed on, over the rising ground and the rolling open moorlands of the Morthwaite foothills until, in the Portmore vicinity, they caught their first glimpse of the tail-end troops of the rebel horse, Thomas wondering whether Janet's father was amongst them. Satisfied, wet and weary, they turned back, duty done.

Nearly exhausted after the extra thirty miles or so, he reported to the Queen that night, and was given a royal kiss of appreciation. He had no complaint to make, but was not long in seeking his couch.

In the morning they were all off betimes, in what was already being ruefully referred to as the Chase About Raid. The weather was improved, dull but not raining.

It was not much more than a score of miles to Peebles and the vanguard of the royal army reached there by midday. It was to learn that Moray's force had indeed spent the night in the town but had ridden off early, up Tweed, westwards.

Townsmen claimed to have heard talk of them making for Dumfries, not Ayr or Lanark.

All pressed on, up Tweed.

Sure enough, at Broughton where that river made its sharp turn southwards towards its source on Tweedsmuir, the tracks of the rebels turned with it. So it looked as though it was indeed Dumfries, a strange choice of destination in the circumstances.

The Queen's host had not climbed far up towards Tweedsmuir when there was a development. Two horsemen, riding hard, came up behind them. They were messengers from the Earl of Mar, at Edinburgh. Word had reached him that Argyll, who apparently had remained at Castle Campbell meantime, was now reinforced by a large Highland host and was moving west in the direction of Stirling.

This news, of course, considerably concerned the royal leadership. Stirling Castle was the strongest fortress in the kingdom. But its hereditary Keeper was Mar himself, who was not therein but holding *Edinburgh* Castle. Who had been left in charge? And was he trustworthy? If Stirling fell to the rebels it would be a dire blow, not only as to its strength and prestige as the senior royal seat, but in that it dominated the only crossing of Forth and so could divide south and north Scotland, Highlands and Lowlands. Even if it did not fall, Argyll, with a powerful force, especially Highlandmen who were notable fighters, represented major menace in their rear.

A council was hastily convened, and it was the almost unanimous opinion that Argyll represented infinitely the greatest threat at this juncture. Just where their own infantry force, under Lords Seton and Livingstone, might be now, none knew, almost certainly not yet at Edinburgh. It was decided that this host here must turn back, unite with the infantry, and make for Stirling. But to keep some pressure on Moray it was felt that a detachment should continue on after him, not to bring him to battle but to keep him, as it were, preoccupied, and to prevent if possible any link-up with Argyll again. They were in Border country now, and this was surely a task for Borderers. Thomas could not do other than volunteer.

A number of other Border lairds present, including Home of Blackadder, agreed to join him, with their contingents, and being the only knight amongst them, Thomas found himself in the extraordinary position of being put in command, by the Queen's decision, of a force of almost eight hundred men, little as he esteemed himself apt for the responsibility.

A hasty leave-taking and well-wishing followed, and with the Queen turning back northwards, Thomas led his large detachment on southwards, with distinct misgivings again.

There followed a very strange interlude such as that man had never before experienced, commanding forty score of fighting men who were not to fight unless they had to, in order to form a presence, a possible threat, playing a watching role rather than an aggressive one, odd behaviour for moss-troopers and Border reivers.

As they rode up over the heights of Tweedsmuir and down into upper Annandale, Thomas considered well. According to reports, Moray had almost twice his own numbers. In this shadowing process, once they were seen by each other, it would not be long before the enemy realised their superiority, and that would almost certainly result in attack. So he devised a plan to confuse the opposition, if possible, dividing his force into four groups of approximately two hundred each, these to ride some distance apart but to keep in touch. By this means he hoped that Moray's people would never know just how many they totalled, with bands appearing and disappearing.

They were well down into Annandale, past Beattock and Moffat, to the river's junction with the Whamfray Water, in the Johnstone country, when Thomas caught sight of their quarry; so it seemed certain that Dumfries was the destination. Why, he wondered? Why there? There must be a reason. Galloway, he supposed, could be a source of manpower. Were the Maxwells, who tended to dominate this West March area, to be allied to Moray? Perhaps it was the comparative proximity to England, Carlisle only some thirty miles away? Moray was alleged to be seeking help from Queen Elizabeth. It might be that such was expected to be sent here?

Thomas kept his distance, for no doubt they would have been observed by now and he did not want conflict. Once he was satisfied that Dumfries was in fact the enemy objective, he summoned his groups together again and led them away eastwards, out of the Annan valley and over into Dryfesdale, to the area north of Lockerbie, where they ought to be reasonably safe from discovery or attack. Here at an isolated and alarmed farmery-hamlet called Balgray, they encamped for the night.

The next day, in separate groupings, they circuited the Dumfries vicinity, establishing the fact that the town was occupied by a large force. No doubt their own presence would be reported therein, but any confrontation was avoided. This was what they had been sent to do; but somehow it seemed singularly unsatisfactory a proceeding. All returned to the hamlet of Balgray.

In the morning, Thomas decided that he must at least try to obtain more information as to Moray's intentions. Ordering his people to continue with their diversionary tactics, he, with only two companions, discarded jacks, helmets and swords and, selecting undistinguished horses, set off for Dumfries itself. They hoped that they would be taken for ordinary local countrymen. The Balgray folk had told him that it was the weekly market-day in the town, so strangers would be the less noticeable.

Dumfries, the "capital" of this south-west corner of Scotland, lay some six miles inland from where the River Nith joined the wide Solway estuary, a fair-sized walled town dominated by quite a strong castle. Approaching it, Thomas and his companions were happy to insert themselves between two of the many herds of cattle being driven thitherwards, for as well as being market-day it was recognised by the local farmers that there would be an army to feed and beef would be in demand. In the circumstances, there was no difficulty for the trio in entering the town, and they continued on with the cattle down to the large open area at the riverside, known as the Sands, apparently, where the sales were held. There, in that crowded, noisy, smelly confusion of shouting men, barking dogs, lowing cattle and general hubbub, their anonymity was as safe as it ever would be.

It was not difficult, or too obvious, to make enquiries, for the talk everywhere was of the invasion of the area by the Earl of Moray's forces, and the welcome they had been given by the Lord Maxwell, from nearby Caerlaverock. This last in itself was valuable information, for Maxwell was powerful, indeed was Warden of the West March. Discreet and seemingly random questioning elicited further details, that as well as Moray, the Earls of Glencairn, Rothes and Cassillis were here, with the Lords Boyd and Ochiltree – but no word of Kirkcaldy of Grange. All were lodging up at the castle, with Maxwell. Their men were behaving reasonably well, considering – Maxwell would be insisting on that, in his own town – but some of the English troops were making nuisances of themselves apparently. Thomas pricked up his ears at that. There were English here in Dumfries? He was told that there were three hundred of them, under the Earl of Bedford, Queen Elizabeth's Lieutenant of the North, and they were awaiting more, ten times that, it was said, and gold with them, much gold.

So that was indeed what brought Moray to Dumfries, Elizabeth's besought aid. If reinforced by three thousand English, and moneys to hire more Scots fighters, the situation would look very different.

Making a sally further into the town but avoiding the castle vicinity, Thomas repeated his enquiries, learning little new but confirming what they had been told at the market. The Englishmen were not popular, and considerable alarm was expressed at the possible arrival of thousands more.

Satisfied, the trio returned to Balgray.

Thereafter, Thomas sent off a couple of riders northwards, to inform the Queen of the position, and to seek instructions.

The days that followed were uneventful, less than exciting. In large groups and small, they quartered that area, the vales of Nith, Annan, Cairn, Dryfe and Esk, from the Kirkmichael and Keir Hills down to the Solway, into Galloway and right to the English border at Sark and Gretna. Their ridings to and fro must have been reported to Moray many times, for they made no attempt to hide themselves, but never lingered in one place for long enough to be challenged in any strength. Fortunately the Johnstone chief proved to be a staunch supporter of the Queen – possibly because he was at hereditary feud with the Maxwells – and so *his* area was secure ground for Thomas's people, and they were able to make their base in Dryfesdale. No word came from the Queen – but equally no new influx of Englishmen crossed the borderline. It was evidently a waiting game for all concerned, that September of 1565.

Then, at last, a royal courier arrived, from St Andrews oddly enough. The Queen had saved Stirling, scattered Argyll's force and taken Castle Campbell. She would now bring her enlarged army down to Dumfries-shire, to deal with Moray. Thomas was to keep the enemy under close observation meantime, so as to inform her accurately when she arrived.

It was into October before the great royal host, now no less

198

than eighteen thousand, with the Earl of Morton joining it with his Douglas contingent – a fairly clear sign that Moray's cause was waning – came marching down Annandale, armies of that size travelling but slowly. And, of course, its progress could by no means remain secret. Thomas heard of its approach three days before it arrived – and so evidently did Moray. For, with no further access of strength arriving from England, it seemed, he finally saw the writing on the wall. He disbanded his force and with his close associates himself departed southwards, with Bedford and the three hundred English troops, to cross the border and on to Carlisle, entrusting himself to the distinctly doubtful charity of Queen Elizabeth Tudor.

The Chase About Raid was over at last, and with it Moray's rebellion. The Queen of Scots seemed to sit the more secure on her throne; and Thomas Kerr thankfully returned to Ferniehirst and his own life again. He had been away from home since August.

15

Janet was pregnant again, with both of them praying for a daughter this time. Dand and young William were in good shape, and all was well at Ferniehirst – save of course that issues and problems over lands and tenants and law-breakers, especially Jedburgh ones, had not conveniently restricted themselves while he was away and had piled up direfully for Thomas's attention. He had been gone for almost three months.

During the remainder of that autumn and the early winter, Thomas was kept busy, then, his problems mainly administrative ones, he being well content that this should be so, although he thought often of the Queen and her ladies, wondering in especial how the marriages were developing, the royal one and Flam's. He could not feel that either were right, the former more obviously ill-fated in his opinion, but the latter scarcely suitable either, with William Maitland twice Flam's age.

As it happened, and surprisingly, it was Secretary Maitland himself who next brought Thomas in touch with court affairs, arriving at Ferniehirst one day at the beginning of March. He apparently had been sent by the Queen to confer with Moray and the other exiled lords, who were now staying at Newcastle-upon-Tyne, and they had met at Berwick-upon-Tweed. On the way back, he had been instructed to call on Thomas and to invite him to the wedding of Beth Beaton who, it seemed, was to marry a northern laird, one Alexander Ogilvy of Boyne, in early April.

Maitland had much to tell. Darnley – Thomas, like so many another, could never bring himself to think of him as King Henry – was fairly consistently misbehaving himself, and the Queen becoming progressively disillusioned, even though she was now pregnant. During the Chase About Raid Darnley had been resentful that he was not put in overall command of the army, and in fact had declared publicly that it was shame when women commanded men in the field. He was drinking excessively, and was frequently helplessly drunken even on official occasions, at one banquet shouting disgraceful and opprobrious accusations at the Queen, so that she had risen and left the hall in tears. She had been unwell in the early stages of her pregnancy; and instead of remaining at his wife's side, Darnley had gone off for ten days' hunting in Fife with some of his unworthy companions, of whom the dissolute Lord Ruthven was the most prominent. And so on. It all made a sad and sorry story.

There had been a parliament held in Edinburgh, notably ill-attended with so many of the Protestant lords elsewhere. The Earl of Bothwell had taken a leading part – he had arrived back from France too late to take any part in the Chase About Raid – at the official opening he bearing the sceptre before the Queen, the restored Lord Gordon, now being allowed to style himself Earl of Huntly, carrying the crown and the Earl of Crawford the sword of state, Darnley being pointedly absent. This parliament had refused to confirm the Queen's bestowal of the Crown Matrimonial on her husband – apparently this was required by law – and he was mortally offended. It had also refused to pass a bill of attainder against Moray, Argyll and the other rebel lords, claiming that they had been only seeking to maintain the established and Reformed religion of the realm. So, in the circumstances, the Queen was having to reconsider her attitudes towards the exiled ones, at parliament's urging. Hence this present visit of Maitland to Berwick, to try to work out some agreement whereby byegones could be byegones and co-operation between Catholics and Protestants established, for the peace of the realm. John Knox, it seemed, had abandoned his quieter attitude and become more virulently hostile to the Queen since the failure of Moray's rebellion. One of the interesting and significant decisions of the parliament had been that an iron stamp of Darnley's signature was authorised, since he was seldom there when documents had to be signed, and legislation and charters were being held up lacking the joint superscription, he being almost totally uninterested in the processes of government. The stamp was put in the care of Private Secretary Rizzio. Darnley's hatred of the Italian was the more intensified.

On a happier note, Mary Beaton's marriage to Ogilvy of Boyne was to be celebrated at Holyrood at the beginning of

April, and Thomas's presence was requested. And Flam sent her good wishes.

All this much occupied Thomas's thoughts, needless to say. But only a couple of days after Maitland's departure, his mind was more direly occupied than ever. For his Uncle Walter of Cessford, who had been in Edinburgh reporting, as Warden of the Middle March, to the returned Bothwell, Lieutenant of the Border, called in at Ferniehirst on his way home. David Rizzio had been murdered, and in the Queen's presence.

Appalled, Thomas heard the details. Whilst the Queen was at supper at Holyrood, with her ladies, Rizzio and one or two others present, Darnley had burst in on them, drunken, with the Lord Ruthven, George Douglas, an illegitimate brother of the Earl of Angus, and three others of Darnley's dissolute companions, including, sadly, Andrew Ker of Fawdonside, one of Cessford's lairds, Ruthven shouting accusations that the Queen was a strumpet, a whore, that Rizzio was her lover and that the child she was bearing was the Italian's, not King Henry's. Rebuking them, the Queen was pushed aside, the supper-table knocked over, and daggers drawn. George Douglas struck the first blow at Rizzio, quickly followed by Ruthven, who actually snatched Darnley's own dagger to do it, and the others joined in, stabbing and stabbing again. Collapsing on the floor, the Italian had clutched at the Queen's knees and gown, pleading for her to save him. But she was held back, and the others there threatened, whilst the twitching body was dragged out of the room, Darnley assisting, and thrown down the stairs, leaving the Queen and her ladies in a state of shock, horror and hysteria. Darnley ordered a palace servant to strip the body of Rizzio of its bloodstained clothing but to leave the corpse lying there at the stair-foot. Fifty-six wounds were later counted.

Thereafter the six-months-pregnant Queen took to her bed, and it was feared that there would be a miscarriage. But she had rallied and composed herself royally and there seemed to be no danger now that she would lose her child. Edinburgh was in an uproar.

Thomas, dumbfounded, decided that he could not wait for the Beaton wedding but must go to the Queen at once. Not that he could do anything effective – although he felt like taking a dirk to Darnley himself – but he had to go and at least demonstrate his support and devotion in this desperate situation, however pointless that might be. Janet, herself seven months pregnant, urged him on.

He was surprised, on arrival at Holyrood, to find how normal-seeming all appeared to be, when he had anticipated a state of general upheaval and distress. The Queen had clearly made a major effort, calmed herself and set an example for all at court. Without seeking to seem lightsome or over-cheerful, she was behaving with every appearance of normality, and others were taking their cue from her. Of Darnley there was no sign.

Thomas's arrival had, in fact, the effect of at first somewhat cracking this determined calm, producing something of an emotional reaction and temporary lowering of defences on the part of the Queen and her ladies. Yet they were most obviously pleased to see him, and in embracing him on welcome tended to cling for a little. All quickly recovered composure, however, and the man took his line from that, endeavouring to keep his enquiries and comments low-key – which was difficult considering what had happened.

The Queen did not, could not, avoid the subject of Rizzio's assassination in her presence, but sought to speak of it, to him, almost as though it was something which had happened to other people, a distressing and shameful event which had to be accepted and come to terms with.

"We must put it behind us," she said, "or it could wreck all, my life, my marriage, my throne's security, the governance of my kingdom. I have thought long on this, Thomas, and made decision. I remind myself that I am a queen, not merely a woman and a wife – aye, and soon to be a mother. So much is at stake, so many could be affected, hurt, if I behave wrongly, foolishly, now I have already made one great mistake. I must not make another."

He nodded. "I understand, Highness. And greatly admire. How hard a part you have to play I can only guess . . ."

"Hard, yes. But not beyond me, I think. Signor Davie's death could, the manner of it, could have split my realm in pieces. Do you see that? Perhaps it was contrived partly for that very purpose. By my enemies. I must see that it does not. Indeed, I would seek to make it help, rather. Use it to bring together not to separate. To heal rather than to poison. You are my friend, Thomas. Can you see it all?"

"Partly, Your Grace. It is a noble decision. You, you will forgive?"

"If I can, God aiding me."

"Will that not be esteemed a sign of weakness?"

"*I* say so," Beth Beaton put in.

"I must risk that. But perhaps it will not. If I forgive sufficient and sufficiently!"

"Sufficient? Your Grace means . . .? Not only your, your . . .!" he did not finish that.

"Not only my husband, no. And those with him. And behind him. For he is being used against me, I think. But others. Many. My brother, the Earl James. My sister's husband, Argyll. The other rebel lords. All these, so that we may make a fresh start. And out of this horror some good."

"If they will have it so," Beth doubted.

"They will, they must, recognise that they owe me much, if I permit their return from exile and the restoration of their lands and titles. They must have their honest feelings."

"My lord of Bothwell says otherwise," Flam mentioned.

"He is a man of action, a fighter, is James Hepburn. He sees matters as a fighter. But there are other ways to win a cause than by battle."

Thomas was as doubtful as the others, but sought not to show it. He was thankful for his father-in-law's sake, to be sure. "They *should* be grateful," he agreed. "And the Lord Henry, the King? Will he be part of this?"

"He must be. It is necessary. We must remain together, at least meantime, Queen and King, husband and wife, until the child is born. For the child's sake. And the succession."

"I see that, yes. That, that constrains you, in the matter. So – what now?"

"King Henry is gone I know not where. Probably to his friend Ruthven's castle, at Perth. That evil man. I will not have *him* back at court. But for the rest, all must be as before all this abomination and horror and sorrow. This is my decision. Pray God that it suffices to bring peace to this realm."

"It must, it must, Your Grace," Ebba Seton said earnestly. "So great a sacrifice on your part. All must see it, and recognise the cost to you."

They left it at that.

*

Thomas had asked what now? He did not have long to wait for his answer. For, two days later, the rebel lords arrived back in Edinburgh from Newcastle. William Maitland had been sent there to inform them of the Queen's gesture and pardon and they had lost no time in translating permission into actuality. They had the grace not to present themselves boldly at Holyrood, the Earl James and Argyll going to lodge in Lord Home's quarters in the High Street, since Moray's house in the Canongate was under forfeiture and occupied by Huntly – to whom it had originally belonged anyway.

When the Queen heard of the so prompt arrival, she summoned her brother to the palace forthwith. She suggested that Thomas should be one of those present to witness the reconciliation process.

It was a strange and distinctly fraught proceeding, inevitably, although the monarch did her best to make it as easy as possible for all. Indeed Thomas, for one, felt that perhaps she rather overdid it, going forward, when Moray appeared with Argyll, to throw her arms around him in affectionate greeting, exclaiming how happy she was to see him.

That man, never demonstrative, scarcely responded in kind, managing only to look embarrassed. He had not, of course, had a French upbringing. He muttered something.

Argyll, glancing at his estranged wife, another of the royal bastards, standing behind the Queen, was a little more eloquent, in his Highland way.

"Your Grace is kind," he said. "Very kind. And, and gracious."

"My grace seeks the peace and well-being of my kingdom, my lord. And that of *all* my subjects. After so much of pain and hurt and sorrow, it is time. I welcome you back to my peace."

Argyll bowed low, Moray stiffly.

"It has been a sorry time," Mary went on. "Much of evil, of savagery. I have been sorely grieved, sorely-tried."

"Yes," the Earl James acknowledged briefly.

She looked at him directly. "Oh, my brother, if you had been here they would not have used me thus!"

Even Moray blinked at that, as well he might, a barbed arrow indeed, for there were rumours that he had known of the plot to kill Rizzio. He coughed. "I ever seek the best interests of Your Grace and your realm," he got out.

"That gives me joy, then. You will find much of opportunity to prove that goodwill hereafter," she assured. "I shall rely on you. And on you, my lord of Argyll."

Bothwell, standing with the Countess of Argyll behind the Queen, spoke up. "They will require to be very active, Highness!" he said, almost with a sneer. "To undo what has been done." He was no diplomat.

"They will not fail me, my lord." That was cryptic and somehow final. Mary was today very much in command. "Now, my friends – refreshments . . ."

Mary's mastery of the situation prevailed that evening, but Thomas found Moray's and Argyll's attitudes less than responsive. In this Bothwell clearly agreed with him, and said so. Reconciliation requires to be more than one-sided.

In the morning Thomas's doubts were reinforced. It was Sunday, and it was not long before word reached Holyrood that Master Knox had preached violently against the Queen and her policies and supporters, and even gone the length of applauding the death of David Rizzio. Moray, Argyll and the other Protestant lords had been present, and had gone off with Knox afterwards.

The Queen was grievously disappointed and upset, Bothwell bluntly declaring that he had told her this would be the way of it, and that she was but asking for trouble with this forbearance and policy of forgiveness. He prophesied that it would not be long before Moray and his friends would be taking over the reins of government again, despite their failure in the Chase About Raid, and the Queen find herself all but a captive in their hands. That, at least, would not happen to him!

When, distressed, Mary asked what he meant by that, the Earl said that *he* was not going to wait for the rebels to render him helpless. He would serve his Queen more effectively. He would leave Edinburgh whilst he could, this day indeed, and go to raise a sufficiency of armed men to come to her aid, much more effective than trusting in forgiveness. No, he would not make for the Borderland at this point, but would go to his own family territories in Lothian, to draw men quickly from the lands of Hailes, Prestonkirk, Morham and the Haddington area, assembling them at Dunbar – which royal castle, although not actually in the Borders, was on the northern edge of the Merse and accepted as a fortress for the Queen's Lieutenant.

Thomas, although he did not care for Bothwell, tended to agree with him in this matter.

Then, to the surprise of all, Darnley put in an appearance, where from he did not say. He came in a peculiar frame of mind, apologetic and yet defiant too, deferential to the Queen herself but arrogant towards all others, playing the misunderstood King. What he said to Mary, in private, they did not know, but she behaved towards him more kindly than he deserved. For the rest, he particularly offended Bothwell, who stormed off to Dunbar shouting folly, folly!

They saw nothing more of the Earl James and Argyll meantime. But that evening Thomas, on his way from Holyrood to his Canongate lodging, was actually challenged by men-at-arms stationed at the palace doors, these wearing the Douglas emblem and therefore presumably the Earl of Morton's people. Since Morton had aided the Queen in the final stages of the Chase About Raid, it was to be assumed that they were here, for some reason, in a protective role, however roughly they behaved. But when, at the outer gates, he came under questioning, not by the palace guards but by men wearing the Campbell colours, he was left wondering indeed. These were unlikely to be here save by the orders of Argyll himself, the Campbell chief. Yet they were evidently in some sort of alliance with the Douglases, Argyll and Morton, then, co-operating now? That would be something new. And why guards on the palace? Puzzled, Thomas retired to bed.

But in the morning, returning, he was more than puzzled, he was alarmed. For he realised that these men-at-arms, reinforced now, he was concerned to see, by Leslies of the Earl of Rothes and Lindsays of that lord's, were not guarding the palace so much as blockading it. He had difficulty in gaining admittance.

Within, he found the Queen and her courtiers much perturbed. They were, it seemed, all but prisoners, no egress permitted. And on whose orders, none would say. It was outrageous, almost beyond belief, but a fact, the reasons behind it unknown.

Strangely, it was Darnley who was most fearful. He declared that it was himself who was being threatened, imprisoned. Moray hated him, Argyll also. And Morton had insulted him, many times, when with the army.

This might well be so. But it did not help the Queen's cause of reconciliation. Darnley was included in her pardoning, their husband-and-wife partnership essential, however superficial, at least until the birth of an heir to the throne. Mary was greatly exercised. She said that she wished that she had gone with Bothwell, before this happened.

Thomas suggested that it might still be possible, not too late to make an escape. Surely there must be some way out of this sprawling palace and abbey precincts, which would be unwatched? The abbey, probably. What about the servants' and kitchen premises? A small group only, perhaps . . .?

Mary agreed eagerly. She sent for one of the Lord Robert's innumerable offspring – he himself was not at the abbey meantime, she having created him Earl of Orkney, and he gone there to survey his new domains. Young Willie Stewart came, and was sent to prospect. He came back to announce that there was indeed an unguarded way out, two in fact, from the former monks' laundry, now unused, and from a storehouse. The former would be best, for it led on to a narrow lane and eventually out into the vegetable-gardens area. He was sent off again to try secretly to arrange for six or seven horses to be available that night, in the gardens area. The Queen and her husband would try to make their escape after midnight.

They all endeavoured to make that day's activities seem normal, although Darnley's behaviour made that difficult. At least they were not incommoded by any visits from the absolved lords, however much in evidence their men. There were only the seven of them to go, it was decided, for the smaller the party the more hopeful of success. The Queen and Darnley; Stewart of Traquair, the captain of the royal guard; Sandy Erskine, a brother of the Earl of Mar, her equerry; Mary Seton as attendant, since they would be passing Seton Palace; one groom; and Thomas Kerr.

Impatiently they waited until all the palace staff were either in bed or pretending to be. Then quietly gathering, darkly clad and with well-wishes from Flam and her mother and Beth Beaton, they set off down back-stairs and kitchen corridors which led to the former monastic premises of the abbey, meeting none. At the disused laundry, Willie Stewart was waiting for them, to conduct them to an inconspicuous doorway and the promised lane. No guards were to be seen, no persons at all.

The alley was equally deserted at this hour, and they reached the vegetable-garden unchallenged. There they found two more of the Lord Robert's odd brood waiting, with the horses. They had only been able to collect six without raising suspicions. Some debate ensued, in whispers, as to who should be left behind, Darnley impatiently urging haste. Ebba Seton solved that problem by suggesting that, since her mistress was over six months pregnant, she ought not to ride astride anyway; therefore she should ride pillion behind one of them, changing over as they went on.

So the Queen mounted behind Erskine, and they rode off, thankfully. They were unlikely to meet trouble now, at this time of night, riding through the empty royal parkland below Arthur's Seat.

It was some ten miles, over the Esk bridge at Musselburgh, to Seton Palace, the magnificent main seat of Ebba's father, and they covered this in just over the hour. They had some difficulty in waking first the guards at the gatehouse and then Lord Seton himself. But once roused, the latter was all concern for his liege-lady, and hot in his resentment against those who forced their monarch into such straits, especially after her great generosity towards them. He promised to muster the strength of his Lothian lands forthwith, to add to Bothwell's force. And he would seek to enrol men from the Lords Elphinstone, Cranstoun, Fawsyde of that Ilk, and other well-disposed magnates in these parts.

Then it was on to Dunbar, another twenty-two miles, avoiding the Douglas lands of Longniddry, Kilspindie and Tantallon, arriving with the dawn at the extraordinary sea-girt stronghold built on rock-stacks rising out of the tides, these linked by roofed-in bridges, the red-stone town crouching nearby.

Bothwell welcomed the Queen heartily, if scarcely her husband, not failing to point out that she should have come with himself in the first place. He already had over one thousand men collected in the town, and would more than double that in the next few days. Thomas had no idea that the Hepburns could raise such numbers. He offered to ride on south-westwards, to muster the Kerr strength to add to the total, and Mary agreed to this gratefully.

So, after only a brief rest, he was off, with a fresh horse, on his fifty-mile journey across the Lammermuir foothills and the wide Merse of Berwickshire beyond, to the Tweed and Teviot dales, weary but determined.

He reached Ferniehirst, after a total of eighty miles in the saddle, not so tired that he could not issue orders for the mustering of men, before collapsing on his bed, with Janet unsuccessfully trying to keep him awake to feed him.

Two days later, at the head of one hundred and fifty moss-troopers he retraced his steps northwards for Dunbar again. It was not so simple a matter for him to raise men quickly, for his lands were wide-scattered and thinly populated in hill country, not the rich and populous farmlands and villages of the Lothians. Another hundred or so, including Cessford Kers, would follow in due course.

The town of Dunbar was like an armed camp when they arrived that evening, Thomas surprised to find fully three thousand assembled. The Lords Huntly, Atholl and Fleming had also arrived. The Queen had sent commands for all leal Lothian lairds to assemble their manpower at Haddington, where Lord Seton would take charge, with his contingent; so it looked as though quite an army would be going to march on Edinburgh for the ungrateful ones to face.

In fact, very soon after the midnight flight from Holyrood, over eight thousand men marched on the capital, the pregnant Queen at their head but Bothwell very much in command, with Darnley an all but ignored and scowling appendage. Such a host was inevitably slow-moving, and could not keep its approach secret, especially as all had to cross Esk at the town of Musselburgh, only six miles from the city, a lengthy process. In the event, the rebel lords proved to be well-informed and, unable to match such numbers in a hurry, fled to their own territories, Ruthven and Morton actually to England, even John Knox departing for Ayrshire. Only the Earl James chose to remain, and he adapted to the situation by coming, alone with the Lord Provost, to welcome his half-sister at the city gates, typically unsmiling but with no appearance of shame. Despite Bothwell's urgings to the contrary, Mary accepted this fraternal greeting without reproaches, reconciliation still her policy. Argyll and Glencairn, it seemed, had gone only as far as Linlithgow, and should be allowed to return; indeed, Argyll, on promise of future support, would be given back his chancellorship, since Morton his successor had chosen to flee.

So, without a blow struck, Mary took over her capital again.

But she was not going to risk another Holyrood discomfiture and now chose the all but impregnable Edinburgh Castle as her lodging, to await her lying-in, Bothwell now the power behind the throne.

Darnley might not have existed, for all the attention paid to him.

16

Not only Thomas, probably, had rather lost sight of the fact of Beth Beaton's wedding to Ogilvy of Boyne, which had been arranged to take place on 6th April. This was only a few days hence now, and with conditions of approximate peace and normality re-established, there was no reason to postpone it. Thomas, an invited guest, felt that it would be churlish not to attend. There was little point in going down to Ferniehirst and then hurrying back almost at once; so, after sending his men home, he decided to do something which had been on his mind for some time. He would use the intervening few days to go to see his father-in-law, at Hallyards, partly for Janet's sake.

Sir William Kirkcaldy had been pardoned, along with the rest, after his failure to ward himself in Dumbarton Castle. He was more appreciative, however, than some others of the Queen's generous gesture, and had not been involved in the recent ongoings in Edinburgh, keeping quietly to himself at home in Fife. Thomas had come to like Kirkcaldy, even though he considered him mistaken in his allegiances; and he was concerned, as of course was Janet, for his well-being.

So he made a journey over to Fife.

At Hallyards Castle, Sir William, living alone, was glad to see him, and eager to hear news of his daughter and grandsons. He seemed to be quite well-informed as to what went on in the nation's affairs, much of it, apparently, with which he was distinctly out of sympathy. He was a strong Protestant and always had been, but disapproved of the way the Protestant cause was being handled, in especial of this latest attempt to constrain the Queen, particularly in view of her forgiving policies. He regretted the Darnley marriage, like so many another, but also the way the rebel lords had used that young man against the Queen; indeed he inadvertently revealed to Thomas machinations in that respect which his son-in-law had not known, including the fact that Moray, in Newcastle, had been informed of the plot to encourage Darnley to have Rizzio murdered, as a means of driving a wedge between the Queen and her husband, and also weakening Darnley's own position – which murder Kirkcaldy deplored most vehemently. But it had evidently been a two-way traffic, for it seemed that Darnley had been in touch with Moray and the other lords before that, offering the rebels his co-operation, and his support for their Protestant efforts, in return for their influence in gaining him the Crown Matrimonial in parliament.

Thomas was disgusted with all this deceit and plotting, and said so. "Surely, sir, you cannot continue to work with those who behave so, and that against their sovereign-lady! No cause borne forward by such shameful means should have the support of honest men!"

The other shook his greying head. "So, at times, I tell myself, lad. Yet the cause itself is good, I am convinced. The Reformed faith is right, necessary for this land, I believe. Nothing changes that, even though the tools to establish it are faulty, not what I would choose. But all that come to hand. I have fought for this all my life, reform of religion. I believed that we had gained it. But now, with a Catholic monarch on the throne, all is in the balance again. You are a Catholic, Thomas, and cannot see it as I do. But try to understand my view of it all."

"I see the Catholic Queen sorely betrayed and traduced, beleaguered, yet risking all for the sake of peace and conciliation, to bring the Protestants and Catholics together, for her realm's sake. Not forcing *her* religion on others. Is there anyone on your side who would do as much? This Deed of Oblivion which she has signed, pardoning all . . ."

"I do not know. I greatly honour and admire Her Grace for what she does, and seeks to do. I should, since I have profited and gained my freedom by it. But can she, a weak young woman, maintain and establish it? Will not those who support her, when they have the power, overturn her clemency? They talk of counter-reformation now. If that triumphs? This Bothwell, who now shouts so loud? Is he to be trusted, in this? Will he be any better than Moray and Argyll?"

Thomas had to admit that he knew not, either. Why was it that it seemed to be always the unscrupulous and violent who rose to power?

Sir William changed the subject. "Thomas, there is something which I have wished to put to you and Janet for some time. To have your feelings on the matter. I am not so young as once I was. I shall not remarry. I have only Janet my daughter, and no son. I have a brother, but he is unwed and in poor health. So there is no heir to my name and estates. Living in the way, and the times, that I do, my life could end at any time. You perceive the situation?"

Thomas muttered the usual disclaimers.

"I must seek to take such steps as I can, therefore. I have grandchildren, God be praised – your sons. How think you? Young Andrew will be your own heir. Could William be mine?"

"You mean . . .? You mean, you might leave your properties to *him*?"

"Yes. But not only my properties. Kirkcaldy of Grange is an ancient name. I would much wish it to continue. If William would adopt the name and arms of Kirkcaldy, instead of Kerr, I would leave all to him. How say you? It would much ease my mind. And make him, one day, not just a younger son but a man of some standing and note."

Thomas hesitated. "This is a great matter, sir. I much esteem your thought. But . . . suppose young Dand was to, to fail. Not to live to manhood. He is a lusty bairn, as is Will. But the young do not always survive their childhood. If Dand did not, Kerr of Ferniehirst would be left without a laird, the line without a chief if Will was to take *your* name and lands."

"I see that, yes. But Janet and you are both young yet. You could have more children. She is pregnant now, you say? There would be others to carry on your line."

"Ye-e-es . . ."

"See you, think on this, lad. Janet and you both. Consider that you could agree to it as a fair prospect if you have another son, or sons, to ensure the Kerr succession. When that is so, I will make William my heir, and he will become William Kirkcaldy Younger of Grange – not before. Will that serve?"

Thomas scratched his chin and nodded, unspeaking.

"There is another point, important. If there are further troubles in this land, as there may well be, and *I* am on the losing side, I could go down, even die, and my lands be forfeited. But if they were destined, by law and charter, to your son, and you a notable supporter of the Queen, they could pass to your keeping instead of falling to the Crown."

"Ah – now I see it!"

"More than that. If *your* side was to go down and mine triumph, Kerr lands could likewise be forfeited, but Kirkcaldy's not. So there would be sufficient for a measure of prosperity for both. You see? For mine are rich lands. Grange itself, this Hallyards, Auchtertool barony, Carden, Pettycurr, Inverteil, and properties in the town of Kirkcaldy itself. Richer than your Border hills, lad. A goodly inheritance. Think on it. Think well."

"I shall, sir, I shall. With Janet . . ."

They left it at that.

In the morning, although the subject was not specifically mentioned again, Thomas was conducted round the baronies of Hallyards and Auchtertool, and adjacent lands, and left in no doubt as to the value of these West Fife and Fothrif properties, with many fertile farmeries, rich pastures, wide woodlands and sundry villages and hamlets. He was duly impressed.

Next day, he rode back to Queen Margaret's Ferry and thence to Edinburgh.

Beth's wedding was held in the Chapel Royal at Holyrood, as had been the Queen's, but at a less abnormal hour and on this occasion there were no hitches, embarrassments and awkward moments. There might just possibly have been, too, had not Bothwell absented himself, for it transpired that, before he met Beth, the bridegroom had been the lover of the Lady Jean Gordon, Huntly's sister, who was now Countess of Bothwell. When that romance had been abruptly broken off, in rather mysterious circumstances, Ogilvy, a personable youngish man, had, as it were, rebounded into the arms of Beth Beaton. They seemed to suit each other very well. And Flam said that Beth had not failed to enjoy her own amorous preludes anyway.

So all went well, and the happy couple, with guests, all – went back up to the castle for the festivities, Holyrood still considered to be vulnerable to attack. None were so rash as to believe that troubles and insurrection were no longer possible.

On this occasion, after the feasting, music and dancing, the bedding ceremony was not curtailed, by popular demand

– although the Queen kindly offered to have it restricted if desired. But Beth was no shrinking lily and her spouse an experienced man and no spoil-sport. So, amidst much helpful advice and encouragement of a cheering throng, the newly-weds were escorted outside from the great hall and into a nearby tower, then upstairs to their bedchamber. This was less large than the company would have chosen for their own edification, irrespective of the bridal pair, but part of the limitations of dwelling meantime in a fortress.

Fortunately there was a small ante-room attached, and into this the ladies present – all except the bride, to be sure – crowded with Ogilvy, whilst the male guests, or all who could pack in, filled the bedroom itself.

Thomas had never actually participated in one of these affairs, rendered, as it were, in full, although he had heard much of them, and thankfully had been spared the like at his own marriage. The procedure was well established. The men undressed the bride and put her on the bed to await her groom, whom the women were disrobing to bring to her. Thereafter, unclad, the couple were expected to fulfil their joining together in matrimony in suitable physical fashion, there before the company, if necessary guided and encouraged by the expert, until achievement, or at least approximate satisfaction by all concerned.

On this occasion everything proceeded cheerfully and expeditiously, with Beth co-operating amiably, slapping too eager male hands but by no means obstructing progress, her clothing coming off without hindrance on her part, she even pushing monopolists aside so that the less forward might have their due share. Naked, she did not disappoint, proving to be most adequately made, slender without being thin, her breasts full but slightly pointed, her hips and bottom satisfyingly rounded. She sensibly made no attempt to hide any part of herself, indeed pivoted round once on tiptoe, arms out, in smiling grace, before being picked up bodily by as many men as could get a grip on her, and being deposited on top of the wide canopied bed amidst shouts for the bridegroom.

The ladies had evidently been equally sedulous and efficacious in their attentions, and brought Alexander Ogilvy in promptly, he grinning and pretending to be shy, seeming to hold back, but exhibiting a well-endowed if hairy physique and competent masculinity. Led forward, to be put on top of Beth, he abandoned his pretended reluctance and showed indeed every sign of appreciation of the situation, she welcoming him with open arms and otherwise. By the facility with which they came together, the impression given was certainly not that the exercise was entirely novel to either.

Loud was the applause, before the company, satisfied at least that all was proceeding correctly, was authoritatively ushered out of the bedchamber by the Queen's Master of the Household, who happened to be Andrew Beaton, Beth's brother, a well-launched nuptials.

A certain excitation engendered by this traditional ceremonial was evident amongst the wedding guests thereafter, and there was a noticeable pairing off and dispersing, by no means all back into the great hall for more public entertainment. Thomas found Flam at his side and leading elsewhere – her husband's duties as Secretary of State and ambassador seemed to keep him at a distance for much of the time. The circumstances could well lead to endangerment of his own marital faithfulness, Thomas recognised, and he rather determinedly steered the affectionate Flam not indoors but on and up to one of the battlements of the fortress where, alean against the parapet, they could survey all the widespread late-evening panorama of city and hills and darkling firth to Fife – and also be surveyed by guards and any who cared to watch.

Even so, some moderate kissing and fondling developed, the man falling somewhat behind his intentions and the young woman obliging. In some concern, presently, he thought fit to assert his better self, and to initiate intercourse on a more general plane, choosing heedfully the subject of Darnley, knowing well Flam's detestation of the man.

"I heard but two days back, from Kirkcaldy of Grange, my goodsire, that Darnley had been in communication with the Earl James while he was exiled at Newcastle," he announced, in suddenly determined fashion. "This regarding the plot to murder David Rizzio and to support the Protestant cause, if the lords would ensure that he gained the Crown Matrimonial. Does the Queen know of this, think you?"

That was successful in diverting Flam's attention. "You say that?" she exclaimed. "Is it truth? Sir William would not lie? No, she does not know of it, I swear. The wretched ingrate!

The dastard! Why, oh why, did she marry him! She has little judgment of men, I think."

"Perhaps. I am concerned that she now seems to favour Bothwell overmuch."

"He is better than Darnley, at least, a man of some strength! But this of the Earl James – he *knew* that Signor Davie was to be slain? He favoured it?"

"Knew, yes, it seems. As to favoured, I know not. But he sent no warning, at least."

"No. It was terrible! A deed that shouts to heaven for punishment! Yet the Queen forgives and pardons. When she believes that her own death was plotted also."

"Her own? Surely not that!"

"Yes. Or so Andrew Beaton says. He heard it from one of the palace servants who was paid to let the murderers up a private stair and in at a locked door. Ruthven it was who urged it on Darnley. That she and the unborn child should both perish. And Darnley then reign as King. But Douglas and Lord Lindsay would not go that far . . ."

"Sakes! How evil may men get! This is beyond all. Even Darnley would never have gone that far?"

"I would not put it past him. He is base, treacherous and wholly selfish. And weak, weak in evil men's hands. And Lord Ruthven his closest and foulest fondling, that monster!"

"Aye. A high-born rogue that. And looks it. Like any death's-head . . ."

"He is sick in body as in mind. That is another of the Queen's worries. Ruthven has been ailing for long – but it does not stop his ill-behaving. She fears that he even may be a leper! And, and associating with Darnley. That could mean . . .!"

"Lord! A leper! Not that, surely. Not leprosy."

"She says that she has seen lepers in France. That she sees similar signs on Ruthven. His skin. And if he could have infected Darnley, her own husband . . .!"

"No, no, that is beyond all. I cannot believe that it could be that. I have seen lepers also. But how could one like Ruthven have got the disease, a noble, rich and powerful? It is the poor who are prey to it, the needy, those who lack food, live in filth . . ."

"She says no. That she knew a countess in France who had it. She was . . . put away. But, it much exercises her. If Darnley could have got it also . . ."

218

"She is sore troubled with that accursed man. I wonder that she does not seek divorce, drive him from her kingdom."

"So say we all. But he has a hold on her. At least until the child is born. He has threatened her that if she acts against him he will publish it abroad that the child is not his, a bastard, and no heir to the throne. And that would be disaster. However false. Her crown might topple . . ."

He stared at her, wagging his head, speechless.

These thoughts effectively banished their former mood and tendencies. Soberly they returned to the great hall.

17

Janet was, of course, much exercised over her father's proposal for their second son, delighted with the idea, and coming almost to hope that the child she was bearing would not be a girl, after all, so that the design could go ahead at once, to the benefit of both families. However, in mid-May, she did present Thomas with a daughter, and both of them promptly forgot the advantages of having another boy in delight over the small charmer they had produced, who seemed to have been born smiling, gurgling and finding the world a joy. They named her Mary.

Some weeks later, on 19th June, the Queen was safely delivered of a son, in Edinburgh Castle, to be named James, Duke of Rothesay, amidst the rejoicing of almost all the nation. There was an heir to the throne. If any had doubts as to parentage, after the Rizzio affair, they did not trumpet them abroad. Indeed, the General Assembly of the Kirk of Scotland made its especial attitude clear, by greeting the news with acclaim and demanding that the heaven-sent new heir must be reared in the Reformed religion, parliament to be petitioned to that effect.

Darnley was little spoken of, and appeared to be lying fairly low, if in low company.

Thomas sent his congratulations and loyal good wishes, and hoped that soon he would have the honour to see mother and son.

Whether as a product of this solving of the succession problem – the English succession also, as it might be – or the fact that Mary had managed to contrive a public reconciliation compact between Moray, Argyll and Glencairn on the one hand and Bothwell, Huntly and Atholl on the other, there was comparative peace in Scotland that summer of 1566, with Morton, Lindsay and Ruthven exiled in the north of England – indeed Ruthven dying at Newcastle, a development which no doubt further aggravated the Queen's fears as to the nature of his disease, however little she might mourn that miscreant. Protestant and Catholic did not exactly agree to accept each other, but they did not fly at each other's throats, especially once parliament had decreed that young James was to be brought up a Protestant, whatever his mother's views. And the Hamilton faction no longer had cause to assert rights as heir-presumptive.

Thomas was glad to be able to devote his time to family, local and Border affairs, without being called on to intervene on the national scene. He was sufficiently busy, as it was.

Then the autumn changed all. At first it was all most pleasant, with the Queen coming down to hold justice-eyres in the Borderland and basing herself at Jedburgh, in the house Thomas had built for her there. She did not bring the infant James with her, leaving him in the care of his foster-mother, the Countess of Mar, in secure Edinburgh Castle, which her husband Mar still held. She looked a little frail, Thomas thought, although that might be the result of childbirth, four months past as it had been. He was delighted to see her, needless to say, also the four Marys, Beth's marriage not having depleted their number, her husband having been found a minor position at court. The Earl James came too, and Bothwell, who was obviously on very familiar terms with the Queen; but he went away the following day to his castle of Hermitage in Liddesdale, on business of his own.

There was no sign of Darnley, but the young women informed Thomas as to the current situation. The wretched man was in no way reformed, they said, but was very little with the Queen, with no co-habiting. Indeed the last time they had been together he had departed saying that that was the last that she would see of him for a very long time. He, in fact, was said to be contemplating going to France. He seemed to be in poor health, which was further concerning his wife – although that was hardly to be wondered at, considering the way he was living, constantly drunken and racketing around with depraved company. The Queen had gone so far as to enquire from Rome as to possible divorce, but the Pope, displeased with her for not heeding his injunction against marrying a Protestant, was proving unhelpful now.

The Queen made a great fuss over the Kerr children, her new status as a mother much emphasised.

So a week passed, the Queen presiding at some of the

senior assizes, sitting in at others, including the Warden's and magistrates' courts, showing herself to the people, but also enjoying sports, archery, hunting and hawking, mainly organised by Thomas – although he judged her slightly less active than heretofore.

Then there was a diversion. A messenger arrived from Liddesdale to inform the Queen that the Earl of Bothwell had been assaulted by a Border reiver he was trying, and stabbed. He was sorely ill in Hermitage Castle.

There was much concern at Jedburgh, with the Queen declaring that she must go to Hermitage – James Hepburn was her Lieutenant of the Border, after all. It was late evening when the courier arrived, and a start at first light was ordered. Thomas was less concerned for the need for this journey, and the haste, but could not say so. Nor could he refuse to accompany the monarch on her long ride. It was almost thirty-five rough, hilly miles to Hermitage. He could, and did, provide tough and hill-trained horses and an escort of moss-troopers.

Fortunately the October morning was crisp, with a touch of ground frost, good riding weather. As well, for the Queen, in deciding who should come with them, only the best horsemen and no women, announced that she would be coming back the same day.

Astonished, Thomas did protest then. It would be over seventy miles, and across the very spine of Lowland Scotland – to which the Queen answered that she had ridden more than that before this. But not over hills of heather and bog and rushing rivers, he countered. But she was determined.

They went over from the Jed to the Rule Water, crossing this at Bonchester, then over high empty moorlands to the Slitrig Water at Stobs, to follow this river up. Now the real climbing started, with the high hills closing in. Up and up they went, by valleys and corries, over swamps of bog-myrtle and alpine meadows, to the lofty heather moors of the watershed, by Penchrise and Shankend Hills and Windyslack, to the ancient Catrail, heavy going for the horses. Then gradually the descent beginning, all the land opening again before them, right to the borderline itself, Hermitage only another six miles.

If the Queen was tired, she did not complain of it, all solicitude for Bothwell.

They found that man, in the grim stern castle, more angry

than ill-seeming, bandaged up but not bedded. Whether he was glad or not to see the Queen, they could not tell – he certainly glared at Moray; but he was eloquent on the cowardly savagery of his attacker, one Elliot of the Park, whom he had been prepared to treat fairly lightly for the usual cattle-stealing and rape when, bursting free of his careless guards, he had dashed forward and plunged a dirk into him, three stabs. Fortunately he had missed heart and lungs, the steel deflected upwards by the breastbone, from the first, the other two lesser strokes to scalp and hand. Now the wretch was hanging from the castle battlements, after suitable expiation. And the guards languishing in the dungeons, to teach them their lesson.

The Queen, all sympathy, insisted that the victim should be in bed and being properly attended to. Protests ignored, by royal command he was put to bed and fussed over. Most evidently Mary had strong mothering and nursing instincts. Thomas felt that it was a pity that she could not find more worthy patients.

It had taken over five hours to come this far, and Thomas was concerned about the return journey. Rough riding as it was, it would be much worse in darkness or even dusk, with hazards and obstacles hard to see; and this was October, with sunset soon after five o'clock and the horses already tired. They had arrived at midday, and in three hours he was agitating to get away, if the Queen was determined to return that night. She was, it seemed, but even so it was after four before he was able to get her to make a move, after she had extracted a promise from Bothwell that he would come to Jedburgh just as soon as he was able to travel – in a horse-litter she advised.

The ride back was grim. There was mist on the high ground now, bringing on an early dusk. Weary beasts stumbled and pecked, and weary riders rode with less than customary care. It was almost dark before they reached the Slitrig Water.

Fortunately Thomas knew the way now, from boyhood, and could avoid the worst pitfalls. But there were still minor hazards, burnlets, ditches, outcrops and the like, and there was much tripping and cursing. The Queen grew very silent.

It was well after ten before they reached Jedburgh, and the Queen's ladies anxious. But they had hot water boiling, for bathing aching limbs. Janet had the same for Thomas.

He slept late next morning, and was eventually wakened by

the arrival of Flam Fleming at Ferniehirst, with bad news. The Queen was ill, not just over-tired, but fevered and in pain. She was crying out, delirious. All were greatly worried.

Thomas went back with Flam to the town, and Janet also. Not that there was anything much that they could do but show their concern.

They found the Queen in a troubled sleep, flushed, restless, muttering, occasionally exclaiming incoherently. The local physician was there, shaking his head over her and mouthing large words and platitudes about fomentations, herbal concoctions and blood-letting. Moray, in charge now, was forbidding all such.

The next day Mary was no better but less vocal and restless, her skin blotchy and hot, with occasional fairly lucid periods, in which she complained of pains in her stomach and loins and itch all over her body.

Thomas, after visiting the sick-room the day following, and seeing no improvement, was surprised that evening to receive a summons down to the Queen's house in the town again. She wanted to see him. When he arrived, it was to find her sitting up in bed, still looking ill but apparently in her right mind. She clutched his wrist with a hot hand.

"Thomas," she got out, "Thomas, my good friend!" Then she ordered Flam and the others out of the room.

"You feel better, Highness?" he asked urgently. "I am sorry, desperately sorry . . ."

"Thomas, hear me. I have a task for you. Only you I can ask to do it, I think. I want you to go to France for me."

"France . . .?" He stared.

"France, yes. You see, I fear, I greatly fear, that I may have the, the dire disease. Leprosy! I much fear it, God help me!"

"No, Your Grace, no!" he exclaimed. "Not that, never that!"

"Yes, Thomas, yes." She jerked at his wrist in her emphasis. "Hear me. I have seen the signs of it, many times. And now see them in myself. I am very sick."

"But not that, Highness. Not the leprosy!"

"Why not? I believe that Ruthven was leper. And has died of it. He was close to my husband. They, they shared beds, I am told! The Lord Henry could have got it from him. He also is a sick man now. And he could have given it to me."

"Highness, this is all but fears and supposition. You are

ill, yes. But it could be a score of ills other than leprosy — a hundred! Do not so torture yourself."

"Have you ever seen lepers, Thomas?"

"Ye-e-es. But . . ."

"There are the two sorts, the red and the white. The white is the worst, but both can kill. And, and disfigure, terribly. I think that it is the red which I may have. These blotches and rednesses on my skin. Perhaps I should not be touching you!" She withdrew that clutching hand. "There is numbness, patches where I feel nothing. I fear . . . I have been less well since my child was born. Pray the saints that I have not passed it on to James!"

Thomas shook his head. "I still cannot think it true. Not you, the Queen!"

"My great ancestor, the Bruce, believed himself leper. It is no respecter of rank and titles! I *may* be mistaken — I beseech my Maker that I am. But I will never know peace in my mind, Thomas, until I learn otherwise whilst this dread is on me. So, will you go to France for me, my friend?"

"I will go anywhere for Your Grace. But, why France?"

"Because of the Order of St Lazarus of Jerusalem. The ancient order of knights which has as its great concern the relief and possible cure of leprosy. It is based in France — indeed, the King of France is always its protector and head. My first husband was that. Which is why I have seen many lepers. The Order's seat is at Boigny, near to Orléans. If I send you to the King of France, with a letter, he will help me. Send you to the knights at Boigny, command them to aid. It may be to send one of them back with you, to me, one knowledgeable in the disease. Our physicians here know nothing of it. Will you do that, Thomas?"

"To be sure. How will I get to France, speedily?"

"Go to Monsieur du Croc, the French ambassador. In Edinburgh. There are always French ships at Leith harbour. He will see that you are taken, and swiftly. He is my friend, appointed through my uncle, the Cardinal of Lorraine. That will be better than seeking a safe-conduct from Elizabeth Tudor to travel down through England. Safer and quicker. And speed, Thomas, is my need."

"I will go, and at once, Highness. Tomorrow, if I can."

"Praise God! I knew that I could rely on you. Tell none here of this my fear — this of leprosy. I, I would not have it talked of. I will give you letters. One to du Croc, one to the King, one a general command to aid you in what you do. They will be ready for you tomorrow."

"Tell me again, Highness, just what I am to do. I am to go to the King of France. At Fontainebleau? Ask him to send me to these knights at Orléans. Boigny, yes. And there to do what?"

"To seek the aid of the Grand Master of the Order. Tell him how it is with me. Ask what I am to do. What can be done. Not only for myself. For my husband. Possibly even my child. He will know. Possibly bring back with you one of his people, who deals with leprosy. Do this for me, Thomas, and I shall be always in your debt. If God gives me life! Tomorrow you will have your letters, my knight-errant!"

All this had obviously all but exhausted Mary Stewart. He left her then, distinctly bemused.

18

Thomas had few problems, at least, about the first part of
his onerous and peculiar errand. The ambassador, du Croc,
agreed that there were apt to be French ships at Leith,
the port of Edinburgh, but these were trading vessels and
might be long enough based there whilst their cargoes, of
wool from the Lammermuirs, hides and salted fish from
Fife, were collected and loaded, so speed was very doubtful.
However, it so happened that a fellow-ambassador, Moretta,
representing the Duke of Savoy, had just been recalled, and
was in fact sailing from Dumbarton in two days' time, to
Nantes in France, and undoubtedly could take Thomas with
him. Nantes was not all that far from Orléans, although not so
near Paris and Fontainebleau. Thomas, who had met Moretta,
a pleasant-enough character, recognised that this was not only
an opportunity for speed but would offer him company on
his sea-journey. He went to see Moretta, an Italian from
Piedmont, and found that cheerful individual quite happy
to have him with him. All was arranged for his voyage in
the French trader, *La Galante*, sailing from Dumbarton in two
days. They would ride west the next day.

So it was the further fifty-mile journey to Dumbarton,
across the waist of the land, the pair chatting easily, excellent
company. The only hint of a rift between them occurred when
Moretta, speaking of his late fellow-countryman, David Rizzio,
indicated that that man could have been quite capable of going
too far with Queen Mary – a suggestion which had Thomas
frowning. The other saw it and quickly changed the subject.

La Galante had been waiting for Moretta, and so there was
no delay in setting sail. Their quarters were scarcely luxurious,
but for Thomas, used to campaigning and living rough, this
was small matter. They were told that the voyage ought not
to take more than four days, in this sort of autumn weather.

For one who was essentially an active man and fairly constantly busy, those days made a strange interlude to which

it took some adjusting, not least in having to swallow a sort of guilt for all this inactivity, as for eating and sleeping too much. He continued to get on well with Moretta, fortunately, and improved the hours by having that amiable character help him to speak and understand better French. Happily they neither of them suffered from sea-sickness, and sailing conditions were on the whole good.

A state of wary non-aggression was in force meantime between France and England, and to the merchanters' satisfaction this more or less ensured safety from attack by English ships, although sheer piracy could never be ruled out. They did see considerable numbers of other vessels on their way down the Irish Sea, and across the mouth of what their shipmaster called La Manche, but they suffered no interference.

Off Ushant and the westernmost tip of France, where they entered the vast Bay of Biscay, cross-tides and the great Atlantic swell did give them some discomfort, but they had only some twenty-four hours of this before they skirted the Belle-Ile and headed in towards the estuary of the Loire at St Nazaire. Up the wide waterway they sailed, then, for another thirty-five miles, to reach the large city of Nantes on the evening of their fourth day, La Galante's home port, after a remarkably trouble-free voyage.

Thomas had been discussing with Moretta how he should proceed from here. Paris and Fontainebleau were two hundred and fifty miles from Nantes, but Orléans considerably nearer, indeed on this same Loire river, Boigny nearby. It seemed rather unnecessary to go all the way to Paris to try to see the French King, just in order for him to send him to the St Lazarus Grand Master at Boigny, when he, Thomas, had Queen Mary's own letter to the said Grand Master. Moretta agreed with him that he ought to proceed direct to Orléans and only contemplate trying to see the King if he had little success at Boigny. The Savoyard said that he would accompany him that far, since it was more or less on his way across France to Piedmont; he could help possibly with the language and directions. This was gratefully accepted.

So they hired horses at Nantes, after leaving the ship next morning, and proceeded eastwards up the mighty River Loire. They had over one hundred and fifty miles to ride, even so, but the roads were good, better than in Scotland, and the countryside pleasing, Thomas much interested in all he saw.

By Ancenis and Saumur, Tours and Blois they went, and exactly one week after leaving Dumbarton they came to the fine city of Orléans, and from there were directed to Boigny.

They discovered this to be a small town, with a large castle or château, much more elaborate and decorative than the Scottish variety and giving little impression of any preoccupation with something so grim as leprosy. Great green-cross banners, presumably representing the Order of St Lazarus, flew from its towers and pinnacles.

Presenting themselves at the gatehouse, Thomas asked the uniformed guards there if this was where he could find Monsieur de Seure. Eyed somewhat doubtfully, he was informed that His Excellency the Grand Master was at present gone to Rome to see Pope Pius. Crestfallen at this, Thomas asked if there was a deputy available. They were told to wait, and a servitor was sent to fetch someone to attend to them.

Presently a handsome young man appeared, wearing an equally handsome golden cloak emblazoned with the green Maltese cross of St Lazarus.

"Are you the deputy Master here?" Thomas asked. "I am Thomas Kerr of Ferniehirst, from Scotland, and this is the Savoyard ambassador to Queen Mary. We seek the Grand Master de Seure. On the order of the Queen of Scots."

Moretta repeated that in rather better French.

Astonished, the young man eyed them. "The Queen of Scots? She who was Queen Marie of France?"

"The same."

"Then welcome, *messieurs*. Are you *chevaliers*?"

Even Thomas was sufficiently informed to know that *chevalier* was the French word for knight. "Yes, sir. I am knighted by Queen Mary. And my friend is a knight of Savoy."

"Not of our Order, Chevaliers?"

They shook their heads. "Is that important?"

"Perhaps not. I am the Chevalier Guy de Senlis. Can I help you?"

"Of that I am unsure," Thomas said. "I was sent by my Queen to see the Grand Master. I am told that he is in Rome. Are you his deputy?"

"No. I am but a humble *chevalier* of the Order. The Chancellor is in Orléans today, but he will be back in the evening. Come. You have travelled far?"

"From Scotland. But today from Blois."

"So. You will require refreshment, then. Leave your horses here . . ."

Led through the splendid château, its salons and galleries and corridors, with their statuary, tapestries and portraits, Thomas saw little to link it with mankind's most dreaded disease. He said as much to their guide.

"We do not have lepers here," he was told. "No lepers may come within a mile of our town, or any town. We have a leprosarium some distance off."

They were well entertained by the knights and brothers, of whom there seemed to be about a score in residence, with many others, they were told, out on their duties of mercy. They were both young and old, all friendly and eager to hear about Scotland, a land which they seemed to assume was all but in the frozen north, and where their fair Queen Marie had astonishingly elected to return on the death of her husband. It seemed that although these men were used to travelling far and wide on missions concerned with leprosy, and two had actually been to England, to somewhere called Burton St Lazars, none had contemplated venturing so far into the unknown, more or less assuming that leprosy would never spread to such cold and remote territories. Education was required, in which Moretta was more eloquent than Thomas.

Chancellor de Bonneval arrived from Orléans before long, a dignified-seeming man of middle years, severe of manner but crisply helpful when he heard of Thomas's quest and requirements. He was duly concerned for Queen Mary, although seeming doubtful that she indeed could have contracted leprosy. But he himself, he pointed out, could not go so far as to send one of their knights all the way to Scotland, lacking the Grand Master's permission. Whether His Excellency would agree to this he could not say, but thought it possible in view of the fact that it was on behalf of their former and much-loved Queen of France. He suggested, therefore, that Thomas went on to Rome, where Grand Master de Seure was conducting negotiations with Pope Pius. He did not see any point in seeking King Henry's intervention.

Thomas was put in a quandary. He had no desire to go all the way on to Rome, with haste being the Queen's urgent plea. But what else could he do? He asked the Chancellor what might be done for relief or cure of the disease, and was given various instructions as to salves, remedies and treatments.

But these were conditional on the patient's state, what kind of leprosy it was, if at all, the stage it had reached, and so on. Without an expert's investigation, all this would be of little value.

Thomas could not go home with so feeble result for his long journey. He would have to go to Rome, it seemed, far distant and difficult as the journey might be.

Moretta was again helpful. It was not so dire a problem to reach Rome. He himself was going more than halfway there, to Chambéry, the Savoy capital. He would take Thomas as far as Nice, where he could take ship to Rome, no great distance. They could be at Nice in five days, Rome in another two.

That decided it. They would leave in the morning – and pray that they did not miss de Seure, perhaps homecoming, on the way. The Chancellor said that there was little chance of that. The Grand Master was having a difficult time with this Pope, and was not expected to be back at Boigny before spring. Sir Thomas could take letters for him, if he would be so good.

So commenced a great riding, of over three hundred miles, mainly in the valleys of great rivers, in a south-easterly direction. The roads were on the whole good still, the weather, for November, likewise. On up the great Loire they went, passing Nevers and Roanne, to Lyon on the Rhône, one hundred miles in two days. Then down Rhône to Avignon, seventy-five miles in one major day. Then, with the Alpine mountains beginning to loom to their left, they turned eastwards instead of south, through Provence, hilly country now, to Aix, another day. Finally, by Cannes and the sea shores, they made it to the port of Nice, in the five days Moretta had promised, Thomas much interested by all that he had seen, and grateful to his Savoyard friend and guide.

Moretta was not finished yet, for he took him down to the great harbour and found a ship to take him to Rome, or at least its port of Ostia. Actually there were many such available, for the trade thereto was the most important on all that coast.

The pair parted in mutual esteem, with Moretta's good wishes for Thomas's errand and the health of Queen Mary.

It was less than two hundred miles by sea to Ostia, and, with a westerly breeze, that was covered in less than twenty-four hours. It was all more timeous than Thomas had feared. He had not yet been two weeks away from Scotland.

He did not think much of Ostia and its surroundings. The port was extensive and busy enough, but it lay in the most dreary marshland country, criss-crossed by choked-up canals, obviously ancient, and littered with ruined buildings, some of ambitious architecture but now all speaking aloud of neglect and decay. However, there was ample traffic between the port and the capital and Thomas did not have to hire a horse but travelled the fourteen miles up the Tiber in an open coach with others from the ship he had come in.

The Eternal City itself, of course, could not fail to impress, with its magnificent edifices, churches, palaces and squares, its strange mixture of flaunted wealth and grinding poverty, its tremendous monuments to the past, temples, statues, aqueducts, mausoleums, arcades and the like. But here too there was evident neglect. And the smells were breath-catching. What Rome would be like in hot weather did not bear contemplating.

Fortunately, two of his late fellow-passengers, being Roman merchants, were able to direct him to the Order of St Lazarus's quarters, for it seemed that the Order had its own palazzo in the city. Here, in an ornate and rambling courtyarded building, he asked for the Grand Master de Seure. He was told that His Excellency was at the Vatican, as usual, talking with the cardinals. But he would be back before long, with nothing achieved. That was declared with evident disgust.

Thomas, provided with food and drink, after delivering the Chancellor's letters, asked what it was that was demanding so much negotiation with the papal authorities. That loosened the floodgates. Pope Pius the Fifth, Michele Ghisleri, fairly newly instituted, had done the unthinkable, appointed a new head for their Order, over the head of the Grand Master, and without consulting their hereditary protector, the King of France, and was seeking to divert all the Order's wealth and properties to him, a kinsman of his own, from Milan, one Jaques de Castallan. He could not achieve this in France, of course, but here in Italy and in other lands around, the papal word was law. Even this house they were in was endangered. It was all so wrong, so shameful, for their ancient Order was not a papal one. It was independent, international, but under the high protection of the Kings of France, and this pontiff had no right so to act.

Thomas was sympathetic, but wondered where the lepers came into all this.

De Seure, when he arrived, proved to be an elderly man of great presence, with a leonine head and keen grey eyes. He was obviously tired and preoccupied, but listened to Thomas's account gravely, read the Queen's letter and asked various questions. He did not dismiss the royal fears that she had either red or white leprosy. Without examination, however, he could not say yea or nay. The blotchiness of the skin and the numbness were certainly symptoms of both – but could also apply to other afflictions. But fear itself could lead to grievous consequences other than the dreaded leprosy; he had seen sufficient of that to know it well. He must think what was best. They must do all they could for the Queen whom they so admired and whose late husband had been their Order's protector. Meanwhile the Chevalier Thomas was their very welcome guest.

If this sounded like delay it proved otherwise, for the Grand Master sent for Thomas that same night just as he was heading for bed.

"I have been considering deeply, my friend," he said. "To do what is most effective and helpful for your Queen. Are you prepared to travel further?"

Thomas blinked. Had he not journeyed far enough, in all conscience? "Further . . .?"

"Yes. To Dalmatia."

He was not very sure where Dalmatia was. But it somehow sounded distant.

"The Queen, Excellency, was very eager that I should not be long away. Haste. She was very ill . . ."

"Yes. But if it is indeed leprosy, she will not die of it quickly. It is a slow killer, although it gives much distress first. You say that she was not ill for long before? Then, if leper she is, she will still be alive when you get back to Scotland, fear not."

Thomas shrugged. "Very well. Why should I go to this Dalmatia, Excellency?"

"For good reason. Two reasons. One is that there, at Dubrovnik, they have, of these last years, done great things in the treatment of the disease, discovered much that is valuable, not known hitherto. So much so that I have lately sent two of my most able knights there, to learn from them. That is the second reason. One of these, the Chevalier Alain

233

Montfleurie, is the best man I have, in both recognising and treating leprosy. If anyone can help your Queen, Montfleurie can. And with what he will have learned at Lokrum, be the better. That is an island off Dubrovnik where there is a leprosarium and monastery where they have discovered so much. I will give you a letter to him, and instruct him to return with you to Scotland."

"You are good, sir. But, how do I get to this Dalmatia?"

"None so difficult, my friend. I have my own vessel at Ostia. Lying there. I shall not be requiring it for sufficiently long yet, I fear, since my task here proceeds but slowly! And my crewmen weary and get themselves into trouble. They could have you in Dubrovnik in three days. It is the best that I can do for you and your Queen."

"Then I thank you, Excellency, and I will do as you say . . ."

The voyage to Dubrovnik was quite the most interesting and pleasurable of all Thomas's long journeying. He learned that Dalmatia was an area of the eastern Adriatic coast, north of Greece, Albania and Montenegro and south of Croatia; and Dubrovnik an independent city-state within it, a republic but ruled by a line of dukes. Not that all this meant much to him. It was apparently a place of mountains coming down close to the sea, with innumerable offshore islands – therefore presumably not unlike the Scottish West Highland coast. The process of getting there was consistently pleasing, for the Grand Master's vessel, a galley, although not large, was quite the most comfortable he had ever sailed in, some indication of the status and prestige of this Order of Chivalry and its leader. Moreover, the journey itself had its attractions of picturesque scenery all the way, the ship hugging the Italian seaboard, past Naples and Salerno to the narrows of the Strait of Messina between it and Sicily, where was Scylla and Charybdis, to turn the mighty cape of Spartivento into the Ionian Sea, across the Gulf of Taranto and up into the Adriatic. And all this in weather conditions which were as good as summer in Scotland, November notwithstanding.

That third day, following the Adriatic coast past Albania and Montenegro to Dalmatia, was the most spectacular yet, all beetling cliffs, with stacks and headlands, honeycombed with caves and backed by fierce white limestone mountains, the Dinaric Alps, barren-seeming but challenging. There seemed to be but little cultivable land between mountains and sea, but many offshore islets were green.

About ninety miles of this and they began to see different conditions ahead. Still the lofty heights soared, but there was more low ground between them and the shoreline, more trees, cultivation of a sort, mainly terraced on hillsides, vineyards, olive and orange groves. Cattle dotted the slopes. Now there were large islands everywhere, to thread, and much coastal shipping.

In the late afternoon, closing the shore now, an extraordinary sight loomed before them, a huge, lofty walled citadel projecting mainly on cliffs, occupying a large promontory, all towers and bastions and ramparts, in gleaming pinkish stone above the blue waters, the mountains rising immediately behind. It was huge, dominant, dramatic, at first seeming to be wholly military, an enormous fortress; but as they drew nearer, there could be seen to be steeples and pinnacles, domes and cupolas, red pantiled roofs and smoking chimneys, rising above the sheer curtain walls. So it was in fact a walled city – Dubrovnik, the city-state. Never had Thomas seen the like.

Approaching from the south-west, less than a mile offshore they had to pass a crescent-shaped wooded island, which the shipmaster declared to be his passenger's destination, Lokrum. But it had no haven suitable for their vessel to berth in, and they would have to go on to the great and busy harbour tucked in on the south side of the citadel itself, from which a small boat would take him back to the island in due course.

They moored in the crowded harbour. The shipmaster, who had been here many times, took Thomas at once, not inside the walled city but along outside the ramparts and round the base of the massive south-easternmost flanking tower of the citadel, to a tall and quite ornate edifice which was the St Lazarus headquarters for Dalmatia – lepers and those constantly in touch with them were not permitted to enter the walled town itself. Stretching out from this, over a high arched bridge, and along the shoreline, built indeed directly from the sea, was a series of sternly functional and identical buildings, rather like warehouses. These were the lazarettes, the leper-houses, with their windows above the tides, from which sufferers could be let down to dip in the salt water, a recommended treatment.

The Grand Master's letter of introduction ensured Thomas's welcome from the St Lazarus brothers here. The Chevalier

235

Alain was not yet back from the island, where he went every day, but would return for the evening meal. The knight in charge here, the Chancellor of the Dalmatian Priory of the Order, was helpful, despite a language problem.

When Alain Montfleurie appeared there was no such problem for, although a French-speaking Fleming, he was fluent in many languages, even some English. Not only so but he was a most friendly individual, quite young, even boyish, genial, laughter-loving and burly. Somehow Thomas had visualised, as an expert on a dread disease, dedicated to the relief of sufferers, a grave, sober man, probably elderly and remote of manner. The two men found each other compatible from the first meeting.

Over an adequate evening repast, they listened to Thomas's explanation of his mission, aided by Montfleurie's translations. All there had heard much of Marie d'Ecosse, as they called her, and there was great concern over her illness and fears of leprosy – although none thought the latter really likely. The Chevalier Alain had seen her once, when she and her husband had visited a leprosarium near Paris. He declared that he would be happy to obey the Grand Master's orders and proceed to Scotland to see the Queen; the experimental work that he was doing here was important, but it could await his return. But he felt that Mary was probably mistaken in this matter. Leprosy was not apt to reveal itself suddenly, in this fashion; it was a slow-developing disease and not nearly so readily transmitted from sufferers as was generally believed. It was a dire and horrible plague, to be sure, but many people, and authorities, dreaded its onset more than they need.

Next day Thomas was taken out, in a small rowing-boat, to the island of Lokrum. It was, like all that seaboard, built of outcropping white limestone, but this here was thickly covered with trees, pines, cypresses, and a kind of wild cherry, as well as planted olives, vines and oranges. It appeared to be about a mile long and not much more than a quarter of that in width.

They landed at a narrow little bay about halfway down the stony south-eastern flank, and his guide, whom Thomas was already calling Alain, led him up by shady paths through the trees towards the crown of the island.

He explained. "There has been a Benedictine monastery here for long. But it is only in recent years that there has been any especial concern with leprosy. It happened that one of the monkish brothers here developed leprosy. Probably he had had it in him from childhood, unknowing. The prior here was fond of him, and did not want to banish him to a lazar-house on the mainland. But he dared not risk other monks becoming lepers through him; so he built this young man a hut for himself beside a pond that there is on this island, not far from the monastery, and there the sufferer dwelt, was brought food daily, and instructed to bathe himself in the sea morning and night, salt water being helpful. However, the coast near this pond is very steep and rocky, and the monk was a poor swimmer. So he did most of his bathing in the pond itself. And in time his condition improved. I do not say that he was cured, but he was much better, the progress of the disease halted. Some called it a miracle, including the fond prior. But the sub-prior was of a different mind, a man of an enquiring nature. He sought a cause."

"The pond water . . .?"

"That, yes. He decided that this was the only difference in treatment the young monk had from the lepers in our leprosarium there in Dubrovnik. They bathe them in sea water, let down in nets from the windows, since most cannot swim. So the sub-prior sought to discover what was in the pond water. He was a determined man, and learned much. The water is not salt, but is brackish. It is fresh water, from rain and a possible spring, seeping down through the rock, the limestone. He decided that this admixture, possibly with salts out of the rock itself, was curing the young monk – or not curing, but helping. He informed our St Lazarus people at Dubrovnik and they began to use large amounts of this water. And it does help many, undoubtedly, although it is not a cure."

"So that is what brought you to Lokrum?"

"No, no. Not just that. But with the monastery here becoming famous for this, members of our Order came here to investigate, from other parts. From lands plagued by leprosy. And they brought their own skills. And so was built up this especial community, college as you might say, for study in the relief of leprosy. And so our Grand Master sent me here."

They had reached the gates of a high-walled enclosure, surrounded by gardens and orchards where men were at work with mattock and hoe. Within the walls they could see the tall towers, gables and belfries of the monastic buildings. As they approached the wide half-moon entrance to the gate itself, Thomas perceived a feature which he knew well, but which he had never seen so placed. It was an aumbry and piscina and holy-water stoup. Practically every Catholic church had such, in Scotland, near to the altar in the chancel; but indoors, not out in the open, set in the walling of a gateway.

"Many of the men working here in the gardens are lepers," Alain explained. "They may not, by law, enter the monastery itself, nor its church; but the sacraments placed here they can partake of and enjoy."

The gateway led to large open cloisters, square on plan, with pillared arcading for walking devotions, off which opened a chapel with brilliantly painted murals of classical figures, birds and decorative designs; also ample monastic premises, refectory, dormitories, auditorium, infirmary, chapter-house and the like, as well as the kitchens, bakehouse, laundry and other domestic quarters of a self-contained and self-sufficient community.

Montfleurie introduced Thomas to colleagues, monkish and knightly. Then he was taken to see rooms where items were laid out, treatments were being prepared and experiments tried, all there being eager to show the stranger from far-away Scotland what they were doing and seeking to achieve for the good of humanity. In one chamber, for instance, the livers of fish were being boiled, each kind in a different cauldron, and the oils therefrom, which rose to the surface of the water, skimmed off and bottled. Apparently oils were very important in the treatment of lepers, not a cure of course but notably palliative. In another, fruit, plums of a special sort brought all the way from India by Turkish traders, were being crushed to produce an even more effective kind of oil called *chaulmoogr*. The dried leaves of mugwort and wormwood were being ground to a powder, to be applied to sores on the skin. More simply, olive oil was being prepared in large quantities.

Much impressed, Thomas was not backward with his questions. "These oils and salves," he said, "they are for healing the sores? Lessening the pain? Giving relief? Not *curing* the lepers?"

"There is no cure for leprosy, save God's holy will! By the time that the disease is recognisable as leprosy, it is fully established. We can only seek to restrain it, to lessen its advance. Little more is possible."

"You mean that the sufferers all must die?"

"Must not we all, one day? Lepers will die, yes, sooner or later. But some of us may live less long! It is a slow killer. We can but delay it, give easement. And seek to prevent its spread to others, in some measure."

"You can relieve the pain something?"

"There is little pain in leprosy – save of the spirit. It is a numbness, lack of feeling, limbs failing, hands and feet becoming as claws . . ."

"My beautiful Queen! If she indeed has it, what a fate! If you can help, in whatever way, whatever measure . . ."

Alain took him down to the pond, a small thing enough amongst the trees, rocky at one end, sandy at the other, the water brownish, with some scum, and less than inviting. It seemed a strange place to be the source of so much enquiry and hope.

"This water?" Thomas said, "You may take some of it back to your lazarettes in Dubrovnik, for lepers to wash in. But we cannot take it to Scotland! What then do we do?"

"This water, no. But I can take other salves, oils, ointments, powders. And we have sought to make powders and salts such as we believe are in this water, to add to sea water elsewhere, which we hope will have a like effect. That is what I have been doing. I am no alchemist, but I think that I have had some success . . ."

They went on the short distance to the very broken shore, jagged white clifflets, overhangs and steep rocky inlets, and saw why the leper-monk had chosen to bathe in that pond. Alain said that there was clearly an underground seepage channel from one of these tidal inlets.

Thomas was gratified, before they left the island, to hear his new friend informing his colleagues here that they would not be seeing him again for some time, for he would be off to Scotland just as soon as the Grand Master's ship could take them. On enquiry, he learned that Alain was assuming that in fact they would sail all the way in this galley. They would have to go back to Rome first, of course, to ascertain dé Seure's will in the matter. But from his letter, he seemed to be anxious to do all that he could for their late protector's widow; and from all accounts he was not likely to be needing any vessel himself over the winter, with his negotiations with the Vatican proceeding so very slowly, if at all. So the galley would probably be available to take them on, and bring himself, Montfleurie, back in due course.

This much heartened Thomas. Not only would it simplify matters considerably, but the galley was an altogether speedier mode of transport than were the heavy trading-ships, not only because of lightness and slender lines but because it had the use of banks of sweeps, long oars, to aid its sails, and so was not so dependent on favourable winds.

Two days later, then, they said farewell to the Dubrovnik knights and set off for Ostia.

19

However excellent the galley's speed, manoeuvrability, and
the comfort for travellers, Thomas was made aware of its draw-
backs when they left the comparatively sheltered waters of the
Mediterranean at the Rock of Gibraltar, and turned northwards into the notably rougher seas of the winter Atlantic.
For the vessel's narrow lightness now had its disadvantages,
making it much less stable in high waves and particularly so
when broadside-on to any deep swell – and such were fairly
prevalent in these waters, especially when crossing the great
Bay of Biscay. The winter, too, was the more evident the
further north they progressed.

Thomas, since the choice was his, elected to turn eastwards,
at Cape Finisterre, and head up the Channel, or La Manche,
instead of making on due north for the Irish Sea. Their galley,
flying the green cross of St Lazarus, would be fairly safe from
English pirates in the Norse Sea, and anyway could probably
outsail and outrow most other vessels. Thus they would arrive
at Leith, not Dumbarton, a deal nearer to home at Jedburgh.

This they did ten days after leaving Ostia, in grey, white-
capped seas now, with warm clothing needed, even for the
oarsmen. Alain was much impressed by his first glimpses
of Scotland, the great cliffs of St Ebba's Head and the
Berwickshire coast, the frowning sea-girt castles of Dunbar
and Tantallon, the vast rock of the Craig of Bass at the mouth
of the Firth of Forth, the isolated conical hill of North Berwick
Law, and then the fertile Lothian plain behind the miles of
sandy beaches. It was all so different from the Dalmatian
seaboard, but spectacular.

On the last day of November they docked at Leith, in a
chill easterly haar. There, from the harbour-master, Thomas
quickly learned news relative to the Queen. She had left
Jedburgh a week ago and was now lodging, not at Holyrood
nor Edinburgh Castle but at Craigmillar, on the southern
outskirts of the city, the seat of Sir Simon Preston, the Lord

Provost. She had evidently been sufficiently improved in health to be able to travel thus far, in a horse-litter, but was still ill. The court was with her at Craigmillar, a large castle, Bothwell, convalescing well, included; but Darnley was not.

Hiring horses, Thomas and Alain, glad of the freedom of exercise, rode up, skirting the city and Arthur's Seat east-about.

There was great excitement on their arrival at Craigmillar, Flam, Beth and Ebba welcoming Thomas as though he had been gone for a twelve-month, and to the other end of the earth, although they had often not seen each other previously for longer intervals than this. It seemed that the Queen had been asking anxiously for him for weeks. She was somewhat better than she had been, they conceded, but grievously depressed and frequently saying that she wished that she was dead. They were all direly worried, and hoped that Thomas's return would herald a change for the better. Despite their evident distress about their royal mistress, Thomas noted that Flam and Beth were not unaffected by the appearance of the Chevalier Alain, whatever his remedial abilities.

With little delay, the two young men were conducted up to the royal bedchamber, high in the main keep. In her great canopied bed the Queen did not so much as look up as they were ushered in. When, at Flam's announcement, she did, Thomas was shocked at her appearance. She was thin, almost emaciated, pale, frail, lack-lustre indeed. But when she saw him, and took in who it was, she changed dramatically. She sat up, arms outstretched towards him.

"Thomas!" she exclaimed, voice thick from little use. "Thomas, you have come! Oh, Thomas, I, I . . .!" She choked on her words then, but continued to hold out her arms.

He went to her, to be clutched and held close – and there was strength in those arms yet. Long she held him, gasping incoherencies, he little more eloquent.

When she sank back, she still held his hand. "I feared, Thomas – I feared . . ." She shook her head. "So long!"

"I had to go far, Highness. Far beyond France. Even Rome. To Dalmatia, near to Greece. To find . . ." And he turned, to look at Alain standing beside the Marys.

The Queen stared. "One, one to help me? Come to my aid? At last . . .!"

242

He nodded. "The Chevalier Alain Montfleurie of the Order of St Lazarus of Jerusalem. Which makes leprosy its especial care." He glanced almost guiltily behind him as he spoke. The Queen had ordered him, that time, not to mention the dread word to others at court.

She appeared not to have noticed. "St Lazarus, yes. Boigny. I sent you to Boigny."

"Yes, Highness. But I had to go on, for the Grand Master was not there. But at Dubrovnik, in Dalmatia, I found what I sought. The Chevalier Alain." And he turned, to beckon that man forward.

"Majesty, your humble and devoted servant."

"Come to succour me?"

"If God wills, yes, Majesty."

"If God wills!" she whispered, shaking her head. "I fear . . ."

"Do not fear, lady. Fear is of the Devil, not of God, the loving God."

Thomas felt that these two should now be left alone. Rising, he gestured towards Alain, and turning to the girls, indicated the door. They all bowed out.

In the nearest chamber on that floor, which had been allocated to the Marys, they waited and talked. All but submerged under questions, Thomas told them of his travels and adventures, of what he had seen and experienced, of the quest for what he sought and eventual success at the tiny island of Lokrum – success as far as his own mission went; whether there would be success in the outcome of it all, remained to be seen.

The girls knew about the leprosy fears now, it transpired; in her semi-delirious state the Queen had not been able to keep it secret. They discounted it, to be sure, like others, but were desperately worried nevertheless about her illness. The physicians seemed to be unable to do anything valid, even to put a name to her ailment, talking vaguely of fevers, post-natal decline, skin infections, muscular atrophy and the like. They prayed the saints that this good-looking young Alain would be better.

For their part, the Marys too had much to tell Thomas. The Jedburgh interlude had been grim. Often they had feared that the Queen would not survive the night, for she said that she wished to die, that she deserved to die – the folly of it! Bothwell had come from Hermitage in a horse-litter and had been given a room near the Queen's. It had taken Darnley, however, eleven days to decide to visit his ailing wife and monarch, and then only stayed the one night before going back to his gaming and carousing and hunting in Glasgow and the Lennox. Now the lords were pressing the Queen to seek divorce, or to destroy the papal dispensation for the marriage, which had belatedly arrived; but she was concerned that this could have the effect of making her son James be declared by some illegitimate. Nothing of the sort could be contemplated until James was duly baptised – if she lived so long. She had been persuaded to come to Edinburgh only because there were more physicians there.

It was some time before Alain Montfleurie appeared. He nodded to the young women.

"Go to her, ladies," he said. "She requires your attentions, I think."

They gazed at him, and then hurried off.

"Well?" Thomas demanded. "What is it? What is wrong with her?"

"I am no physician, my friend. I cannot say just what her sickness is. Much of it is of the mind, I think. But this I *can* say – your Queen is no leper."

Thomas drew a great breath. "Thank God!" he got out. "Thank the good God." He gripped the other's arm. "You are sure, man?"

"Sure, yes. I have seen sufficient lepers to know when one is not. Your lady has not the signs of it. Some skin affliction, yes. Painful sores – but those are not of leprosy. I will give her oils and ointments for that. But she is clean, and no leper."

Thomas, quite overcome with relief, sat down on one of the girls' beds. "You, you told her?"

"To be sure."

"And . . .?"

"She is much moved. I left her in tears. But they are tears of joy and deliverance, I think. Easement of mind. So – I sent her ladies to her. She will need them . . ."

"What now, Alain? What now?"

"I judge that she will grow greatly better now, her sore fear removed. I will leave her salves and lotions to apply. Her physicians will do the rest. She has what she needed from me – the assurance that she is no leper."

"To have brought you all this way, for those few minutes!

But – so worth it! So joyful an outcome. You do not think . . .? She will not go back to fearing it?"

"I think not. I am sure of it. For she *wishes* to be quit of her fears. And she is a woman of spirit. She accepted me as knowing it all, accepted my questioning. Answered me eagerly. Allowed me to look, to inspect her person. The fact that you have brought me from so far to see her in itself will assure her that I know much of the disease . . ."

"Yes, that is true. This is so good. Will you remain with her, for some time?"

"It is not truly necessary. A few days, perhaps. Just to see that she does not go back to fearing. Not attending her, for there is little that I can do that her physicians cannot do better. Just to wait a little."

"So – then you can come with me to Ferniehirst for a day or two. My home in the Borders. I must see my wife and children. I have been away from them for too long. Come with me, and then come back to see the Queen before you return to Dalmatia. I would wish you to see my Janet and the bairns . . ."

"Might I not be more profitably employed here, waiting, with these agreeable young women?" That was asked with a grin.

"Fleming and Beaton are both married, and Seton has taken vows of chastity!" Thomas informed solemnly.

"Ah! Then perhaps I had better come with you." Alain fetched a mock sigh, then smiled again. "As I would wish, my friend. To come with you."

"Tomorrow, then, we ride south. If the Queen permits . . ."

There was a joyous reunion at Ferniehirst next evening, and the visitor made much of. No grievous problems had arisen there in the interim. Janet was her loving, attractive and competent self; and the children a delight, even in their squabbles. Four days of enjoyable daylight activities and long evenings by the fireside in homely but excellent relaxation, with songs and ballads, lyre-music and story-telling. Then the two men returned to Edinburgh, Thomas assuring his family that he would not be gone for long this time.

At Craigmillar Castle they were astonished to find the Queen and court gone. They had moved to Holyrood the day before, it seemed, at the royal decision. Unexpected as this might be, it was surely a good sign?

It was better than that, when they arrived at the palace. Even Alain was surprised to behold the difference in Mary Stewart, Thomas amazed. In those six days she had become a new woman – or at least a fair return to the woman she had been before her illness. She was still thin, of course, but there was colour in her cheeks, sparkle in her eyes and a lift to her voice, her bedchamber abandoned by day, mistress of her court again. She greeted Alain and Thomas as though they were her saviours. Clearly she was rid of her fear, and with it much of her bodily ailing. Alain had been right about the mind.

The Marys, and others, called it a miracle.

As proof of the Queen's sudden recovery, they learned that she was actually planning to go to Stirling in a few days' time, there to hold the delayed christening of her son James, something she was obviously concerned about. She declared that Thomas must attend this important event, the first step in establishing the full status of the future King of Scots, and possibly of England also. She invited Alain likewise, but that man regretfully excused himself, saying that he should be off on his long voyage back whence he had come. He could not leave the Grand Master's galley too long at Leith; and he had been told that the winter storms were much more apt to occur in these northern waters in January and February. If he left now, he would be back in his own place for Yuletide, God willing. With Her Majesty's permission, he would sail the next day.

The following morning, then, nothing would do but that the Queen herself should accompany the Chevalier, with much of her entourage, down to Leith to see him off. It was the first time that she had ridden in the saddle since Jedburgh. She had heaped Alain with gifts.

Thomas was quite sad to see his friend depart, for they had grown close. But at least he could offer some acknowledgment of gratitude. He said that he would discover if he could in any way be instrumental in getting a branch of the Order of St Lazarus established in Scotland. Oddly enough, one of the occasional courtiers, Sir James Sandilands of Calder, a brother-in-law of Flam Fleming, Master of the Hospitaller Order of St John, told them that there had in fact been a Grand

Priory of St Lazarus in Scotland, based on Linlithgow, Lanark and Elgin, and concerned with leprosy; but it had died out for some reason – and in fact the Order of St John had inherited some of its properties. No doubt it could be revived, the Queen assisting. Robert the Bruce, her ancestor, had introduced it.

So the galley sailed off to warmer climes, Alain hoping that he might be able to return one day.

On the morrow, the Queen said, they would go to Stirling.

The christening of young James Stewart, so long postponed, was as notable an affair as it was significant. This did not wait for the arrival of the splendid gold font which Queen Elizabeth was sending, as baptismal-gift, and which was taking an unconscionable time to appear; she was one of the godparents, the other two being the King of France and the Duke of Savoy, all inevitably represented by ambassadors, the Count de Brienne for France, du Croc for Savoy, while the Earl of Bedford, for England, refused to come into the Chapel Royal at Stirling Castle because the ceremony was to be held in the Catholic rite. This applied to the Scots Protestant lords also, so quite a gathering stood outside that chill December day, despite many of them being dressed in especial finery, at the Queen's orders and expense, Moray in green, Argyll in red, Bothwell in blue.

The child, now six months old, was scarcely a beautiful infant, sallow of skin, awkward of limb, with a tongue too large for his mouth; but great-eyed and searching, somehow looking too old for his years. The Count de Brienne carried James into the chapel, between two rows of courtiers bearing flaming torches, followed by Catholic nobles bearing the traditional basin, laver, cross and salt. The principal celebrant was the Catholic Primate himself, Archbishop Hamilton of St Andrews, assisted by the Bishops of Dunkeld, Dunblane and Ross. At the font, the Countess of Argyll took over the infant, as representing Queen Elizabeth, however unofficially, the little prince behaving well, indeed seeming most interested in all that went on. There was no sign of the father, although Darnley had been invited to Stirling for the occasion, and was in fact in the town. The Queen proclaimed her vows for her son in quietly assured tones.

Thereafter, with Protestants and Catholics coming together again – although the Countess of Argyll was informed by

Reformed clergy that she would have to do public penance for her part in the proceedings, there was feasting, fireworks and dancing, with masques. In one of these last occurred something of an international incident, when in a skit performed by Frenchmen, the players at one stage turned their backs on the Earl of Bedford and the English contingent, and, putting their hands behind them, waggled them like tails, a reference to the French claim that Englishmen were born with tails.

To end it all, the Lord Lyon King of Arms, after trumpets, officially proclaimed the child as James, High Steward of Scotland, Duke of Rothesay and undoubted heir to the throne of one hundred kings – and one Queen-Regnant.

Mary, satisfied, ordered a return to Holyrood, and preparations for Yuletide. To celebrate all this, and the great improvement in both her health and in the affairs of her realm, she now authorised the pardon of Morton and the others involved in the Rizzio murder plot, and their return from exile in England.

Thomas, rejoicing that he could leave her so much more like her former self, asked and obtained permission to depart from court and go home for Christmas. Darnley had not returned to Edinburgh, and all at court were now talking about a royal divorce.

20

It was February, and Janet pregnant again, before Thomas
had any sure news about the Queen and her affairs, other than
the general gossip of the countryside – which was sufficiently
highly coloured admittedly, with talk of Darnley now being
gravely ill at Glasgow, suffering variously from smallpox,
pustulation or syphilis, near enough to death's door for the
Queen to go to visit him – but not to stay long at his bed-
side. She preferred to nurse Bothwell, apparently, although
that man was now said to be almost wholly recovered from
his wounds. The infant James was being kept under secure
guard at Holyrood because, allegedly, before he became so
ill, Darnley and his curious friends were supposed to have
concocted a plot to seize the child, have him declared King
and crowned, and Darnley to rule as Regent – just what was
to happen to the Queen was not specified: probably slain but
certainly overthrown.

At Ferniehirst they tended to discount much of this, although
there might be some truth behind it. But Thomas reckoned that
if the Queen had indeed been in any danger, or her child for
that matter, she, or her Marys, would have communicated
with him, knowing how much he had her welfare at heart.

Then, on the evening of 10th February, very definite word
did come, brought by Ogilvy of Boyne, Beth's husband. And
dramatic, not to say shocking, it was. Darnley was dead – and
not of any disease but, astonishingly, seemingly of gunpowder.
He had died in an explosion at lodgings he had been moved
to in Edinburgh, at a tenement which was part of the former
Collegiate Church of St Mary in the Field, commonly known as
Kirk o' Field, which had somehow been blown up, presumably
by gunpowder. It was all most peculiar and mysterious. But
the outcome was certain enough. King Henry Darnley was
dead, and the Queen was a widow for the second time.

It was obvious, of course, that it could, and would, be
assumed to be murder. By whom was à matter for speculation,

and there would be plenty of that; but since Darnley had few friends and enemies innumerable and powerful, there would be no lack of possible suspects. Indeed there had been rumours of a plot to dispose of him for months, ever since Rizzio's death, and the names of Bothwell, Morton and even Maitland, Flam's husband, had been linked with it in the common chatter, with what justification none could tell. But now that the wretched Darnley was indeed dead, slain, tongues would be wagging furiously and fingers pointing. And the Queen, it seemed, feared that some of the fingers would point her way, as possibly involved in some measure, her disenchantment with her husband known to all. So she was seeking to gather round her the truest and most reliable of her supporters, as protectors from possible distressing developments. And Thomas Kerr, named her protector frequently, was summoned to her side.

He went back with Ogilvy, in distinctly anxious frame of mind. Much in what he had been told worried him. He did not mourn Darnley; that sorry character was surely little loss to the land or to its monarch. But repercussions there were bound to be. The explosion at Kirk o' Field would be seen to be more than any accident. Apparently it was on the Queen's orders that her husband had been installed there, she not wanting him at Holyrood. Why there should be explosives, gunpowder, stored in such a house in the city, he could not imagine. And admittedly there were many who would have wished him away. But who gained most by his death? Bothwell was apparently the name most suggested – and Bothwell was now accepted as being very close to the Queen. And he was the sort of man who would be apt to have few inhibitions. Morton of course was now back in Scotland, and he was fully as unscrupulous, perhaps more so, and was known to hate Darnley, who had alleged that the Rizzio murder had been his planning. The trouble was that the Queen was surrounded by lawless, violent but powerful men; and her judgment was by no means always faultless. What a situation for a young woman in her early twenties to find herself in.

Even to Thomas's mind, prejudiced as it was in the Queen's favour, her judgment appeared again at fault when they arrived at Holyrood to discover that the new widow was not there now, but had gone to Seton Palace for archery and other sporting contests. He had scarcely anticipated her to be genuinely mourning her husband, but some gesture in that direction would have been wise, and generally expected no doubt. This uncaring attitude towards the man she had made King, although honest, was hardly politic and would not help in the circumstances.

It was only some ten miles to Seton, near the fishing burgh of Cockenzie down the Forth shore, so the two men rode on, in the half-dark of the February late afternoon. Ebba's father's main seat was one of the finest in all Scotland, a palace indeed, the family fortunes long securely based on the twin foundations of fine agricultural land and coal-winning, many profitable coal-heughs being nearby.

At Seton, Thomas became a little less critical. According to Flam and Beth the Queen was here on the advice of physicians, who said that after her recent illness she ought to get away from the atmosphere of charge and counter-charge, tension and alarm which now prevailed in the city; and this was near enough at hand to be available for official decisions, if such were required. Also the monarch *had* instituted the traditional forty days of court mourning, even though few folk took that very seriously in the circumstances. Darnley's body had been embalmed and was now lying in the Chapel Royal at Holyrood, to be interred in the crypt there in due course.

All this relieved the man's mind in some degree, although he found the courtiers assembled at Seton displaying little sign of gloom or even concern; indeed a musical evening was in progress when he arrived. But there was clearly intense interest and speculation as to the details of Darnley's death and who was responsible and involved, Bothwell's name being the most commonly put forward.

That man himself, in no way abashed apparently, was very much to the fore, all but monopolising the Queen and behaving as though he was the host there, rather than the Lord Seton. In consequence, although Mary greeted Thomas very warmly and expressed her gratitude for his coming, he did not see her save in Bothwell's presence, and so could only utter formal and inadequate representations and comments, condolences being scarcely called for.

However, he was able to converse privately with the Marys – and learned much to further surprise and mystify him. Flam was indeed bursting to tell him.

"Darnley was *not* blown up!" she declared. "He was strangled!"

Blinking, he stared at her. "Strangled . . .?"

"Yes, strangled. The house was blown up, yes – we all were awakened by the noise of it, like thunder. But his body was found eighty or so paces away, untouched by the explosion. No burns nor blackness. And still in his nightshirt. But his throat had been choked, throttled, wrung!"

"His tongue was protruding!" Beth added gruesomely.

"But . . .! This is crazy – mad! What could be the reason for that?"

"We believe that there may have been two plots," Ebba Seton put in. "One to blow him up and one to slay him otherwise."

Thomas shook his head, bewildered. "And both on the same night?"

"Yes. Darnley was to come to Holyrood the next day. That had been arranged by the Queen. The blowing-up would not have been possible then. And the previous nights the Queen had stayed in the same house. In a bedchamber below Darnley's. But this night was Bastien's wedding-masque – the Queen's French page. At Holyrood, and she had promised to go . . ."

Beth broke in. "When we all left, with her, we saw the other Frenchman, Paris, who was Bothwell's page before, standing outside the house. He was all blackened with grime and dust – the gunpowder. He had been aiding in stowing the gunpowder in the cellars of the house. The Queen said to him how begrimed he was and asked why. But he only shook his head . . ."

"Bothwell's Paris!" Thomas knew the man well enough, former body-servant of the Earl, and now seconded by him for the Queen's service. "Then, you think . . .?"

The girls glanced around them, anxious not to be overheard. "Bothwell, yes – the gunpowder. With Archibald Douglas of Whittinghame and Sir James Balfour," Beth said. "But the Queen will not hear of it. We think it certain."

"You mean that Bothwell and these others made up a plan to kill Darnley by blowing up this house with gunpowder while he lay abed? But, if so . . .?"

"Yes. So we believe. But it went amiss. Someone must have warned Darnley. Discovered the gunpowder in the cellars.

Told him. For he had been lowered out of his bedchamber window. In a chair, on a rope, by his servant Taylor. The chair and rope were there. Others must have been waiting, watching. And they then moved in and strangled him. Taylor too. His body was found beside him. With Darnley's furred bed-robe."

"Lord! I can scarcely credit it! And you say that the Queen does not?"

"Not Bothwell's part. She holds him guiltless. The gunpowder, yes – that is evident. But not Bothwell."

"She believes that it was all intended otherwise," Ebba said. "That she was to be slain too. And Bothwell would not do that. She had slept in this house the nights before, and would have done that night also had she not remembered her promise to attend Bastien's masque at Holyrood. She believes that the plot was to kill her and Darnley both. Then to have the infant James crowned, and to rule in his name . . ."

"But that was said to be Darnley's own plot. To slay the Queen and become Regent for the new young King."

"Yes. But others could think of it also. The Hamiltons, perhaps? Whose duke is next in line to the throne. Their Edinburgh town-house is next door to this one at Kirk o' Field."

"I say it was Bothwell," Beth insisted. "Paris is his creature, not the Hamiltons'. He had known that the Queen was not to sleep in the house that night – for Bothwell went with her to the masque. And he wants her, Bothwell does – the Queen!"

"But he is already wed . . ."

"He talks openly of divorce. Or . . . I would not put it beyond him to have Jean Gordon blown up also!"

"I do not like the man," Thomas said. "But I cannot believe quite so ill of him as all this."

"My father judges him villain," Ebba said sadly. "But I do not know."

"Moray? The Earl James is not here? What has he to say about it all?" Thomas wondered.

"He went off, the day before. To see his sick wife, he said. In Fife."

"Discreet man!" Beth commented.

"So – what now?"

"There is to be enquiry. For the Privy Council. By the Sheriff of Lothian." Beth snorted. "And who is the Sheriff of

Lothian? Who but James Hepburn, my lord Earl of Bothwell, Lieutenant of the Border and Lord High Admiral of Scotland!"

There seemed to be little to be added to that.

The court remained three days at Seton, mourning little in evidence, and then returned to Edinburgh. It was to find that placards had been put up in the streets, a device introduced but recently from France, declaring that Bothwell and Balfour were guilty of the murder. The Sheriff of Lothian duly took action against this disgraceful placing of painted papers in public places, promised dire penalties, and presently had James Murray of Tullibardine arrested for the offence, on somewhat vague grounds. Bothwell then held his required investigation over the dead body of Darnley, and fairly speedily pronounced the expected verdict that the royal victim had died at the hands of ill-wishers unknown, after the demolition of premises at the former Collegiate Church of St Mary in the Fields, perpetrators also unknown.

Thereafter the corpse could be decently interred in the Chapel Royal crypt, the law of the land satisfied.

Not all were satisfied, however, for Bothwell had his enemies, and there was considerable concern over his increasing influence with the Queen. A quite powerful group of nobles appealed to the Privy Council to arraign Bothwell before the high court of parliament, claiming that they had evidence that he and his associates and servants had, with the connivance of certain of the garrison of Edinburgh Castle, abstracted large quantities of gunpowder from the Master Gunner's stores therein and carted it away by night, for purposes undisclosed. In the face of this demand, the Council could not do other than advise the Queen to call a parliament, required anyway in the circumstances, giving the traditional forty days' notice.

Thomas, who was entitled to sit in parliament both as Baron of Ferniehirst and as Provost of the Royal Burgh of Jedburgh, took the opportunity to return home for a spell, concerned with Janet's pregnancy and delivery date, to add to his other anxieties. He could not believe that the Queen was well advised to place so much trust in Bothwell.

Janet, as ever, succeeded in distracting her husband's mind from court affairs. And in due course, at the beginning of April, she presented him with another daughter, amidst general rejoicing. They named her after her mother.

On 11th April, all being well with mother and child, he set out again for Edinburgh, for the parliament, in company with other Borders representatives, their talk all about how Bothwell was going to get out of the accusations of purloining gunpowder from Edinburgh Castle. However, if any there worried on the Earl's behalf, they need not have done. For that man had his own methods of meeting such challenges.

Arriving at the capital, they found the city to be more or less occupied by no fewer than four thousand armed Bothwell men-at-arms, Hepburn retainers and Border moss-troopers, there allegedly for the protection of the Queen and parliament. Not only so, but he had prevailed on Mary to have young James sent for safer keeping to Stirling Castle again, in the care of the reliable Earl of Mar – which meant that the latter's position of governor of *Edinburgh* Castle was conveniently vacant, and available for Bothwell to appoint thereto one of his own associates, Sir James Cockburn of Ormiston, presumably with the Queen's agreement. And as a result, none of the castle's garrison would be available for questioning over abstracted gunpowder.

To emphasise realities, next day, when Her Grace went in procession to open the parliament, she rode through streets densely lined with Bothwell's troops all the way – and it so happened that not a few of the parliamentary representatives had difficulty in presenting themselves at Parliament Hall. When the Queen reached there, she was led in behind James Hepburn himself bearing the royal sceptre, Argyll with the crown, and Crawford carrying the sword of state. In the proceedings which followed, no mention was made of gunpowder, Kirk o' Field, nor accusations of any sort. It was mentioned by the Chancellor that certain disreputable persons of the lower sort had been apprehended, put to the question and duly executed thereafter, over the sad death of the late King Henry Stewart, their beloved Queen's husband, and justice done. Then it was on to more important business – such as the ratification to the Earl of Bothwell of the captaincy of the royal castle of Dunbar, and an act forbidding the putting up of placards, bills and tickets of defamation in city streets and elsewhere.

It proved to be the most expeditious and briefest parliamentary sitting for many a year.

That night Bothwell held a personal party in Ainslie's

Tavern in Edinburgh's High Street, by special invitation, no women present but a sufficiency of the important and powerful of the land, including nine earls, eight Commendator-Bishops, unnumbered lords, barons and officers-of-state – Thomas Kerr not invited. What was said, done and decided upon there was not publicly divulged; but servants thereafter whispered that the Earl of Bothwell proposed to divorce his wife, apparently by mutual consent – they had been married only a short time – and offer himself as husband for the widowed Queen, who obviously now required a strong hand at her elbow, all present there to support the proposition. Some said that a paper was signed. This became known later as the Ainslie Bond, in facetious reference. And since Argyll, Morton, Huntly, Rothes, Glencairn, Cassillis and Sutherland were present, plus Maitland the Secretary of State, the occasion was not to be dismissed as mere idle flourish.

James Hepburn was riding high.

21

Away in his Border hills, Thomas was not very well situated to hear detailed and reliable news of what transpired in other parts of the kingdom. For the next two weeks he was sufficiently busy and taken up with his own affairs, and also out of touch with any travellers, to remain fairly ignorant of any developments at court, content with the assumption that if his presence was required by their monarch he would be sent for – his lack of sympathy with Bothwell, and the Queen's seeming preoccupation with the man, perhaps subconsciously contributing.

Then, on 26th April, St Mark's Day, this lack of information and concern was abruptly and upsettingly changed. News he had in plenty.

It was Ogilvy of Boyne again, but this time he brought with him his wife and Flam Fleming, both young women in considerable agitation. They came to Thomas for help, if that was possible. The Queen had been abducted, taken captive.

Scarcely believing his ears, Thomas sought to make sense out of the flood of disjointed statements flung at him. It was Bothwell's doing, that at least was clear. And she was now a prisoner in Dunbar Castle, that also. They wanted him, Thomas, to raise a force of Borderers and go to rescue her. The rest was very incoherent.

Eventually, with Ogilvy's assistance, he managed to obtain a reasonably clear picture of what had happened. The Queen had had a sudden and brash demand from Bothwell that she should marry him. No preliminary suggestions, no warning given. Taken aback, she had told him that this was absurd. She had been widowed for only two months; and he was married to Jean Gordon. But he had insisted that it was necessary, for her and for her realm. The nation needed a strong and resolute handling, and she was not providing it, could not, on her own. He would divorce Jean. She had already agreed to it, he said – indeed she was considering marrying another.

Most of the nobility would back him, he declared. It was the obvious course, and necessary.

The Queen, at a loss, said that she could not say yes or no, there and then. She must have time to think. And she wanted to see her son. She would go to Stirling and think on it. Bothwell had stormed off, angry.

That was almost a week ago. She had gone to Stirling, taking them, her Marys, with her. They had stayed two days at the castle there, and one day at Linlithgow Palace, on the way back. Then at the bridge where the Gogar Burn joined the River Almond about six miles west of the city, what seemed like an army had descended upon them. It was Bothwell, with fully eight hundred men, mounted all. He told the Queen that he was going to take her to Dunbar, only herself, none to accompany her. Despite her protests and pleas, he had carried her off, alone, leaving them and the rest of her party to hasten on to Edinburgh with the astonishing news.

"The man is mad!" Thomas declared. "Her Grace – what an ordeal! This is beyond all. What is to be done? What is *being* done for her relief?"

"Nothing," Beth said. "None seem able to do anything. Able, or willing! We told Argyll. And Glencairn. And Cassillis." She glanced at Flam. "Even Will Maitland. But they all made excuse. Said that it was a grievous offence, *lèse majesté*, probably high treason. But they could do nothing. They had no large numbers of men at hand, near the city. It would take time to assemble sufficient support to challenge Bothwell's hundreds. Huntly might have done something – but he was up in his own country of Aberdeen. Atholl gone to his, at Dunkeld . . ."

"If only the Earl James had been here," Flam interrupted. "He would have done something. He is a strange man, but he would not suffer this, for his sister. But he is gone to London, to Queen Elizabeth, on some mission . . ."

"Ebba has gone to her father," Beth informed. "But Lord Seton does not have many fighting men. So we come to you."

Thomas looked from one to the other, wordless.

"You *must* help!" Flam exclaimed. "*You* will not fail her?"

"We knew that we could rely on you," Beth added.

Her husband shook his head, doubtfully.

"But . . . what can I do?"

"Go to her aid. With your Border moss-troopers. Go to Dunbar . . ."

"But . . . Dunbar is one of the strongest holds in the kingdom! Built on rock-stacks rising out of the sea. All but impregnable. An English army could not take it from Black Agnes, even with cannon. And I have no cannon. Moss-troopers could do nothing there."

"You could go, at the least. Challenge Bothwell. Say that you must see the Queen . . ."

"Perhaps he intends her no harm. He is a headstrong, violent man, yes. But he may intend no real evil." That, from Thomas Kerr, sounded distinctly feeble.

"James Hepburn is not a man any woman is safe with, even a Queen!" Beth declared. "I know! With the Queen wholly in his power . . .!"

Thomas tugged at his chin. "What I can do, I know not. But I will go, yes. To Dunbar . . ."

"And we will come with you," Flam announced.

"How many men can you raise quickly?" Beth asked.

"I see no point in taking many men," he told them. "We cannot *take* Dunbar Castle. And you say that Bothwell has near a thousand? *I* cannot find such numbers. Nor near it."

"But a company, even one hundred, would be of some worth, seem better than just a handful."

"Very well. I will muster what I can. We will ride tomorrow . . ."

Early next day, then, they set off, with one hundred and twenty men, north by east, fording Teviot at Ancrum and Tweed at the Ruther Ford. Thomas might have raised more given a little longer, and had his uncle Ker of Cessford weighed in with his people; but that man was Warden of the Middle March, and Bothwell was Lieutenant of the Border, and therefore his direct superior; to proceed against him with Border riders was more than Sir Walter could stomach, save by actual command of the Queen.

At Smailholm they picked up a few more men, then on to cross the wide Merse, by Greenlaw and Polwarth and Duns, and so to ford Whiteadder at Cumledge, and through the ultimate eastern moors and foothills of the Lammermuirs, to descend to the coastal plain at Oldhamstocks and Innerwick, a good sixty miles.

All fell silent as they neared the red-stone, red-roofed town of Dunbar and the strange, towering castle beyond, even Beth

Beaton, realities becoming suddenly apparent. They were now tired, of course.

But more telling was the recognition that, apart altogether from the daunting aspect of that frowning, sea-girt fortress, clearly all the eight hundred and more of Bothwell's force could not crowd into the castle. Therefore some quite large number, possibly the majority, must be quartered in the town itself – and they themselves must either thread the narrow streets or circle the outskirts thereof, in order to reach the castle gatehouse. Also, their own approach was bound to have been observed from the fortress for some time; seven score horsemen would be entirely obvious. And seven score confronted by seven hundred was a sobering thought.

Clearly no sort of challenge was to be considered. Thomas, the Kerr banner, of a chevron and three stars on red, flying beside him, warily led the way round the town, from south to north, at a seemingly confident trot.

Well before they reached the downhill approaches to the gatehouse, mounted men were appearing from the town in ever-growing numbers, in no order or formation as yet but obviously ready to attack the newcomers if so commanded from the castle. Thomas pretended to ignore them, his followers less apparently assured.

Dunbar Castle was unique in Scotland, an extraordinary arrangement of keeps, towers and bastions, starting on a spur or bluff but projecting out into the sea on the tops of stacks of rock of uneven size and height, the whole linked together by what were in effect covered stone bridges or galleries. The landward base was protected by two outer walls which formed a semi-circle, the first of which was long and dropped to the harbour, the inner shorter but higher. Behind these, a massive circular bastion stood on the cliff-top, threatening, dominant, from which a bridge-like extension thrust out across the tide to the first of the squared keeps of the castle proper, on its rock-stack. This arrangement was repeated seawards to the other stacks soaring above the waters, that between the first and second towers being the widest gap, and which was in fact the entrance to the town's harbour, an access which could be closed at will by the castle's garrison by lowering a sort of portcullis, thus enabling the lord thereof to decide who should enter and who should leave, this having the additional benefit of ensuring payment of one-tenth of the catch from all the local fishing-boats using the harbour.

The gatehouse and only entry into all this was down on the low ground beside the harbour itself. Here there was a channel cut in the rock, artificial this, into which the tide was led, to form a moat, and over which a drawbridge could be lowered and raised, a portcullis behind. Clearly there was another gatehouse in the second and higher perimeter wall behind. Two flags flew over this, one bearing the device of Hepburn, strangely like that of Kerr at a distance, the other the Queen's own Lion Rampant. Thomas, despite his preoccupation with the present situation, marvelled at the arrogance of James Hepburn as he led his company downhill to the harbour-side. By now there were hundreds of men, horsed and otherwise, coming along behind his last files.

They were hailed from the gatehouse parapet well before they reached the ditch and salt-water moat. "Who comes unbidden and armed to my lord of Bothwell's castle of Dunbar?"

"I do – Kerr of Ferniehirst," Thomas shouted back. "And I understand this to be a royal castle, Queen Mary's?"

That was not answered. There was a pause. Then, "What does Ferniehirst seek here?"

"To speak with the Queen's Grace. As is my right."

"Her Grace is indisposed."

"The more reason that I speak with her. Here are her ladies, whom she must require."

"I will speak with my lord of Bothwell."

"Do that. And tell Her Grace of my coming." Putting a bold face on it was the best that he could do.

They waited then. There was some altercation going on behind, amongst the Kerr riders and those coming from the town, but Thomas ignored it.

The interval was lengthy – but of course distance to travel in that unusual castle could be extensive. Then, at last, a strong and haughty voice was raised from the gatehouse.

"Kerr, what brings you here?" That could be only Bothwell himself.

"The Queen's business, my lord. I wish to speak with her."

"Any business for the Queen you can leave with me, Kerr."

"I think not, my lord. This is Her Grace's privy business. As you will see, her ladies are with me here."

"I have provided women for the Queen. She needs no other."

"How do you know what she needs, my lord? When you have not heard the business?" He took a chance. "My lord Earl of Moray, Her Grace's brother, returns from England." The Earl James was said to be the one man Bothwell feared.

There was the slightest pause. "Do you come from him? What does he want?"

"My message, my lord, is for the Queen."

"Why does Moray not come himself?"

Thomas took another chance, distinctly alarmed that he might be wading in too deep. "The lords are assembling men. And ships." That last was risking it indeed. But if Dunbar Castle had a weakness, it was from cannon-carrying ships.

Another interval whilst Bothwell digested that. Then, "I am to wed the Queen. Moray and the others must accept that."

Thomas glanced at the girls. He took a deep breath. This exchange was taxing, in more than the shouting. "That is not *my* concern, my lord. My message is for the Queen."

He was almost surprised at James Hepburn's next call. "Very well. You may see Her Grace. But only for a short time. She is not well. And leave your crew there. I will inform her."

Thomas sighed with relief. He turned to Ogilvy. "I will take your wife and Flam with me. I hope that he will let them in. You, keep my men in hand here, if you can. Come."

The girls, excited, complimented Thomas on his skilful ingenuity; but he shook his head, anything but confident, even as they heard the drawbridge creaking down.

At the gatehouse, there was no difficulty, for Bothwell had gone, and the guard did not contest the admission of the two women.

They were led across the outer bailey, in under the second gatehouse, and up steps cut in the naked rock to a postern door in the first of the bridge-galleries. There, they were handed over to a superior servitor who, bowing politely, took them on along this corridor, through the vaulted basement of the first square keep and beyond to another gallery-bridge, longer this, with doors opening on to a parapet-walk, this above the harbour entrance. They passed many lounging men-at-arms, who eyed the girls leeringly.

262

In the second keep they were conducted up a turnpike stair to the first floor where more guards stood outside a doorway. After knocking, there was a call to come in.

Entering, they found themselves in a private hall, tapestry-hung, with a fire blazing. The Queen sat beside the fire, obviously tense, and Bothwell stood behind her chair. There was no one else in the room.

At sight of them, Mary Stewart started up, to run forward and throw herself into Flam's arms, where Beth joined them in a convulsive, clutching embrace. Bothwell frowned. Almost certainly he had not intended the girls to be present. He remained where he was.

Presently the Queen disengaged herself and turned to Thomas, holding out her arms, wordless. Bowing, he went to her, no more eloquent than the others. She held him tightly.

Bothwell coughed. "Well, Kerr – your message?" That was all but a bark.

"My message, my lord, is for the Queen's ears alone." He was a deal less sure of himself than he sounded.

"There can be nothing that the Queen's betrothed must not hear, sir!"

That, of course, put Thomas in the quandary he had feared all along. Invention and contrivance can only take one so far. Blessedly, Beth came to his rescue.

"My lord," she said, "surely you do not prevent your sovereign-lady from speaking privately with her women!"

"Her Grace has no need for women's talk with *you*. There are women here for her comfort."

"Nevertheless I *do* wish it, James," the Queen got out. Her voice was strained, quivering. In that moment, Thomas knew that she was frightened of the Earl now, whatever attraction he may have had for her before. A hot anger boiled within him.

"Then – yonder corner!" Bothwell pointed to a window-embrasure in the thickness of the walling. "Speak there. Kerr – come." And he gestured towards the other end of the room.

The two men eyed each other there, hostility undisguised.

"This message? What of it, Kerr?" the other rapped.

Thomas had something of an inspiration. "The women know it. *They* will tell the Queen," he said, and turned away.

"Do not play with me!" the Earl jerked. "Do not force me to mishandle you!"

"As you have done Her Grace, my lord?"

"Watch your tongue, curse you!"

"I watch the Queen, rather. She is not here of her own wish – that is clear. She is unhappy. You constrain her, the woman and the monarch! The price for that will be required of you. Treason!"

"Fool! We are to wed. She has agreed it. I will wear the Crown Matrimonial, which that weakling Darnley failed to win. So – watch what you say, Kerr! Or it is you who will suffer!"

"The lords will have something to say to that."

"What lords? I have their bond."

"A bond given in their cups, in a tavern! The Earl of Moray will know the worth of that, I think! And *he* signed no bond. They muster men, the Protestant lords. And not for your wedding, I think!"

"Enough! I have enough of this. You will go now, all of you – and be thankful that I *let* you go!" Bothwell left him, to stalk across the hall to the women, to the door they had entered by, and flung it open. "Here, to me!" he called to the guards. "Take these back whence they came." He turned, to go and grasp the Queen's arm. "Come – this will tire you. These leave." That was rough, commanding.

Mary Stewart looked from her Marys to Thomas and shook her head helplessly, hopelessly, but did not resist Bothwell's forceful pressure. He drew her off towards the further doorway.

The guards came to usher the trio out, the girls all but in tears, Thomas fists clenched.

They found that no real trouble had developed down before the gatehouse. There was nothing for it but to turn and ride off, unhappy as they were about the situation. Thomas at least felt that perhaps some small good might arise out of their visit, for he believed that his bringing in of the Earl of Moray's name, the Protestant lords and their mustering, into the talk, in however necessarily general and vague terms, had in fact worried Bothwell. It might be that the man would therefore think again, amend his behaviour in some degree, treat the Queen better, for fear of possible consequences.

Beth emitted something between a gulp and a snort as he mentioned this. "Too late!" she got out. "The brute-beast has already raped her! More than once. To ensure that she weds him. She could bear his child!"

Flam wailed something incoherent.

Thomas stared, drew a long breath, and kicking heels into his horse's sides, spurred abruptly ahead, features working, to be alone with his thoughts and emotions.

22

The girls, when they got back to Ferniehirst, decided just to remain there meantime. Beth had her husband with her, and Flam's Will Maitland was off somewhere helping the lords to muster men, Ebba with her father at Seton, Mary Carmichael home in Lanarkshire. So there was little point in returning to Holyrood. And they were very welcome with the Kerrs.

Not that they made a very cheerful company, all too much concerned for the Queen's well-being and desperately frustrated that there seemed to be nothing that they could do about it. Thomas, remembering his own remark to Bothwell about ships being assembled to descend on Dunbar, wondered whether in fact he might seek to put this purely imaginary move into effect, go to Leith and try to persuade shipmasters to provide vessels. The trouble was that the vessels in the port would be mainly, if not all, merchanters, without cannon. And the source of cannon readily available would have to be Edinburgh Castle – which Bothwell had of course put under the keepership of his friend Sir James Cockburn. Also, to be sure, Bothwell was himself Lord High Admiral of Scotland, and all naval ships under his command.

Merely to assemble more men was obviously not the answer; their visit to Dunbar had only emphasised the impregnability of that castle.

What the lords' mustering might produce was an unknown quantity; but unless they were provided with artillery their army would also be ineffective – and land-based cannon, in the past, had failed to reduce this fortress.

So, ridiculous as it might seem, the Queen's friends, like Bothwell's enemies, appeared to be helpless in this situation.

Then, in early May, there was a surprise. A messenger arrived from Edinburgh, sent by the Queen herself. If her Marys were still with Thomas at Ferniehirst, she wanted them to come at once to Holyrood, where she had returned with Bothwell the day previously. The divorce was in hand

and the banns of marriage were to be called in four days' time, the wedding itself to be celebrated one week later, on 15th May. She was going to require her ladies.

This news and summons, astonishing as it was, by no means relieved the hearers' minds, although it did at least mean that Dunbar Castle was no longer a problem. But the Queen's evident acceptance of the marriage left them the more unhappy. Likewise Bothwell's as evident confidence that, betrothed to wed the monarch, he could outface all opposition. His decision to move to Edinburgh was totally unexpected. They wondered whether what Thomas had said to him had in fact contributed towards this development, producing a speeding up of his plans.

The girls had to go, of course, in whatever frame of mind. But Thomas himself came to a decision that on this occasion he could not, would not, accompany them. The thought of having to witness his beloved Queen's wedding to the man he now hated, was too much to contemplate. He even doubted whether he could be in Bothwell's presence without coming to blows; and for that matter, the Earl himself might well take action against him. He would be no asset at this wretched wedding, and must stay away.

He saw the Marys, and Ogilvy, off with a heavy heart.

The next few weeks were dramatic and fateful ones for all Scotland, and unhappy ones for many, including Thomas Kerr, not present at Holyrood in body but seldom far from it in mind, wondering, fearing. Janet and the children no doubt found him difficult, although he sought to keep himself occupied, busy. Rumours and talk did reach the Borderland, of course, much of it contradictory – of the strange, hole-in-corner royal marriage, of the Queen's tears, of Edinburgh in the grip of Bothwell's men-at-arms, of cannon-fire from its castle against an attempt by a smallish attacking force, of the notable absence of lords from the capital although there were accounts of them assembling their powers all over the kingdom, and so on. However much truth there might be in it all, most assuredly trouble loomed ahead, trouble of a different sort and scale from what already prevailed.

Then, two weeks after the Marys' departure, there was another surprise, the arrival of Sir William Kirkcaldy, no less, at Ferniehirst. This was Janet's father's first visit, strangely enough; he was a man always much involved in the nation's affairs, frequently to his own disadvantage, too honest to compromise. Because he was a strong Protestant, he and Thomas were apt to be on opposite sides; but that did not prevent them from liking each other.

Now Sir William came in some urgency and with a request. He wanted Thomas to go to Crichton Castle in South Lothian. This was one of Bothwell's own family seats, next in importance to Hailes, and where he had apparently taken the Queen immediately after their wedding. They were there now. It was a strong place, but not nearly so strongly sited as Dunbar. The Lords of the Congregation, as Kirkcaldy called them, had now gathered together a large army and, more vital than its size, they had managed to equip it with cannon. This meant that the force had to be very slow-moving, the artillery being drawn by plodding oxen; but they would be at Crichton in a couple of days. And there they would pound the castle to rubble.

"With the Queen inside!" Thomas exclaimed.

"That is it," the older man said. "That is why I am here. I do not love the Queen's religion but in all else I am her loyal subject and wish her only well. So, she must not be killed, or injured, by this bombardment. God forbid! But . . ."

"So . . . ?"

"You are Her Grace's friend. She trusts you, all know. I want you to go to Crichton, to speak with her. And quickly. Speak with her in private, alone. Tell her that she must win out. Leave the castle, under any pretext. Not Bothwell. So that she escapes the cannon-fire."

"But . . . how is this to be done? Bothwell keeps her close by him. If she escapes, so will he."

"This is why I have to come to you, Thomas. I can think of none other who might be able to do it. The Queen will pay heed to you. And you are a man of wits and ability. And, I think that you do not love Bothwell! Get her out of Crichton before the cannonade starts, by any means you can devise. If Bothwell learns of it and flees also, it is unfortunate. But better that than that the Queen should be endangered."

"That I agree. Has she her ladies with her?"

"No. The word is that Bothwell would not have them with him. They were left at Holyrood. But Crichton is where the Lady Jean Gordon is, his wife up till a few days back!"

"Lord! The shame of it all. I do not see how I am to effect

this, sir. Bothwell may not even admit me to his castle. After Dunbar . . ."

"The Queen will see that he does. That is why it must be you, Thomas. She calls you her protector, does she not?"

"A lame protector indeed! But . . . well, I will do what I can, little as that may be."

"You can do no other, Thomas," Janet put in. "That unhappy woman! The fates seem ever to work against her."

"You must go quickly. I left the lords early this morning, at near to Peebles, coming from the south-west. With those cannon, they will not move more than a dozen miles in the day. They will be at Crichton in two more days. So we must ride at once."

"Father! Not tonight!" Janet protested. "You will be weary. You have been riding all day already. You cannot ride again, all night . . ."

"I can and will, girl. With a fresh horse. I am not an old done man, yet! These May nights are light . . ."

They left, then, in a couple of hours.

Crichton Castle sat on a shelf of the deep green valley of the upper Tyne Water, seven miles west by north of Soutra Aisle, a site of great beauty and considerable natural strength – but not as against cannon-fire, for there was higher ground above the shelf, to the south-east, from which the castle could be bombarded. Curiously enough, in the circumstances, not much more than a mile away as the crow flew, in a parallel valley, the twin towers of another castle, Borthwick, could be seen rising above the intervening shoulder of hill, in unusual proximity for two fortalices.

Thomas and his father-in-law arrived on that higher ground about two hours after sunrise, after a difficult ride through the night-bound hills, the older man tired indeed. Already the morning smokes were rising from the castle chimneys.

"There you are, then, Thomas," Sir William said. "I will wait, hidden up here, until I see that you win entry. Then I go to join the lords, who should now be near to Carrington or Arniston. God grant you success!"

"I will need His aid, I think!" He pointed. "Yonder is Borthwick Castle tower-tops. The Lord Borthwick I know. He is a good Queen's man. I might seek to have the Queen to go there."

"Yes. That would serve. He is a good man – Master of the Ordnance, he is. I knew him at Edinburgh Castle."

Leaving Kirkcaldy hidden behind gorse bushes, Thomas rode down openly to the castle on its grassy shelf.

This was a much smaller and more compact hold than Dunbar, but strongly placed, a steep slope dropping away from it on two sides, a moat protecting it on this east and south sides. There was no gatehouse here, but Thomas was challenged from the parapet of the main keep well before he reached the ditch.

"I come on the business of the Queen's Grace," he shouted. "Of urgent moment."

Here there was no argument. He waited, none too hopefully.

When a voice reached him from the keep again, surprisingly it was a woman's – but not the Queen's with its French accent. "My lord of Bothwell is still abed. I am Jean Gordon. What is your business with the Queen, sir?"

"I am Kerr of Ferniehirst. And I have important tidings for her, on the realm's business."

"I have heard of you, Sir Thomas. A good Catholic, they say. But my husband . . ." She amended that, ". . . my *late* husband, guidsakes! *He* may be less welcoming!"

"My business, lady, is with the Queen's Grace, not with my lord of Bothwell."

"To be sure. But he will perhaps perceive it to be his also!" That was distinctly tartly said. "I will admit you, Sir Thomas. But you must needs deal with James Hepburn yourself!"

This at least was slightly more hopeful. He waited until, presently, the drawbridge clanked down for him.

When he crossed it, he found a tall, good-looking young woman awaiting him at the bridge-end, strong-featured and younger than he had anticipated. This was the present Huntly's sister.

"You look as though you had ridden far, Sir Thomas," she greeted him. "At this hour, you must have ridden through the night. From Ferniehirst? If so, the tidings must be important indeed."

"They are," he agreed. "Will you kindly inform Her Grace?"

She eyed him frankly – she gave the impression of being a very frank character. "I should inform my lord first," she said. There was just a hint of emphasis on that "should".

Thomas wondered. "He is not . . . with the Queen?"

"Ah, no. In this house, Her Highness sleeps alone! He may be awake now, but was not when I left him."

That took a little digesting. "You mean . . .?" He hesitated. This woman had been Bothwell's wife up until a few days past. And in this castle she had been mistress, possibly still was. Had the divorce been little more than in name? She could well resent the Queen's presence. And still sleep with her former husband?

He took one of his chances. "A pity to disturb him?" he suggested.

"Perhaps. The Queen herself may be still asleep."

"She will not thank us for delay, I think."

"Very well. Come, you."

She led him across an inner courtyard and up the stairs of a flanking tower, to knock on the door of an upper chamber. A voice answered, and she entered, signing to Thomas to wait.

In only a few moments she was back, and beckoned him within.

The Queen was sitting up in bed, alone. At sight of him she cried out, "Thomas! Thomas!" And held out a hand to him.

He went to her, to bow low and to kiss that hand, but she drew him closer, the arm encircling him, exclaiming emotionally. He found himself patting the royal shoulder.

It took a little while for coherent words to come – by which time the Lady Jean had left them and the door closed behind her.

"Highness," he said, leaning back somewhat. "Here is joy, to see you! You are well?"

"Well . . . as I may be. In this coil! I, I . . ." She shook her lovely red head. "How did you win in? For I am a prisoner, no less!"

"The Countess, the Lady Jean, admitted me. My lord of Bothwell is still asleep. The hour is early."

"Ah, yes. Jean Gordon has her own parts to play here, I have found!"

"Yes. Your Grace, you must get out of this hold. And quickly. Sir William Kirkcaldy, my wife's father and your friend although he is against our religion, came to me, to tell me. The Lords of the Congregation, as he calls them – Morton, Glencairn, Cassillis, Rothes, Boyd and the rest – they have now gathered a large army and are coming here. And they have cannon. They intend to batter down this castle. It cannot withstand cannon-fire. *You* could be injured, possibly slain, if the Earl of Bothwell does not yield. And he is not the man to yield, I judge. They, the lords, are near at hand now. So you must win out. Before they come."

"Dear God! How can I do that, Thomas? He will not let me go – that I swear."

"At night? This coming night? Would the Lady Jean help, think you?"

"Not in that. Not in so great a matter."

"Could you not make your escape otherwise? From a window perhaps? To the steep hillside into the valley."

"All the windows have iron grilles. Yetts, you call them. I could not get out."

"There must be a way, somehow. Then you could go to Borthwick Castle. It is not far away. I would be waiting for you. The Lord Borthwick would aid you then. I could go warn him . . ."

"And what would you go warn Borthwick, Kerr?"

Thomas jerked round. Bothwell stood in the doorway, in a bed-robe.

Thomas swallowed. "My lord!" was all that he could think to say.

"The gate guard told me that my foolish former wife had let you in, Kerr. You are a troublemaker, by God! But you will make no more now, I think! What is this of Borthwick?"

Thomas thought rapidly. He could not hope, now, to extract the Queen from Crichton without Bothwell's knowledge. But she must be got out, at all costs. If Bothwell himself had to escape with her, so be it. Her safety was what mattered, in the end. For that no price was too high.

"My lord," he said, "the Protestant lords come. Come here. A great force. And with cannon. They are not far off. I have it on the best authority. This hold cannot withstand cannon-fire. *You* know that, as do they. The Queen must leave, and swiftly. I am suggesting that she goes to Borthwick."

The other stared.

The Queen spoke, if falteringly. "James, what is to be done? I . . . we must be gone. Sir Thomas . . ."

Bothwell cut her short, unceremoniously. "How far off are they, Kerr?" he demanded.

"They were near to Peebles yester morning. By now they

could be at Arniston or Carrington, a dozen miles away, no more. And their scouts a deal nearer."

The other man paced up and down that bedchamber, frowning. Then he halted. "We must leave, yes. Borthwick will do as well as other, meantime. Until I can gather my strength. Who leads them?"

"The Earl of Morton, I think."

"Curse him! After Darnley . . .! You, Kerr – this is no tale you have devised? To get us out of this house? Who told you of it?"

"My wife's father, Kirkcaldy of Grange."

"M'mm." That seemed to impress. He turned to the Queen. "Get ready to move," he said, ordered. Nothing more clearly demonstrated their relationship. "Kerr, come with me."

There could be no point in arguing, in these circumstances. With a sympathetic glance at the Queen, Thomas followed the other out.

Told to wait in the great hall of the keep, and offered no hospitality, he was nodding over the table, the sleepless night beginning to have its effect, when Jean Gordon came in, and finding him unattended promptly sent for refreshments for him. She stayed to chat with him, assuring that it was not she who had told the Duke of his presence there, but apparently one of the guards.

Thomas picked her up on that reference to a duke, especially as she had, as it were, seemed to make something of a mockery of the style. He learned that the Queen had, in fact, created James Hepburn Duke of Orkney on their marriage – no doubt at his insistence. What her half-brother, Robert Stewart, *Earl* of Orkney, thought of this, who knew?

Thomas told her of the imminent danger to Crichton – of which, it seemed, her late husband had not yet troubled to inform her. She thanked him for warning her and said that she would make her own arrangements for safety – an independent-minded woman. There were rumours abroad that she pursued her own love-life, husband or none.

In mid-forenoon Bothwell and the Queen were ready to move. There was no sign of the Lady Jean, and when Thomas referred to her, the new Duke shrugged and made no answer. But clearly Thomas himself was expected to accompany them to Borthwick. With a small escort of five men, they set out, slantwise, downhill into the valley, to splash across Tyne and climb the other slope to surmount the ridge between the valleys. Borthwick Castle, tall and stern, with its two great linked towers, soared on a spur of the hillside before them, its black and white banner flapping above it.

They rode down into the Gore Water's valley, to approach this imposing stronghold. Here there were no signs of especial vigilance or watchfulness, the drawbridge down and no guards to be seen. The visitors rode through the gatehouse-pend unchallenged.

As they dismounted in the courtyard, two youths came out to greet them, cheerfully respectful towards Bothwell, whom they obviously knew, and clearly interested in his attractive female companion. Thomas they all but ignored.

Bothwell cut short their welcoming, and curtly asked if the Lord Borthwick was at home, and if so to be taken to him. One of the boys, perhaps sixteen years old, looking surprised, led him off, leaving the Queen and Thomas with his companion, who eyed them questioningly.

It was an extraordinary situation, for the Queen of Scots to be left to stand there, waiting.

"Is Her Grace not to be taken within?" Thomas demanded.

"Her Grace . . . ?"

"Yes. This is the Queen's Grace. I am Kerr of Ferniehirst. Are you a Borthwick son?"

The youth was staring at the Queen in astonishment. "I . . . I . . . Yes. Your Grace. I crave pardon! I did not know . . ."

"It is no matter," she told him. "You are . . .?"

"Will Borthwick, Highness. Younger, of Crookston."

"Ah, Crookston. Not my lord Borthwick's son, then."

"Kin, Highness. That was my cousin Will, Master of Borthwick, who went with my lord Earl. But . . . come, Your Grace."

They were conducted round the far side of the twin towers to a flight of steps which led up to a platform from which a wooden gangway stretched across a gap to a doorway in the thick walling at first-floor level, a gangway which could be withdrawn into the building and thus prohibit all access. As they crossed this, a heavily built man of late middle years came hurrying out to meet them, full of apologies for a seeming inadequate reception for the monarch. This was John, Lord Borthwick, Hereditary Master of the Ordnance. He nodded to Thomas, whom he knew.

The Queen assured him that no offence was taken; any fault lay with her husband.

They went inside, through the thick walling, into an enormous high vaulted hall with minstrels' gallery and huge hooded fireplace. Here Bothwell was pacing up and down. Wine and provision was hastily set before them.

The situation was explained, the two youths, both named Will it seemed, gazing wide-eyed. No Lady Borthwick was in evidence.

The information that the Protestant lords were provided with cannon much concerned Lord Borthwick, who was in a better position than most to know what cannon-fire could do to even the stoutest stone walling, if within range. And here at Borthwick, artillery could be sited fairly close by, unfortunately. He shook his greying head gloomily.

"This hold will not stand against cannon," he declared.

"It is Crichton they come to bombard, Kerr says, not Borthwick."

"If they learn that you and Her Grace are here . . ."

"If they do, it will take time. To get heavy cannon down that hill and across Tyne, then up and over the ridge and across Gore. Time that I need . . ."

"Time for what, my lord?" Thomas asked.

"Time for me to assemble my strength again. To muster, at Dunbar. Then, we shall see what they can do with their cannon! They will learn what it costs to tangle with James Hepburn!"

"Then you do not stay here, James?" That was the Queen.

"No. I do not. But you do. Meantime, I have work to do, man's work. Borthwick will guard you. I will go to Dunbar, swiftly. Muster my men. Call on all support. And come back to deal with Morton and these others."

"And if they come against us here, with their cannon?" Borthwick asked.

"You will tell them that we are gone. Both of us. They must not know that the Queen is still here. Speak with them. Keep Her Grace hidden, secure. I want your word on it."

"Yes, yes. But if they bombard? I cannot hold out."

"They will not. When they learn that I am gone and they think the Queen with me. Why bombard *you*? Forby, they may not come here at all from Crichton. They will not *know* that we have come here."

"So be it." Borthwick turned. "Your Grace's safety is the prime matter. You will be secure. So long as it is not known that you are here . . ."

So it was arranged. Bothwell and his small escort would depart, and take Thomas with them – for apparently he was not to be left with the Queen. Anyway, that man did not see what else he could usefully do for her, at this juncture.

She was conducted to an upper chamber by young Will of Crookston.

But arrangements can go awry. Before Bothwell could leave, a watchman from the battlements came down to inform that horsemen had appeared on the ridge between the two valleys and were watching this castle. Presumably they were the scouts of the lords' force, well in advance; and it looked as though they had somehow discovered that their quarry had come here. Someone at Crichton might have betrayed them.

Bothwell cursed. If he rode off now he would be seen and could be intercepted. His five-man escort was too small to protect him from any fair-sized scouting party. He should have gone earlier.

James Hepburn was a man of decision, whatever else, and he came to one quickly. He would wait until night, and slip away under cover of darkness. But meanwhile he would send his escort off. They were of no use to him here now, merely drawing attention to his possible presence. If they were intercepted and questioned they would say that he and the Queen had already gone to Dunbar. That would be best.

So the five were sent off, told what to say, however doubtful they might be. At least Thomas did not now have to leave with Bothwell, since alone he could be a danger to that man. Instead, he sought a couch, to make up for that sleepless night.

When darkness fell on the land, incomplete as it was in June, the new Duke of Orkney had that gangway extended for him, and slipped out, alone. He was going to make for the Black Castle of Cakemuir, three miles due east, a lonely small tower of one of his own vassals, Wauchope by name, and there get a good horse for his ride to Dunbar; also an escort, in case . . .

The morning dawned on a new situation. All around Borthwick Castle, in the valley and on the heights surrounding, an army was in process of establishing itself, great numbers of men and horses, with the banners of lords and lairds. There was as yet no sign of cannon; no doubt they would be arriving later.

Lord Borthwick was very doubtful as to the best procedure, finding his house all but under siege. He was inclined to go out and speak to the leaders of this array, many of whom would be friends and associates of his own – although Morton certainly was not – demanding to know what this meant, surrounding his castle with armed force. But the presence of the Queen therein was a restraining factor. He had more or less promised Bothwell to keep her hidden; and he did not want blatantly to lie to these lords, with the risk of being found out, then or later. Just to remain silent, however, was scarcely possible in the circumstances, and would imply guilt of some sort.

Thomas would have advised that his host ignored Bothwell's directions, and went out to inform the lords that the Queen was herein but that Bothwell had gone. But the Queen herself was against this, strangely enough. She said that these lords were no friends of hers, and would almost certainly take her prisoner; that Morton, said to be the leader, was one of the greatest rogues in her kingdom. She had no wish to fall into *his* hands. Better with James Hepburn who was now, after all, for better or for worse, her husband.

Thomas, who was prejudiced against Bothwell, would have disputed this last, but felt that he had no right to do so to his monarch. And Borthwick tended to agree with her.

Their indecision was cut short by a long horn-blast from outside. Going to the window of the Queen's chamber, they could see that a group of men in half-armour, under the banners of Douglas, Lindsay, Leslie and Boyd, had approached the gatehouse, on foot, and were calling for the Lord Borthwick.

That good man, distinctly apprehensively, went down to confer with them, from the parapet. Thomas remained with the Queen.

It was some time before Borthwick came back, little more happy. They were suspicious and difficult, he declared. Morton was their spokesman and not an easy man to deal with. He had said that they had been informed that Bothwell and the Queen had come to this castle, from Crichton, Bothwell who had treasonably abducted their liege-lady and held her in duress. They demanded that he be delivered up to them, as members of the Privy Council. He, Borthwick, had told them that Bothwell had been here but had now left. He had not mentioned the Queen. But they were disbelieving, although he swore that it was true. They had retired meantime but gave no impression of being satisfied. They had made no threats, but . . .

Thomas wondered about his father-in-law. Sir William would presumably be with these lords, possibly advising them – for he was the realm's foremost soldier, with great experience of the foreign wars. What would he be telling them? Would he guess the truth? And what would his loyalties be now? Would it be he who had advised that they came to Borthwick? It *had* been suggested, between them, yesterday.

All waited.

Around midday what almost certainly all were waiting for, eventuated, heralded by a curious rumbling noise. It was the arrival of about a dozen heavy cannon, drawn slowly by teams of lumbering oxen, moving into position on the higher ground to the east and, nearer, the lower ground beside Borthwick Church to the west, but all muzzles pointing at the castle. The message was entirely clear.

With Borthwick at a loss to know what to do, Thomas volunteered to try to improve the situation. Let him go down and talk with these lords, from the gatehouse. It might serve nothing but could scarcely make matters worse.

Their host was thankful for any help. The Queen besought Thomas to ensure that he gave no hint that she was still there. She wished now that she had gone with Bothwell in the night.

He descended to the courtyard and went to climb to the gatehouse, accompanied by the young Master with a horn to blow.

Their summons brought a man whom Thomas recognised as the Master of Lindsay. He shouted his identity and declared that he wished speech with Sir William Kirkcaldy of Grange, whom he understood to be with this company.

The other waved a hand and went back.

Thomas had quite a wait before his father-in-law appeared. Unfortunately the red-bearded Earl of Morton came with him. This complicated matters and meant that words would have to be carefully chosen.

"Sir William," he called, "I hoped that I might speak with you. My lord of Bothwell and the Queen came here from Crichton, I with them. Yesterday. But he departed again, last night. For Dunbar, he said. Where they were before. To raise his strength. If you have come for them, you are too late."

"Borthwick has already told us that, Kerr." That was Morton. He had a particularly grating voice. "You did not summon us just to hear it again?"

"I wished to assure you that it is the truth. My lord of Borthwick judged you disbelieving."

"*I* believe you, Thomas," Kirkcaldy said. "But we are concerned for the Queen's safety. If she has gone again with Bothwell, she is still endangered." That sounded carefully worded also; which could imply that reservations were held.

"Bothwell may indeed have gone. But he may not have taken the Queen," Morton declared.

"Why should he leave her here, my lord?" Thomas was having to think hard and fast. "Does he not ever seek to hold her secure by him?"

"That is true," Kirkcaldy said helpfully.

But Morton was still suspicious – he was a suspicious man by nature. "If he goes to raise men, he could well do without a woman."

There was no answer to that.

"We are concerned to restrain him," Sir William called. "We have heard that he plans to gain possession of the young prince. To use the Queen to gain him. From Mar, at Stirling. Her Grace to demand to see her son, then to seize him. So that he will have in his power both the monarch and the heir to the throne. So endeavour to rule all." That was difficult shouting. "That must not be."

"He said no word of this."

"He would not." That was Morton.

Thomas felt that the sooner this encounter was ended, the better. It had been a mistake to seek it. "I but wished to assure you that Bothwell is not here," he called. "It is to be hoped that you will now leave this place." He raised a hand in salutation, and turned to young Will Borthwick and gestured to lead the way down into the courtyard.

He told the Queen and Borthwick what had transpired. He wondered whether to mention the suggestion that Bothwell might be considering the seizure of the young Prince James, but decided that he must. The Queen was much perturbed about this, taking it rather differently from Thomas's expectations. She became the protective mother; but revealed this in an announced determination to rejoin Bothwell just as soon as possible, and not to allow him to go anywhere near Stirling Castle without her. She would see that her son was safe, at any cost to herself. Thomas would have thought that she might have sought rather to put herself in the hands of these lords, his father-in-law in especial, and asked to be taken to Stirling to be reunited with the child, and defy any efforts Bothwell might make to grasp them. Instead, she was the more determined to escape from the castle here that night.

Borthwick shook his head, but could not say her nay. After all, she was the sovereign.

All that afternoon and evening they awaited developments; but none were apparent. More troops arrived, that was all. Patrols made intermittent parades round the castle's external walling, and as the evening advanced, camp-fires were lit. But no further approach was made by the besiegers, meantime. What they were waiting for was anybody's guess. Possibly they were themselves largely undecided, divided as to reactions.

The Queen at least was sure of her course. She would leave as soon as she might without danger of being apprehended. But she was worried as to how this was to be achieved. Unfortunately one of the points where the lords had posted sentinels was in full view of the keep door and gangway entrance, and vice versa. So anyone emerging here and crossing the gangway would be seen. Whether the June night would be sufficiently dark to hide anything such was debateable. Her escape obviously had to be secret. And there was no other door to this stronghold's main building.

She discussed this with Thomas and the two youths – who were much intrigued and excited over having their so attractive young monarch to wait on. The Lord Borthwick tended to absent himself, probably prudently. It was the Master who came up with the suggestion that the Queen could escape unseen by lowering herself by a rope from one of the windows on the far side of the keep, which could not be overlooked. Then he would lead her to a small postern door in the outer walling, which would take them down into the ravine of a burn, part of the defensive site. By proceeding up the floor of this ravine, in the burn itself perhaps, they could get out presently on to the open hillside, under cover as it were. Horses, of course, could not be used. But perhaps Her Grace could not risk the descent from a window?

Thomas was doubtful about this, but the Queen was not. Of course she could and would do it. How far would she have to walk, to get to the Black Castle of Cakemuir?

No more than three miles, the youngster assured. He would lead her there himself.

She would require different clothes, Mary Stewart declared, practically; she was not clad for climbing down ropes and walking night-bound moors. Young Crookston, not to be outdone by his cousin, said that he had extra gear here which might serve, if Her Highness did not object to wearing it. She was about his height, although rather differently shaped elsewhere. His offer was accepted.

Thomas, needless to say, declared that he would accompany the Queen to wherever she elected to go.

Fortunately it was a dull evening, threatening rain, which ought to help an escape attempt. Even so, they waited until after midnight, when vigilance in the surrounding camp should be at its lowest. The Queen appeared, her tall and fairly slender figure looking suitably boyish in young Crookston's clothing. The Master had found a length of rope – his father was all but washing his hands of the entire affair, judging it ill-conceived – and they tied a number of knots in this, at intervals of about one foot, to give hands and feet a grip. Then they anchored one end of it securely to a leg of the massive hall-table, which would remain stable, and, opening the chosen window, paid out the rope. The drop was about twenty-five feet to the ground.

The escapers could see no sign of sentinels or patrols, from here, in the gloom, and trusted that this applied in the reverse direction. On this side, beyond the walls, there were no nearby overlooking mounds, only scrub and gorse on the edges of the ravine, rising beyond, less steeply, to the open hillside.

The windows had wooden shutters at the foot, which were openable, with fixed glass above. The young Master climbed out first, to lower himself carefully down the rope, hand-over-hand, to test it. At the bottom, he did not call up, all very secret, but tugged the rope as signal.

Then Thomas aided the Queen up from the window-embrasure, through the opened shutters and over the sill, alarmed for her safety, telling her to hang on to his hand until she had her feet steady on one of the knots, not to hurt herself on the stonework, especially her knuckles, not to look down, and so on. But she seemed entirely confident and commendably agile, and went over and down as though practised in the business. Without pause she lowered herself, with no slips nor gropings, surely the first time that a reigning monarch had done the like. In less time than it takes to tell, she was tugging the rope as signal for Thomas to follow.

Will of Crookston had wanted to come also, but the fewer the better, and he was left to pull up the rope and close the window shutters.

Thomas descended without difficulty, feet holding him off against the masonry, and the trio congratulated themselves thus far.

The Master led them across to an inconspicuous little doorway between lean-to outbuildings of the courtyard, massive of timber, and barred. Quietly he unbarred this, they praying that it would not creak. They passed through.

Slantwise down into the ravine beyond they went, seeking to go silently through the nettles, bay-herb and bracken, alert for loose stones. Soon they were at the burnside, to turn upstream. It was a small rivulet to have created so deep a gully. Its chuckling murmur overlaid the sounds of their going.

Perhaps a quarter-mile they were led up this, the ravine shallowing. Then Master Will thought that they could risk climbing the higher eastern slope, amongst the gorse bushes and outcrops. They went slowly, for there were sheep scattered hereabouts and they did not want any sudden fright amongst these to give away their presence. Near the top, the youth advised that they hold back, crouched behind a bush, while he crept forward to spy out the land. The Queen seemed almost to be enjoying this adventure, holding Thomas's arm.

Will was soon back, to announce that as far as he could tell there was nobody about up here, the way clear ahead. It would be rough going over tussocky grass and short heather, with two or three burnlets to cross, but nothing to cause them any real trouble.

In fact, once their eyes had become accustomed to the gloom, it did not seem very dark at all, and they had a minimum of tripping over obstacles. Apart from alarmed cattle lumbering away, and grouse and peewits disturbed, they had the moors to themselves.

The Black Castle, a modestly sized fortalice of L-shaped tower-house within its barmekin and courtyard, stood in its own little valley of the Cakemuir Burn, remote amongst the foothills. After about an hour's walking, they approached it cautiously. Only one light showed.

The caution was in case the lords had sent a party here, although why they should do so was not evident. The Master offered to go ahead and prospect.

He came back presently with surprising news. There were none of the lords' men; but the Earl of Bothwell was still there. Why he had not proceeded on to Dunbar, the youth did not know, but the guard he had spoken to said that he was at present asleep. The place's laird had, however, gone off yesterday, presumably to raise men amongst the other Bothwell properties in this area.

This information had its effect on Thomas. He had no desire to fall into Bothwell's hands again. Escorting the Queen was all very well, but in the Hepburn's grip he would be unlikely to be of any help to her. But she was determined to rejoin her husband, not out of affection now but for the sake of her throne and the child apparently. And, of course, she might be pregnant again. Thomas still would have preferred to see her abandon Bothwell and come with him, possibly to safety at Ferniehirst. Or he would have conducted her to Stirling. But she said no, better her way, much as she appreciated all his help.

So they said farewell there on the dark moorland, a strange parting, the Queen clinging to him for moments, then resolutely pushing herself away. Will Borthwick would take her to this tower-house and then come back to him. What would *he* do? Thomas said that he might as well go back to Borthwick with the Master, get back into the castle as they had left it, and then in the morning seek to depart, openly. His horse was there, and he did not think that the lords would have any reason to detain him, especially with Kirkcaldy one of their leaders.

The man watched her go, in a confusion of emotions.

The return to the castle was as uneventful and secret as their outward passage. Lord Borthwick was relieved to see them back, alone, the more so when Thomas announced that he would be gone soon after daylight. The castle could then return to near normality.

When at length Thomas, mounted, took his leave, and the portcullis was raised and drawbridge lowered for him, he was picked up by the sentinels and taken, at his own request, to his father-in-law. This time he saw him, not alone, but with Morton not present. He assured them, on his honour as a knight, that neither Bothwell nor the Queen were at Borthwick now and that there was no point in this army waiting here. Dunbar was where their quarry could be looked for. This was accepted by his hearers and no hindrance put in the way of his departure, for they had nothing against him personally.

Thankfully, if distinctly wearily, he turned his beast's head southwards, for the Gala Water, Tweed and Teviot, a man who had done his inadequate best.

23

Quite astonishing was the speed and significance of events which followed. Thomas had been back at Ferniehirst only four days when Ogilvy of Boyne arrived there once more, sent by the Marys, to inform of dire events. The Queen was a prisoner still, but not at Dunbar, and with different gaolers. There had been a confrontation of armies, rather than a battle, and Bothwell had lost in it. He was now fled, none knew exactly where.

All this was almost too much to take in, at first telling. Thomas wagged his head, all but disbelieving.

Ogilvy provided more details. The Lords of the Congregation had left Borthwick and gone to Edinburgh, or at least to its outskirts, for its great castle was held by Bothwell's friend, Cockburn – although it was said that he was thinking of changing sides. And from Dunbar, Bothwell, with only a moderately sized force, had come against them, picking up the Lord Seton and more troops on the way. The lords had moved out to meet him, and just south of Musselburgh, at the hill above Carberry Tower, the two armies had faced each other. This was two days ago.

It had, apparently, been a strange encounter, with neither side eager to make the first attack, both hoping for reinforcements at this stage, and the Queen at least hoping that battle could be avoided. The lords, under a banner depicting a tree with the dead Darnley lying beneath it and the infant prince kneeling before the corpse, and the words "Judge and avenge my cause, O Lord!" writ large, were in theory under the command of Morton; but in fact Kirkcaldy of Grange, the seasoned soldier, controlled their strategy, and, being the man he was, sought actually to avoid fighting at all, if possible. Du Croc, the French ambassador, came to act as go-between, and there was considerable parleying and to-ing and fro-ing. Bothwell challenged any opposing lord to single combat, but objected to volunteers as being beneath him in rank until the

Lord Lindsay offered to fight. But the Queen was against this. She was urged to abandon Bothwell and place herself in her lords' hands, Kirkcaldy himself coming out alone to speak to the Queen to this effect. Bothwell, recognising that he had the enemy's best leader at his mercy, called on one of his men to shoot him there and then, but the Queen, perceiving it, screamed, and commanded the man to be gone.

All this frittered away the day, with no large reinforcements reaching either side; but the effect was to Bothwell's disadvantage, for as time went on and evening fell, his people began to trickle off, singly and in groups. Before long, it was evident to all that if there was actual fighting, the lords must win.

Then, to the surprise of all, at the Queen's urging, Bothwell rode off in the general direction of Dunbar, and Mary Stewart was left alone, to yield herself into the hands of the Lords of the Congregation. They had taken her to Craigmillar Castle, as being safer than Holyrood should Bothwell make another effort to retrieve her, where they placed that banner of Darnley and the child in front of her window. She was there briefly reunited with her Marys, but the next day she was parted from them and led off, she had thought to Stirling Castle to be united with her little son, but in fact to considerably further off, to Loch Leven Castle in Kinross-shire, an island stronghold of one of Morton's Douglas kinsmen, where she was now held prisoner.

Flam, Beth and Ebba Seton had sent him, Ogilvy, here to tell Thomas all and seek his help.

Astonished, bemused, Thomas sought to get a grip on this involved situation, or at least its salient points. The Queen was no longer in Bothwell's power – but she was, of course, still married to him. She had been taken to an island castle, from which presumably it would be difficult to rescue her. So the lords controlled the monarch and therefore the kingdom, possibly also the young prince, if Mar was siding with them. And Bothwell was still at large and almost certainly would be endeavouring to amass another and more effective fighting force; given time, he would undoubtedly make another bid for supreme power.

So what was to be done, if anything? The Marys expected Thomas to do something, it seemed, their strange faith in his abilities puzzling. Perhaps even the Queen herself did. Ogilvy had no suggestions.

Two preliminary moves were all that he could think of, at this stage: to go see two of the men involved, on either side, the Lord Seton and Sir William Kirkcaldy. From these, he might gain further information and possible guidance.

Janet agreed that he had to go, and try. She assured him that her father was loyal and trustworthy, and if he had anything to do with the Queen's state, she would be a deal better in his friends' hands than in Bothwell's.

So the next morning, with Ogilvy, he set off northwards again.

They rode direct to Seton Palace, which in fact lay only a few miles from the so strange battleground of Carberry Hill, east of Musselburgh. Thomas was quite prepared not to find Ebba's father at home; he might have been captured by the Protestant lords, or he might have gone to join Bothwell again – although these two had never been friends. But Seton was there, and greeted Thomas warmly.

He was loud in his disgust at Bothwell, in his behaviour towards the Queen, in his handling of the recent travesty of a battle, and the consequent decline of the royal cause; also of his desertion of his wife on the field itself. Not that he was not thankful to see her out of the man's hands. But this of Loch Leven was bad, bad.

Thomas agreed with all that, but sought the other's detailed anxieties.

It was Morton who worried him, Seton said. Morton was a scoundrel, in his opinion, scum – and like scum had risen to the top of these Protestant lords, in the long-continued absence of Moray. Of them all, he was the least to be trusted and the most unscrupulous. And it was to *his* cousin's hold that the Queen had been taken, the heir-presumptive to Morton's earldom, for that man had only daughters. So Sir William Douglas of Lochleven would not go against his cousin. And two of Morton's closest colleagues amongst the lords, Lindsay and Ruthven, enemies of the Queen both, had been sent as her gaolers. So clearly Morton was now in complete control of the monarch, a most alarming development, personally and nationally. She was little better off with him, if any, than with Bothwell.

What of parliament and the Privy Council, Thomas demanded? Could these august bodies not exert their lawful authority?

The Protestant lords had both in their control, and the lords were dominated by Morton.

"Is there any chance of rescuing the Queen out of their hands, then?" Thomas asked. "This Loch Leven Castle — I had never heard of it before. It cannot be so powerful as to defy all taking?"

"It is its situation," Seton explained. "It sits on a tiny island near the north-west end of the long loch, half a mile from land at Kinross town. To assail it would demand a fleet of boats — such as will not be had on that loch. And cannon, to get near enough, would have to be floated on rafts. I cannot see it as possible."

"Bothwell, then? He could not take it either?"

"I think not. He it is that they will be thinking of. The largest force cannot do aught against an island."

"So-o-o!" Thomas breathed a sigh. "You have no advice, my lord? No notions as to what might be attempted?"

"Think you that I have not considered it at the fullest, man? Morton knew what he was doing when he took the Queen there. I see no way out."

He paused. "And she *may* be none so ill there. She is at least safe from Bothwell. Morton will wish to hold her, to gain power, no doubt. There would be no gain in harming her. And he cannot keep her shut up for over-long."

Thomas looked doubtful.

Seton told them that his daughter and the other Marys were still at Holyrood, so far as he knew. So the pair rode on through the June evening to Edinburgh.

The young women's reception was flattering, but troubled Thomas in that all of them seemed to think that now he had arrived everything would improve. He must take them to this Loch Leven Castle, they declared. The Queen needed them, and *they* could not pose any threat to her gaolers. And once they were there, they might be able to devise some means of escape. Could the Queen swim, did he know? None of them were very sure.

He stared at them. They were not serious? It was half a mile from the shore.

That suggestion died a death.

He told them that he was going to visit his father-in-law at Hallyards in Fife, to see whether he could usefully advise. They were all a bit doubtful about this, looking on Kirkcaldy of Grange as in the Protestant camp; but he assured them that he was a loyal subject and the Queen's well-wisher, only at odds with her over religion. They could all call at Hallyards on their way to Loch Leven.

So the following morning all four Marys and the two men rode off, westwards, for Queen Margaret's Ferry over to Fife. Flam's husband, the Secretary of State, was as usual elsewhere.

Using the ferry across Forth it was no more than twenty miles to Hallyards, and they reached there soon after midday, and were fortunate to find Sir William at home. What he thought of his son-in-law's escorting of the young women about the land he did not say, but treated them all courteously. When Thomas got on to the subject of the Queen and guidance, he did however indicate that he would prefer to talk in private.

Alone, the older man admitted that he was not happy about present developments. Morton was his least favoured amongst the Protestant lords, and Ruthven and Lindsay not much better. It was most unfortunate that the Queen had fallen into *their* hands, harsh, power-seeking, arrogant men. Her Grace was to be pitied in the men who sought to control and use her – the weak, petulant Darnley; the unscrupulous and domineering Bothwell; and now these. At least there was no likelihood of her present captors seeking to marry her!

Thomas asked what chance there was of getting her out of Loch Leven Castle, by force or by guile or by negotiation? The other was little more optimistic than had been the Lord Seton. Certainly not by force; that could be ruled out. By guile, he was not hopeful; Morton and the others would not be easily hoodwinked or outwitted. Negotiation – well, that would depend on what was on offer, and who did the negotiating.

What did Morton and these others intend? Thomas wondered. What was their objective in holding the Queen? Why had they not taken her to Stirling Castle, the most secure royal fortress in the kingdom, where she would be reunited with her son?

That was ominous, Kirkcaldy agreed. It was what *he* had advised, and Maitland and Argyll. But Morton had more or less taken all into his own hands, used his large force of Douglases to have his way, and to constrain the Queen and take her to Loch Leven. He admittedly must have some aim in view, other than keeping her secure from Bothwell. He had talked earlier of abdication . . .

"Abdication! The Queen abdicate!" Thomas exclaimed. "This is crazy – mad! Why should she? And what would that serve? She is the undoubted monarch. Only she."

"It would be to make the infant James King, and to rule through the child as Regent."

"Lord! Morton Regent!"

"Perhaps not himself. But some other, as figurehead, it could be. To rule through him." That sounded less than confident.

"But . . ." Thomas wagged his head. "This beyond all." He paused. "Moray . . .?" he asked. "What of Moray? Where is he in all this? The Queen's own brother. He was the most powerful man in the kingdom. He is your friend, is he not?"

"I would not go so far as to say friend. I have worked with him, and recognise his many qualities. He would have made, I think, a good king. A pity, perhaps, that his mother, Margaret Erskine, Mar's sister, and the late King James were not married – as Moray claims they were, in secret, but has no proof – and so Mary would never have been Queen-Regnant. As it happens, the said Margaret Erskine is now mistress of this Loch Leven Castle, for she in the end wed Sir Robert Douglas thereof, Morton's cousin. Their son, the present laird, Morton's heir."

Thomas stared.

"Moray remains in England," Kirkcaldy went on. "Why, I am not sure. He went on an embassage to Queen Elizabeth. Some say that he has even gone to France. He was to tell Elizabeth that Queen Mary was not involved in Darnley's murder. For Darnley was, to be sure, Elizabeth's cousin once-removed. But he has stayed away. Perhaps he had also to go tell Catherine de Medici of France."

"It may be that he has his reasons for staying away?"

"Yes. It may be that with the Bothwell marriage and all its inevitable troubles, he wishes others to take the action, leaving *his* hands clean. Then, when all is quieter, he will return and take charge."

"Think you, then, that he *knew* of this plan of Morton's? Perhaps even devised it, at a distance. If his mother is one of the Queen's gaolers."

"I do not know." But Kirkcaldy sounded troubled.

"This talk of abdication, then? It could be *Moray* who could become Regent?"

"It is possible."

"And you, sir? Would you approve of that?"

"No, lad. I would not. But who am I? I am useful to these lords when there is fighting to be done, armed men to lead – a trained soldier. But otherwise I am only a laird of very modest importance." He shrugged. "But I am the Queen's loyal subject. I have sworn allegiance to her. I do not approve of this talk of abdication."

"So – what can be done?" Thomas demanded.

"If I knew, I would tell you, lad. We can only wait and see how matters proceed. That may sound feeble to you. But I see no clear course meantime."

"Bothwell may raise a great army, and challenge Morton again."

"He may. But that will not get the Queen out of Loch Leven Castle."

They could only leave it at that, however unsatisfactory.

Loch Leven was about seven miles to the north. They spent the night at Hallyards and rode on next morning, Sir William but doubtfully wishing them well, Thomas meanwhile debating procedure once they reached there. Presumably there was nothing for it but to try to hire a boatman to row them out to the castle. That might well not be so simple as it sounded, for all thereabouts would be beholden to the Douglases and might well have received orders to allow none to approach the island. Kinross town could be expected to be entirely under Douglas control, so their reception there might be doubtful. They would have to go warily, and seek to adjust to circumstances.

The loch, very large for lowland Scotland, lay at the western foot of a spur of the prominent twin Lomond Hills and was the source of the River Leven which flowed eastwards through Fife – the names Leven and Lomond and Levenach or Lennox all coming from the same source, the Gaelic word meaning river. The loch was four miles long and about half that in width, fairly shallow and dotted with small islands, seven of them, the largest, at the south end, having the ruins of the Celtic Church monastery of St Serf, tutor to the more famous St Mungo. But the islet the visitors sought was much smaller and two miles further north, near the top end, where nestled the town which gave name to the shire and sheriffdom.

This was no very large community, and when the new-comers reached it the place seemed to be populated with idling and unruly men-at-arms, for whom the sight of the four young women was an evident diversion and challenge. Their two escorts sought to counter this by calling out "A Douglas! A Douglas!" a device which, however fraudulent, did have sufficient effect as to keep the assaults purely verbal.

Down at the loch-shore there was a haven of sorts with a stone jetty and a few small boats tied thereto or beached. Five islets lay some way off, but there was no question as to which was their goal, for the castle-keep, in reddish stone, rose tall and square within its curtain walls and flanking towers, dominant, the red heart and white mullets on blue of Douglas flapping on banners above.

With that in view, the six of them eyed each other, their problem all too apparent. That their well-beloved Queen was immured just out there affected them all notably.

There were a few cottages near the haven, from the doors of which the riders were being watched. Dismounting, Thomas went to ask whether any there had a boat to take them out to the castle. Four men he asked, all of whom either eyed him blankly or made curt refusal. He offered generous payment, declaring that he had important word for Sir William Douglas. This produced no results.

Flam then suggested that further away from the castle and town they might find a fisherman or boatman less afraid to take them, even though it meant longer rowing. This seemed a possible solution, and they set off southwards round the western shore of the loch. They recognised, of course, that their presence would be seen and noted from the island.

This west shore, they discovered, was perhaps the least hopeful, for it was consistently flat, marshy and reedy, and they could see no villages or even houses. Frequently they had to ride quite some way inland to avoid inlets and bogs; but always they came back to the water's edge.

The further south they went the further it would be to row back; and they began to wonder whether they would have been better at the far and eastern side, two miles away, which seemed to be less flat, and where they could see the odd house. However, at the extreme southern end, they did come on a group of cot-houses, screened by trees, with another stone jetty and two boats, this directly opposite the St Serf's island, for which it presumably had been a ferry-base.

Here also, on enquiry, they gained no help, only suspicious looks. Thomas strolled down to the pier, with the idea of purloining one of the boats for themselves, which he and Ogilvy could row the two miles back to the castle; but unfortunately no oars were in the boats, nor visible elsewhere. So that notion came to nothing.

They rode on round to the eastern shore and up it, making for what seemed to be a small village they could see perhaps a mile up. They would there be about as far from the castle-island as they could get, owing to the shape of the loch – though whether that was hopeful or the reverse was doubtful. However, well before they reached this, Ogilvy called out and pointed. Behind them, half a mile off, a group of perhaps a dozen horsemen were spurring fast. It was too much to hope that these were unconcerned with themselves.

Soon it was so obviously pursuit that they reined up to await the party, all seemingly armed. Two young men led men-at-arms. These were both handsome, and might be related.

"Who are you who circle our loch so boldly?" one of these shouted, the elder by his looks. "And why?"

"Do we require permission to ride the open land, sir? I am Sir Thomas Kerr of Ferniehirst. With friends."

"Ha – I have heard of you, sir. One of the Queen's men."

"Are not we all?" That was strong. "All the Queen's subjects."

"M'mmm. Yes." The two young men looked at each other. They rode closer. "Have you come here to spy out the land?"

"Spy? Why should we spy, sir? And spy what in our sovereign-lady's realm? And who are you who ask?"

"I am George Douglas, Younger of Lochleven. And this is my kinsman, Will Douglas."

"Ah. So you, or your brother Sir William, are presently hosts to the Queen's Grace."

"Well . . . yes. Her Grace is in our house."

"We have come for speech with her. On her realm's business. These are the Queen's ladies-in-waiting."

The pair eyed each other again, obviously embarrassed. "Our orders are that none may have speech with Her Highness." The speaker could not have been more than twenty years.

"Whose orders, young man? Not the Queen's, I think!"

"My lord's orders. The Earl of Morton's, sir."

"And does the Earl of Morton outrank the Queen's Grace?"

The younger spoke. "Sir, we do only what Sir William tells us. *He* sent us after you."

"Then pray take us to him, to Sir William Douglas."

The young men looked uncertain. But Thomas had spoken authoritatively throughout, and they were clearly unhappy as to their position. George Douglas shrugged.

"Very well, sir. And ladies. Come with us."

So, escorted by the Douglas men-at-arms, they turned and rode back whence they had come.

Beth spoke up, to their guides. "Her Grace – is she well? I am Mary Beaton, wife to Ogilvy of Boyne, here."

"She, she keeps her room, lady. We think her not in the best of health."

"She is almost certainly pregnant. And should be most heedfully cared for. She needs her ladies." That was Flam. "I am Mary Fleming, sister of the Lord Fleming and wife to the Secretary of State."

The young men looked the more ill-at-ease. They rode on in silence.

When they got back to the Kinross haven, the Douglases told them, distinctly apologetically now, that they must wait there while they went out to consult the laird. No one was allowed out to the island, they said, without express permission. They could only protest, watched over by the men-at-arms.

It was quite some time before George Douglas returned, alone, looking more troubled than ever. "Sir William's salutations, Sir Thomas, and ladies," he got out, jerkily. "But Her Grace is indisposed. She is confined to her chamber and cannot see anyone. Any message you have for her, she will receive . . ."

"But – her ladies! She should have, she *requires*, the attentions of her ladies."

"My mother attends her. And there are other women."

"At least let us speak with her," Ebba pleaded.

"I am sorry, lady. But none are to be permitted to land on the island."

"Let us row out in your boat," Thomas said. "If we cannot land, we could speak with the Queen, from her window or tower-top."

"I am sorry. But it is not possible."

"This on the orders of your brother?"

"And the Lord Ruthven. He, he waits on the Queen."

"*His* father, the leper, was a scoundrel! It seems that the son is no better!"

Douglas shook his head, silent.

"Tell me – the Earl of Morton, your cousin. Does he act thus alone? Or does he do the bidding of another? Another, who perhaps we may approach?"

"I know not . . ."

"You must have heard your brother and mother speaking of these matters? The Earl of Moray, perhaps? He also is your mother's son, is he not?"

"Yes. He has been away in England and France. But he comes home shortly. He will be here . . ."

"Here? You mean, to Loch Leven? Then he knows that the Queen is here?"

"He will, yes."

"So he has remained in touch with Morton throughout?"

"So I understand it, sir. But they do not tell me of these matters."

"I understand, yes." That was perhaps more emphatic than the admission itself warranted.

They had no paper and pen to write letters, nor had Douglas. So all they could do was to give messages of devotion, affection and loyalty to him in the hope that he would pass them on to the Queen. He appeared to be an honest, even likeable young man, and they could only trust him.

Sadly, there was nothing more that they could do. Kirkcaldy had been right, and their journey fruitless. They returned to Hallyards, to admit as much.

The Marys, depressed and uncertain as to what they should do now, decided that they should go back to Holyrood meantime, to be available should conditions improve for their mistress. Perhaps when Moray returned? Thomas would escort them that far, before going home. And Ogilvy said that he ought to go north to his Buchan lairdship meantime, where his brother was acting for him, whether Beth accompanied him, or not. They made a frustrated little party as they rode southwards.

24

Thomas, amongst his Border hills, heard only rumours about the national situation in the days, extending into weeks, that followed: of Bothwell's efforts to assemble a powerful force and of the reluctance of his vassals and friends to join him, after the fiasco of Carberry Hill; of the Queen's continued immolation at Loch Leven and of her alleged ill-health; of the lords collecting at Stirling, around the infant prince, but doing nothing in particular; of Mary's supporters waiting, as he himself waited. Everything seemed to be hanging fire, this late June. Thomas, by now, had little doubt why. All were waiting for the arrival on the scene of the man who had masterminded this situation, from however far off, the Queen's half-brother James Stewart, Earl of Moray. It was interesting and significant that, of all her numerous other half-brothers, including the Lord Robert, now Earl of Orkney, none appeared to be prepared to do anything; only this one – and he ominously.

Firm news did not reach Ferniehirst until mid-July, with the unexpected arrival of Kirkcaldy of Grange himself. He came, in a way reversing the position of Thomas at Hallyards earlier, to spy out the land, sent by the Lords of the Congregation to try to gauge the extent of Bothwell's army-raising in the Borderland, and, as a military man, to assess the possibilities of reducing Dunbar Castle, seen as Bothwell's base and an all but impregnable strongpoint.

Kirkcaldy told Thomas and his daughter of sad developments for the imprisoned Queen Mary. She had miscarried of twins and was now sunk in despair and lethargy. Morton and the lords had prepared a document of abdication and were to put it before her for signature. Preparations were even being made for the coronation of the infant James as King of Scots. A Regent would be appointed, but his identity was not proclaimed – but almost all anticipated that it would be Moray, whose return was expected at any time. It seemed that Mary's reign was all but over.

Thomas was distressed and angry, and almost accused his father-in-law of complicity in the Queen's betrayal and troubles, of insincerity in his professions of loyalty. But the older man forestalled this by declaring that he was against any abdication. He had let the lords know this. He had agreed to this mission of investigation anent Bothwell because he believed that Bothwell was as much a disaster for Mary as he was for the kingdom in general, and the sooner that he was eliminated from the scene the better for all. Thomas could not really disagree with that judgment, at least. With Bothwell gone, Mary's friends would be quit of an incubus, and many would rally to her cause, he was convinced – Huntly, Home, Atholl, Sempill, Maxwell, Herries and more, as well as Seton, Fleming, Livingstone and Carmichael, the ever-faithful ones. Bothwell, whom the Council had outlawed for his part in the Darnley murder, was an actual danger to any allegedly linked with him, for any supporter of an outlaw was himself outwith the law. Bothwell must go.

Kirkcaldy declared that after that bugbear was disposed of, he would be prepared to co-operate with any worthwhile attempt to aid the Queen. In return, Thomas agreed to help him in his present task.

So for three days they rode up and down the Borderland, or at least the East and Middle Marches, for the West March held no support for Bothwell, under the dominance of his enemies the Maxwells. They went as far as Hermitage itself, and into most of the Cheviot valleys, making discreet enquiries. And they discovered everywhere a notable lack of enthusiasm for Bothwell and his call to arms. That Earl had sullied his reputation by his inadequate leadership at Carberry and his desertion of the Queen there; also his outlawry had its effect. The Borders were not going to rise for their Lieutenant.

Satisfied in this at least, the pair then disguised themselves as travelling cattle-buyers, and headed north-eastwards across the Merse for Dunbar, through the Home country. Sir William made good company, knowledgeable about lands and families and especially strong on the doings of the past, military in particular. They got on well, Thomas learning much.

They reached Dunbar town in late afternoon and spent the evening visiting taverns and harbour-side ale-howfs, under the towering walls and stacks of the frowning fortress. Both men being cattle-rearers on their estates, they were able to talk knowledgeably about the trade, and they did not get any impression that they aroused suspicions that they were not what they seemed. And in conversation with the local farmers and fishermen they learned much that was of value. Bothwell was, in fact, not here, but had gone off into the far north country, Aberdeenshire and Buchan it seemed, no doubt to try to raise the great Gordon manpower of the house of Huntly. He had left Dunbar Castle under the command of one of his vassals, Whitelaw of that Ilk, with a strong garrison, as well as many men-at-arms in the town. The stronghold, all asserted, was well equipped and supplied to withstand siege.

They had to drink much ale before they sought beds that night.

In the morning, they surveyed that mighty sea-girt fortress from various viewpoints, seeking to make themselves inconspicuous. Kirkcaldy's trained eye noted its many strengths, other than the obvious ones, and its precious few weaknesses. Only from the sea, he observed, could the place be effectively threatened, by cannon-carrying ships, and even then the final storming would be exceedingly difficult. Dunbar Castle would be a hard nut to crack.

They rode away southwards again, quest over.

When Sir William left Ferniehirst next day, Thomas sought a promise from him to send him any information or guidance which might enable him to help the Queen. He might learn something from the lords. Anything which could bring aid, comfort, release, for their so-wronged monarch. He obtained his assurance.

It was two weeks later that a letter reached Thomas from his father-in-law. It did not offer any counsel as to how the Queen might be succoured but it did at least bring him up to date on developments – and sad for Mary Stewart they were. In her helplessness and dispirited state, she had been forced to sign a deed of abdication – the Lord Lindsay, who had been instrumental in achieving this, boasting in his cups . thereafter that he had threatened her with death if she did not sign, and saying that she did not even read the paper. Little James, at thirteen months, was immediately proclaimed King by the lords gathered at Stirling, and the coronation hastily arranged for 29th July – which was, in fact, the day that this letter arrived. There was still no sure word as to who would be

Regent for the child; which must surely mean that all awaited Moray's return. He had been away for over four drama-filled months now, and was expected back at any time.

The last part of the letter announced that Bothwell had failed to arouse the north-east and the Gordons, and had sailed off to the Orkney islands, his new dukedom, asserting that, as Lord High Admiral still, he would return with a fleet and army of tough Northmen to assert his rights and rescue his wife.

Thomas, and Janet also, could by no means accept the idea that Mary was no longer Queen of Scots. Just because, under vile duress, she had been forced to scrawl her signature on a piece of paper. She had been Queen since she was a week old, duly anointed and crowned. None, surely, had the right to dethrone her, certainly no group of power-seeking lords. She was still their crowned sovereign, then, to whom all had sworn allegiance. For themselves, and for multitudes of others no doubt, she was monarch, and would remain so, whatever was said and done at Stirling.

Be that as it may, however, there seemed still to be nothing that they could do to aid her. No amount of brain-racking produced any practical or possible plan or device.

So much now seemed to depend on Moray. If, as seemed possible, even likely, all was being done at his direction, how much better off would be his half-sister on his return? Moray surely was an unsubstantial straw to clutch at in this situation, they had to admit, however able a man he might be.

Thomas felt himself to be a poor creature, a feeble friend indeed to the Queen who called him her protector, as he passed those unhappy summer months in his Borderland, minding his own and the town of Jedburgh's affairs. He sent a letter to the Marys at Holyrood – if they were still there – informing them of what Kirkcaldy had told him, but with no suggestions as to action.

It was almost a month later when a second letter arrived, sent from the port of Leith. It was hastily written, to the effect that he, Kirkcaldy, was being sent north with four ships-of-war to Orkney, to try to persuade the islanders not to support Bothwell, and to capture the man himself if at all possible. He was not over-sanguine as to the success of this mission. But he added a very small note of hope as regards Mary Stewart. Queen Elizabeth of England was much upset, apparently, over the treatment meted out to another Queen-Regnant, however critical she was of Mary herself, and had sent her envoy, Throckmorton, north to tell the lords so. She was even suggesting that the little prince should be sent for safe-keeping to England until all the disturbances were over. This was not likely to be greeted with acclaim at Stirling; but since Moray had been seeing much of Elizabeth over his months in England, it was possible that he might obtain better treatment for his half-sister when he returned, in consequence. Incidentally, Throckmorton was to urge Mary's divorce from Bothwell.

Before this, general rumour and gossip had it that a form of coronation for the infant prince had been held at Stirling, Morton bearing the sceptre, Glencairn the sword and Atholl the crown. Few amongst the ordinary folk of the land accepted this as anything more than a play-acting, a gesture by the lords; Mary was still their Queen, however ill-done by.

Then the waited-for tidings went round the Borderland. The Earl of Moray was back, the strong man and Queen's brother. Now there would be developments, a decisive hand on the helm of state.

The whole kingdom waited, eager for news.

It was Ogilvy of Boyne who brought Thomas his information, sent as before by the Marys – who were no longer at Holyrood, it seemed, Ebba with her father at Seton and Flam at her husband's house of Lethington, near Haddington and only a few miles from Seton, with Beth Beaton and himself with her. So they were all still in touch. It was Secretary of State Maitland himself who had given his wife the latest news; he was having to play a difficult and almost two-faced role, sympathetic to the Queen yet the servant of the Privy Council, which was of course dominated by the Protestant Lords of the Congregation; he would resign, but felt that he could be of more use retaining office. His information was that Moray had visited the Queen at Loch Leven, and she had greeted him lovingly and with relief. But that he had not promised her release, implying that it was beyond his power to do so, against the wishes of the Privy Council. So she had urged him to accept the regency, if it was offered to him, so that he *would* have supreme power in her kingdom. Then she would be freed; and she had promised that she would be guided by him thereafter, even allowing him to retain the title of Regent for *her*, rather than her son, until the matter of Bothwell was out of the way. She had besought him not to think of doing Elizabeth's bidding and sending her little son to England. He, Maitland, had no least belief that Moray had ever contemplated such a thing; but also that he had no intention of obtaining the Queen's release from Loch Leven. Almost certainly it was on his orders that she was there, in the first place.

Thomas digested all this with near-despair. Not that he could claim real disappointment, for he had never built any great hopes on Moray, a cold-blooded realist in his opinion; but this betrayal of his sister whilst pretending to cherish her, took a deal of swallowing. It was small consolation to learn that the Queen's health and spirits had picked up considerably, in her belief that her brother would help her.

Ogilvy had brought a message from the Marys. Would Thomas join them in a visit to Moray himself, to try to persuade him to at least improve the Queen's conditions, perhaps move her to Stirling Castle where she would be more comfortable and with her son; and to allow them, her ladies, to attend on her again? This surely he could do at no cost to his ambitions?

Thomas, with no desire to speak with the Earl James, could scarcely refuse this request. He agreed to return next day with Ogilvy, to Lethington.

Secretary Maitland said that he would accompany them and seek to ensure that they won into Moray's presence; and when they picked up Ebba at Seton, her father also offered to go with them, to add weight to their pleas – although he was not optimistic as to results.

So they made quite a party to ride westwards, with an escort of Seton men-at-arms, late in August. It was St Ebba's Eve, which the young women at least took as a good omen. Stirling was some fifty miles from Lethington, so they halted for the night midway at Seton's castle of Niddry, near to Linlithgow, where next morning they collected the Lord Livingstone, their former colleague's father, at his house of Callendar. The more impressive the deputation the better.

Stirling town, where the Forth narrowed sufficiently to bridge its width, was full of the retainers of the many lords assembled there, and idle soldiery seldom make for placid conditions; they were quite glad to have their armed escort to win them passage through the crowded, narrow, climbing streets and wynds of that hilly burgh, to the great rock-crowning fortress, premier stronghold of Scotland's ancient monarchy.

Secretary Maitland's presence ensured their entry at the castle gatehouse; but gaining what amounted to an audience with the Earl James – who was now being styled the Regent Moray, the second to bear that title, for the Bruce's nephew, Thomas Randolph, Earl of Moray, had so acted for the child David the Second – was less easy. Actually, since there had been no parliament to confirm the regency appointment, or for that matter, the infant's elevation to King – or Thomas and these two lords would have been entitled to vote – Moray was not yet legally entitled to the style. But clearly such small matters did not weigh heavily in the present situation. There was no sign of the baby James.

The callers had to wait until evening, carefully avoided by the other lords in residence, before there came a summons to the presence. Significantly perhaps, this was held in the royal apartments. Moray was alone, unsmiling, stern and looking older than his thirty-six years. Here they were face to face with the undoubted ruler of Scotland. It was, to be sure, his royal father who had built these splendid apartments, in one of the finest edifices in the land. Did legitimate birth count for so much as did blood?

They had not expected any warm welcome and they did not receive one. Moray's bow to the ladies was brief, even though Flam was his own sister's daughter, and his eyeing of the men all but frigid.

"You wished to see me?" he said flatly.

"Yes, my lord." Seton being the senior there, in years as in rank, spoke first. "We understand that you now exercise the fullest authority in the realm, and so we approach you on behalf of the Queen's Grace. She is . . ."

"The Queen's Grace is my sister, my lord. I am well able to consider matters on her behalf unaided."

"That is good. Then we can hope for speedy improvement in her situation?"

"Her situation is well enough. She is safe and cared for and improving in health."

"But she is to all intents a prisoner, is she not?"

"I do not esteem her so."

Flam spoke. "My lord and uncle, Her Grace is denied the

attendance of her ladies. Of whom we here are three. Always we have been with her, waited on her, for a score of years, since we were all but children. This is unkind, surely?"

"Unkind for whom, Mary? The Queen – or yourselves!"

"Both. She needs us."

"I think that you over-rate your services! My sister is well attended at Loch Leven. My mother, the Lady Douglas, cares well for her. And there are other women. Forby, that castle is a small one, lacking room for numbers of folk. You would all be scarcely comfortable therein."

Thomas took him up on that. "That is part of our contention, my lord. Strong Loch Leven may be, but it *is* too small a place to immure the Queen's Grace. Unsuitable. And on that small island, restricts her woefully. There are other strong places, less prison-like." He emphasised that phrase. "If Her Grace's safety is so threatened. This Stirling, indeed, the strongest in the land. Where she could be with her son. A mother's right, surely?"

Moray eyed him coldly. "Your concern may do you credit, Sir Thomas. I understand that you have already visited Loch Leven, making representations. On whose authority I am unaware!" So he was well-informed, was James Stewart. "Her Grace is well cared for, I tell you. I am not unconcerned for her security and well-being."

"Security from what, my lord? Is it the Earl of Bothwell? Now that he has fled to Orkney, there can be little to fear from *him*, for some time, at least. Who else must the Queen be secure from?"

"Those who would use her against her realm's and her own interests, sir." He frowned. "But this inquisition grows tedious. You have my assurance that Her Grace is well cared for. Is there anything else, to the point?"

Thomas Kerr had a stubborn streak to him. "Would you deny that the Queen is presently held captive, my lord? Which is surely a grievous assault on her royal person. Which must, I think, greatly concern other monarchs, in particular the Queen of England? This cannot be good for the realm. Would it not be better, if she cannot be freed entirely, to instal her here in her own royal castle of Stirling?" That shrewd thrust cut home, witnessed to by the quick narrowing of those grey eyes.

"Her *son's* castle! I would remind you that the child James is now King of Scots. Perhaps you have forgot?"

"Parliament has not said so, my lord."

"Parliament will do so. The Council has to act for it meantime, as is its right and duty."

William Maitland spoke, his voice troubled. "My lord, my wife and her friends but seek Queen Mary's personal welfare and comfort. Not to debate affairs of state." Clearly he was anxious not to be considered by the Regent as himself any sort of dissident. He glanced warningly at Thomas.

"Then you can leave well content, Mr Secretary. The Queen's interests, and I hope the realm's, are safe in my hands. I bid you a good night." And with a curt nod, he turned and left the chamber.

They filed out, a deal less than satisfied.

All agreed thereafter that they should get out of Stirling Castle forthwith, the August evening not so dark that they could not reach Livingstone's house of Callendar. They made a silent company.

When Thomas went his own way next day, after passing through Edinburgh where Moray was being proclaimed Regent from the Mercat Cross with full royal honours, he left three unhappy young women, each reacting in her own fashion – Flam hurt and vocal, Beth hotly angry, Ebba silent but with tears not far away. They would all remain in touch with each other, but none made pretence of hopefulness.

25

It was 6th October and another saint's day, Adamnan's, before
Thomas heard directly of important national developments –
not that these had anything to do with the Queen's state. It
was Sir William Kirkcaldy again, come to see his daughter.

He had come, he announced, from the siege of Dunbar.
When this surprised them, he informed that he was not
long back from Orkney – where he had failed to apprehend
Bothwell, who had in fact fled to Denmark, presumably to his
Anna Throndsen – when Moray had decided to try to take
Dunbar Castle, indeed had been waiting until his, Kirkcaldy's,
return to help in the attempt, flattering but not particularly
welcome. So it was promptly back to his four ships in Leith
haven, to load them with powerful cannon, and set off down
Forth again, whilst the Regent took his army by land. The
castle had in fact yielded after four days – not so much on
account of the bombardment, he judged, because the garrison
had cannon also, and they could keep the ships at a distance,
but because the attackers had made sure that the defenders
knew that their master, Bothwell, had fled overseas. Whitelaw
of that Ilk, the captain of the fortress, had wisely decided that
there was little point in continuing to hold out, and had traded
good and honourable terms for himself and his men in return
for capitulation. So Bothwell's last strength in Scotland was
gone, and that adventurer could surely now be dismissed as
any threat, marriage or none.

Would this result in the Queen's release from bondage,
Thomas wondered, to be sorrowfully informed that his father-
in-law feared not. Moray had not specifically said so, but the
indications were that he was afraid that a rallying of the
Queen's friends, and particularly the Catholic nobles, would
follow should she be set free, with possible upset to his own
position and the Protestant cause. He was, however, calling a
parliament for 15th December, at Edinburgh, which perhaps
should at least better conditions for Her Grace.

Incidentally Kirkcaldy revealed that Moray had re-appointed him to his former position as Captain of Edinburgh Castle, which Bothwell's friend Cockburn had yielded up.

Thomas took the opportunity to urge the older man to use his evident influence with Moray to improve the Queen's living conditions, if nothing more, in especial to allow her Marys, or one or other of them, to be with her. Kirkcaldy said that he would do that, certainly.

It was two weeks after this that a letter came to Ferniehirst from Flam Fleming. This announced that one of them had indeed been permitted to go to Loch Leven to be with the Queen, but only one. Since she and Beth had husbands to think of, and Mary Carmichael was still away in Lanarkshire with her father, Ebba Seton had gone. They hoped that somehow Ebba would be able to smuggle out letters or messages to them, and even be in a position to help possible escape – how was not suggested. She, Flam, had given Ebba a ring to give to the Queen, presented to her in France, depicting the lion and mouse of Aesop's fable, and implying that though the mouse was small and weak, like themselves, it could perhaps gnaw through the cords which bound the lion, Her Grace. Pray that it could be so. Ebba had also taken with her some extra clothing for their mistress, embroidery thread, soap and the like, even playing-cards, which might aid a little in making captivity more bearable.

This was, at least, a small step in the right direction, whether of Kirkcaldy's doing or otherwise.

Moray in due course issued his summons to a parliament on 15th December, sent in the style of His Grace, the Regent, Thomas receiving his as due. So James Stewart was now even adopting the royal designation.

This parliament, needless to say, the first for so long, was the subject of nationwide anticipation and speculation. Although it would be in no way representative of the common people of the kingdom, save through burgh commissioners, it would, or should, give some indication of how others than the lords and great ones felt about what had been done, and the grass-roots attitude towards their Queen. There were hopes, but also fears – and the latter were widespread. It was commonly being said that the entire idea of having this parliament was to pinpoint and trap the Queen's supporters. That those who expressed themselves in favour of Mary and against her forced abdication would thereafter be arrested and imprisoned, so ensuring that there would be no leadership available for any rising in the Queen's favour.

Thomas recognised all too clearly the possibility of this, and it could not but cross his mind to wonder whether he himself should attend. But he dismissed the thought as craven, unworthy. If the Queen's friends so behaved was there any hope for her? He had a duty to be present. But he did perceive the possibility that others might well stay away. He comforted Janet, if not himself, by pointing out that he at least had a voice to speak for him, in her father, if there were reprisals on the Queen's supporters.

Holding the parliament in mid-December was in itself a deterrent for many from all over the land, for even though the winter snows might not yet have closed many of the passes through hills and mountains, the rains could have made rivers swell and fords become impassable, and turned valley-floors into quagmires. It was no time for long-distance travel for any but the toughest.

When Janet, with the children, saw Thomas off for Edinburgh, she could not wholly hide her fears for his safety, good at that as she usually was.

Arrival in the city tended to confirm these fears. The streets were full of armed men, but they were all, so far as Thomas could judge, the retainers of the Protestant lords. That evening, he saw none of the people he would have looked for as the Queen's supporters. They might be there, but prudently keeping themselves private meantime. He called in at Holyrood, but found the palace and abbey all but deserted, even the Lord Robert and his multitudinous household absent. Moray, apparently, was lodging up at the castle. Thomas felt, that night, almost like a stranger in a strange land.

In the morning, up at Parliament House where he arrived early, it was the same story. As the seats and rows gradually were occupied, he perceived precious few whom he could identify as likely to be the Queen's active well-wishers; indeed comparatively few of any sort, with the benches only sparsely occupied. He had wondered whether to sit with the burgh representatives, as Provost of Jedburgh – thinking that perhaps these might be more sympathetic towards their liege-lady – rather than in his usual place as Baron of Ferniehirst; but he saw so scant a company of burghal commissioners, other than Edinburgh's Provost and magistrates, who could hardly absent themselves, as to make any such move there pointless. Right up until the trumpets sounded outside, to herald the arrival of the magnates and officers of state, the hall was half-empty.

When the lords filed in, Seton, Fleming, Livingstone and Herries were there, but notably few others whom Thomas had hoped to see. And, significantly, not a single representative of the great house of Hamilton. Of the earls following, Huntly, Eglinton and Atholl appeared, with some doubtfuls such as Glencairn and Cassillis, but no sign of Sutherland, Marischal, Montrose or Crawford. Argyll, it seemed, was still Chancellor, and came to take his place at the chairman's table. Thomas had expected him to be replaced; but whether this was a good sign or bad remained to be seen. Otherwise, the earls', lords' and commendators' seats were solidly Protestant-occupied. In a kindly gesture, Kirkcaldy of Grange came to sit beside his son-in-law.

More trumpeting announced the arrival of the Regent. The Lord Lyon King of Arms and his heralds appeared, and signed for all to stand. Then Morton bearing the sceptre, Rothes the crown and Mar the sword of state filed in, to lay their symbols on the Chancellor's table.

To a final fanfare, Moray stalked in, as ever sternly dignified, all but regal indeed despite his sober clothing. He strode to the throne, without a glance left or right, and, nodding curtly to Lyon, sat down.

The King of Arms then announced in ringing tones that this was a duly called and convened parliament of the Three Estates of the Realm, assembled in the name of James, King of Scots, on the authority of his Regent, James, Earl of Moray here present. He bowed to the throne. All might now sit. He gestured towards the Chancellor, and went to take his place behind Moray.

At his table Argyll both looked and sounded nervous, shuffling papers and glancing about him. He cleared his throat.

"Your Grace, my lords and commissioners," he began, "this parliament is called for the better government and well-being of the kingdom. Much is required of it. There has been misgovernment, unlawful actions and usurpations, of major scale, since last parliament sat." He was reading this out hurriedly. "It is necessary now that steps taken to right this misgovernment and grievous tyranny should be approved and enacted by the Estates of the Realm and so made lawful. But before the business of this assembly commences, with His Grace's approval, I call upon the Commendator-Bishop of Moray to open the session with prayer."

Thomas, for one, gasped, and glanced at his father-in-law. Patrick Hepburn, kinsman of Bothwell, who had so recently succoured and sheltered that earl at the Bishop's Palace of Spynie, near Elgin, was perhaps the last cleric he would have expected to perform this present duty, to be here at all, and not only to be prepared to co-operate but to be accepted by the ruling faction. This was significant indeed.

The bishop came forward, to pray briefly but explicitly, and very much in the Protestant idiom, that Almighty God would bless the hearts and minds of all present and enable them to support the right, uphold the wise steps taken for the realm's weal by the King's Regent and Privy Council, and to uphold the true religion. Amen.

That left no doubts in anyone's mind as to what was expected and intended. Bothwell's extinction as a force to be reckoned with could not have been more clearly emphasised.

The Chancellor resumed, eyes still on his papers. "Firstly, three items to be passed as lawful and perfect. The former Queen Mary's abdication. The elevation to the throne and coronation of James, Duke of Rothesay and undoubted heir to the throne. And the appointment of his uncle, James, Earl of Moray, to be Regent. All as agreed and enacted by the Lords of the Privy Council."

He had barely got the words out when the red-bearded Earl of Morton shouted, "Approved! Approved!"

Half a dozen Protestant lords were on their feet immediately to second that.

Argyll duly noted it. "Any contrary motion?" he asked flatly.

Thomas, on the edge of his seat, sighed with relief as Lord Seton rose.

"My lord Chancellor," he said carefully, "I scarcely think that we can so briefly accept these vital matters of highest importance in the realm's affairs without further debate and explanation."

"Are you putting forward a motion, my lord? If so, what?"

A growl arose.

"I seek information, my lord. But if a motion is called for at this stage, I move that we should debate the validity of the Queen's alleged abdication."

Lord Fleming's seconding of that was lost in shouts of opposition from all over the hall.

Argyll thumped his gavel half-heartedly for silence. "A motion has been proposed and seconded. Also a counter-motion. Who speaks?"

"I do." That was the Lord Lindsay. "None, I say, may speak with greater surety. Since *I* presented and read the deed of abdication to the Queen and watched her sign it. With Lord Ruthven, present, as witness. And Sir William Douglas, also present."

"I confirm that," Ruthven called out.

"Are you satisfied, my Lord Seton?"

"Scarcely that, Chancellor. Much has been said since then about duress. Threats made against the Queen's person, to force her to sign. I have heard . . ."

"Said by whom?" Lindsay interrupted. "Bothwell, and his like? Rogues, and men of ill-will. To make trouble. How can any so say who were not present?"

Lord Ruthven spoke again. "My lord Chancellor, should you not warn the Lord Seton that making such wicked and unprovable accusations here, before so many, could result in action being taken against this lord?"

That produced strong, indeed menacing applause.

Seton raised his eyebrows. "I have heard it said that one who *was* present wished to come here to testify. I refer to the Queen's Grace herself, who is declared to have requested permission to come from Loch Leven to speak herself to this parliament. A request which has *not* been granted."

That produced a major disturbance in the hall. Argyll had to bang his gavel loud and long.

"You are not satisfied, then, my lord?" he asked, unhappily.

"No, I am not."

"Nor am I." That was Livingstone.

"This lord talks of hearing this and hearing that," Morton accused. "Hearsay. Idle gossip. Parliament requires more than that."

Applause was vociferous.

"You wish to put the issue to the vote, my lords?" Argyll asked.

Seton looked from his few friends to the so hostile gathering all around, and shrugged. "What use?" he demanded wearily.

"Very well. I declare the motion carried. Move to the next business."

Thomas could not contain himself, even though Kirkcaldy laid a hand on his arm. He jumped up. "My lord Chancellor, this is against all reason and justice! Parliament must not be muzzled thus! The Queen's Grace and her cause are to be upheld – for to most of this nation she is still their sovereign-lady. Do not forget that. I say . . ." The rest was howled down.

Argyll beat his gavel again. "Sir Thomas Kerr, I must rule you out of order!" he declared. "If you have a motion to put forward, state it. Otherwise, sit down."

Thomas hesitated. "I move, then, that this parliament discusses the validity of the coronation of the infant James, Duke of Rothesay, since it was done without the express agreement of the Queen, the prince's mother, the authority of parliament, or even of the full Privy Council – members of which, here present, were not consulted."

That, although it provoked angry murmurs, did give momentary pause as men eyed each other. Who would, or could, answer that?

It was Moray himself who did, and who had not spoken hitherto. The monarch, or Regent therefor, was an integral part of the Scots parliament, unlike the English, and although he did not preside, overlooked all and could end any session by rising and walking out. He was entitled to speak, like other members.

"Such motion is incompetent for this parliament," he announced authoritatively. "The Privy Council has the right and duty to act in the nation's interest at all times when parliament is not sitting. As then. If all members of it cannot be reached, with speed, before an urgent meeting, then a quorum is sufficient. I myself could not be reached, on that occasion. As others. But I accept the decisions made. The urgency was vital. The Queen had demitted the throne, and signed a deed of abdication. Her signature can be seen, on proper application. It is undoubtedly hers. The throne of Scotland cannot remain vacant, not for one night and one day. That is the unchallenged law of this nation. So a new monarch had to be proclaimed forthwith. And crowned at the soonest thereafter. No time to await the arrival of distant lords of council, myself or others. My lord of Morton, and the others gathered at Stirling, acted correctly. This parliament can endorse their actions or seek to amend them. But it cannot question their validity."

It was not often that James Stewart made so lengthy a statement.

Perhaps Thomas should have been satisfied in that he had provoked such a cogent pronouncement from the Regent, but he was not. "Then all hangs on whether the Queen signed that abdication document under duress, and so makes it of no worth . . ."

"That matter has already been dealt with. And I am not to be put to the question by members here, as you should know. My lord Chancellor, I request that you bring Sir Thomas Kerr to order."

Argyll coughed. "Yes, Your Grace. Sir Thomas, you transgress the rules of parliament. Sit, you – or my Lord Lyon will have you conducted from this hall."

Muttering, Thomas sat.

After that, there was no more discussion of the three-fold acceptance of the abdication, coronation and regency. They moved to the next business. This took most there by surprise. It was a motion, put forward by Morton, that since evidence had come to light that the former Queen was aware of, indeed art and part in the murder of her late husband, the Lord Darnley, she should continue to be detained in the castle of Loch Leven whilst the matter was enquired into.

The commotion this aroused went on for some time, the more so in that it seemed that the Chancellor himself appeared as disturbed about it as any, and clearly had not known that this was to be brought up. There were cries for elucidation from around the hall, with Herries on his feet demanding a withdrawal of the infamous allegation of guilt and Huntly requiring proof or retraction. Argyll had difficulty gaining quiet. He glanced for guidance at Moray.

"My lord of Morton," he said, when he got no help from the throne, "this is a most serious assertion, of which I had not been given warning. Since it is in the form of a motion before the house, I cannot refuse it, if seconded, and . . ."

He had to pause as numerous Protestant lords rose to second. "As I say, I cannot refuse to hear the motion, as Chancellor. But I can and do say that, as *Argyll*, I deplore it, and would counsel that the allegation be not proceeded with."

Morton, still on his feet, grinned. "I have the right to raise the matter and will do so, since it bears heavily on the kingdom's welfare. Evidence has come to light, which puts the former Queen's guilt beyond doubt. This parliament should know of it."

Almost everyone there looked from Morton to Moray. The latter could undoubtedly stop this, if he so desired. He sat, inscrutable.

Thomas was not the only one who was astonished at Morton's move. For that man, himself, was suspected by almost all as having taken a leading part in arranging Darnley's death. At the farcical enquiry into Bothwell's alleged complicity in the matter, Morton had supported Bothwell, and his own concurrence had been mentioned. Was this now some effort to absolve himself officially?

The Chancellor shrugged. "Proceed," he said, frowning.

"A common man, one George Dalgleish, tailor to James Hepburn, Earl of Bothwell, coming from Dunbar Castle, after its fall, was apprehended, with in his possession a silver casket belonging to Bothwell and bearing his arms. It was locked, but on a key being made, was found to be full of letters, written to the said Bothwell, in Queen Mary's own hand-of-write. These letters were written from Glasgow, before Darnley's death, indeed while the Queen was attending on her sick husband, and most clearly in one she reveals that she knew of the plan of Bothwell to have Darnley done to death, indeed wished the project success. That casket and the letters are in my safe keeping."

Huntly jumped up. "I protest, my lord Chancellor! Such dastardly accusation cannot be accepted by this parliament. It would require fullest proof, display of the documents, verification that they were indeed in the Queen's writing and not forgeries. I move that this entire wicked motion be ruled out of order."

Seton, Livingstone and Herries rose to second that.

Argyll shook his head unhappily. "I would agree, my lords, if the motion itself depended on the authenticity of these alleged letters. But as I see it, the motion was that the

314

Queen's Grace should be continued in ward at Loch Leven Castle until the matter be enquired into. That is competent for this parliament to decide, it seems to me." And he glanced again at the Regent.

That man nodded briefly.

"Is it then the will of parliament that the motion be passed? Or rejected?"

There was no need for a counting of the votes. Although not a few abstained, the obvious majority present voted yes.

It was evident now to all that no good would come for the Queen in this parliament, and that her friends were wasting their time in attending. This was still further emphasised when Morton was again on his feet, with a motion that, in consequence of the clear misgovernment of these last years, in no time coming should any woman be admitted to public authority in the realm, or function in the government. This extraordinary proposal produced so much outcry and hubbub that even the imperturbable Moray found it too much, and, rising from his throne without a word, stalked out, thus closing the session.

Kirkcaldy, taking Thomas's arm, led him quickly away, once the earls had filed out, by a side door of Parliament House and down into the Cowgate, a low-level street to the south where few of the parliamentarians would be likely to come for some time at least, and thence westwards, to climb to the castle on its rock by steep wynds and stairways, this to avoid any encounters and possible attacks by those who might have disapproved of his stance in the proceedings. He expressed the opinion that it had been unwise, in the circumstances. Thomas, for his part, demanded to know whether the older man approved of what had transpired, in so obviously a managed and manipulated parliament, of Morton's behaviour, of Argyll's so evident fears and subservience to Moray, and of the Regent's own attitudes. His father-in-law confessed that he was not happy about it all, but pointed out that the entire present situation was fraught with difficulties for all concerned, and that Moray, with the responsibility now of ruling a divided nation, had to pick his way most carefully. This, needless to say, did not appease Thomas; but there was no point in coming to verbal blows over it. He and Janet's father were on different sides in the nation's divisions, but they liked and respected each other.

Nevertheless, Kirkcaldy urged his son-in-law's departure from the castle, and Edinburgh, just as soon as possible, indeed that very evening, for it was not at all improbable that Morton's Douglases, and others, would be after him. He had made himself altogether too prominent in his support of the Queen, spying out Loch Leven, approaching Moray personally at Stirling, and now today's confrontation. Morton was an unscrupulous enemy to make, and Thomas would be a deal safer in his own Borderland.

Recognising this to be sound advice, the younger man gave up his projected attempt to see Moray again here in the castle that evening, and in the December dusk, slipped out of the fortress, heavily cloaked and as inconspicuous as possible, to head southwards. He ought to get as far as the Soutra hospice amongst the Lammermuirs for the night, dark as it was.

He would have been better to have stayed at home, as Janet had advised, he recognised now.

26

That winter and early spring of 1568 were, strangely enough, the most peaceful and uneventful of any since Mary Stewart had returned to her homeland over six eventful years before. There were no risings or disturbances, plots may have been laid but none came to anything, Moray ruled wisely, if sternly, and well – save perhaps in the matter of his sister – and seemed to keep even Morton in hand. Only, the poor Queen remained prisoner, and her friends sorrowed.

Thomas got occasional word of her, for Ebba Seton was still with her, and managed to smuggle messages out of the island-castle from time to time, and, incidentally, through the agency of young George Douglas himself. Apparently that young man was coming more and more under the Queen's spell – which was a hopeful sign in more ways than one, for it meant surely that Mary was improving in health and spirits for her old magnetism to be asserting itself. So much so, indeed, that it was said that the Lord Ruthven even, one of her principal gaolers, was in love with her now and suggesting marriage. The messages Ebba sent were that escape was not impossible. They must be prepared for it.

Then, in mid-March, there came news of a positive nature. George Douglas himself had arrived at Seton Palace. He had been expelled from Loch Leven Castle as a danger, too much enthralled by the Queen for his mother's peace of mind. However, before he had left, he had managed to make an arrangement with one of the serving-men, who happened to be betrothed to a young laundry-maid who was ferried out to the castle daily to wash the inmates' clothes. The girl was to delay her return to the mainland one evening, until after dark, on the pretence of being unwell. She was to change places with the Queen, Ebba Seton assisting, Mary to don the laundress's clothing and, her features covered on account of the alleged sickness, the servitor would have her rowed ashore in the girl's place. If Lord Seton and a party, with horses, was to be secretly waiting nearby, then the escape could be completed. The messenger who brought Thomas this exciting information said that the Lord Seton, with George Douglas, had already left for Loch Leven-side.

The news had Thomas hurrying to have his horse saddled and be on his way to Seton Palace.

He found Flam and Beth at Seton, Ogilvy having gone with the rescue party. The plan was that, once they had picked up the escaped Queen, they would ride with her first to Niddry Castle, Seton's stronghold near Linlithgow, after the crossing of Queen Margaret's Ferry, and after she had rested there – for with long imprisonment on the small island she might well be somewhat frail and unfit for long riding – bring her here to Seton.

Not knowing just when the expected escape attempt would be made, there was little point in Thomas proceeding on to Niddry. He would just wait, with the young women.

They had not very long to wait. Lord Seton arrived back that evening, with Ogilvy, both much dejected. The rescue project had misfired, and the Queen was still in Loch Leven Castle.

It was all most unfortunate, for the attempt had almost succeeded. The Queen, dressed as laundry-maid, had got into the boat and been rowed ashore where, hidden, George Douglas awaited her. She had kept her face covered with a scarf, and only mumbled when the two boatmen spoke to her, the accompanying servitor explaining that she was unwell. But when preparing to land, to clamber over the side, the scarf had slipped, and she had raised hands to keep it in place. And those hands, even in the dark, had given her away, long-fingered, slender white hands, not at all those of a washerwoman. The boatmen, about to aid her out, perceived it and reached to uncover her face, to reveal her true identity. She had pleaded with them not to take her back to the castle but the men, afraid of what would happen to them, especially afraid of the Lord Ruthven's fury, had said that they must, their very lives could depend on it. But they had agreed, probably mainly for George Douglas's sake, not to say anything of the escape attempt to the castle's occupants – this they had assured Douglas on their eventual return to the mainland.

So it was failure. However, George Douglas had told Seton

that another attempt could be made, if his brother and Ruthven did not know of this one. He had concocted the plan of returning openly to the castle, to say his farewells. He would pretend that he was going to France and could not leave without saying goodbye to his mother and brother. While he was at the castle he would try to arrange with his cousin Will to make another attempt, and to tell the Queen. He himself would have to leave again, but Will, who also greatly admired Her Grace, could possibly contrive it.

Disappointment was general, hope deferred.

Thomas returned to Ferniehirst.

It was four weeks later, to the day, 29th April, that Ogilvy arrived again. There was indeed to be a renewed attempt, on the night of 2nd May. It was Sir William Douglas's birthday, and there would be some celebration at the castle which might well help by distracting attention. Seton and an escort, with George Douglas himself, were to be in position again that night. Would Thomas join them?

Thomas certainly would. They rode at dawn next day.

With fresh horses at Seton Palace they set off with its lord, George Douglas and an escort. The size of this was the subject of debate. Seton, one of the richest lords in the land, could have taken hundreds; but the more inconspicuous they remained, the better. On the other hand, they might need a sufficiency of armed men, if the rescue was successful, on the way to Niddry and the crossing of Forth, especially if the Queen's gaolers discovered the escape fairly quickly. And there was always the problem of ferrying large numbers across the firth. It was decided that a score would be best which, with horses, could all get aboard one of the large scows at the Queen's Ferry.

Timing was important too. They did not want to arrive in the Loch Leven area too early, to be seen and reported on. Just when Will Douglas would be able, if at all, to contrive the attempt, was itself uncertain; presumably it would have to be well after dark. At the beginning of May sunset would be about nine in the evening, and such darkness as followed perhaps two hours later. So they should probably try to arrive at the foot of Loch Leven at, say, an hour after sunset, and then head carefully northwards, George Douglas to go on ahead to prospect.

On this occasion Flam and Beth were not to be left behind. While they recognised that they could be of little help in any actual rescue, they could at least wait at the foot of the loch, and provide female company for the Queen, which she would surely be needing if the attempt was successful – and they were both as good on horseback as any men.

The party rode to reach the narrows of Forth at Queen Margaret's Ferry in the early evening, and had no difficulty in getting the ferrymen to put them across to the Fife shore. Thereafter, they came in sight of the loch rather earlier than intended, and so delayed in the low hills to the south until well into the dusk. Then they left the young women, with a couple of guards, in woodland near the access to St Serf's island. George Douglas pressed on, alone.

Fortunately it was a dull evening and so darkness would be early. They moved slowly on up the west side of the loch, glad now that it was all but uninhabited.

When they could see the few lights of the town of Kinross glimmering about a mile ahead, they halted and dismounted, to wait. But quickly, not the most patient of men, Thomas Kerr grew restless. He would go on, he said, on foot. Seek to remain hidden. Link up with George Douglas, perhaps. Be on hand to welcome the Queen if or when she got across. Had Douglas said just where the escape-boat would intend to come in? Not, presumably, at the town jetty?

Seton did not know, but guessed that they would want to land somewhere more private. Better to wait here for Douglas.

But Ogilvy supported Thomas. Help might be needed at the landing. It was not so dark that they would not be able to see a boat heading for the shore – so others might see it also. The presence of one or two of them might be useful – not many, or they would be obvious. He would go with Thomas.

This was agreed, and the pair went forward. They reckoned that it was around ten o' clock.

It was a difficult shoreline to cling to, on account of reedy inlets and marshy edges. But at least there was fair cover, with bushes and scrub and tall rushes, however muddy and wet they became. They went cautiously, startled themselves when they put up flapping flights of disturbed waterfowl.

It was strange how much lighter it seemed over the water

than on the land, the former seeming to glow palely with some inner translucence as though it had swallowed the last of the daylight, the latter all shadows and gloom.

They did not want to get too close to the town jetty. Presently they came across a slight eminence in the wet flatness, a mere hummock, bush-grown, and decided that this must serve as look-out post. Climbing this, they were again startled, this time when a dark figure rose up before them out of the scrub. But it proved to be only George Douglas, who had chosen the same vantage-point.

He told them that he had no positive news. He would have liked to have found a boat to row out in the dark to the castle, to prospect the situation there, but feared that if he was spotted this could endanger the entire attempt. He had crept along to the jetty and found some men waiting there beside the boats – these no doubt boatmen who had ferried guests out for the birthday celebration and had not been allowed to remain on the island for security reasons. So he hoped that Will would not seek to come ashore there.

The trio settled to wait and watch. This was as good a spot as any, Douglas averred.

They had a long wait, or it seemed long. The night appeared to get no darker – although that may have been their night-vision improving. Whether this was good for the venture or otherwise was questionable. They listened to the night birds' sad calling and the occasional sleepy quacking of mallard from the reed beds. They tried not to let sleep overtake them. Thomas and Ogilvy had ridden far that day.

Nevertheless it was Ogilvy who roused the other two, exclaiming and pointing. At first Thomas could see nothing new, but Douglas perceived it, and pointed also, eagerly.

Then Thomas discerned it, a low-lying darker shape on the water, half-right of them, and much nearer land than he would have looked for, close enough to see that it was moving shorewards.

"Will has chosen to come well to the south," Douglas declared. "A longer row, but well away from the town. A poor landing, but less chance of being seen. We have not seen him because of the island's dark background. From this point. But . . . this is good indeed!"

"They are quite close in. We must go meet them . . ."

That was not so simple, on that indented, marshy shoreline, and with doubts as to just where the boat would come in. They hurried off, stumbling, splashing, plowtering, sometimes having to retrace their steps.

The boat appeared to be nosing along the shallows, seeking a landing-place. Glimpsing it now again, Thomas's heart sank. He could see only two figures aboard, both very much male-seeming and both rowing. Was the Queen not there, after all? Or was this some other boat?

After a little, George Douglas, reaching a spit, not of sand but of firmer mud, halloed and called out, "A Douglas! A Douglas! Here!"

He got a prompt answering hail of that clan's rallying-cry. Thereafter there was an exchange of calls, less than shouts, to bring the boat in to this spot.

Thomas, peering, saw only the two men.

Then, as the boat's prow grounded, one, obviously young Will Douglas, stood, shipping his oar, to bend and raise up what seemed to be a cloak. And then a person who had been hidden beneath it, and beneath the stern seat where usually nets would be stored. Clearly, even in that half-light, it was a woman.

Thomas let out a great sigh, and plunged forward into the water. "Highness!" he cried. "Your Grace! Thank God!"

"Thomas! My Thomas!" The Queen held out her hands, her arms. "Oh, Thomas . . .!" Her voice broke.

There were ample and eager hands to aid her ashore, amidst a spate of greeting and exclamation.

George Douglas cut this short. "Come!" he urged. "Quickly. The boat may have been seen. I have horses. My brother's. Hidden inland. Who are you?" That was to the second man in the boat, evidently no local fisherman.

"I am John Beaton, Younger of Creich. My father is at the castle."

"He aided me. And Her Grace," Will explained.

Thomas had heard of the Beatons of Creich, in Fife, kin to Beth. One of them, probably this young man's aunt, had been one of the many mistresses of the Queen's father.

"Come!" George Douglas insisted.

They moved from the water's edge, Thomas taking the Queen's arm to aid her through the puddles and mire. She clung to him, obviously much moved, but silent and ever glancing behind her. No doubt she could scarcely believe that she had indeed won free of that dread castle and island.

At first George Douglas seemed doubtful about his direction, hesitating and peering this way and that. Then, coming on a track of sorts, he seemed to know where he was and swung off along the track, southwards. Soon, in a hollow, they came to three horses tethered to hawthorn trees. The castle horses were stabled on the mainland near the town, there being no room for such on the castle-island. George had apparently had no difficulty in collecting these.

It seemed that John Beaton was not planning to go back to the castle and the birthday festivities. If the Queen's escape had been discovered, and himself seen to be missing, he could be in trouble. His father, he reckoned, would not greatly blame him, but the others would. He would throw in his lot with the Queen's party.

George Douglas was impatient to be off, although Will was less concerned now. In the party atmosphere, it seemed, he had been able to collect Sir William's keys from where they were kept, and to use them to lock the main and postern gates of the castle behind them, and then had thrown them down the mouth of one of the guardian cannon; so even if the Queen's absence was discovered that night, Ebba Seton failing to hide it, any pursuit would have great difficulty in getting out to look for them.

So, with six of them now, it was two to each horse at this stage, Thomas taking the Queen up pillion behind him. They trotted southwards, reckoning that it would be around midnight.

It did not take them long to reach Lord Seton's group, to great joy and welcome. And thereafter Flam and Beth greeted their mistress with tears of happiness and relief. It was a cheerful and voluble company which rode onwards through nightbound Fothrif for the Forth crossing.

The ferry was a dozen miles off, and they were there well before sun-up, too early for the ferrymen to be risen and on duty. But Seton, in these circumstances, was not going to wait on their convenience. He had them roused, in the Queen's name, announcing that if they did not take his party across forthwith, he would man their scow with his own men-at-arms and forgo payment. There was much surprise but little dissent. Indeed, some of the oarsmen made loyal gestures towards the Queen, which pleased her.

On the Lothian shore, remounted, they headed south-westwards now the four miles to Niddry, a strong castle considerably larger than that of Loch Leven or Hallyards, standing just south of Winchburgh and long in the possession of the Seton family. Here, secure for the moment, they could rest and eat.

The Queen expressed no desire to sleep – she had had sufficient of sleeping and inaction over these last sorry months. She looked thinner, more fine-drawn, pale, but she had recovered her spirit and seemed remarkably well considering her lengthy ordeal. The talk went on. There was so much to say, to recount, to explain, to speculate upon.

But after a while, Lord Seton pointed out that decisions were called for as to the immediate future. While they were safe enough here meantime, the last thing wanted was for them to be besieged in this castle. The lords at Stirling were only twenty-five miles away, and the news of the Queen's escape would not take long to reach there. He suggested that they should ride for Seton Palace without much delay, and there seek to muster an army. Dominance in East Lothian was shared between himself, Bothwell's Hepburns and the Red Douglases. The last-named would be inimical, but the Hepburns probably would not. After all, their chief, although overseas, was still married to the Queen; and they would have no love for Moray and his supporters. It was easy to reach the Borderland from there, where Sir Thomas could raise his Kerrs, and neighbouring clans; possibly the Homes would join in, although their lord's affiliations were doubtful.

Strangely, however, the opposition to this course came from the Queen herself. She had thought much on this situation, she said – she had had ample time for thought. And she had come to the conclusion that, if she won free, she should make for the south-west, in the first instance. It was the Hamiltons that she saw as target. They were one of the largest and most powerful houses in the land, yet for long they had taken no active part in the kingdom's affairs. This out of pique and resentment, no doubt, for their chief, the Duke of Châtelherault, was next in line to the throne after her son, and they thought that he, Châtelherault, should have been given the Crown, rather than having a woman to rule. She had heard it said, too, by her gaolers, that he greatly resented Moray and felt that *he* should have been offered the present regency; after all, he had been Regent once when she was a child. So he might well be prepared to try to put down Moray, if offered inducement. And the Hamiltons could raise great numbers of men. Moreover, the loyal lords such as Fleming, Carmichael, Sempill, Somerville, Maxwell and Herries were based in the south-west, in Lanarkshire, Ayrshire, Dumfries and Galloway. Cassillis might join in; and Eglinton, even Glencairn. And there was Lennox, the late Darnley's father; he did not love *her*, that was sure, but he hated Moray and might well be prepared to co-operate to topple him. She believed that a great alliance against Moray, who undoubtedly had contrived the present situation, was the first priority. When he was removed from power, then they could plan the future with more confidence.

There were some doubts about this programme, not least from Thomas Kerr. But the Queen was set on it, and she was their sovereign-lady again; and the last thing anyone there desired was to start by countering the monarch's expressed wishes. It was agreed that the move should be south-westwards, to Hamilton. But meanwhile, Thomas would go off on his own, south-eastwards, to raise his own Border folk, and if possible the Homes, and bring them to Hamilton, as swiftly as was possible.

So it was parting company again, but this time with hopes uppermost.

Thomas rode fast, for home.

27

It was nine days later that Thomas saw the Queen again, at Hamilton Palace, beside the town of that name, where the River Avon joined the Clyde in mid-vale, and was made flatteringly welcome – and not only for himself; he came with no fewer than four hundred Borderers, Kerrs, Kers, Scotts, Elliots, Turnbulls and Rutherfords, with more to follow, a notable force of hard-riding moss-troopers, satisfactory augmentation of the host already assembled there. No Homes, however, their lord having decided to throw in his lot with Moray.

Thomas was surprised, in fact, at the numbers encamped in the parkland around the great palace, thousands obviously. Considering how short a time had elapsed since the Queen's escape it was remarkable how many had rallied already to her side. It looked as though her decision to come to the south-west had been a wise one. Apart from the Hamiltons themselves, who had mustered to the number of almost three thousand, with the townsfolk available, there proved to be as many again belonging to other lords. It was astonishing how quickly the word had got around, for all these to have assembled. There were some unexpected adherents. The Earl of Rothes, for example, who had hitherto been on the other side. Argyll the Chancellor was there, and the Earls of Eglinton, Montrose, Cassillis, the Lords Fleming, Carmichael, Boyd, Herries, Somerville, Sempill and Livingstone. There was even an archbishop and a bishop; James Beaton, Archbishop of Glasgow, who turned out to be a half-brother of their John Beaton, and whose rise in the Church had been extraordinary even by the standards of the day, from sub-deacon, deacon to priest in one month, next month a bishop, and then, aged twenty-seven, archbishop. The other prelate was Châtelherault's illegitimate brother, James Hamilton, Bishop of Argyll. Huntly had come, but meanwhile had gone north to raise his great Gordon manpower.

The Queen's cause looked hopeful indeed – although some of those present may well have temporarily joined it for reasons other than loyalty, for instance because they were being neglected by the Regent Moray, Rothes probably in that category.

Thomas felt that the Duke himself was a doubtful ally. Elderly now, and no strong character, he had not lifted a hand to help the Queen, his cousin, in all the problems and crises of her reign. And his eldest son, the Earl of Arran, had conspired against her – although he was now locked up as a madman. Two other sons, however, the Lords John and Claud, the latter usually styled Lord Paisley, were better, and appeared to admire the Queen. And it so happened that one daughter was wed to Huntly, another to Eglinton. So perhaps the balance was weighted in the Queen's favour.

There was news of the Regent. He was known to be at Glasgow, holding justice-eyres. The Queen had sent him a message and proclamation, declaring that she denounced the abdication document as false, obtained under dire threat and duress; that she had resumed the Crown and throne; that she called on him, Moray, to renounce the so-called regency and to come and make his peace with her, and all would be forgiven, for the realm's sake. There had as yet been no reply from him – but it was known that he, too, was assembling forces on Glasgow Green.

The Queen was being given varying advice; indeed there were too many advisers. Some said to proceed at once, in strength, and strike at Moray before he had fully mustered his strength. Others said to wait, for Huntly's Gordons and Argyll's Campbells. Others again urged that Moray and Glasgow be bypassed and an advance made on Dumbarton Castle on the Clyde estuary, which Lennox held, although it was a royal castle. If they could win over Lennox, who was of course related to Queen Elizabeth Tudor, this could help Mary's cause. Still another advice was that they should avoid Moray, and head direct for Stirling, there to seek to take that fortress, which would be under-manned, surely, in this situation, demand that its Keeper should yield it to its rightful owner, and the young James be handed over to his mother. Mar, the Keeper, could scarcely refuse this, it was held; and once the child was in Mary's hands, Moray's regency became pointless.

The Queen, privately, sought Thomas's view on all this. He had few doubts. The Stirling suggestion he dismissed as a folly; that great citadel was the strongest in the land, and only sustained and heavy cannon-fire might reduce it – and they were not going to bombard buildings containing the infant James. He did not quite see the worth of making for Dumbarton. His preference would be to wait here for a while. He recognised the problems of keeping large numbers of armed men, of differing loyalties, standing idle; but the access of strength they would gain with the arrival of the Campbell and Gordon reinforcements would well outweigh that. More men would come also from the more remote Border valleys in a day or two. The Queen's army might well double in numbers, and more. And Moray was unlikely to attack them here, in the heart of Hamilton country.

Mary Stewart seemed impressed by this counsel.

However, other voices prevailed, especially Châtelherault's. The Duke looked on himself as obvious commander of this army; and certainly he had more men present than anyone else. He was in favour of marching on Dumbarton. That way, not only could they draw in the difficult Lennox, and the south Highland clans he all but controlled, the Buchanans, Grahams, Colquhouns, but they could meet the Campbells, if possible, who would be coming from southern Argyll, their lord said by crossing the Clyde shallows near Renfrew. So they would gain a Highland army – and the Highlanders, whatever else, were notable fighters.

So, on Wednesday, 13th May, a great host was on the move north-westwards, fairly slowly, for by no means all were horsed, with instructions left for reinforcements to follow on. There had been much debate about the route to follow to Dumbarton – for Mary was convinced that this fortress would yield to her, and it would provide a very strong base and would control the Clyde ports, to which aid could come to her from France, if necessary. Some felt that they should head east-abouts round Glasgow town, ford Clyde at Carmyle, and on by Dennistoun and Bishopbriggs before turning west by Bearsden and Kilpatrick to the beginning of the estuary. But this of meeting the Campbells, who had been instructed to cross much lower down Clyde at Renfrew, was considered to be a great advantage, and this meant following the south side of Clyde, almost to Rutherglen and swinging due westwards, following the line of the tributary Water of Cart, by Paisley to Renfrew, thus avoiding Glasgow to the south, instead of the north. It would make a thirty-mile march altogether, two days.

The earls and lords were reluctant, to say the least, to be led by the Duke of Châtelherault, elderly and indecisive, and there was argument and offensive remarks, to the Queen's distress. However, fairly soon after they had passed Cambuslang there was some alarm amongst their advance guard, under the Lord Claud Hamilton, at the sight of a large company ahead, on foot and oncoming. But this proved to be the first of the Campbells, arriving earlier than expected, from the Cowal and Loch Fyne area, a very welcome addition to their strength and with news of more to follow from further north. Now, Argyll, the Chancellor, seemed to be the obvious choice as overall commander, and to still argument the Queen appointed him Lieutenant-General of the Realm, there and then. This decision was reinforced by the fact that the Campbells expressed themselves, withal in the Gaelic, as averse to serving under any lowland Hamilton. The Duke was angry, but the other lords were supportive; and the Queen then named the Lord Claud as leader of the van, which seemed wise, as he was a spirited young man and moreover knew the ground they would be traversing, since as Lord Paisley he owned much of it. This appointment somewhat mollified his father. There was altercation, also, as to who should lead the cavalry, this motley collection of the Queen's supporters, as usual, riven by their own family and clan jealousies. The earls assumed that the leadership should be theirs by right, although none were experienced in actual warfare, as distinct from local feuding. Lord Herries, however, had served in foreign campaigns, and was moreover a Borderer, if from the West March, and used to forays across into England. So, since a large part of the horsed force was composed of Border moss-troopers, it was grudgingly accepted that he should lead the horse. If it had been a reigning King instead of a Queen in charge, of course, all this debate and squabble would not have arisen.

They had left the Clyde and were making westwards for the valley of the White Cart in the High Crosshill area when the Lord Claud himself came spurring back from the van, to announce that there was a large force approaching, half-right, an army indeed, which must have crossed Clyde at the Glasgow Green fords. It was much horsed and bannered and could only be Moray. And little more than a mile away, hidden hitherto by the low Langside Hills.

A hasty council-of-war was held. There was no real divergence, now, as to strategy. They had to do battle. By no possibility could they retire, or seek to avoid the foe, especially as almost certainly they would be much the larger host. The Queen, although as always reluctant for bloodshed amongst her subjects, had been advised that her future would be decided by parliament or by battle. So now she declared, "By battle then – let us try it," to the cheers of those who could hear.

But tactics were another matter. And here they had to be guided largely by those with local knowledge of the ground, that is, the Hamiltons, the Lord Claud himself the most urgent. He declared that it was not where he would have chosen to fight an engagement – but then the same should apply to the enemy. Between them and the opposing force lay the Water of Cart, with low hills both sides and some marshy ground flanking the river. Whoever controlled that river-crossing, he averred, had the advantage. He asked permission to make a dash down, with the van, and secure this.

Argyll acceded, and the younger man hurried off.

They were now committed to fighting on this site, however much some of them wondered whether a better battleground could not be found somewhere nearby, even if it entailed some manoeuvring. They moved forward for the shallow Cart valley.

Soon they could all see the opposing array, or some of it, the small hills and ridges of the area somewhat obstructive as to view. Reaching the crest of one of these low ridges, which the Duke called Cathcart Hill, they could discern that at least the Lord Claud had gained the River Cart with their vanguard, without opposition, and so could control the crossing. So far so good.

Across the Cart they saw that the enemy had now taken up position around the village of Langside. Nearby, and closer to the river, was a rather more prominent ridge, with a steeper face towards the south, that is towards themselves. If they could win that, they could be in a position to more or less dominate Moray's force below. It was agreed to attempt this. But since the enemy were nearer to it than they were, Moray might well perceive the tactical importance of it and occupy it first, especially if he saw the Queen's host making in that direction. A diversion was called for therefore, to distract the foe. Herries and the cavalry wing should ride ahead, splash across Cart and then encircle this Langside Hill to the west, where they would be largely hidden from the enemy, who would therefore not be able to gauge their numbers and intentions, and so be apt to remain stationary in their present position round the village. Then, if the Lord Claud crossed the river also and took his force east-about, to threaten the village position from that quarter, Moray would see the danger of being caught between two horns, outflanked, and be put very much on the defensive, or even, possibly, decide to retreat. What they would wish for was for him to retire towards the Clyde itself, which they had already crossed, and where the Queen's army might be able to pin them against the great river, presenting a major problem for them.

That was the tactical decision. Thomas Kerr was less confident than some. It seemed to him to be assuming overmuch inaction and passive waiting on the part of Moray. If, as was almost certain, he had experienced soldiers with him there, they could see the possibilities and dangers equally well as themselves. Morton would be there, a trained fighter. And if they had Kirkcaldy of Grange, the best soldier in the land . . .!

Argyll ordered advance by the main body, down to the River Cart. But before they moved, he urged the Queen to remain there on the crest of Cathcart Hill, where she would be safe and could oversee all, with a small reserve force which could be sent to the aid of any, if required. This seemed good counsel; and the Queen chose Thomas Kerr to remain with her, although he would have wished to go with Herries and the cavalry, inactive watching not being his preferred role. He would command the reserve, with his Kerr moss-troopers. The Duke stayed beside the Queen also.

This viewpoint, in fact, could hardly have been bettered for the area under scrutiny. They could see most of the terrain involved, except behind Langside Hill itself; indeed they could see far beyond, to the Clyde, and the steeples, gables and roofs of Glasgow town, the great cathedral of St Mungo prominent. Mary, who had grim memories of Glasgow and of Darnley there, shook her head over the prospect.

Watching, they saw the main array reach the Cart and commence the crossing, so far with no evident forward movement of the enemy. Thomas wondered why they had not moved down to contest the crossing. It seemed the obvious first move. He did not voice his doubts to the Queen.

They saw the Lord Claud's van, across now, dash off eastwards on their encircling move. They could no longer see Herries's wing, which had disappeared behind Langside Hill. The entire area they had to deal with was in fact comparatively limited, less than a mile in each direction embracing all.

Argyll's force, fully five thousand strong, was certainly not in haste to cross that comparatively minor river, the watchers wondering what delayed the bulk of them. Perhaps, nearer to the enemy, they could see something not visible from this hill? The Queen and Châtelherault were discussing this, when Thomas called to them and pointed half-left. Men were appearing along the crest of Langside Hill, half a mile away.

They were assuming that Herries had quickly achieved this his first objective, and that this was what Argyll had been delaying for, when something about the ranks appearing on the hill struck Thomas as odd. There were no horses to be seen. This surely was strange. Admittedly the far side of the ridge might be steep, but not too much so for some of the cavalry to have mounted it. Moss-troopers were used to taking their mounts up rocky Border hills.

Then he perceived something else, not at first evident at that range. It was like a fringe of forest, bare winter forest, rising above those ranked men. He cursed. Those could only be pikes, long-shafted spears, used by infantry for close fighting and forming defensive squares. And their army had no pikemen. These, then, were the enemy. Moray, or Morton or Kirkcaldy, had not waited so idly, as they had assumed, but had sent a force on foot, unseen, to occupy Langside Hill.

The significance of this was not lost on the watchers. That hill was tactically important. And it meant that the enemy was confident enough to be taking the initiative.

They were wondering what Herries would do now, whether he would assail that hill from the far side, or attack the main enemy force at the village, in flank, or just return to rejoin Argyll, when a Hamilton laird rode up at speed to inform the Queen and Duke of astonishing news. Argyll had fainted away, at the side of Cart, and was unable to continue in command. The Earl of Eglinton had taken over meantime. It was suggested by the Hamiltons that the Duke should now assume the leadership of the main force. This was the reason for the delay at the river. The Campbell clansmen were unhappy, and reluctant to proceed without their chief.

Astounded, the hearers stared at each other. None had ever heard the like. Thomas remembered the Chancellor's strange and nervous behaviour at the last parliament, and his obvious fear of Moray. Perhaps the MacCailean Mor, the great Campbell chief, was a man of dreads and panics? But the Queen said that she had heard that he was subject to occasional fits of epilepsy.

Huffing and snorting, the Duke hurried off to take command.

Thomas, more concerned and troubled about the outcome than ever, would have wished to go and take a more active part, but felt that he could not leave the Queen. Besides, what could he do in these circumstances to improve the situation, with all these arrogant nobles seeking to exert their authority?

At last the main army was across the Cart, and advanced towards the village area – but the kilted Campbells were now seen to be in the rear, not in the forefront. Fighting could be seen, distantly, to be going on well to the east, which would be Lord Claud engaging the enemy's left flank, as intended. Then Herries and the cavalry appeared from behind Langside Hill. So he had not attempted to storm that eminence, presumably holding to the original plan to threaten Moray's west flank.

A little cheered, the watchers were then surprised to see the advance of their main force come to a halt, halfway to the enemy's position. There was a pause, and then a quite large detachment, possibly about one-third of the whole, dismounted and, including the Campbells, moved off to their left towards the hill, in what must be an attempt to storm it.

It was, in a way, a sound move of the Duke's, in seeking to dispose of the threat of those massed pikemen up there, who could charge downhill and assail his army in flank. But, as the rest of the main body remained stationary, where they were, evidently waiting to see the outcome of this storming attempt, the matter took on a different aspect. This inaction could endanger all, discount any advantage gained by the twin east and west threats of the Lord Claud and Lord Herries.

Impatient, concerned, but unable to affect the issue, Thomas, and to a lesser extent, the Queen, fretted.

The climbing of that hill had to be done on foot, rocky and

broken as the ascent was, and it appeared to the watchers to take an unconscionable time. And all the while those below waited. This was the most dilatory battle Thomas could have imagined. Only the wings were so far doing any fighting; but how long they could keep that up, unsupported by the centre, was anyone's guess. Desperately the Queen's cause needed an experienced and able commander to take charge. Why were all the soldiers on the other side?

Then, as the hill-climbers reached the summit of the ridge and began to try to come to grips with the pikemen – and obviously found it difficult to get past the dense frieze of long spears – there were two developments. The crackle of hagbut-fire sounded, the hagbutters evidently standing behind the pikemen, adding a new dimension to that struggle – the Queen's people had no such weapons – and at the same time the main array of Moray's force began to advance from the village area, trumpets blowing, banners flapping, heading down directly for the Queen's stationary host, with a sizeable cavalry detachment swinging off westwards to counter Herries's attack.

It was real battle at last.

The situation was a distinctly complicated one. Although the Queen's was undoubtedly the larger host, it was split into four. So, in a measure, was the Regent's; but these were all closer together, in touch, and the detachments not so large; also they had a base in the village itself, as a stronghold where comparatively few men could hold off larger numbers, protected by houses and walls. Moreover, as Thomas at least well recognised, they had more effective leadership. And that quite large part of the loyalist force up on the hill was being wasted, to a large extent, and suffering severely from the hagbut-fire, making little or no impact on the situation. A much smaller defensive line further down the hill could have protected their main force from an attack by the pikemen in flank. The Duke's array should not have been waiting there for the enemy to descend on them; surely they could have at least divided into two, so that the initial horsed charge of the enemy against them could be, as it were, engulfed and assaulted from both sides as well as in front. But it was, of course, easy to play the general from up here, safe and out of the thick of it.

Easy it might be, but desperately galling and frustrating for a man of Thomas's temperament. He paced up and down like any caged lion, however unlionlike he felt in this ineffective and passive course.

They could clearly hear the clash of arms, punctuated by the crack of the hagbuts, the shouting of men and the neighing of frightened and injured horses, as the two sides met. Now there was no clarity in the situation down there, only a chaos of struggling men, rearing and falling horses, the noise equally confusing, horrible. The Queen wrung her hands, uttering little cries.

Thomas raised his eyes to the further scene, the background, around the village. If Herries and the Lord Claud could make an end there, join up and drive down on the enemy's rear, then the day might yet be saved. But there was no sign of that coming about.

For how long that terrible mêlée continued across Cart was not to be calculated by the watchers, time in the circumstances having little relevance – save in the matter of allowing for any helpful development in the rear, the enemy's rear. It was, eventually, with a sinking heart that Thomas indeed saw development in the rear – but it was the wrong one. People in the Duke's force were beginning to trickle back towards the Cart. If that further developed . . .

Sadly, it did. More and more men, on foot, were leaving the fight to make for the river, many wounded, undoubtedly, stumbling and falling, but by no means all. And when some mounted men joined them, the watchers feared the worst. It could, of course, be that they were being *sent* back to hold the crossing secure – but if so, that implied that the leadership was contemplating retiral, perhaps only to behind the Cart, but retiral, retreat, nevertheless; in other words, a measure of defeat. It was a dire sign, either way.

The Queen herself saw it as such. "Thomas – oh, Thomas! Look! They fail, they fail! No, no – they must not! Never that. Let us go down. With your men here. If I went amongst them? We must stem this flight. If *I* went . . ."

Eager as he was to be active, Thomas shook his head. "No, Highness – no!" he exclaimed, in turn. "Look! More and more are turning back. You would not halt them, fear-crazed men in a battle. You would be overwhelmed, swept aside. My moss-troopers here would not alter anything now – save perhaps to hold the crossing of that river, if there is general retirement." His main and over-riding duty and concern **was** to guard the Queen's person, all else subservient.

"Let us do that, then. It may something help. Keep the crossing . . ."

At least it was not inaction.

They rode down, a compact group of some two hundred, swords drawn at last, the Queen in the midst.

Nearing the river, quickly it was apparent that the idea of making a stand on this side of it was by no means foremost in the minds of those leaving the battle. It was self-preservation that preoccupied, flight – and there were many more now thinking that way. Thomas attempted to rally some, but was ignored. Priorities were otherwise.

By the time that they reached the waterside it was clear that only a rearguard action was being fought by the Duke's force, disentanglement the prime aim. The two flanking attempts could not be seen from this low ground. But up on Langside Hill there was withdrawal downwards now also, the men there no doubt perceiving that retiral was in the air.

Thomas shouted to the Queen to remain on this south bank, making no bones about commanding the monarch. Then he splashed most of his men across, to take up position, two-deep, facing what was left of the battle, in a line, leaving a sizeable gap between for escapers. He thought of driving forward, in the traditional wedge formation, into the heart of the fray, instead of waiting here to defend the ford, but that would mean leaving the Queen unprotected – and she might well follow them. And it would mean smashing through the inextricable tangle of battling friend and foe; and he was uncertain as to whether it would do any good at this stage anyway. He remained where he was.

But if *he* did not approach the battle, the battle approached him, for all the time the drift was towards the river. And when all the Campbells and the others came running down from the hill, it was not to join in the fighting now but to make for the ford also.

That finished it. Save for a few stalwart fighters, breaking off the engagement was general. The retiral became a rush, all seeking to save themselves, lords, knights, men-at-arms, infantry, making for that river, which must seem something of a safety-barrier, horsemen even riding down others.

Thomas and his men were all but swept away in the

panic-stricken tide, holding their line with great difficulty. It was only when most of the Queen's people were across, leaving behind a hell of yelling and groaning wounded, flailing horseflesh and littered corpses, that he turned and gestured his men back over – but not before he had glimpsed his father-in-law amongst the group of lords under the Lion Rampant standard of the Regent. Both sides were flying that flag, this day.

With the Queen again, there was great and urgent dispute going on, some lords pleading with her to be gone before she was again captured, others seeking to form a front here, protected by the river, shallow as it was. Thomas was joining this defending party when there was a diversion.

It was the unexpected arrival of Herries, with the Lords Fleming and Livingstone, who had gone with him and the cavalry. From their assault on the village base they had seen that their main body was in trouble; and leaving their force under his kinsman, the Lord Maxwell, he had dashed back to the Queen's side, to see what best he might do. Now, discovering the full extent of the reverse, he was in no doubt, and took charge forthwith. There was no possibility of regaining the day now, he declared. They must disperse, and fight another day. The Queen's security was all-important. The Hamiltons could look after themselves, in their own country. The other groups and contingents must find their own safety. He, and sundry others of her closest supporters, would take Her Grace at once down into his own safe country of Dumfries and Galloway meantime. They would raise a new army there, and resume the struggle thereafter.

There was, in fact, little disagreement over this course – amongst those who were prepared to wait and consider it, however briefly – no one putting forward better. Except, strangely, from the Queen herself, who said that she thought that she ought to make for Dumbarton Castle, none so far away, that great stronghold where she would find refuge. It was more central in the land, and it commanded the Clyde estuary, from which she could gain aid, by sea, from the Highlands, from France, even from Elizabeth of England, who would not be prepared to see a sister-monarch put down thus. There was opposition to this, however, many there pointing out that there were a score and more of enemy-occupied miles to cover to reach Dumbarton, and even if they reached there safely, Lennox was highly unlikely to yield up the castle now. Few there had any use for the Earl of Lennox.

There was no time for debate. The enemy advance guards were already at the other bank of the river, so close, and the Regent's main force was re-forming, to move down to it. Once they actually started the crossing, their own slender defensive line would not hold them back for long, Thomas the first to admit it, however good his moss-troopers. Herries, the most determined and authoritative voice there, had his way. He would take the Queen due southwards, and immediately. Those who wished could come with them – so long as they were good horsemen! It would be a long and hard ride.

Thomas, of course, was going to accompany the Queen. But she had a different course for him. Her Marys had been left at Hamilton Palace. Thomas was to go and get them and bring them on to her. They could not be left there; and she wanted them, needed them.

Where to bring them, then, Thomas demanded?

It was Herries who answered. To Terregles, his seat near to Dumfries, he said. The Queen would be there, safe. Now – off with them, whilst they might.

There was no time for any leave-taking. Herries, Fleming and Livingstone rode off with the monarch without backward glance, others following. Thomas, hand raised in salute, turned to call in his moss-troopers. As he did so, George Douglas, who had attached himself to Lord Seton since the Loch Leven escape, announced that that good lord had been wounded and captured. He had tried to save him but could not. Shaking head, Thomas told him to come with him to Hamilton.

They left that sorry field of Langside, Thomas Kerr angry, angry.

28

So far as they could tell, they were not pursued over the eight miles to Hamilton. It was almost dusk when they reached there – to find the Duke and many of his people there before them, and in process of moving out again. The palace was vast but not a strong place. Cadzow Castle, nearby, which had been the earlier Hamilton seat, was much more defensible, if it came to assault.

So Thomas had no need to disclose the sorrowful tidings to Flam and Beth. He was surprised to find Ebba Seton there with them. Apparently the Douglases had ejected her from Loch Leven Castle after the Queen's escape, and she had made her way to Niddry, and there learned that her father and the others had taken the Queen to Hamilton. So she had followed. It was grievous to have to tell her that her father was a captive, and injured. At least Flam could be informed that her brother was safe and with the Queen.

There was no question as to procedure now. All were for rejoining the Queen at the earliest, even though it meant all-night riding.

Obtaining fresh horses, the escapers from the battle were joined by the Lord Claud, who had managed to bring his vanguard men back safely and who declared his intention to accompany them southwards. This was a welcome addition, for he was a likeable and effective young man, the best of his family; moreover he knew this countryside, as Thomas and the others did not, and they were going to require a guide through the nightbound hills to the south.

They set off with little delay, George and young Will Douglas going with them. The girls were unhappy, saddened over the disaster, but at least glad to be going to rejoin their beloved mistress. Ebba asked them all to pray for her father, as they rode.

Their route, Hamilton said, would best be by Cadzow and

Glassford Muirs to Strathavon, then up the Avon Water into the Glengavel Hills and so over to the Douglas Water. Thereafter they must cross the high shoulder of Cairn Table and so come down to Sanquhar. After that it was the straight road down Nithsdale to Dumfries. His hearers could by no means take all that in, but they did gather that it would be a lengthy and taxing ride, in the half-dark. As well that the Marys were all good horsewomen.

It was not long before it was very apparent to all that they could not have done much of this without Claud Hamilton, going by byways and tracks rather than roads, through a country of low hills, up and up on to the high bare moors which cover so much of the centre of lowland Scotland. Apart from the town and castle of Strathavon, a Hamilton fief, which they rode through around midnight, its streets deserted, they seemed to be avoiding all haunts of men. May nights in that country are never very dark and the mirk did not greatly trouble them; but direction and identifying features and routes would have confounded them, especially amongst the sheep- and deer-tracks of those high moorlands. Even Hamilton faltered sometimes, apologetically, but always recovered his sense of direction.

They halted to rest, more for the mounts than themselves, in the small hours, at a stream-side which their guide declared was the upper reaches of the Douglas Water. Here the horses drank. Ahead of them now was a long ascent, he said, by an ancient drove-road which climbed over the western shoulder of the mighty hill of Cairn Table, the highest in all this area. Once over that they would be into Dumfries-shire, with the great Nith valley ahead, Maxwell country – although they would first come to the Crichton castle of Sanquhar; but the aged Lord Crichton was kin to Hamilton, and a good Queen's man, and they could rest there. But that was still a score of miles.

In fact, despite the long climb up, this was the easiest part of their journey, for they were on a drove-road now, one of the many well-trodden routes which criss-crossed the uplands to take the great cattle-herds to the low-country markets. So the way was clear, with no real obstacles, and drinking-places for cattle, and horses, available.

In the half-dark, the shoulder of Cairn Table was hardly recognisable as such, merely seeming to be a very long, slightly curving area of short heather. Then they were sloping gradually but consistently downhill, into Nithsdale, dawn breaking behind them.

Weary, they reached Sanquhar Castle, on a high bluff above the Nith, just as the sun was rising – sixty miles, Hamilton said, good going for night-time riding. It was a fine place, large, within outer and inner courtyards. They were challenged as they approached the gatehouse, and the Lord Claud shouted his identity, which swiftly was resultant in the drawbridge being lowered for them and the portcullis raised. Hardly were they into the gatehouse-pend than the portcullis clanged down again behind them and they heard the creaking of the bridge being raised. The Lord Crichton was evidently very much security-minded.

They saw why, moments later. The outer courtyard, large as it was, was filled with horses, lathered and obviously long-ridden. Thomas recognised amongst them the pure white mare Seton had given to the Queen. So the Herries party had reached here also, and halted.

In great excitement the young women hurried across the inner court and within the keep, Flam falling into her brother's arms. The Queen and her company were eating a hastily provided meal, having arrived barely an hour earlier, come by a different route but approximately the same distance, tired also.

Mary Stewart herself seemed dispirited rather than merely fatigued. Clearly the disaster at Langside had greatly grieved and depressed her. She greeted her friends in a flood of tears, which was not like her, clutching the young women convulsively, her voice broken, incoherent, sobbing out dire details. All was lost, she cried, all lost.

Partaking of the provender, Thomas, George Douglas and Claud Hamilton sought to reassure and cheer her. One battle lost was not the war. No great proportion of Her Grace's adherents had been engaged. With better and more experienced leadership, the tide would turn. It had been too soon after her escape from Loch Leven to assemble full support; and so on – all of which no doubt the other lords had already told her. But she remained unresponsive, dejected.

After eating, a council was held as to immediate moves. Herries, who was very much in charge now, was for immediate onward flight. He was much afraid of pursuit. After all, it

341

would soon be known by Moray that they had fled southwards. He would not be satisfied until he had the Queen safe in his own Galloway uplands, a country remote from the rest of Scotland and having its own concerns and allegiances. But the enemy would be well aware of that also, and they might well be followed. So despite old Lord Crichton's urging to stay at Sanquhar awhile, at least until the Queen and her ladies were rested, also their horses, he was for off. Most there agreed with him.

The general view was that they should proceed down the long Nithsdale, to Dumfries, straightforward and comparatively easy going for their beasts, so much better than the land they had recently covered, and then turn south-westwards into the Galloway hills. But Herries urged otherwise. If it was easier for them, it could be easier for any pursuit likewise. They would be expected so to go. Instead they should swing off south-westwards from *here*, into the empty hills of the Glenkens, and make their way down to his country by remote and little-known ways, rougher riding admittedly but a deal safer. He would wish to instal the Queen in his main castle of Terregles; but this might well be anticipated by Moray and the others, and therefore he suggested that they should head first for a secondary and older place of his, the Tower of Corrah, on the river called the Kirkgunzeon Lane, amongst the Fells of Criffell. From there he would send to discover whether it was safe to go to Terregles, nearer to Dumfries. None there were sufficiently knowledgeable about this outlandish and little-known country to make better suggestion.

So, only allowing their mounts brief rest and fodder, they took leave of Crichton, forded Nith, and headed south-westwards into a maze of hills and valleys which Herries called the Euchans, over from the Euchan Water to the Scaur Water, and thence by the headwaters of the great River Ken, down which they rode to Loch Ken, over a score of very rough miles. They had to go comparatively slowly now, because of the state of their mounts; but at least the many heights they surmounted permitted them to see that there was no pursuit. Down long Loch Ken they made their way, another fifteen weary miles, to Crossmichael, there to turn off, eastwards now, to ford the Urr Water at Haugh of Urr, and, exhausted, man and beast, came to remote Kirkgunzeon and the comparatively small castle of Corrah, the original seat of the Herries family. Not only the women were almost in a state of collapse. They were over a hundred hilly miles from Langside.

That company, of nearly fifty, sorely taxed the facilities and provision of the Tower of Corrah, but none were critical of this shelter, comfort and provender, so thankful were they all for sleep and relief from riding. But before Herries himself slept, he sent a messenger to Terregles, a dozen miles away to the north, to ascertain the situation there, an establishment more suitable for the support of large numbers.

It was late next morning before most of them roused themselves, hungry now and more like themselves. Sadly, however, the Queen was no more cheerful nor more hopeful, despondent indeed as to her future. Herries was quickly talking about rallying his own people to the last man, the Maxwells in their many branches, the Johnstones, the Jardines, the Kirkpatricks, the Irvines, the Macullochs, the Hannahs, the Agnews, and the other clans of this country, at Terregles; but the Queen showed little interest. The defeat in the field, so soon after her long imprisonment, seemed just to have been too much for her.

They were still awaiting word from Terregles and Dumfries when Mary Stewart came out with her decision. No mustering of armies meantime; there had been sufficient of bloodshed. She would go to her sister-Queen, Elizabeth of England. Elizabeth would help her, would not have her kinswoman and fellow-monarch, anointed and crowned as she had been, put down thus by subjects. She had influence with Moray, and could bring pressure on him. She, Mary, had in fact sent John Beaton to her at Whitehall, from Hamilton before the battle, acquainting her with her escape from Loch Leven, and of her determination to regain her throne. Elizabeth would help her.

Almost without exception all were appalled at this suggestion. Elizabeth Tudor was well known to be self-seeking, untrustworthy, devious. To put herself in that Queen's hands would be a greatly mistaken move for Mary. Almost certainly she had already supported Moray with money and advisers. He had spent much time at her court before going to France. She was, they could never forget, Henry the Eighth's daughter, Scotland's greatest enemy since Edward the First.

The girls and Thomas added their dissuasions. But to no

avail. The Queen averred that if she saw Elizabeth in person, all would be different.

They pleaded against this. Send a letter, an envoy, if she wished; but not herself go over into England. Offer Elizabeth every inducement, but not to leave her own Scotland.

Mary was adamant. She had thought long on this; she had had much time for thinking. If force of arms failed, she would go to Elizabeth. Arms had very much failed. She would go.

Herries tried another approach. If she must seek help from outside Scotland, let her send, or even go, to France. She had been Queen of France, and her de Guise kin all but ruled there. They would be much safer, more trustworthy allies, the Auld Alliance rather than the Auld Enemy. If go she must, she could sail from one of their Galloway ports, Stranraer or Garlieston.

No, Mary would not go to France; not yet, at any rate. It was almost seven years since she left there, with such high hopes. It would be humiliation indeed to have to go back, seeking help, rejected by her own people. Better Elizabeth than that.

Unhappy, all waited.

It was one of Herries's sons who arrived back from Terregles. There was a large family of them, apparently, no fewer than five sons and seven daughters. This one came from their mother, to declare that all was well at Terregles. Many of the Herries men-at-arms had returned safely there from Langside, and there was no word of any pursuit. His elder brother, who had been with his father and left in charge of the men when Herries had hurried off to the Queen's side, had told her that survivors said that Argyll had been captured, but promptly released by Moray – which seemed very significant, and perhaps made his fainting fit the more suspicious. Also, the Lords Home and Ochiltree, on the enemy side, had been wounded. Lord Seton was not thought to be seriously injured. Casualties amongst the Queen's forces were thought not to have numbered more than some three hundred.

A move was made northwards. Terregles, the barony and parish, lay not far west of Dumfries, where the Cluden and Cargen Waters joined Nith. The castle was a much more impressive establishment than Corrah, where their hostess proved to be equally impressive. Agnes, Lady Herries in her own right, had brought the title and lordship to her husband, this Sir John Maxwell, second son of the fifth Lord Maxwell;

and this Terregles had been his own, Corrah a Herries place. The lady welcomed the Queen in almost motherly fashion, and promptly put her to bed, declaring that what she needed was sleep, sleep and more sleep, this process only to be interrupted by suitable feeding, at intervals.

Others there were not averse to like treatment.

Whilst the Queen slept, Herries himself, Fleming, Livingstone and Thomas discussed the position. All were against this project of going to England. Perhaps when the Queen was rested, and in some better frame of mind, she would heed them. A much greater army could be raised than was at Langside, and with Herries in command could very likely reverse this sorry situation. But if she insisted on going, they had to recognise that she was their sovereign-lady and would have to be obeyed. What, then?

They could not all just ride with her to the border and say goodbye. Nor perhaps put her in a boat and say farewell. She was a Queen, and the way must be prepared for her. If she was determined to go to London, envoys must go on ahead to inform Elizabeth, the approach made in dignified fashion. The two nations were not at war at the moment, and there should be no serious obstacles to travel. Fleming said that he would be prepared to go, as envoy. But meantime her immediate reception in England should be arranged. This was the West March of both countries, and the headquarters of the English West March were at Carlisle – as the crow would fly, a mere forty-five miles to the south. The governor there, the English Warden, was the Lord Scrope; but he was seldom in residence at Carlisle in peacetime. His deputy, Richard Lowther, was known to Herries, from Wardens' meetings, and seemed a reasonable man. They could send a messenger to him requesting an escort to meet them at the borderline, to receive into England Queen Mary, who was on her way to visit her sister-monarch in London. So all would be done in decent style, without risk of border guards behaving roughly or discourteously to the Queen, as they might well do in the state of clan feud and raiding which prevailed there. But let them hope that, rested and restored, Mary might be more amenable to reason . . .

Alas, that was not to be. Mary Stewart, so unlike her normal self, was impervious to all pleas and representations. She would go to Elizabeth, and without further delay.

Flam and Beth were especially saddened. For although Ebba Seton said that she would go with their mistress, *they* were both married women now, and although their husbands were understanding as to their commitments to the Queen, this of going away to England for an unspecified length of time was scarcely to be considered. So it had to be parting again. As for Thomas, he was profoundly grieved.

Decision accepted, Herries sent off his messenger, protected by men-at-arms, to Carlisle, acquainting the deputy governor there of the Queen's intentions, and requesting that an English escort be sent to the border, at Gretna, to meet her and escort her to Carlisle Castle.

Meantime, as they waited, Mary was concerned about her important journey, about her appearance, and as to clothing therefor. She was still wearing what she had been dressed in when she had escaped from Loch Leven, anything but queenly wear and now much travel-stained. Unfortunately Lady Herries was a large and bulky woman, and her daughters only girls. Nothing at Terregles was suitable; and the other Marys had hurried south in only what they were clothed in. However, Sir John Gordon of Lochinvar, with them from Langside, and one of Herries's friends and neighbours, declared that his wife was remarkably similar to the Queen in build, tall but slender; he would go and fetch some of her clothing. It was some twenty miles to Kenmure, Lochinvar's castle.

It was scarcely a cheerful company that waited at Terregles, despite Agnes Herries's hospitality and efforts.

Gordon arrived back in the evening, with an assortment of gear, with which the Queen expressed herself as well pleased. This would serve very well until she could have her wardrobe replenished in England.

In the morning, they were all further exercised by the royal announcement, at breakfast, that she wanted to be on her way forthwith. No, she would not wait for word to come from Carlisle. She had had a vivid dream that Morton, Lindsay and Ruthven, who had so maltreated her at Loch Leven, were now close at her heels, and this time they would not spare her life. She must be off, at once.

Herries, urging delay, pointed out that crossing the border into England was not something which could be achieved, as it were, casually, without permission and co-operation. Both sides maintained guards, apt to be aggressive; and the local people were notably unruly, living by robbery and violence in what was known as the Debateable Land. Eager individuals, or raiders, might slip across in darkness, undetected; but that was no way for the Queen of Scots to enter Elizabeth's England. They should wait for Richard Lowther's response and escort. That man would probably come himself for the royal visitor.

No, Mary Stewart said. She had had enough of waiting. She would be off, if not across the borderline, then by water. They could sail across the Solway Firth, could they not, with no questions asked? To quite near to Carlisle. Let them do that.

To further objections she raised a hand. This was her decision, her royal command. Let it be arranged, forthwith.

So, while Herries sent a courier down to the little port of Dundrennan, the nearest which was sufficiently secret and yet available for sailing despite the difficult Solway tides, final preparations were made. The Queen further concerned them all by declaring that she was going to have her long and lovely red-gold hair cut short. It was too kenspeckle for secret travel, and was indeed in a wretched state anyway after all the neglect and difficulties of the past days. It must go. Ebba Seton, who had always dressed Mary's hair, now had the sad task of shearing it off. She did not cut it quite so close as her mistress sought, and kept some.

Dundrennan, with its abbey, now in fact Herries's property since the Reformation, with its Commendator his second son, lay about twenty-five miles south-west of Terregles, indeed not so very far from where they had come from Corrah. The parting with Lady Herries and family was emotional.

At Dundrennan Abbey, most of it now more or less abandoned, while Herries went to see to the boat and its crew of oarsmen, the Queen wrote another two letters, one for Deputy-Governor Lowther, in case he came in person to Gretna to escort her to Carlisle, another to Queen Elizabeth, which she besought him to forward, announcing that she was on her way. These she entrusted to Sir John Gordon, to take to the crossing at Gretna. Then they all moved down the side of the Abbey Burn, to the fishing-haven, where a quite large fishing-coble was moored, awaiting them. They made a silent party now, with the Solway Firth, wide and blue ahead of them, seeming almost as ultimate a crossing as Rubicon, or Styx itself. Thomas Kerr, for one, scarcely trusted himself to speak.

This was separation, then, severance, the ending of so much, for his Mary-Queen to be leaving her own country, after almost seven so eventful years, with her future so uncertain, leaving behind not only her realm and subjects, her friends, but her infant son. If Elizabeth Tudor failed her, as he feared she so well might, would Mary ever come back, ever be able to come back? Or would she go to France, and they possibly never see her again?

The company divided into two, very uneven as to numbers, the few who were going to accompany the Queen into England, at least as far as Carlisle; and those who must stay in Scotland. Herries, Fleming and Livingstone would go, and Ebba Seton; George Douglas, who was hopelessly in love with Mary now and had more or less burned his Loch Leven boats behind him, elected to go also, although young Will did not. These, with some servitors and the boat's crew, made up eighteen in all. The rest stood, wordless.

Mary Stewart turned to face these, beautiful features working. "My dear ones," she said. "My very dear ones! What am I to say to you? What to tell you? My faithful, loyal, loved ones?"

Flam, ever impulsive, flung herself forward, arms outstretched, bursting into tears. The Queen embraced her, stroking her hair.

Beth moved in, set-faced.

An arm around each of them, Mary Stewart looked over at Thomas, shaking her head, Ebba looking on, biting her lip.

He came to them, and reached out to grasp all three, speechless still.

For long moments they stood thus, eloquent enough in their silence.

The Queen found voice first. "Thomas . . . Tom Smellum! My protector! Who will protect me now? This is hard, hard. But I must go, must try. Pray for me, Thomas – and remain my protector, my warden, thus."

He could only nod.

"All of you," she went on. "I will need all your prayers. Till, till we meet again."

"May that be soon, soon," Thomas got out, with fervour even if without conviction.

"Yes, soon. Who knows . . .?" Her voice broke.

That choking of hers seemed to release the man's tongue. "Highness, wait at Carlisle. Until you hear from Queen Elizabeth. In case . . . she will do nothing. Or little. As I fear. Then you can return quickly. Back where you belong. To make another and better endeavour. We will be busy. All of us. In more than praying. We will gather a host, to await you. Much greater than you had back there. Too soon, it was. A host. I swear it! Then you will triumph. For the people love you. Do not go further than Carlisle."

"I have written to Elizabeth . . ."

"A letter. Paper, only. And you may be at Carlisle before the letter is. Thus."

Yes, yes, the girls clamoured, drawing back a little. Go no further.

All around the cry was taken up.

The Queen shook her head. "We shall see. Learn what Elizabeth says. Meantime, alas, we part. But . . . only in the body. Not in mind, not in spirit. It is but *au revoir*, my friends, only that, not goodbye." She kissed them, all three, and again. "You will not . . . forget me?"

That last undid all the firming of emotions, all the strengthening of resolve. The girls dissolved into tears again, and Thomas sterned his features to what he hoped was suitably masculine immobility. The Queen herself pushed them away from her, and turning, all but ran down to the waiting boat without looking back.

Lord Fleming came to embrace his sister, and then followed the others of the boat-party down to the waterside. There was no cheering, no calling out and exclaiming in that farewell, only silent gazing, much of it misty.

Nor was there any lingering now. Once all the passengers were aboard, the fishermen cast off at once and thrust in their long oars, as though anxious to get this over as quickly as possible. Out of that burn-mouth and into the wide firth they pulled.

It was only when they were well clear of the land that the Queen turned in the stern to look back, well beyond any sight of her features. Then, after a little, she raised her arm high. She did not wave nor gesture, but held it up straight, and for long, almost as long as they looked, Mary Stewart's final salute to her native land.

The watchers stood there until the boat was a mere speck, lost against the loom of the Cumbrian mountains.

Historical Note

Mary Queen of Scots has been accused of lacking judgment. Certainly her decision to flee into England seeking Queen Elizabeth's aid was ill-judged. Unfortunately she did not wait at Carlisle. As we all know, she was given no aid, was taken prisoner on Elizabeth's orders, and remained a captive for nineteen years before suffering execution on her sister-monarch's command. Other misjudgments admittedly occurred; but it must be remembered, as so often it is not, how young she was and inexperienced, at least in matters of state and policy, only eighteen when she came back to *rule* in Scotland, not just to reign. It is frequently forgotten that she was Scotland's only Queen-Regnant, why she is called Mary Queen of Scots, not Queen Mary of Scotland, not the Queen of a monarch but the monarch herself. And the period was one of the most difficult in even Scotland's story, with the Reformation newly established, and the Counter-Reformation still a distinct possibility, and she a firm Catholic.

Sir Thomas Kerr did not indeed forget Mary. When she was imprisoned in England, he actually led an armed invasion of that country, in an attempt to press Elizabeth into releasing her. When this failed in its objective, he and his father-in-law held Edinburgh Castle in the Queen's name – for when, two years after Langside, the Regent Moray was assassinated by a Hamilton, Kirkcaldy of Grange turned against Morton and the others and threw in his lot with the Queen's party, which still hoped and existed. When the besieged were eventually obliged to surrender, after pounding by heavy cannon sent up from England for the purpose, with Morton now ruling Scotland in the child James's name, Kirkcaldy was executed. Thomas, escaping death, was banished the realm and his estates forfeited. He was in exile for some years on the Continent, then, on Morton's death, he was able to return home, and had his lands restored by the young King James, now ruling his own kingdom. He died two years later.

His son, the Sir Andrew Kerr knighted in infancy, became the celebrated Dand Kerr, a favourite of King James, whom he took to England with him in 1603, on attaining the United Kingdom throne, and who was created the first Lord Jedburgh. Another son, Robert, also went to London's court, and was created Earl of Somerset, who changed his surname to Carr, and got into serious trouble with his monarch, was tried for murder, with his wife, but eventually pardoned.

The Queen's Marys have been the source of many stories, tales and ballads, by no means all accurate. Seton remained with her royal mistress during the years of captivity, eventually retiring to France and entering a nunnery. Fleming's husband, Maitland of Lethington, joined Thomas and Kirkcaldy in Edinburgh Castle, falling foul of Morton, like so many others, and took his own life thereafter rather than face execution; his widow remained one of the Queen's loyalest supporters in Scotland. Beaton, apart from alleged involvement in an incident over the royal jewels, seems to have faded out of public life.

Happily, there are still Kerrs at Ferniehirst, the present Marquis and Marchioness of Lothian, Lord and Lady Jedburgh, who allow the public to visit that picturesque Border stronghold, and even stay in it. This novel was really their idea.

N.T.